Dracula's Demeter

Dracula's Demeter

Doug Lamoreux

COPYRIGHT (C) 2012 DOUG LAMOREUX
LAYOUT COPYRIGHT (C) CREATIVIA

Published 2014 by Creativia
Paperback design by Creativia (www.ctivia.com)
Cover art by Cover Mint
ISBN: 978-1497500389
This book is a work of fiction. Some names and incidents are suggested by the novel, Dracula, by Bram Stoker, a work entirely in the public domain. All other characters and incidents are fictitious, original, and drawn from the author's imagination, and are not to be construed as real. Any resemblance to real persons, living, dead, or undead, is purely coincidental.

For
Lydia Rose

Acknowledgments

- Jenny McDonnell – without whom there is nothing.
- Bram Stoker – who wrote the beginning and the end; in hopes he enjoys this... middle.
- Andy Boylan – vampire expert, for his knowledge of blood typing.
- Aaron Christensen – for his horror knowledge, writing skill, and willingness to suffer early drafts.

A Penultimate Moment as Prologue

THE old man was crying. The wind tossed his wispy hair and fanned the tears running down his tortured face. He twisted his hat in trembling, arthritic fingers and begged the young woman to forgive him.

The *where* was the village of Whitby, on the Yorkshire coastline of the North Sea. It was quite like any other English village. One horse-cart streets separating red-roofed houses, jammed together and atop one another like hurriedly stacked boxes, protected by cliffs rising so steeply to the east and west one could stand upon either and look across without seeing the town. The river Esk wound a sharp S approaching the southern viaduct, straightened north through the village, then broadened to the harbor and sea. Oddly, because of Whitby's position in this valley, though the sea lay to the east, the villagers could only see her by looking north. On the eastern side of the river, atop the great steps rising in a slow curve from the pier drawbridge, overlooking the harbor and out to sea, there stood the ruins of Whitby's ancient Abbey. On the same field, nearer the harbor, stood the parish church. Surrounding the church and stretching across the field to the cliff's edge above the harbor, was the massive village cemetery. Of all the places visited

A Penultimate Moment as Prologue

in the telling of this tale, it is most appropriate the story begin there, in the company of the ancient dead.

The *when* was simpler; a gray Friday evening on the 6th of August, 1897.

The *who* was the old man (locals agreed, he was nearly a hundred) tearfully making his case. He was a Scotsman by birth, a whaler by trade, retired from the sea. With him was the young woman to whom he poured out his rapidly beating heart, the charming Mina Murray.

Mina was in her usual place, the church cemetery, when the old man came upon her. Nothing strange there, the hilltop graveyard was virtually the village park. Serene walking paths ran all through the grave rows with stone benches interspersed. Everyone in Whitby, residents and tourists, eventually wound up among the tombstones, invigorated by the breeze, to investigate the histories of the dead, to sneak off to the dilapidated Abbey (said to be haunted, as ruined churches must be, by a mysterious *lady in white*), or to while away the day from that beautiful vantage point, commanding a view of the village, the harbor and out past the Kettleness headland to the sea.

Since her arrival in Whitby two weeks prior, it was routine for Mina and Lucy Westenra, the friend with whom she was staying, to escape their rooms at the Crescent and stroll these quiet paths. And, when Mina walked alone, to rest upon a bench she'd chosen as her favorite near the cliff's edge. There, to quietly consider her troubles.

Lucy, always of an excitable temperament had, since Mina's arrival returned to a frightening old habit of walking in her sleep, but with a determination Mina had never witnessed before. The last few days Lucy's *night walking* had all but reached a fever pitch. Mina was desperately worried. Add to that, her overwhelming fears for her fiancé... Jonathan Harker was far away in Transylvania completing an important business transaction. His work allowed only infrequent letters and his last, two weeks since, had been so disappointing, a single line from Castle Dracula saying he was starting for home. Nothing more, and no news since. It was unlike Jonathan. Mina missed him terribly and longed for his return. So the walks, and the contemplation.

Not that there was always solitude.

It was there at her bench visitors paused, sometimes to pass a pleasant moment, sometimes to pass the day, the coastal guard and his technicians installing their new search light, the locals, the touring visitors and, of course, the seamen.

There were in fact *three* seamen; the old whaler mentioned and his crusty sea cronies. (These two were absent just then, while the Scotsman was crying, but they were usually at his elbows.) The seat she'd chosen as her favorite was, Mina discovered, their *liars' bench*. Rather than chase her away the old men took her in, delighted for fresh ears upon which their stories were again new, and ever since had daily regaled her with tales of the sea. Mina called the old whaler 'Sir Oracle' because the other two fawned over him, laughed at his jokes, agreed with his obvious lies, and egged-on his endless tales. Often they did nothing but sit in the cemetery all day and talk. Many days she did nothing but sit and listen.

As much as the old man gabbed rarely did he talk of personal matters; until that day. With his compatriots absent, perhaps because they were absent, Sir Oracle went on, like water through a burst dam, with his heartrending story.

In his hundred years, he'd seen a wife and three sons to their graves. One son remained, a sailor too, in his late sixties and still at sea. Sir Oracle knew neither the port nor the part of the world his 'babe' presently occupied, but clearly he wanted him home again. In the meantime, he made his home in Whitby with his widowed granddaughter (daughter of the son at sea). She was an only child, her mother having died in childbirth, and he and his son traded the role of 'father' whenever the other went to sea. Both returned to sailing when she took a husband. Both resumed the role of 'father' when her husband met his end. They'd cared for

A Penultimate Moment as Prologue

each other all their lives. His story, one of great love, was sadly punctuated with great loss and the ravages of death.

Now the old man was crying, regretting cynical comments made over the past few days. He'd ranted about the tombstones, a startling speech as Mina remembered. He'd called them 'lies carved in stone' and the families 'liars'. He'd offered examples, graves marked, 'Here lies so and so – lost at sea in such and such'. Then leveled his charge, "If they were lost at sea, how d' they lie here?" His tirade became a melancholy soliloquy on the sadness of life – and death.

Now the poor thing was apologizing with all his heart. But the more he struggled for her forgiveness, unnecessary in the first place, the more dire became his talk of looming eternity. He interrupted himself, trying to explain these portents of doom, until the tears cascaded down his pale cheeks. Mina was so desperately sad for the confused old man she felt she too would cry.

Then he fell silent, took a breath to the toes of his old leather boots, and collected himself. He smiled, with clouded eyes, and said, "But I'm content." He wiped his tears with his hat. "My life is here. Solid ground 'neath me tired old feet an' a roof o'er me head. I've my granddaughter to care for me, an' I for her. An' her dad comin' ageeanwards home. Dear Gog, I hope he's comin' home soon." Then Sir Oracle, staring out to sea, whispered, "I'd like to see him ageean - 'efore I die."

"I'm content," he said. But there was resignation in his voice. "For it's comin' to me, m' deary, an' comin' quick. It may be comin' while we be lookin' an' wonderin'. Maybe it's in that wind out o'er the sea that's bringin' with it loss an' wreck, an' sore distress, an' sad hearts."

"Look!" he cried. "Look!" He gestured at the roiling sky. "There's somethin' in that wind an' in the hoast beyont that sounds, an' looks, an' tastes, an' smells like death. It's in the air. I feel it comin'." His hair danced in the wind. He raised his hands. "Lord, make me answer cheerful, when my call comes!" He mouthed a prayer and Mina could only feel for him. He gently shook her hand with his gnarled claw, blessed her, and said, "G'bye." Then he turned and, as he started across the cemetery, angling for the long stairs, whispered, "So many steps... so many steps... 'efore I'm home."

Mina watched him go tears running down her cheeks too. She was the essence of vibrant youth, with a front row seat to the debilitating effects of time. As Sir Oracle reached the stairs, she couldn't help but wonder what it must feel like to be so old – so near to death.

Not far from Mina's bench, the eastern cliff curved away. Wind, weather, and time had undercut that portion of the rise. The underside had fallen away and with it several graves had fallen to the harbor below. Outside the harbor, on this side, a great reef ran for half a mile straight out from behind the lighthouse. A lone buoy bobbed there and, in heavy seas, the sound of her bell drifted like the cry of mourners on the wind. The old man had spoken of a local legend that when a ship was lost at sea that mournful bell was heard.

A pall settled over Mina, the effects of Sir Oracle's tearful pleas, the sadness of the bell and, as she shook off her reverie, the appearance of what looked a frightening storm approaching over the sea. The clouds, gray all day, were darkening over Kettleness and the sea was growing black.

Mina saw the crippled old whaler, hobbling down the long stairs (she'd counted them once, 199 steps in all). He was passed by the young coastal guard racing, in the opposite direction, three steps at a time from the harbor below. She hurried to dry her cheeks (her handkerchief a gift from Jonathan) before the guard arrived. He usually paused to greet her before going about his business. It was her duty to save the gentleman any embarrassment.

The coast guard reached the top of the stairs and waved as he caught his breath. But, instead of approaching, he turned to the sea. He was carrying a spyglass which he lifted to study the horizon.

"I can't make her out."

A Penultimate Moment as Prologue

He hurried to Mina's side, nodded a greeting and returned to the glass. Mina followed his gaze to the sea beyond the harbor. The approaching storm and an odd mist that had suddenly arisen made visibility difficult but, straining, she saw it now too. A long way off, a sailing ship bobbing on the sea.

"I can't make her out," the guard repeated. He turned the lens following the ship, scanning her billowing sails, tracing her masts, patiently waiting for one of her flags to unfurl in the winds gusting at sea. "She's a Russian!" he finally called out. "She's a Russian by the look of her."

He saw it now, the solid white, blue and red bars of the Russian flag whipping atop her main mast, and a yellow banner, their Imperial flag, flying on the mizzen. A small house flag, denoting the owners, flew beneath but its details were beyond the reach of his glass. Still there was no doubt, the ship was Russian. But what in God's name was she doing?

"But she's knocking about in the queerest way," the guard said. He'd never seen the like and reported her movements to calm his own nerves. "She doesn't know her mind a bit. She seems to see the storm coming, but can't decide whether to run up north in the open, or to put in here. Look there again! She is steered mighty strangely." He shook his head inviting Mina to share his alarm. "She doesn't mind the hand on the wheel and changes about with every puff of wind." He lowered the spyglass and solemnly declared, "We'll hear more of her before this time tomorrow."

Chapter One

THIRTY-EIGHT nights earlier, Tuesday, 29 June, 1897, in Transylvania, in eastern Austria-Hungary where... a flying shadow beat the air with its leathery wings.

Below in the country dark, the trees, the black ribbons of river, the rolling fields... turned into sparse, barren foothills, then rose to rugged peaks frowning down upon the beaten road heading northeast from Bistritz, Austria-Hungary to Bukovina, Romania. The flying shadow flitted, rolled, darted down then up again, stroking the air as it soared over the narrow, rocky Borgo Pass, the juncture in that dusty road offering men their last opportunity to escape the dreaded unknown and return unharmed, sane, to their world of daylight.

Its wings worked rhythmically, unceasingly. The flying shadow issued a shrill scream and climbed above the craggy slopes of the Carpathian Mountains, higher still beneath the fading moonlight to the broken battlements of an ancient castle. Its only approach from the ground was a disused coach trail on the north leading to a narrow courtyard. From the other sides the castle was impregnable. Massive windows in its walls, out of reach of sling, bow or cannon, looked out from the rock upon which it was erected, sloping sharply away to the east, and falling to a precipice to the south and west. The shadow dove, soared low over the dilapidated,

Chapter One

seemingly deserted stronghold, and disappeared between her towers. An instant later, a tall man emerged from the darkness - in its place - and strode the castle rooftop.

He was clad in flowing black from head to foot. His thick hair and tremendous mustache were both a dark iron-gray. His full cheeks, as the moonlight hit him, were ruby-red beneath pale white skin. His lips were intensely red and marred with maroon splotches of drying blood. Even his eyes, like burning coals, seemed buried deep in swollen flesh. The tall man, like a filthy leech, was gorged with blood. This thing was Count Dracula.

He stepped noiselessly to the edge of the roof and leaned over the parapet. With keen eyes and ears he saw and heard a pack of wolves, monstrous even from that height, padding and panting about the dark courtyard. Earlier he'd found it necessary to summon them to put a young Englishman in his place and to help that *guest* understand exactly who commanded there. He smiled at the memory and his sharp, oddly protruding teeth dented the surface of his bloody lower lip.

The wolves, his children, had served their purpose. Now, with a courtly gesture, Dracula released them. He closed his eyes and relished their melodic howls, clamorous at first then fading, as one by one they abandoned the courtyard and mountainside, returning to the dense wooded foothills. A remarkable stillness overtook the land.

Dracula stared out over his Transylvania, his empire, his lifeblood for the last four hundred and fifty years. To the west, where the valley was backed by the peaks of jagged mountains, the cracks in their rock faces studded with ash and hawthorn. To the south, where the expanse of distant hills, bathed in moonlight, melted into the velvety blackness of the peasants' fields. Endlessly beautiful but devoid of life. The land, despite the fresh blood on his lips, was drying up.

His decision was the only one possible. He would leave his homeland, travel to distant shores, insert himself into a modern world ignorant of superstition and its protections; a world begging to be fed upon. He knew also he'd chosen his new home wisely. The British Empire controlled one-quarter of the world's population; one-quarter of its land. If Transylvania could no longer sustain him, where but England did a conqueror belong?

His journey had been long-planned. Through the machinations of the greedy and the stupid an estate awaited him in London, a receiver awaited in Whitby, and the ship that would carry him in Varna. The well-paid gypsies, the Szgany, were encamped below. In the morning would come the Slovaks to aid them. In darkness, on the voyage ahead, he would sleep... and bring to full flower his great experiment.

Among his growing powers was the ability to communicate with lesser beings; animals, yes, and those especially compliant humans. For centuries he'd wondered at their sensitivity to his thoughts and tested the distances at which subjects could be influenced. It was necessary, for he would require assistance in his new home.

To that end...

He'd been weeding through the voices of humanity that floated on the wind, deciphering, selecting the speakers and their thoughts over ever-increasing distances. Once he'd *learned the trick*, the miles melted like wax and the words rang like bells. Among them, he found that one particular voice. He heard his subject, read his thoughts and, finally, learned to actually experience his subject's surroundings. When he could hear and feel in the man's place, the Count turned the table. He returned his psyche on the same mental stream and gave the subject his thoughts, his words. This experiment had one goal; absolute obedience. Body and soul, this man would serve Dracula.

The one selected for greatness, a nobody called Renfield, had just over a month since been hospitalized for a mental breakdown. He was morbidly excitable, suffered periods of melancholy and, with his great physical strength, was quickly judged a danger to himself and others. None of that mattered to Dracula. Renfield

Chapter One

had a pliable consciousness. It was no coincidence the sanitarium was just outside of London.

So began the instruction. He stressed secrecy, loyalty, obedience. He had even *suggested* a hobby. With the natural streak of cruelty he'd found in the subject, Dracula's suggestion was taken up eagerly. It became a need and, soon after, an obsession. The hobby? Simply that Renfield should catch and collect flies.

Renfield was instantly rebranded a lunatic. His hobby, in two short weeks, drove his attending psychiatrist, a smarmy know-it-all called Seward, to demand he cease and desist. On Dracula's order, Renfield begged for three days more to purge himself of his horrid collection. And, of course, the bleeding heart doctor relented.

Seward had played into Dracula's hands. The flies were merely a means to an end and had, by then, served their purpose. To continue the game, the Count had only to send Renfield another suggestion. Within a few days, the flies had greatly diminished. In their stead, hidden in a box from Seward's prying eyes, the lunatic had collected several fat, juicy spiders.

Atop his castle, Dracula stretched his white hands to the stars (a gesture that seemed to fix him into stone) and, across distant land and water, called to his servant. From far away, he heard Renfield's whispered reply, "Yes, master. I await you!"

The moon was all-but gone and the first streaks of dawn broke over the mountains. Dracula climbed onto the south parapet and slipped head-first over the side. His sharp nails gripped the roughly cut stones, the toes of his boots dug into the crevices where time and the elements had crumbled the mortar or washed it away. He took in the heady vista of the shadowed countryside and crawled lizard-like down the outside of the castle.

He paused in his descent by a tall, deep, weatherworn window, the bedroom of Dracula's guest, and peered in at the Englishman. He slept fitfully, across the heavy bed, still wearing his disheveled clothes. The Count's eyes gleamed and he laughed silently. He thought of his three *wives* in flowing white, somewhere within, even now making their way to their resting places. His women and his guest alone together. He congratulated himself on the fate he intended for Herr Jonathan Harker. He crawled on to another window, a storey below and to the left, raised the sash and disappeared inside.

The web-filled room was scantily furnished, an ornate bed, a table, a high-backed arm chair, all covered in thick dust. In one corner a great pile of gold rose from the floor like a mountain in a child's sandbox; chains and ornaments (some jewel encrusted, many tarnished) and, mounded amongst them, gold and silver coins from countries throughout Europe and the East; Greece, Turkey, Hungary, Austria, Italy and Britain, all ancient and covered with dust – for long had it lain there unmolested.

He opened a heavy door in the opposite corner, strode through a passage to a circular stairway, and descended. The stairs were steep and treacherous but he glided down without a sound. At the bottom was a tunnel heavy with the sick odor of old earth newly turned. At its end, he opened a heavy door and entered a ruined chapel. The roof was broken, vast walls fallen away, and its graveyard long since been abandoned and forgotten. Until now.

These grounds had, recently, been dug over; the earth placed in great boxes piled throughout the chapel by the Szgany, on his orders. Between these boxes, in two places, steps led down to in-ground vaults. He passed the stairs to the first two, containing fragments of old coffins and piles of dust, and descended the second staircase to another set of vaults. At the base he entered the crypt on his left. He examined the remaining boxes, stacked within, the last of a total fifty being readied for removal by the Slovaks in daylight.

Count Dracula sighed in satisfaction.

His own box lay as he'd left it, close against the wall, atop newly turned soil, open and partially filled with earth. Beside the box leaned its cover, pierced sporadically with tiny holes, nails in place at its corners ready to be hammered home.

Chapter One

Dracula climbed into the box. Bloated, he belched and an eructation of blood escaped his lips and ran in a crimson rivulet down his chin. He drew his cloak about him like a shroud and lay back atop the cool soil. He drew the lid up and over his box and, exhausted with his repletion, closed out the sliver of light stealing into the vault from the stairway door.

Tomorrow, he and his boxes would be taken from his castle home; from the kingdom where he lived, ruled, and died. He would be taken from his haunted Carpathian Mountains where, following his death, he had been – unborn – to live again. He would leave the Transylvania he loved but that could no longer support his kind. Tomorrow, Count Dracula's new life would begin.

Chapter Two

THE taste was awful!

There was no other word for it. Had he been home Nikilov would have pinched his nose (like his late mother when she wanted the little boy *he used to be* to swallow a nasty elixir). Now, fifty years later, in public - in a public house - he couldn't. So he took the spoonful straight from the labeled bottle. The quacksalver's answer to his uncooperative heart. He shook his head to down the dose. Awful!

Getting old, he thought, and tired. But he had no right to complain and wouldn't. Getting old was part of God's plan too.

"Captain?" the Innkeeper inquired, teapot in hand. Nikilov cleared the path to his cup. He sipped the fresh, steaming brew that, after the quack's tonic, tasted better than it had all morning. He stowed the heart medicine in his coat pocket and returned to his charts. His ship sailed at noon – and he had his course to consider.

* * *

An ancient stone wall surrounded Varna, fifty miles south of Romania, in northeast Bulgaria. Inside, the wooden houses of the Ottoman coastal town were packed along narrow, winding streets leading to one place; the largest port on the western Black Sea.

Chapter Two

It was Tuesday, 6 July, 1897, and Trevor Harrington had made his way to Varna in hopes of finding an out-bound ship, passage off the continent. He hated the thought. Sailing was outdated, dirty, and took an eternity with one plague after another; cramped quarters, danger of fire, seasickness, inedible food, and illness. He dreamed of one of the sleek steamers replacing sailing vessels around the world. But it was only a dream. As he neared the harbor, the young Englishman had to face two cold facts. Sailing was cheaper than steam. And he had precious little money.

Harrington was on the lam (a phrase just come into usage). Over the last four days and nights he'd had a hard, first-hand lesson in its meaning. Actually, as fugitives went, he could have been in worse shape. The territory was unfamiliar but Harrington was not completely lost. He'd spent ten months studying in Bukovina (a Romanian city on Transylvania's eastern border), a year walking there from Spain, and he spoke six languages. He was fine... but his clothing needed help.

Harrington normally looked the dandy. But a night in a vineyard, after four days afield without a bath, had been hard on his attire. His hat was irreparable. His brown pinstripes had gone to smash owing to mud and grass. The watch pocket on his red silk waistcoat had been ripped by underbrush. His collar was embarrassingly limp, his silk braces needed a brace, and his four-in-hand tie was out of hand. All would have been lost were it not for the occasional brook to rinse the grit from his hair and the ache from his sunburned face and hands.

To his good fortune, Harrington found a public house outside of Varna's harbor. He wasn't a drinker but, in a port town, what better place to learn which ships were to sail. He dusted his pants, adjusted his tie and stowed his hat in his kit. He forced his chin up (off his put-upon collar), his chest out, and entered the pub.

* * *

The innkeeper, and the men holding up the bar at his elbows, examined Harrington with frowns and whispers. Bulgarian was not among his fluent languages. While most eastern European tongues were similar, the Englishman heard only slang and gathered he'd made a poor impression. Still, he smiled and bid them good morning. He soon discovered the bookends spoke Romanian and German (languages he savvied) and that both spoke the landlord's Bulgarian. A round robin was established and their glasses refilled. Harrington took tea. Satisfied his coin was genuine, the innkeeper and company agreed to help if they could and Harrington learned the name of an outbound ship.

"Demeter," one of the old boys said. The others agreed. "Demeter, a Russian schooner, sails today. For England, I believe."

It was grand news. Harrington hadn't hoped for a vessel bound for his homeland and found himself wondering if his luck might not have turned. He had no idea how far until he followed their stares to a rugged, man of the sea alone in the corner.

"Her captain," one whispered. Prodded by the landlord, he added, "Nikilov."

He wore a blue coat with shining brass buttons, a matching waistcoat and trousers, a white pin-striped blouse and wrinkled blue tie. Worn black boots scuffed the floor, and a beaten hat lay at his elbow. He was sixty-like, clean shaven, wind-burned and sun-baked. He studied several maps, unrolled atop his table, as he sipped from a china cup.

Harrington gulped his own tea, nervously crossed to him and, in his admittedly rusty Russian, introduced himself.

Without looking up, the captain said, "You are not from here."

He confessed he wasn't, stumbled explaining his presence and, omitting his reason for needing to be gone, asked for passage aboard his ship. With a disinterested wave, the commander muttered, "No passengers. Private charter; cargo only."

"Please, captain," Harrington blurted, remembering four nights since, the rough days between, the brothers Gabor and their red-faced father on his heels with blood in their eyes, eager to shoot

Chapter Two

him like a dog. He shuddered. "I do not mean to offend. But it is important I leave Varna. I can pay you."

"You do offend, young Herr. Your Russian offends my ears. I speak English."

"I am sorry."

He waved away the apology and the apologist. "I cannot help you."

Harrington would not be put off. He grabbed the nearest chair and impudently sat. "Please, I beg you! It is vital I get to England."

The captain looked up, stinging him with electric blue eyes beneath exploding white brows. "Is that true? Must you get to England? Or is it merely vital you leave Varna?" The young man hesitated. "It does not matter. We are contracted for cargo only. It would be illegal."

"I would pay whatever you demanded."

"That is ridiculous. You have no idea what I might demand. I pray, Herr...?"

"Harrington. Trevor Harrington."

"I pray, Herr Harrington, you guard your soul more carefully than your purse. I cannot offer passage. But you are in luck. I am not a bandit, so you will get away without having your throat cut."

"Do you need crew? I could work for you. I'll be no trouble."

The captain studied the man, who looked intelligent but did not understand the word *No*. "Would you be any use?"

"Excuse me?"

"I am not concerned with trouble. I can handle trouble. Would you be any use? Have you ever been to sea?"

"I crossed the English Channel - once."

The captain made a noise, either amusement or disgust, Harrington wasn't sure, and shook his head. "I already have ballast."

"I'm not a sailor," Harrington said, talking rapidly to head-off rejection. "I'm a scholar. But I am strong. I'm not afraid of labor. I know a good many things."

"Why must you leave? What laws have you broken?"

"It isn't a matter of broken laws," Harrington said bitterly. Then, in for a penny, he finished the thought. "It's a matter of broken hearts."

The captain sipped his tea and smiled sadly. "I had a heart once, Herr Harrington. It too was broken." He frowned and pushed the thought away. "You would be useless; teats on a boar." Then he paused, struck by an idea. He lifted a finger and, staring at Harrington, stabbed down at the top-most map on the table. "Tell me something, anything, about this spot – that I do not already know – and I will sell you passage on my vessel."

Both looked, following the finger to the map.

"The Dardanelles." Harrington cleared his throat.

"Yes. As it says."

He cleared his throat again, buying time. "Uh, with the Bosphorous, uh, they make navigation possible between the Black Sea and the Mediterranean."

"You think I do not know that?"

Harrington held up his hand, pleading. "The waters..." he said, trying to remember something he'd read. "The waters of the Dardanelles flow in two directions; from the Sea of Marmara to the Aegean via a surface current and in the opposite direction via an undercurrent."

Nikilov smiled. "That is good. You are smart, young Herr. But – I already know that too." He waved him away and returned to his cup.

It wasn't fair, Harrington thought, rising to go. What in the name of blazes could he tell a sea captain about the Dardanelles? Then, as if a lamp had been lit, he shouted, "Lord Byron!" He turned back to the captain, ignoring the eavesdropping trio at the bar. "Lord Byron."

Nikilov shrugged his ignorance.

"In May of 1810, Lord Byron, British author and poet, swam across the Dardanelles. An event he immortalized in Canton the Fourth of his poetic masterpiece Don Juan, eh, published in 1821."

Chapter Two

The captain growled with his eyebrows. "Why would I care about this?"

"I don't imagine you do. The question is, did you know of it?"

The captain stared, then laughed a rumbling laugh (the landlord and his book-ends joined in). He jumped up, clamped Harrington's jaw in his rough hand and demanded, "Are you healthy?" He squeezed so hard Harrington had to open his mouth, jerked his face toward the lantern and, squinting, examined his teeth. Satisfied, the commander released the pressure but maintained the hold on his jaw. With a threatening thumb he pulled down on the flesh of Harrington's cheek, abandoning the role of dentist for that of ophthalmologist. His eyeball bulged and Nikilov stared in. He repeated the process on the other side.

Though startled and embarrassed, Harrington understood. He'd read of it. The captain was looking for signs of illness, conjunctivitis perhaps. Emigrant passengers had to pass physical exams before traveling to prevent the spread of disease; often holding up passage for days. The captain was expediting the process. "You look healthy enough."

Nikilov released his numbed face, then rumbled again, "Lord Byron!"

* * *

In the end, the captain charged a steep but fair price for passage. Nikilov was taking a risk. Harrington recognized it and would have paid more. He left the pub with a note ordering he be shown aboard, and a warning to be squared-away by eleven-thirty as they sailed at noon with him or without.

The last had been unnecessary. There was nothing in Bulgaria, or Europe, Harrington needed more than to be gone. For all he knew, his pursuers were right behind and he'd have been mad to be taken so near to an escape. He would get aboard and out of sight. Buying a new hat could wait until he was safely back in England.

The harbor entrance was separated from the city by a large warehouse that, at that moment, featured a queue of men trailing out its open door. At a table inside, a bald, muscular seaman was swearing blue fire at the line of would-be sailors. Things looked to be going badly. The Englishman considered the note in his hand and moved on, hopeful of finding a less excited ship's officer. He turned the seaward corner of the building and the chaos of the harbor came into view.

To the far right lay a web-work of piers extending from the quay, forming a marina of working ships, fishing boats, and pleasure craft of every shape, rig, tonnage and color, flying flags of every nationality presently considered a friend, moored or at anchor. Several knockabouts (one with no bowsprit, another rigged with the mast forward) tacked in, passing a steamer leaving a gray trail as it tacked out. A ketch, across the inlet, was making ready for sea. Behind it, lay several two-masted schooners (lumber and grain haulers) at anchor, their sails furled, their masts poking the sky like skeletal fingers; one taking in cargo, the other discharging. A larger barque rested idly on this side toward the harbor entrance. To the sea, a long pier and breakwater jutted south protecting all from the sporadic ravages of nature. It culminated in a lighthouse at the harbor mouth. Back his way, tied astern of the barque, a pulling cutter (*Harbor Pilot* painted across her bows) bobbed on the water. The sky above was filled with sea birds singing to the work. All across the quay, dock workers, sailors, and civilians walked and talked, stood and strolled, labored and lounged under the morning sun.

As exciting as Harrington found it all, still it was merely background.

What grabbed his attention despite the harbor's activity was an imposing ship's figurehead; a beautifully carved sculpture decorating the prow of a three-masted schooner before him and stretching down the dock to his right.

For centuries, bow ornamentation exemplified the wealth and might of ship owners; weighing tons and twinning the sides of the

Chapter Two

bowsprit. Following the Napoleonic wars, while still beautiful, they went out of style as massive works of art, shrank in expense and pomposity, and reverted to their original purpose - to proclaim the name of the ship to an illiterate society. The scholar studied this figurehead, captivated. Most, Harrington understood, were either female or bestial but this specimen was both. The Greek goddess of the crops and fertility, her gold hair wrapped in a halo, gazed out over the harbor's waters. She wore a crimson gown, off her shoulders, with the head of a wild boar resting between her exposed breasts, their bodies intertwining. A basket of vegetables occupied her near hand. A torch staff was gripped in her other, extended to symbolically light the darkness ahead. Harrington had found her, the Greek goddess and the Russian schooner that bore her name; *Demeter*.

While she wasn't the work of art her figurehead was, *Demeter* was beautiful. More, she was the answer to Harrington's prayers. She was thirty meters long, perhaps thirty-five, with another ten for the bowsprit and mizzen boom; over 150 feet. Her three masts rose over twenty-five meters, nearly 90 feet, into the air. She was dark brown at her rails and altered in hue as you descended the side of the ship; brown to auburn, to burnt umber, to sienna, maroon and finally bright crimson at the water line. The effect was startling - as if the ship were bleeding into the sea.

Less-than-startling was the loading process. Harrington expected the bustle to be concentrated around the soon to launch ship. But it was not. The activity about *Demeter* was, for want of a better term, anemic. On her bow, chutes slanted from the bulwark to the deck and open fore hatch. There they sat – unused. Likewise, on the dock, a trapeze was in place to swing cargo aboard, ready but idle. Harrington continued down the dock past workers, sitting and smoking, past several others at midship carrying sacks marked *silver sand* up the gangplank. They moved steadily, in no rush, gained the deck then disappeared. On the stern, this side of the ship's wheel, many identical sacks were stacked; more sand. Two men, a big one in a white blouse and one with no shirt, lifted these (with no urgency) and passed them through scuttle holes in the deck.

Harrington shouted up, inquiring if either was an officer, but they paid him no mind. The scholar was at a loss when a third man appeared at the rail, combed his fingers through black bangs clawing at his eyes and, in Russian, asked Harrington what he wanted.

"You are a ship's mate?"

"Second."

"I'm to hand this to one of the ship's mates," Harrington said, waving the captain's note. The man just stared, so he added, "It is from your captain."

Suspicious, the second joined Harrington on the quay. He read the note, eyeing the Englishman warily. "I did not think we were carrying passengers." He returned the slip. "Did you show this to the first mate? The bald one?" He crooked a thumb at the warehouse.

"He didn't appear in the mood."

The second laughed. "No, he rarely is." He started back up. "I will prepare your cabin. Remain here until I call."

'Here' was beside the ship, in the open; a place Harrington had no desire to be. He chose instead to disappear into the shadows between the warehouse and the harbor pilot's shack, until the second permitted him to board. It was his first lesson in the danger of disobeying orders.

A din erupted. There came the turn of heavy wheels, the crack of whips, the wild cries of panting horses, shouts - and singing. A startled Harrington looked up to see a riot of force and color rounding the warehouse in a blur of insane speed. It was a monstrous ornate wagon that would have been at home in a carnival caravan. It was filled with a cargo of wooden boxes, and (jovially singing!) men, was pulled by four draft horses, and bore down as if Harrington were its target. The driver, a mustachioed gypsy, grew wide-eyed as he spotted the man in their path. He yanked on the reins and shouted. Harrington dove out of the way. The

Chapter Two

horse team missed him by inches as the wagon ground to a halt, its boxes groaning, its men shouting. But the incident wasn't over. Two other wagons, the ladder-sided leiter-wagons of the country, followed in single file parade; loaded with identical stacked boxes, pulled by eight massive horses each and driven, not by gypsies, but by Slovaks. The driver of the second shouted and reined his horses in just before they collided with the lead wagon. The driver of the third halted his team and only avoided running into the second.

"Cor blimey!" Harrington sputtered. It was a guttural expression he'd picked up in London; hardly gentlemanly but it fit the moment. He jumped up covered in fresh dirt. "What do you think...? You almost killed me!"

The horses stamped and panted.

The first driver, carrying a rifle, left his seat on the Englishman's side. He was a Szgany, a gypsy, one of six climbing down. They were attired in high boots, puffed pants, colorful vests, wearing bandanas or wide-brimmed hats. They were weatherworn, tattooed; several wore neckerchiefs, several ear-rings. The driver, the largest of them, took the lead horse by the bridle to calm him.

The men aboard the other wagons climbed down too. These were Slovaks; glorious looking barbarians with baggy dirty-white trousers tucked into high black boots, puffed linen shirts, and massive leather belts studded with brass nails. Several wore long mustaches and all long hair beneath huge cowboy hats. Most carried rifles.

Why the Slovaks and Szgany were together was anyone's guess. But their number was imposing, their weapons threatening, and their silence frightening. None appeared ready to apologize. In fact they ignored Harrington completely. For his part, the Englishman got a bad feeling. Despite the bright sun, it was as if a gloom had descended over the dock. He quickly decided Falstaff was right, discretion was the better part of valor. He would do without an apology. He brushed himself off and renewed his search for shadow and anonymity.

The bald first mate and his prospective sailors, having witnessed the tumult, funneled back into the warehouse. Harrington, loitering, heard an argument taking shape (in bleats of Romanian and Russian). The mate shouted, "What the hell are you talking about?"

"What I said. I'm not going."

Another voice added, "Nor I."

"You signed the book. And you. You both agreed to sail."

"We changed our minds."

"In twenty minutes? You were eager to sail twenty minutes since."

"In five minutes, if you must have it!"

"Something's changed in the last five minutes? What? What's changed!?"

"Do you not feel it?" The anger was gone. The man was afraid. "There is something wrong here. Something is dreadfully wrong. And it was not here, this feeling, five minutes ago. I quit!"

"And me."

Two seamen, their kits shouldered, walked out and away from the port. No sooner were they gone then, inside, the mate was arguing with another. "What did you say?"

"I said, if this ship is screwy, I want more money."

Even from outside, Harrington recognized the thud of flesh – and a crash. Someone was struck and had gone down like a ton of bricks. "There's nothing screwy about this ship!" the first yelled. "Those are the wages. Plus all the goddamn grief you can swallow. If you want the work, sign the book and grab your kit. If not, get the hell off the quay!"

Another sailor stormed out. Holding a swelling eye, cursing, he threw his duffle over his shoulder and walked away. Harrington watched him go, then scanned the dock from the schooner to the gypsies and their cargo of boxes, wondering what he'd missed. What had happened in the last few minutes that suddenly nobody wanted any part of this voyage?

Chapter Three

WHILE tensions cooled in the warehouse, they heated up on the dock. The Bulgarian laborers, happy lounging before the gypsies arrived, were impatient to unload the wagons. They were suddenly, strangely nervous and wanted those boxes off their quay.

Their supervisor led three men to the rear of the Szgany wagon and immediately began moving the caskets, seven feet long, two and a half wide, two high, by the rope handles on either side. In their haste, they thumped the first box heavily on the tail of the wagon. The leader, complaining of the weight, dropped his end hard on the dock. His co-worker had no choice but to follow. The Szgany driver clouded. He waved his rifle and shouted for them to watch what they were doing. When the supervisor shouted back, the row was on. Sides were quickly drawn; the port workers behind their leader, the gypsies and gun-toting Slovaks behind their Szgany boss.

Harrington had a front row seat. The mate and his would-be sailors, again, looked on from the warehouse. The second descended *Demeter's* gangway while several of his hands watched from the deck. The harbor pilot's door flew open and, shouting, two others joined the fray. The first was the surprisingly spry harbor master, who looked sixty, but ran as if he were twenty years younger. Well behind him was a bespectacled, flesh-ball of

Chapter Three

a man dressed like a toff and waving a handful of papers. The pilot reached them first and, growling, demanded the reason for the conflict.

Chaos ensued as men shouted in Bulgarian, German, Russian, Romanian (and several Romany sub-tongues). The Szgany was livid about the inept handling of the boxes. The Bulgarian resented being told his job. The pilot wanted order in his port. The second wanted his ship loaded (the first agreed, goddammit!). The rotund solicitor, introduced as Herr Leutner, in the interests of the Transylvanian noble that owned the boxes, wanted the wagons inventoried before anything was moved. Leutner wanted that done now so he could sign and go.

The harbor master won and order was restored. The ship's crew returned to stowing sand, the first mate to finding sailors. The men on the dock stood at ease while the pilot, Herr Leutner, the supervisor, the big Szgany, and the ship's second conducted the inventory.

The wagons held fifty boxes, matching the manifest, of common earth for unspecified (and to Harrington quite unimaginable) scientific purposes; to be delivered to the consignee, a solicitor called Billington, of 7, The Crescent, Whitby, England. What the matter was with English soil that it was necessary to ship dirt from Transylvania, the scholar had no idea – and no more interest. The second would soon be free and he would have permission to board.

One further incident, however, occurred before the cargo was safely loaded.

The supervisor and his mate carried a box to the rig lifting its fellows to the schooner's deck. There, as if they hadn't trouble enough, the leader tripped and fell. His end smacked the solid masonry of the quay, the box split at the corner, and dirt spilled out. His partner had no choice but to let his end crash as well.

The Szgany driver leapt from his wagon and stormed them, shouting curses, with blood in his eyes. Both drew back in fear. The gypsy inspected the damage then stood with an enormous sigh of relief. He turned and slapped the Bulgarian supervisor to the ground. While he lay stunned, the gypsy slapped him again. He turned his rage on the second man and only the intervention of the other Szgany prevented his thrashing.

When the harbor master stepped up this time, the Szgany refused to back down. Waving his rifle, he shouted that the boxes had been entrusted to his people and warned everyone within hearing he and his comrades would shoot the next man to mishandle them. The pilot pleaded there be no violence. The solicitor thanked the Szgany leader, saying he appreciated their efforts on behalf of his client. He waved an envelope with a broken red wax seal, correspondence from his client, as proof of authority and added, "The harbor master, I'm sure, will see all is gotten aboard safely."

The pilot bowed curtly. "It will be done, Herr Leutner." He admonished the Bulgarian for his stupidity, his laziness, and threatened to fire him and his men on the spot. He ordered them all back to work – and with the utmost care.

The matter was finished. The Szgany and Slovaks, at their leader's insistence, unloaded what remained in the wagons. The Bulgarians saw the boxes aboard and, once there, the ship's crew (the shirt-less one laughing, the massive one shaking his head, and now a third man grumbling and nervously crossing himself) joined in loading them into the hold.

With their wagons empty, the supervisor thanked the big Szgany and bid him and his men good day. He was wasting his breath. The gypsy, still carrying his rifle, moved to the edge of the dock. His men, and the armed Slovaks, followed. Silently, they lined up beside the ship on either side of the gangplank intending, it appeared, to remain until after the schooner's departure.

* * *

The troubles on the quay were echoed inside the warehouse. Another sailor had quit, for no discernable reason, and the first was ready to explode.

Chapter Three

Everything about Iancu Constantin, *Demeter's* mate, was explosive. He not only looked like a hard-boiled egg, he was one; with gray-streaked eyebrows that, depending on the light, looked red, or brown, or black above small, closely-spaced eyes that seemed always to be issuing a threat. His mouth was angled so that, even when he laughed, he seemed to be sneering. He wasn't laughing now.

What a morning it had been! He rubbed his aching dome because it wasn't over yet.

He'd received word their cook, Dimitri Andreev, was sick and could not sail. The same report said the ailing man had done them the favor of finding his own replacement. When the stand-in arrived, the mate nearly had a heart attack. The new cook was ancient as hell, decades beyond useful sea-going years, and a clamorous Scotsman to boot. Constantin rejected him unequivocally. But to the first's surprise, the old boy, called Swales, not only stood his ground but returned fire. He relayed his extensive experience and insisted there was no better ship's cook in Varna, in Bulgaria, or on the Black Sea. Constantin relented. He signed the old man, advised him to make do with their provisions or see to extras on his own, and warned him to be ready on time. Heaven fall or hell freeze, they sailed at noon.

As usual, several hands from their last voyage had disappeared with their pay. Replacing such was rarely a problem but, today, signing those few was proving impossible. Following the excitement on the dock, one seaman after another backed out claiming there was *something wrong*. It was the damnedest thing Constantin had ever seen.

He still needed crew and was down to his last two applicants. What a pair they were! Constantin turned his book on the table and handed a fountain pen to the first; a wiry sprout, more boy than man, with short blonde hair peeking from beneath a black knit cap. The lad hesitated, pen shaking, staring at the page as if he couldn't remember his...

"Name! What is your name, son?"

"Uh, oh, Funar," the boy squeaked, all nerves. "Umm, Rada Funar."

"Write that." The lad stared at the book. "Do not worry. Many cannot write; just make a mark."

"Huh?" the boy croaked.

"Make an ex!" he growled impatiently. "Tick the page, for Christ!"

The terrified lad hurriedly forged an X. Shaking his head, Constantin grabbed the pen and pointed through the door to the second atop the gangplank. "That is Mr. Eltsin. Do what he says."

The lad nodded. He grabbed up his kit bag and hurried out, across the dock, and up the gang.

"Nothing bigger willing to sail with you?"

The question came in a ridiculous falsetto! The mate glared up at the questioner – unable to believe his eyes. He'd just weeded through one unimpressive queue of applicants but this fellow, the last body standing... Bless Nikolay! This one took the cake.

* * *

The damaged box had been hammered back together, the earth replaced, and it and its brothers loaded. Harrington too was safely aboard and in his cabin with no more thought of the incident. Neither he, nor the crew, understood how significant that box might have been.

Had the same error occurred with one of the other caskets, a moment of horror might well have erupted on the quay. And a drawn-out tragedy of terror, that day being set into motion, may well have been avoided. Forty-nine of the wooden boxes contained nothing more than moldy earth, taken from the chapel graveyard of a ruined Transylvanian castle. The fiftieth held... something more.

* * *

Chapter Three

The last two hands signed, the pencil-thin deck boy and the odd-looking sailor (with the alarming falsetto and a soiled shirt), stood beside the fore hatch watching the bustle on *Demeter's* deck. They would have done forever, ignored by the crew, had not the second mate spotted them and barked an order. In response, the mountainous seaman appeared; an intimidating Russian named Olgaren, with a barrel chest, the chin of a bull mastiff and a melon head radiating tufts of untamed red hair. Eltsin, the second, ordered him to escort the hands below to store their gear and to return them top-side double quick. Olgaren tossed a sausage-fingered salute and reached for one of the seaman's two kit rolls.

"No!" the new sailor squeaked, coming unglued. He clutched his bags as if Olgaren were a thief. "I'll take them!"

Olgaren looked a question with dull cow eyes. The new *man* matched his lady-like voice; petite, with gray-streaked hair draping down his back. Were it not for the monstrous black mustache, waxed at the tips, hiding the lower half of *his* face... Olgaren shrugged and turned to the other, a snippet of a boy. Funar ogled back in fear and hugged his own small kit to his chest. Out of shrugs, and more than willing to let them carry their kit if that's how they'd have it, Olgaren started away. He led his charges astern, aft of the midship deckhouse, through, and below to the crew's quarters.

From the moment they entered the between-decks, any time he was below, Olgaren's life was a misery. Olgaren was six-two. The overhead of every below deck and between-deck space aboard *Demeter*, except the forward hold, stood at six feet. Their voyages echoed with sounds of his head thudding the overhead beams, his muttered curses, and the laughter of his mates (heartless bastards all). Between-decks, his bowed back and the top of Olgaren's bright red hair were always on display.

"You are lucky," Olgaren said, sluggishly. He indicated the empty cots and storage places. "We are short crew. Everyone gets a bunk." They selected theirs while he warned them not to touch anything they did not own and suggested (without explanation) they not get too comfortable. He finished muttering, "We are needed topside." Then, hunched, head down, he led them back up.

* * *

The second reported them shipshape. Which, for this voyage, meant the vessel was damned near empty. The stores, water, food, and rum, were on deck, in the galley larder, and in the holds as was convenient to the captain's will and the cook's whim. The client's boxes were in the fore (and a few in the midship) hold. And, because her load was so light, a great deal of sand ballast had been taken on throughout all three holds. "Ready for departure."

Captain Nikilov returned aft where his first was conversing with the steersman. "Mr. Eltsin reports the ship ready. The crew?"

The mate led the captain from the ears of the steersman, beneath the main boom, to the starboard rail. "I've raised a ship's compliment, captain," he said. "But they are no compliment to you. We have the bodies to sail but we're damned short of sailors. I apologize, sir."

"Mr. Constantin, you do yourself an injustice."

The first shook his head. "No, sir." He stared over the rail at the harbor, searching for the words, then over the starboard bow to the breakwater, beyond the lighthouse at its southern-most tip, and into the Black Sea brilliant with the high sun. "Four hands disappeared with their pay; leaving us with three. Replacing them has been... difficult. Many applicants; few worth considering."

"No experienced men?"

"Some... signed. But they walked off. Said there was something wrong with the ship. One of them, I don't know the bastard's name..."

Nikilov frowned. "Mr. Constantin."

"Your pardon, captain. But he said, within hearing of the rest, this ship was screwy. I almost..." The mate paused.

Chapter Three

Nikilov studied his junior, imagining what he'd *almost* done. Constantin's loyalty and devotion were well known. So was his temper.

"I signed five," the first said. "Two have not reported. Late as it is, I doubt now they will."

"Three will do," the captain said, ignoring his own doubts. "We have nothing for cargo and I expect only summer seas. Where are they?"

Constantin led the captain to the front of the deckhouse and scanned the deck and above. He spotted three men in the square-rigging and pointed to one, the odd one, halfway up the fore mast. "That's Smirnov," he said. "A Russian."

Nikilov followed Constantin's hand aloft to the slightly built man with the outrageous mustache, his feet entwined around a mast spar, his hair tied now in a bright blue bandana. "A man of the sea?" the captain asked. "Seems little to him, save hair."

Constantin nodded, unable to disagree. "He acts as odd as he looks." Returning to the deck, he pointed beyond the fore hatch into the bow. The second mate had brought the hour-glass forward (a half-hour glass really; stored at the helm to keep the ship's time) and was showing it to the new boy. No doubt explaining one of his many duties. "The lad with Eltsin is Funar; a Romanian."

The captain took in the thin blonde in cap, jersey, and boots; all too big for him. "What are you planning to do with him?"

"If he does nothing but swab the deck or hand out the rum, he'll free up an able hand."

The captain stared hard at his first. "A pipsqueak and a child. I've never seen the like."

"I have no explanation, sir," Constantin said. "No one in Varna would sail with us."

Cognizant he wore his emotions on his sleeve, Nikilov diverted his stare to the sky and held it until his brow unfurled and the fiery feelings ebbed. Only then did he return his gaze to the deck and the new deck boy. He watched the delicate-looking lad take the fragile timepiece in hand (wondering which would break first) and follow the second aft. Nikilov sighed and nodded his assent, if not his approval. "He'll do," he told the first. "But I am not convinced he's old enough. Leave him off the manifest. We will pretend he is not here."

"What about customs? If he's not on the manifest. . . "

"Yes, Mr. Constantin, it is a problem. You brought a child aboard my ship. When the time comes, you will be responsible for hiding him from the Turkish customs officials."

"Aye, captain."

"You signed five. Two failed to appear. Two are useless girls. I hold my breath in anticipation of your fifth recruit."

The mate looked as if he wished he were – anywhere else. Then, aware procrastination would only make matters worse, cleared his throat and began. "Dimitri Andreev fell sick this morning and could not sail."

"We have no cook?"

"We do. He sent his own replacement. What could I do but sign him?"

"Please, Iancu, tell me he has been to sea before? That he wears a man's boots?"

"He does. He has been wearing a man's boots. . . for a long time."

What, Nikilov wondered, did that mean? He met the mate's gaze and decided against asking. It had been a strange morning as it was. But omens, good or bad, were tools of the devil and he would not take the bait. The time to cast off was at hand and, as they could not delay, he would shake off the gloom trying to drown him and go to sea with a positive attitude; thankful for the crew God had provided. For surely a loving God had provided his crew – and his cargo.

Chapter Four

THE owners of *Demeter* had, without the captain's consent, rented his ship under strange conditions. She was to carry no passengers (and, officially, she did not) and no cargo save the boxes already aboard. Of course, the ship could, and normally would, carry a great deal more. The obstacle of lost revenue had been overcome when the client agreed to pay the difference for the weight they might have carried. Which meant Nikilov's hold was filled with tremendously expensive dirt.

The contract also stipulated the ship embark for England that day, *no later than noon;* which gave them another problem. Sailing off the dock would have been preferred. But they were square-rigged on the fore, necessitating a full and well-trained compliment of hands, a favorable tide, and narrow wind conditions. The Lord may have provided Nikilov with a crew but they were thin. And providence had left the commander empty-handed in regards to the wind and the tide. The gaffe-rigged main and mizzen sails might have done the trick under such conditions but the risk of damage to the ship, the cargo, and the dock made the thought distasteful.

The harbor pilot was consulted as it was his job to guide ships through the dangers of entering and leaving the harbor (the most

Chapter Four

challenging part of any voyage). And, though Nikilov remained in command, to offer his expert advice regarding the local port.

"We've crew enough to sail," the captain said. "But, without a wind, not enough to sail her off."

"We're in no hurry," the pilot replied, "if you wanted to wait for the tide."

"The owners say no later than noon, no matter what. Can we warp her out?"

"Aye. I can pull some men off a barque we're loading. But they'll need be paid."

"So far, money is the only thing about this voyage that is not an obstacle."

"Right then. We'll kedge you out."

Orders were passed and soon, with her sails lowered, the pilot's cutter was put into service. Four men, double-banked, rowed the small boat to *Demeter's* outboard side, while Nikilov's men headed to the schooner's bow. Together, they began laying the kedge.

* * *

In his cabin, Harrington felt the ship move. It was an odd sensation to move while standing still. Followed by the sense he was levitating; for the floor – solid beneath his feet – suddenly felt fluid. There was no doubt, they were off and a flood of relief passed through him. He had escaped Europe with his life.

But the relief was short-lived for the movement of the ship was confusing. On top of the floating sensation, which he felt already was going to take acclimation, their movement seemed to be oddly – lateral. Harrington grabbed the top bunk to steady himself. Yes, he was certain. The ship was going sideways.

* * *

The kedging was in full vigor.

A hawser line had been affixed to a light anchor and handed over into the cutter. The boat crew rowed the anchor as far out as the line allowed, several hundred yards to the seaside, then dropped it to the harbor-bed.

The hawser's loose end had been held aboard *Demeter* and attached to the bow capstan; the hand-winch that lifted the ship's anchors. Poles, standing-in for the shorter hand spikes, were slid horizontally into the capstan's crown. Nikilov's men, like slaves on a mill wheel, walked the bars around winding in the line. With the anchor set in the harbor-bed, the tightening line pulled the ship from the pier into deeper water.

In short order *Demeter* drew near the pilot's cutter and, when the line was nearly vertical, the captain hollered, "Mr. Constantin, back the topsail."

The main gaffe-rigged top sail was pivoted to catch the light breeze, stem their drift, and save the distance they'd gained.

* * *

Leaving aside his crossing the English Channel, Harrington's sea-going experience consisted of sitting in that cabin in that port. There he remained, as it had been made clear the crew didn't need him underfoot. The real reason, of course, was neither he nor the captain could risk his being seen on deck.

He'd even planned to skip the evening meal; not that that was a tremendous sacrifice. He was too on edge. And how could he eat with Ekaterina on his mind? No, he warned himself, don't think about her now! Anyway, with the floor moving, it seemed sensible to wait for sea legs before burdening his stomach. No, he wouldn't be eating. It was best he leave his head, his heart and his stomach to themselves for a time.

Then he was thinking of Ekaterina again. Damn blast it to hell! No one in her family, not her father, the vaunted Lord-high Mayor, nor her muscle-bound, blockheaded brothers, would listen. They

Chapter Four

were hunting him like dogs mad on the scent and fully intended to murder him. What was the use of thinking about her!

He moved to the cabin's sole porthole, intent on getting his mind off the girl and, while he was at it, solving the mystery of the ship's movement. And, assuming it was desired and not a precursor to their sinking, for a last look at Varna and a farewell to the turmoil Europe had brought to his once boring life. He peeked out and saw two things immediately. First, the ship was moving – by the head slightly, but mostly to the starboard – sideways, and the dock and everything on it were gradually receding as they inched away. Second, was an explosion of activity on the dock.

Several new wagons, horses, gentlemen, laborers (some flashing rifles) appeared, seemingly from nowhere, moving across the pier in a wave. Behind them, their commanders appeared, authorities in political and para-military uniform. Among them, obviously in charge, was His Honor, the Lord-high Mayor Gabor and his sons. The brothers, shotguns in hand, looked the quay up and down while the mayor stared, scowling, at the departing *Demeter*.

Harrington ducked. He couldn't have been seen from that distance, but knowing that didn't convince his racing heart. Running for his life may not have been heroic, but it had been the only response available. Escape had never been his intended means of returning home much less by a long sea voyage. They were his only means. Now he could only hope that he had escaped.

* * *

"What does this mean?" one of the seamen grumbled. It was the man who had crossed himself when the dock workers fought. He'd wandered from the capstan to stare at the activity on the quay where more armed men had appeared searching and shouting. Others, their leaders no doubt, stood in confrontation with the gypsies guarding the seaside berth they'd just vacated. The sailor crossed himself again. "There is something wrong here," he muttered. "Something wrong with this voyage."

Funar was at his elbow. Fear shown in the boy's eyes; fear and sadness. He gripped the port rail and stared across the widening distance at the chaos. Smirnov joined them as well, ogling the scene.

"Are we going to get away?" Smirnov squeaked.

"I do not know," Funar replied, all but whispering.

"Get away?" The seaman grumbled, eyeing both with annoyance and suspicion.

"Popescu, get back to your work!" It was the first mate, enraged. "You know better."

The seaman glared daggers at the two new hands then, grumbling, returned to the capstan.

"Funar! Smirnov!" Constantin barked. He pointed to their untended push-poles between the other slavishly circling crewmen. "You also! Your business is here. If you want to work the dock, jump over and swim back! Or I will gladly throw you!"

Funer reddened and, with a last frightened look at the port, hurried back to his labors. Smirnov glared over his monstrous mustache and strolled back defiantly. The mate filed their responses for future reference.

The kedging anchor had been hauled up, the line rowed out and dropped again by the boat crew. *Demeter's* hands, including Funar and Smirnov, were again pushing round the capstan, pulling the ship further from the dock and nearer the sea.

In mid-harbor Nikilov found a breeze to bring the fore, square-rigged top sail into use. At the mouth of the harbor he found the wind to sail. At the breakwater lighthouse he ordered one of the ship's anchors dropped and the sails adjusted again. He thanked the pilot, who replied with his wish for the ship's good voyage.

Paid and content, the pilot returned to his cutter. His crew raised their small sails and, tacking back and forth, leisurely worked the harbor's waves back to the dock.

* * *

Chapter Four

On the quay, the Lord-high Mayor Gabor had finally (distastefully) accepted the word of the Szgany leader that there were no passengers aboard the schooner just put to sea. "My master has chartered the vessel privately," the immovable gypsy insisted. "She carries no passengers and no cargo save what we loaded aboard."

Gabor may as well have taken his word for it. The man, and his armed compatriots, were still aligned along the dock and meant to stay as long as they considered their cargo in jeopardy. The mayor had come to Varna hoping to track a deceitful Englishman, not to engage in armed conflict with a motley group of gypsies and barbarians who had never heard of Trevor Harrington. The cutter returned its master to the quay where the pilot, without taking the side of the Szgany and Slovaks, agreed with their position. He reassured Gabor the departing ship had no passengers. The mayor gave the order and his sons and their hired hunters retreated.

When they were gone, the pilot returned to his shack, and the quay cleared of all threats, the lead Szgany turned and looked out to sea taking in *Demeter* for the last time as she brought her sails around. He nodded, content they had met their commitment. He told his compatriots as much, thanked them and wished them well on their journey back to Transylvania. Then he stuck the barrel of his rifle into his mouth - and blew the top of his own head off.

The last incident of any consequence to occur that day on the Varna quay was the lifeless body of the Szgany leader toppling off the dock into the harbor with a barely audible splash. There, like the paint scheme on the just-departed schooner, he bled into the sea.

*　*　*

With her sails unfurled, Captain Nikilov ordered his crew to weigh anchor and at noon, Tuesday, 6 July, 1897, the Russian schooner *Demeter* – oblivious to both the storm of impotent authority and the bloody suicide that had seen them off – sailed from the port of Varna. Powered by an east wind, they moved safely out around the breakwater into the Black Sea and steered a course S.S.E. down the Bulgarian coastline. As a matter of record, they carried a crew of five hands, a first and a second mate, a ship's cook, and the captain. Unofficially, and therefore not recorded in the manifest, they carried a deck boy and, secreted in his quarters, one English passenger.

Not one of those aboard had any idea that in the dark quiet of the ship's forward hold - they carried something else entirely.

* * *

Dracula awoke, as always, in the dark. But there the centuries-old routine stopped. Usually his timed emergences from hibernation were an awakening in the silence of the tomb. But now a flood of sensory thrills overwhelmed him.

The first was an acute sensation, something he felt rarely; pain. It intrigued him. Despite the cramped quarters of his box, he lifted a hand and dabbed at his forehead. His hands were coarse, broad, with squat fingers. Hairs grew in the centers of his palms and his long, fine nails were cut to a sharp point. They were hardly tools with which to conduct a sensitive investigation in darkness. Yet, they proved to be up to the task. For he immediately located and, with the tip of his index finger, quickly identified the source of his pain. A deep gash marred his high forehead, just right of center, below the hairline. The wound – over two inches in length by the feel – gaped in the middle and was encrusted in dried fluids. Someone had injured him while he slept.

His mind raced quickly over the possibilities; those who in any way might have had the opportunity. The Szgany and the Slovaks, of course, as they had handled his transport. He rejected them. They were loyal – to the death. Theirs.

Then it came to him. Harker! Somehow that damned Englishman had... But no matter. He gave a fleeting thought to his brides, the mistresses of Castle Dracula into whose care Jonathan

Chapter Four

Harker had been left. They would collect the debt. He would pay for this wound – in kisses.

Satisfied with that thought, he forgot Harker. He concentrated instead on the other sensations; the water rushing by beneath him, the creaking wood all around, the shouts, laughter, even singing, distantly above. He felt the keel roll gently, felt the wind in the sails driving the ship, down at the head then up again, down at the heel then up again, defying the surging waves.

He laid his hands to his sides and closed his eyes. His plan had come to fruition. He was at sea and all was well. The voyage of Dracula had begun. The shores of an unsuspecting England lay ahead.

Chapter Five

WEDNESDAY morning, 7 July, brought sunshine and a stronge wind driving *Demeter* south through the western Black Sea. It failed, however, to bring an appetite to the ship's only passenger. Neither Harrington's stomach nor his head found a good reason to break his fast and, when the dinner bell rang, he refused again to partake.

The Englishman decided instead to leave his berth in search of his sea legs. He wasn't complaining. He had fine accommodation; a bunk-style bed (he preferred the upper and used the lower as a chair), a chair he used as a desk, and a desk he didn't use at all. There was a box for storing his kit, a shelf above each bed (he had more books than clothes) and his own lamp which he'd burned the previous night past the ten o'clock call for *lights out* without anyone appearing to care. It was comfortable – for a prison. But with land a day behind, Harrington wanted out. For sanity's sake he needed his mind on other things; to meet the crew and shake off Europe and the last year of his life.

Not surprisingly, the men were less than eager to share themselves with a stranger, let alone a foreigner, despite his ability, to varying degrees, to speak their languages. Their moods were uneven. Sometimes they laughed and sang (two played instruments; an accordion and a violin) but the music seemed rushed and the laughter hollow. Often they whispered or were simply

Chapter Five

silent as they went about their tasks, on edge without seeming to know why. Even learning their names was like pulling teeth, particularly among the Russians; followed by the monumental task of trying to comprehend them.

Take, for example, the ship's captain. His first name, Harrington learned, was Mikhail; a common enough Russian name. (The crewman that divulged it swore, if it got back to the master, he would deny having done so, and added a whispered warning, "God save the soul of the fool who uses it to his face.") But Russian given names had drastic variations depending upon the user. The formal *Mikhail* would be used in business relations and on official documents. The shortened *Misha* by friends and family. The more affectionate *Mishenka* by parents and grandparents. Or, should someone wish to be rude, the variant *Mishka* could be employed. The captain's patronymic name, Sergeyevich, was derived via a rule that added either *-evich* or *-ovich* to his father's first name, Sergei. This had for most of his life been (as the Anglo's would have it) the captain's last name. The combination, Mikhail Sergeyevich, was used formally with unfamiliar people; other ship's masters, older members of his family, government leaders.

Until only months ago the captain, like most of his countrymen, had no surname. In the first ever Russian population count, just completed, the census takers issued surnames. These were based on the names of the family's eldest father. The captain, whose grandfather Nikolay (no relation to the current Emperor of All the Russias) was still living, with the wave of a census taker's pen, would thereafter be known by the government-approved moniker, Mikhail Sergeyevich Nikilov.

Among the new, most widespread Russian surnames were: Ivanov, Petrov, Vasiliev and Nikitin; all to answer the question, as charmingly posed by the Russians, "Whose you are?" Harrington was just thankful there were no women aboard. Female names, he understood, added *-ovna* or *-evna* to their father's name, or took their husband's names, or took the husband's paternal family name (often the same as their village). Harrington shuttered. The masculine names were difficult enough.

* * *

While Harrington wrestled with Russian monikers, someone (outside the knowledge of the others) wrestled with a stern scuttle hatch.

Until that moment, it was dark as the grave in the aft hold. Not as quiet, for there was the rush of water passing on either side and, being the deepest, most-stern part of the ship, the squeaks, creaks, and tension-filled groans of the lines behind the bulkhead working the ship's rudder. But it was as dark. Then one of two overhead scuttle holes came open and a glow of amber stole in from the between-decks companionway above. A lithe form slipped through and quietly drew the lid closed.

The interloper, a thin shadow, carried a cloth-wrapped bundle and paused at the base of the ladder, straining to see the layout of the compartment in which he had no legitimate business. He moved quietly, feeling his way around the stacked sand ballast to the middle of the hold. He paused again to hug the bundle to his chest.

The ship rocked jarringly. He replanted his feet to keep from falling, and inhaled to keep from... He felt suddenly nauseous, seasick, homesick. But he did not regret his choice. He was where he wanted to be; where he needed to be. But enough. Time was short. Someone on deck would miss him and he needed to get back.

He groped among the bags of sand until he found a space that would serve. A hiding place invisible to a sailor going about his business. Having found it, with great care, he tucked the bundle out of sight. He felt his way back to the ladder, lifted the hatch and, finding the companionway clear, climbed out and pushed the lid back into place.

The aft hold was dark again.

Chapter Five

* * *

That night, of his first full day at sea, Harrington had the opportunity to practice their names when he joined the crew for supper in the mess. His companions consisted of three Russians, the big Moisey Olgaren, Feliks Petrofsky, and Pasha Amramoff, who had all sailed with this captain for many years, and a Romanian, Bogdan Popescu (who nobody seemed to like), that had been with them for several voyages. One mate was present, the Russian second with the threatening bangs, Georgiy Eltsin.

The first, Constantin, who normally ate with the crew was that night supping with Captain Nikilov in his quarters. Ippolit Smirnov, the mustache with a small Russian attached, was on duty at the wheel. The deck boy, whom Harrington had yet to meet or even see close up, was absent. Likewise, the old cook, who laid their meal out in silence then vanished like a ghost. Whether or not old Swales' disappearing act was a comment on the night's repast, Harrington did not know.

What he did know, or quickly discovered, was how badly he'd misjudged his readiness to eat. Watching the experienced sea dogs stuff themselves with salted pork, grease gravy and hard biscuits overspread with gobs of butter, as the table pitched and rolled to the movement of the sea, only made it worse. Four bites and the Englishman's stomach began to rumble. Harrington inhaled deeply...

Then, out of nowhere, Olgaren slapped the table with the flat of his hand. The explosive BANG made Harrington jump. He stared, ogling the massive Russian. Olgaren lifted his hand – and the flattened remains of the two-inch cockroach he'd killed.

Harrington excused himself and rapped his shin getting away. He threw his hand over his mouth to stifle a cry, and his stomach's impending return, and stumbled hurriedly from the mess to a chorus of derisive laughter.

* * *

"I've sailed 'round the waarld!"

Harrington heard the shout over the rushing water below. He breathed deeply, watching the white caps swirl in cold blackness, then forced himself to look up, through bleary eyes, at the speaker on the deck beside him. It was Oliver Swales, the old cook.

In the dim light of the half moon, and the dimmer light of the kerosene lamp on the fore mast some distance away, he was little more than a shadow; but a bent and recognizable shadow. He lit a match and put it, flickering in cupped arthritic fingers, to a short-stemmed pipe in his teeth. Then he loudly repeated the boast, "Aye, lad. I've sailed 'round the waarld!"

Harrington, folded over the pinrail, his head dangling above the sea, breathed deeply. He ran a kerchief across his lower lip and dabbed the tear-filled corners of his eyes.

The cook continued to bluster. "I've whaled in the bitt-er north o' the German Sea. Hauled sisel from the Grand Turk, coffee from South America, pushed wheat down the flooded Nile, an' drank Bumboo in the West Indies. I've sailed from one end o' God's creation t'other an' seasick was me only constant companion." His clay pipe clicked against his teeth. "Aye, lad, seasick was me constant companion."

Harrington dabbed his mouth again, flushed and overheated, but with that undeniable sense of relief that comes after you've... Anyway, he felt a good sight better and was – at least temporarily – sure of his stomach. He pushed up on the rail. He turned slowly, for despite the calm sea the deck was in constant motion, and leaned his rear against the bulwark. Etiquette dictated he reply, but nothing came to mind. His mouth tasted of sick stomach. Better to keep it closed.

The old man, wispy white hair, round red face, drew hard on his pipe, puffed an aromatic cloud of smoke, and pointed over the side of the ship. "No' a comment on me cookin', I hope?"

Harrington shook his head to assure him it wasn't.

The cook laughed a congested, smoke-filled laugh. The Englishman's frown was lost in the darkness, or the cook ignored it, but

Chapter Five

he slapped Harrington on the shoulder in a fatherly way and went on as if there'd been none. "Ye've nowt to be embarrassed fer, lad. Most people throw up after eatin' their first meal aboard. Some struggle for days t' keep food down; long, gruellin' days they are. I've seen folk, masel', bedridden fer the crossin', virtigo, nausea, strugglin' to rise for one reason an' one reason only, to puke their guts out an' fall back abed. I've seen men so o'erwhelmed w' seasick they starved t' death durin' the voyage. An' who could blame 'em? Who could eat? How could ye eat? How could ye swallow down pulled pork flesh, bloody rare roast beef, fish stew - with some o' these crazy bastards eatin' heads an' all right in front o' ye. With the ship bouncin' up an' down, jostlin' with the waves. The deck rockin', forward and aft, starboard to port; pitchin' an' rollin', pitchin' an' rollin'...."

Harrington spun round and, heaving from the bottoms of his curled toes, vomited over the side again. Between the spasms, somewhere behind, the cook's timber laugh grew distant.

* * *

His stomach empty, his dizziness mostly abated, his mouth rinsed and lips again wiped clean (thanks to one of the rain barrels on deck), and his shirt and waistcoat realigned, Harrington cautiously maneuvered the port companionway, beside the midship deckhouse, toward the back of the ship, intent on returning to his cabin and bunk. Suddenly his rented prison cell didn't sound so bad.

He paused at the rear corner of the deckhouse, listening to the ship's bell ring. It was followed by Smirnov's scratchy falsetto, "Eight bells and all's well." Then, under his breath, the added, "'Cepting for Popescu late again to relieve the watch."

Harrington peered round the corner. In the pale lamplight, he could just make out Swales bending Smirnov's ear at the ship's wheel. Harrington rolled his eyes and leaned against the shadowed bulkhead. He'd had more than enough of Swales for one night.

Better to return forward and wait him out. Surely the old cook would go below soon.

Demeter rode the dark water with relative ease, pitching and rolling only slightly, with an occasional yaw at the bow, as they cut a path to the southwest. The night's warm breeze blew gently in the billowed canvas of the sails. He reached the battened forward hatch and pulled up, groping for the main mast, when the ship carved into a particularly robust wave. The deck leveled and one of the jib sails snapped like the report of a gun. Then came a sound Harrington knew well. Somewhere in the dark starboard bow he heard someone being sick.

Harrington felt for them. The pit of his stomach still rumbled. His nose and throat burned. He still felt the attending exhaustion. Yet, forgive him, he was secretly glad he wasn't alone. Someone else, poor soul, knew what he had gone through (his stomach gurgled); was going through. And, in this cruel world, who really wanted to be alone? He moved forward, wondering whether he might be of more assistance than the obnoxious old cook had been. If nothing else perhaps offer moral support.

He reached the bulwark even with the fore mast's heavy rigging, grabbed the pinrail to steady himself against the toss of the deck and, in the moonlit bow, made out the form of the deck boy. He was leaning over the starboard rail and anchor, as Harrington had earlier, fiercely throwing up into the sea.

The Englishman waited quietly, not wanting to startle him, until the emesis had run its course. Then as the gasping boy took in air, and wiped his wet eyes with one sleeve and his besotted mouth with the other, Harrington called out, "Don't worry, lad."

The boy started, looking up in abject terror.

Harrington saw little in that light, but he felt the young man redden with embarrassment. "You're not alone," he said, trying to reassure the boy. "Believe me, I know."

Actually he didn't. For the boy, apparently, felt like running. That's exactly what he did, without a word, bolting past the stupefied scholar and vanishing into the shadows aft of the deckhouse.

Chapter Five

In the distance, Harrington heard the steersman shout Funar's name. The call went unanswered. Then he heard the deckhouse door slam shut.

Harrington was flabbergasted. He had by no means intended to frighten the boy. If anything he'd been trying to offer the comfort he had himself been denied by that supercilious cook. A fleeting notion to follow and apologize was as quickly overruled by his own ailing stomach. His head, a slight dizziness returning, made a motion instead that he forget the deck boy and adjourn to his own bunk. His shaking legs seconded it. The motion passed without further discussion.

Chapter Six

THE routines of sailing were interrupted on Thursday, 8 July, by two odd incidents, back to back, aboard *Demeter*.

The morning bloomed bright and Harrington, feeling brighter, came up for a breath of sea air. The captain and mate were chatting near the steersman. Olgaren was coiling a line at the foot of the mizzen mast. (Calling it a rope, the scholar had learned, was a grievous shipboard sin.) The others were amidships, in the main mast shrouds, doing what sailors did with the sails. The Englishman didn't pretend to know, but as it was explained afterward -

Smirnov, his impressive mustache, and his same filthy shirt, had been in the rigging only once. That morning he was going up to work. Two experienced men, Petrofsky and Amramoff, held a friendly debate over which would go with him.

Both were able-bodied seamen. Like paper dolls, only their heads distinguished them, but those differences were striking. Feliks Petrofsky wore his black hair like a gentleman, greased and parted mid-crown. He had large brown eyes and was the quietest man Harrington had ever met. Pasha Amramoff was the ship's carpenter and, until the arrival of the odd Smirnov, the ship's character as well. Amramoff was a laugher, whose pointed beard and round explosion of yellow hair made his head look like one

Chapter Six

of the edible iced-cream cones Harrington had seen under *Cornet with Cream* in his mother's 'Marshall's Cookery Book'.

Petrofsky won (or lost) the debate and went up the mast with the new man. Their mission was to fit a line, called a vang, into place to prevent the top of the main gaffe sail from sagging downwind. This could have been done by dropping the sail but, with a warm breeze, a clear sky, and a calm sea, the mate thought it a beautiful day for Smirnov to work among the clouds.

Petrofsky had climbed the spar to the leech edge of the sail, while Smirnov waited on the mast to pass the vang through the block and down. Harrington watched for several minutes before he realized Funar, the deck boy, had gone up as well. He clung, halfway up the shroud, watching the real sailors above like a trembling baby spider in a web. The Englishman had to hand it to the lad. With nothing but a few lines and thirty feet of air separating him from the other stains on the deck, he ignored his fright and courageously showed his heels to those below.

Then Swales appeared. The old cook, bent and belligerent as usual, barged out the deckhouse door carrying scraps for the sea. He paused, scowled, then took in the three above. He started violently and shouted, "Carrie!" Swales dropped his pail. "What are ye doin', my pretty? Michty me! Get down, 'efore ye break yer gob!" To whom and for what he was hollering, Harrington hadn't a clue. Nor, by their looks, did the startled seamen from quarters high and low.

That was the first odd incident. Strange as it was, it ought not to have caused the second.

Petrofsky, at the peak of the gaff spar, between main and main top sails, was as curious as the rest about the old cook's cater-wauling. Craning his neck, he let both his attention and his feet slip. Petrofsky fell.

He would have fallen to his death had he not acted. Known as the ship's 'marlinspike', Petrofsky carried the metal rope tool for which he'd been named on a lanyard round his wrist when on deck. As he toppled, he flipped this into his hand, swung rapidly, and drove the spike through the foot of the top sail. For a breathless instant he dangled fifty feet above the deck like one of Jules Léotard's trapeze acrobats, arms stretched between the pin he'd stuck through the sail and the gaff vang in his other hand, still held by the alarmed Smirnov on the mast who was struggling to support his weight.

"Swales, what in the..." The captain's rant was interrupted – by Smirnov, shrieking like a woman, on the verge of being pulled off the mast.

The shrouds, Harrington knew, were no place for him. The others could climb, but to what end? Amramoff, at the pinrail, waiting for the mustache to pass the line down when the cook shouted and things went pear-shaped, had no way to help from below. Swales shook himself from whatever caused his outburst and, embarrassed and angry, stared helplessly. The captain, mate, Olgaren were there. Eltsin lashed the wheel and joined them. Other than Popescu, who'd stood the watch and was abed, all were there. But what could they do?

Then the main top sail tore. Petrofsky had no choice but to yank his marlinspike free and trust to Smirnov. He did, and swung on the vang like a buccaneer before the main sail, while his partner fought to hold on to the line and the mast.

The first mate jumped into the rigging and started up. But Funar was well above and, to everyone's surprise, doing more than watching. He'd climbed even with the swinging Petrofsky and worked inside the shroud. Clinging with one elbow and one knee, the sprite of a lad grabbed Petrofsky with the other arm and leg and drew him safely into the shroud. There, they found the vang biting Petrofsky's hand. They freed the miniature noose (which, ironically, saved his neck) to find salvation had come at a price. Petrofsky's hand was torn. Only his leathery skin prevented the rending of thumb and forefinger. Constantin arrived and, with Funar, helped Petrofsky down.

Smirnov was shaking like a leaf. Following hard, he jumped over all to escape the rigging, and fell the last eight feet to the deck. He

Chapter Six

was on his feet immediately, holding his aching back, and staring wide-eyed as the others helped Petrofsky. The marlinspike uttered not a peep, while Smirnov cried out again and ran (his aversion to heights no match for his fear of blood).

The crew ignored Smirnov's antics now Petrofsky was safe. Instead, as if someone had thrown a wet tarpaulin over them, they shared silence and darting glances. To end the gloom, Eltsin slapped the marlinspike's back, stole a look at his bleeding hand, and whistled.

Amramoff laughed (Amramoff was always laughing) and said, "Good thing Popescu is below. He'd be shaking beads; thanking the Lord and blaming the devil in the same breath."

"He'd blame the ship's curse," Olgaren said. Save the breaking waves and wind snapping in the sails, the deck went silent. Reddening, the big Russian added, "Not me. Popescu says there's a curse."

"That's enough!" Constantin barked. "The only curse... is this ship's cursed hands, not watching their work! Let us be about it."

As all returned to their business, Harrington noted the deck boy missing. He observed too words passed between captain and cook, though he heard only a snippet.

"I need not tell you, Swales, that man was almost -"

"Aye, cap'n," the cook nodded. "I apologize, sir. I had no wont to skeer anyone. I thought I... seen somethin'... I could no' have seen. I do no' gawm what come o'er me. T'won't happen ageean."

Nikilov dismissed him, wondering if the mate hadn't made a mistake signing the old fellow. His presence amounted to one more thing he'd need to watch over as...

"Which of you is the doctor?" Harrington asked, interrupting the captain's thoughts.

"No doctor," Nikilov answered simply. He signaled the mate and, together with Eltsin, headed back to the wheel.

Harrington stared after them, agog the vessel carried no physician. Apparently, it was a ship's policy no one be injured. Then he heard Swales, booming again, ask Petrofsky if he needed help

54

below. The marlinspike, arm clutched, bloody bandana wrapped round his hand, shook his head and started for the deckhouse. Swales followed, muttering to Harrington as he passed, "The cook does the doctorin'."

"Indeed! If you could use a hand, I've read quite a little about medicine."

"Come," Swales said. "If ye wish." He picked his pail back up, disposed of the scraps and, with Harrington, caught up to the patient. The injured Petrofsky led the way below. The hobbling cook and the scholar trailed dutifully after.

Concerned, the captain watched the parade. Just who and what had he let aboard his ship?

* * *

Neither during his death-defying moment aloft nor after, as they headed between-decks, had Petrofsky uttered a word. (Come to think, Harrington was not certain he'd ever heard the man speak.) Now, in the galley, forced to answer questions, the secret to the marlinspike's silence was revealed. Petrofsky spoke with a stammer. Not that it mattered to Harrington; many did. But a stuttering Russian (with their sharp and exacting diction) was something to hear. And, though none had ever mentioned it, the condition embarrassed Petrofsky enough he chose to keep mum.

Swallowing his pain was a discipline that might come in handy, Harrington thought, when the cook advised the sailor the wound needed stitches. "We'll play hell fightin' infection w'out," Swales said, biting his unlit pipe. "An' ye don't want gangrene." Petrofsky took the news in the same manner he took everything; quietly.

Permission was received for four rations of rum; three for Petrofsky to imbibe and another to disinfect the wound. The surgery tools were got: soap and fresh water, clean towels and linen, a spool of stout line, one fish hook, and both a file and a pair of pliers borrowed from the ship's carpenter. While Harrington tore the linen and Swales filed the barb off the hook, Petrofsky drank

Chapter Six

rum. While the scholar cleaned the wound and the cook sterilized the hook and pliers, the sailor drank a second ration. While the Englishman doused the oozing injury and Swales threaded the hook, the Russian downed his third ration and talked his head off, slurring his words, but with no sign of a stammer.

To skip the sordid details, sewing the wound was bloody, painful, and Petrofsky passed out half-way through. But the surgery was a success. The stitches were doused a final time and bandaged. Then Harrington and the first carried the unconscious marlinspike to his bed where he remained for the rest of that day and night.

Harrington returned to the galley. They'd performed the surgery on the dinner table and it was only right to help Swales clean it before the next meal. Constantin lagged behind. He'd noticed the door to the forehold untied and, knowing that should not have been, decided to investigate.

* * *

The mate reached for the hold door – as it came open. To his surprise and annoyance, Smirnov stepped out. "What are you doing there?" Constantin demanded.

The wiry Russian looked over his ridiculous mustache with glistening eyes. He wiped his hand down the front of his dirty shirt, cleared his throat and, in that high voice the first was already coming to loathe, chirped, "Nothing." As an afterthought, he added, "Sir."

"You left the deck after the marlinspike was hurt. You came down here? Why?"

Smirnov stared back dully. "Just... looking about."

"What does that mean?" Constantin's beady eyes dissected the new man. A thought occurred, the tension slipped from his hard features, and the first smiled (though it looked like a sneer). "You were bothered by what happened to Petrofsky, I saw. You were sickened by the blood – and ran away, yes? For a moment, yes?"

Smirnov looked confused, but answered, "Yes, sir," all the same.

"Life on the sea can be harsh."

"Yes, sir."

"It is thanks to you, you and Funar, that Petrofsky is alive."

"Yes, sir," Smirnov repeated with a shrug.

"You did well, despite your fear and excitement."

The sailor merely shrugged again, seeming not to understand the compliment. Constantin frowned, concerned the man he'd signed was not only odd but an idiot. It mattered not a whit. They were at sea and Smirnov was one of their hands – whatever his short-comings. "Let me tell you about life aboard this ship," the mate said. "This you will *not* shrug off. The first rule is: you do not go where you do not belong. Do you understand?"

Smirnov nodded slowly. "Yes... sir."

"You have no business in the hold."

The seaman stared with heavy eyelids taking in the hold door as if he'd never seen it before. For an instant Constantin thought the bastard was going to shrug again, but he finally managed a nod and another, "Yes... sir."

"Very well. Back to the deck and your duties."

Smirnov stroked his mustache and started away with his usual irritating stroll. Constantin watched after him until he was up, filing the myriad questions running through his head, then turned to study the door. He slipped into the forehold.

All was quiet with just a sliver of lamplight stealing past him down the steps to reveal everything in its place; sacks of sand, boxes of dirt, barrels of oil, nothing more. He considered descending for a thorough look but decided against it. There was nothing that did not belong; nothing but a nagging feeling. Yes (he would admit it). Something *felt* wrong in the depths of the ship.

Then came a new feeling; embarrassment. He was being ridiculous!

Back in the companionway he secured the door. Smirnov had taken to the hold in a moment of cowardice. As long as that moment came after, and not during, the incident, what did it matter to him? The first returned to the deck where the red and

Chapter Six

orange brilliance of the sunset washed over him and drove away the gloom which had overtaken him in the hold. His lungs filled with fresh sea air and, in spite of himself, Constantin felt an overwhelming sense of relief.

* * *

The sun dropped below the horizon; a red ribbon floating on the waves. It sank into a blue evening and disappeared into a black night. In the forward hold, in his box, the nearly translucent lids covering Count Dracula's eyes opened. He gasped as his fitful sleep ended.

He was listening... more intently than ever to sounds from far away; psychic and sonic waves riding the ether as this vessel rode the sea. Had been listening, for days, to the incessant buzzing of flies, the flapping of their cut-glass wings, the cooing of the lunatic, the whining of the self-important doctor led like a lamb to find the whole affair such a nuisance. Listening to Seward's awe and surprise, when Renfield's *sick* hobby blossomed. It was amazing how much noise spiders made, skittering, spinning, feeding. Dracula smiled, remembering.

Soon the psychiatrist, so far away, had forgotten all about the flies. For Renfield's spiders were a growing nuisance. "You must get rid of them!"

"Ohh, but Dr. Seward..."

"And you needn't look so very sad. You must get rid of some of them, at all events. Three days! Same as before. Three days to get rid of some of these spiders."

Renfield responded, as always, by scribbling in his little notebook; maniacally ciphering, adding, subtracting, multiplying, dividing until the world went away. Not wise that, giving a dangerous lunatic a fountain pen! Then silence – as the scribbling stopped.

Hadn't the *crunch* and the *squish* that followed been entertaining! When a carion-bloated blowfly flew into the room, was snatched in mid-air by the aggravated patient, held up (at Dracula's insistence) to ensure the doctor an eyeful, and popped into Renfield's mouth as if it were a sweetie.

"Renfield, my heavens! That isn't the thing! Ohh, that isn't the thing, at all."

Then, from his cold box of earth, from the sea, Dracula capped the rousing success of the experiment by merely whispering, "It is delicious! It is very good for you."

No sooner had the words left his lips than, thousands of miles away in Purfleet, they left Renfield's. "But it's very good, Dr. Seward! Very wholesome. It's life. It's strong life. And, ohh," the lunatic swooned, "it gives life to me."

Many such nights of similar puppet-theater! Back and forth upon the wind. Now again, tonight, over the water, over the miles, Count Dracula heard the voice of he who would serve.

As with the flies, Renfield had put his obsession with the spiders behind him. The good doctor insisted. But Dracula was generous and his excellent servant deserved a hobby. Didn't he? Now the vampire listened as the curtain went up and Renfield introduced his east London psychiatrist to his most recent *suggestion*.

"It's a common sparrow, Dr. Seward. Nothing wrong with that, is it? Just a sparrow, just a pet."

"What of your other, eh, pets?" Came the reedy and superior reply. "Oh, I see. They are... Your spiders and flies... their number seems greatly diminished."

"I must tame the sparrow, mustn't I? It's simple really. A spoon of sugar to tempt the flies... a handful of flies to sate the spiders... Spiders to, oh, so simply, tame the sparrow."

In repose, Dracula nodded his approval and whispered, "The blood is the life."

Over the miles Renfield repeated it, "The blood, Dr. Seward... The blood is the life."

In the dark, Dracula listened to the lines straining, the masts creaking, the wind in the canvas. He heard the waves slap the ship, the water rushing by. He felt the keel roll as the bow rocked. The earth bed was cool on his back. The mold stung his nose.

Chapter Six

Then came another odor – heavy, metallic and, as recognition dawned, unrelenting. The smell of human blood.

He lifted his hands, felt the confines of his box, and drew a breath. Blood was always in the air, surrounding him as the sea surrounded this ship. But this was different. This was on the air like pollen; not dulled by the usual layers of fat and tissue, not racing under venous and arterial pressure but quiet like the waters of a pond. Blood, in the open. Someone aboard the ship was injured.

Count Dracula felt the hunger; the burning need for blood.

He pushed up with his palms and the nails squealed at the corners of the box. But the sound, like a warning whistle, gave him pause. He pulled his hands back, making fists. No!

No. There was a plan – and it would be carried out. The bloodlust had to be quelled, for the ship needed to reach England. He clenched his teeth, forced his hands to his sides, and closed his eyes. He had to be patient. No matter what – the ship needed to reach England.

Chapter Seven

FRIDAY morning, 9 July, a rum-clouded Petrofsky sulked, feeling sorry for himself, over his untouched breakfast. Twenty stitches in a hand that throbbed like burning hell, lost beneath layers of linen bandages, and his first duty that morning would be to climb up and repair the sail he'd damaged yesterday. They'd left port with just enough men to sail. Injury or no, they could not spare him.

"Coffee or tea?" Old Swales hovered with a kettle in each hand.

Petrofsky smiled weakly. He appreciated the cook, and the bookworm, tending his hand but why the old bastard had busted on deck hollering, and sending him off his perch, in the first place, he didn't know. "C-c-c-offee."

"I thought ye hated me coffee?"

"I d-d-d-." Petrofsky gave up and nodded. "The... water is a-a-awful... it renders the... tea in-in-in-sipid. C-c-offee's so bad it h-hides it."

"My coffee? Michty me, that's where the lie comes in! Other cooks buy cheap mixes o' spoiled beans, chicory, an' rat shite. Parch it, grind it; is nigh undrinkable. This here's from South America!" Swales grunted his disgust. "Ye'd better eat. There'll be beef for dinner, but dinner is a long way off. An' ye've some healin' to do."

Chapter Seven

Petrofsky, sulking again, considered asking what yesterday's shouting had been about – but let it drop. Swales was too old to sail, was mad as a goddamned hatter and, like as not, had no idea what he'd been about. What difference? His hand still ached and he still had a sail to repair.

* * *

In the afternoon, bored and wanting to be out, Harrington decided to give himself a tour of the ship. He reached the deck, as his luck would have it, as the men were called to rum.

Rum was long-believed good for a seafaring man's health, grand for his attitude and, as on most sailing ships, was rationed to the crew daily at company expense. *Demeter's* brew lived aft of the deckhouse, under the eyes of the steersman, in two elliptical oak barrels three feet high and two feet front to back. Each banded barrel held half a hogshead; one tapped, the other waiting.

The men had partaken every day since leaving Varna. Harrington, passing at the right moment, was pulled into line by Swales for his first experience. As usual, the scholar took the opportunity to ask questions. "Why rum? Don't Russians drink vodka?"

"Jings, lad! It's no' drinkin'," Swales said. "It's the daily ration."

"Vodka?" Olgaren butted in. At his size, who would stop him? "When Captain Nikilov went to sea as a youth, every ship carried state-manufactured vodka. He dislikes vodka – intensely."

"He does not even like the word," Amramoff added.

The men crowded Harrington.

"The seas abounds with ships' crews drinking rum. Captain Nikilov is as good as any of them." Olgaren leaned, threatening. "Are you saying he is not?"

"No!" Harrington shouted.

Constantin, at the tapper, shot beady looks of annoyance. He was, by seafaring terms, a good mate. He kept to himself or the officers and avoided being free with the crew. He dispensed the ration without caring for the duty and never, under any circumstances, drank with the men before the mast. "Step up," he ordered the line.

"The Englishman has something against our captain!" Amramoff said. Then, turning to the passenger, asked, "What have you against our captain?"

"Nothing," Harrington said. "I never suggested anything of the sort."

Tense silence followed... before the crew burst out laughing. Olgaren slapped Harrington on the shoulder with a meaty hand. The scholar righted himself, then joined them. As the laughter died, Amramoff explained, "He offers rum because the captain is a godly man."

They were laughing again. Harrington looked a question at the cook.

"An' you a scholar!" Swales said, with his familiar derisive grunt. "Do ye not know alcohol evaporates as it ferments? Most lose aboon two percent, no' more. Rum loses, what, eight, ten percent? It's called the *angels' share*. The captain's rum gives the angels a larger share. Just what ye'd expect from a righteous man."

"They are having fun at your expense. It means they like you," the mate told Harrington. He held out a mug. "*They* like you."

The crew fell about. As the red-faced Harrington accepted his rum, it dawned that if he didn't catch wise it would be a long cruise indeed. The thought reminded him of a question he'd never asked. "Mr. Constantin, how long will the journey take?"

The first glowered and shrugged his shoulders.

"I realize you can't know. I'm asking how long the voyage ought to take."

The mate examined him as if he were stupid. "It is not up to us. We are subject to wind and weather." To end the discussion, he growled, "We will get there when we arrive."

* * *

Chapter Seven

His conversation with the first went so well that, following his ration, Harrington resumed his self-guided tour – out of the ornery gentleman's way. He soon found himself in the crew's quarters.

The room had one unlit oil lamp, no porthole and, save for a sliver of light stealing in from the companionway, was dark. There were beds to spare with *Demeter's* shortage of hands; ten permanent bunks, top and bottom, and hooks for hammocks should the need arise. Eight bunks had their heads against the starboard hull and two, for the mates, sat parallel with the inside bulkhead. Above each was a shelf for personal items (books, letters, playing cards, a rosary, trinkets from exotic ports, even a photograph from a family gathering) and, at the foot of the mates' bunks, cupboards for each man's kit. There were two chamber pots... with matching odor.

The door across the companionway led to the mess. "Come in!" Swales boomed as Harrington tried to pass unseen. Whispering, the cook added, "Have a drink w' me."

Harrington could think of nothing he wished to do less. "I was under the impression that, other than the ration, the captain disallowed drink?"

"Aye, he does. So be quiet!"

Hooking his arm with an arthritic claw, Swales dragged him in.

The mess featured a table, little else. Beyond was the hot galley where Swales did the cooking. Cups, dishes, tins, and jars filled the shelves. Burnished pans hung shining from the overhead. The main attraction was a sand-filled, metal bin stove, four feet wide, chest high. He built his fires atop the sand, beneath iron frames that supported the kettles. A stovepipe chimney extended from the hood, through the deckhouse roof but, mostly, wind blew the smoke back into the galley. Smoking was forbidden below and galley fires were disallowed in the night, foul weather or rough seas. Beyond the galley was a larder and Swales' bunk.

"O'er here, lad." Swales lifted a bottle by the neck.

"I'm not much of a drinker, actually," Harrington said, sitting at the long dining table.

"Excellent!" The old man laughed, stirring the air with the bottle. "'Cause this is no' much o' a drink. What's the matter, ration no' sittin' well? Take a mug o' water with ye. Mix it; make a grog."

He poured and they lifted their glasses. Swales drank deeply then sighed. Harrington sipped, twisted his lips, puckered, then coughed. "What is it?"

"Golden Mediasch, a wine o' Transylvania." The cook laughed. "Aye, poorish!"

"No. It just causes a queer sting on the tongue."

"Which is joost how ye gawm it's inferior." Swales plopped down opposite and poured another glass. "All Transylvanian wine is shite. Their wine makers are dirty, lazy bastards. No discrimination. They mix their grapes, the green, the ripe, the o'er-ripe." He waved his twisted hand and grunted in disgust. "An' the pressing, my Gog! Near naked men dance barefoot t' bagpipe music, stompin' carelessly picked fruit w' all their force. Feature thaat!" He shivered. "Everythin' aboon it's wrong. An' so does the whole o' the country prepare their wine!"

"If you are so contemptuous, why drink it?"

"When ye bring drink aboard b'hind Nikilov's back, ye smuggle when the smugglin's good. Ye bean't choosey."

"I should think, to justify it, the reward should be worth the risk."

Swales laughed. "Ahh, shall we talk o' risk? Yers?" The old man stared knowingly. "What put ye aboard this ship, lad? Unless I miss me guess... a wee lass, right?"

"How do you know?"

"What could it be – at yer age? An' ye talk to me o' risk! If ye wont nowt but trouble, laddy, grup to anythin' with wheels or teats."

"Is that why you're at sea?"

"I said yer age." Swales laughed, short and hollow. Then he grew serious. "Old men like masel' go to sea only to keep what they have or 'cause there's nowt left."

"And you?"

"I'm tryin' to keep what I have; a daughter an' a father."

Chapter Seven

"A father, still?"

"Nearly a hundred, if he's still livin'. Me last letter was a year ago. I want t' see me father ageean 'efore he goes. An' me daughter. Ye've no idee how much ye can miss a daughter. No idee how much a heart can hurt."

"There, you are wrong."

"Oh, aye?"

Harrington threw back the Mediasch, swallowed hard, took a deep breath and stared into the old man's eyes. "Mr. Swales, are you now or have you ever been related, in business with, or close friends of the Lord-high Mayor of Bukovina?"

"Bukovina I know. Ne'er heard o' him."

"A rather large fish in a very small pond."

"Bean't they all? An' he, this mayor so high, has... a daughter?"

Harrington nodded dismally and tapped the rim of his empty glass. Swales obliged and the Englishman drank. "A lovely little thing... And her father hates me."

"All father's hate their daughter's lovers."

"He wants me dead."

"Most father's want their daughter's lovers dead."

"He and his sons tried to kill me."

"Thaat's more original."

"They shot my hat." Harrington drained his glass again. "They cursed me; called me a swine." He took a long, deep breath. "Accused me of making her pregnant."

"I'd have shot ye masel' – and no' missed."

"But it wasn't true. It isn't true. It can't be."

"Oh, aye? Ye look healthy to me."

"Yes. But it's not possible." Harrington shook his head. "I never... we never... ever."

"So, it could no' be true from yer side?"

"Nor hers! She was no liar. She loved me. And wasn't her name Ekaterina? From the Greek Katarios! Does it not mean *chaste*? If she's with child, who's? If she's not, why were they shooting?"

"Ye did no' ask?"

"Herr Gabor was not disposed to discussing it. Instead, they went a-hunting."

"So, ye've gone a-sailin'?"

"I've scarpered," Harrington confessed.

* * *

Harrington sipped and Swales drank until supper time. It wouldn't be much. Swales preferred dinner as the main meal, with the evening repast simple; coffee, tea, bread and butter, a soup. To stifle the grumbling, he added raisins or molasses. Who could complain while eating a sweet?

As seven o'clock approached, six bells by ship's time, the wine-filled Harrington rose to leave. Wanting nothing to do with food, he thanked Swales and went on deck. There, tippled but trying to look sober, the English passenger wandered forward.

The old beakheads (or *heads*) of the grand 17th century sailing ships, the ornate platforms under the figurehead from which sailors worked the bowsprit sails, were long gone. Yet the bow of *Demeter* retained one of the heads' important features; toilets. These were holes in the deck, on either side of the bowsprit, through which waste could be dropped into the sea.

Harrington roamed, stiff-legged, to the bow for a breath of air and a peek at the setting sun. What he got was a peek at the startled deck boy in a squat, covering himself, doing his business over the starboard head hole.

"Oh," Harrington said dully.

Funar jerked his head up and stared at the Englishman staring at him. He yanked his cap down to cover his face, and hollered, "Go away!" with the high-pitched shriek only an adolescent could conjure. Harrington, startled and embarrassed, retreated aft, imploring the boy to beg his pardon. In response he got another beleaguered, "Go away!"

The poor lad, Harrington thought, hurrying aft. Every time he saw Rada Funar, it was in some god-awful embarrassing situation.

Chapter Seven

No wonder the boy never approached him in daylight. At this rate, Funar would hate his guts before they ever officially met.

* * *

In secret, Smirnov again slipped into the dark forward hold. He had no business there (and had been told so), but crept in all the same. What his mates didn't know would not hurt them. What Smirnov did not know was that evil incarnate lay in a box not twelve feet away.

Count Dracula's eyes snapped open. He gasped, clenched his fists, and inhaled. His chest rose nearly to the lid. His mind raced wildly as his senses stretched beyond the molding dirt, the wet wood, the stale air of the makeshift coffin. He smelled something. . . that pricked him like needles.

There was someone in the hold nearby.

But something more disturbed him. He could hear the blood surging through the veins of the crew. He could still smell the blood of the injured man. But, beyond these, he smelled something – unique. Not new, he'd smelled it before in his homeland, but unique. An odor unto itself. He inhaled again deeply. Yes, he'd smelled it before and recognized it. Blood. . . impure, tainted. He growled under his breath. Then, unable to contain it, hissed outwardly. The Count's eyes gleamed red in the dark. His teeth snapped together in bloodlust. Still he knew he must control it; more he must quell it. He had to reach England. Which meant, no matter what the urge, he had to remain in his box. But the temptation, the intense longing. . . The bloodlust. He could smell. . . menstrual blood.

There was a woman on board the ship.

Chapter Eight

THE master of *Demeter* was a creature of order and habit. Weather permitting (a phrase that preceded all shipboard activities), the cook was expected to have his stove fire lit by four bells, six o'clock, each morning. All crew members, save the night watch, not hindered by sickness, were to be up no later than seven. And Saturday was created for cleaning and airing the ship. That Saturday, 10 July, was no exception.

Most lubbers feared sailing because of the thought of foundering, but the primary cause of shipboard mortality was disease. Even successful voyages often ended with disastrous survival rates. Cholera, typhoid fever, measles, chicken pox and dysentery thrived in the dirty, damp quarters. The only way to avoid their spread was to clean and air the ship. Constantin handed out assignments, ignoring the crew's grumbles until he got to Popescu. The abrasive Romanian made the mistake of growling too loudly and was reassigned to polishing the chamber pots (or shite pots as Swales so gracefully dubbed them).

Popescu's description has been saved... for he was the last person anyone would want to meet. He grumbled every moment he was not being holier-than and only laughed at other's expense. He had a widow's peak over a heavy brow, mud brown eyes, and a pointed nose that nearly met his pointed chin. He was religious

Chapter Eight

without a hint of spirituality (he crossed himself nearly as much as he swore) and superstitious with no discernable beliefs.

So the cleaning commenced. Eltsin, on the watch, swept the deck ahead of Petrofsky who swabbed with one hand. Swales, going over the galley, mess, and his quarters, boiled water for Smirnov who'd been ordered to see to the laundry. Amramoff collected carbolic acid from the forward hold (a place he no longer cared to enter for the strange feeling it gave him) to assist Funar in scrubbing the crew's quarters. They would work around Olgaren who, just off the watch, had curled up in a corner on the floor; a snoring mountain. (When an opportunity for sleep arrived, a sailor took it.)

* * *

Nikilov, below to inform their passenger that he too would need to clean and air his room, was delighted to find the Englishman already carrying his mattress on deck. "I'm impressed, Herr Harrington. Thank you."

"Happy to do my part, commander."

"I wish all of my crew shared your attitude. Tell me, are you a religious man?"

"No, captain. I'm not."

Nikilov went rigid. "Really," he said dryly. "You do not believe in God?"

"I believe in that which I am able to see and touch."

"Then I will pray, Herr Harrington, this voyage forces you to touch God." As he turned for his cabin, the captain added. "By the way, we reach the Bosphorus in the morning; a situation we've discussed. Following that inspection, everyone will be on deck for worship services. On this ship, regardless of your beliefs, you will be expected to keep the Sabbath. Do I make myself clear?"

Harrrington considered religion a mix of mysticism, fear, and wishful thinking. But, as the captain *had* made his expectations clear, regardless of his beliefs, there seemed little to be said. So he said nothing. He nodded his understanding and continued top-side with his mattress.

* * *

As maniacal about the cleaning as he was his religion, Nikilov personally procured soaps from the great factories in Marseille for the voyages out and those of London's Lever Brothers for the return trips. It was a sack of this special mortar and pestle-ground soap powder that Smirnov toted up now. Creating a base of operation near the fore mast, he collected the items he'd need; a large tub, a ladle borrowed from the kitchen, and a pile of the crew's dirty laundry. He half-filled the tub with the cook's boiling water, cooled it slightly with fresh water, added a liberal dusting of soap, stirred it with the ladle (what Swales did not know would not hurt him) and started scrubbing.

Lines had been stretched from the main mast to both port and starboard shrouds upon which to hang the laundry and bedding. Sea air took care of the rest.

"In the old days," Eltsin told whoever was listening, "they washed and hung their clothing below. Had no idea they were killing themselves. Unhealthy that, steam and moisture below. Nothing dried, made people sick."

"L-Like Smirnov's sh-sh-shirt," Petrofsky said. He turned to the mustachioed launderer. "Makes e-everyo-o-one s-s-sick to sm-smell you."

The petite seaman waved the marlinspike away.

"He's right," Eltsin said. "You are washing everyone's clothes. Wash your own."

"Mine are all right."

Eltsin stared. Something about Smirnov, beyond his ludicrous mustache, was not right. The men teased him mercilessly for his frail physique and falsetto voice, his emotional outbursts and, now, for doing women's work. It made one wonder. But it was nonsense. The world featured all manner of people. Still, something about

Chapter Eight

Smirnov, aroused Eltsin's suspicions. One moment the seaman appeared ready to burst, the next he was all but asleep on his feet. His posture, his way of moving... was odd. The fellow was hiding something.

"L-L-Let's have it," Petrofsky said, grabbing Smirnov's shirt from behind. The small sailor held the front of his blouse with both hands – screaming.

"That's enough," Eltsin said, halting the skirmish. "Petrofsky, unhand him." When he did, the second turned on the new man. "Mr. Smirnov... I order you to wash your shirt. Take it off... now."

* * *

The day flew for the crew; less so for Harrington. With his bunk long back together, his cabin clean, and bored with reading, the scholar decided to finish his tour of the ship by snooping in the one place he'd yet to go - the holds. He'd never been because he had no business there, but he'd paid his passage, hadn't he? Girded with the idiotic notion he deserved to see everything, he slipped quietly down the scuttle outside his cabin door.

Harrington was singularly unimpressed as he passed, by matchlight, through the aft (what Swales would call "the aftest abaft") and midship holds. They contained heavy silver sand for ballast, a handful of the dirt-filled boxes from Transylvania amidships, and little else. Near ready to call the tour ended, he passed quietly through the communicating door into the fore hold.

Larger than the other compartments, it stretched forty-three feet to the ship's bow and, because the between-decks did not extend forward, was twelve feet high. A six foot stair allowed access through a door from the end of the between-decks, and a twelve foot ladder from the battened hatch in the deck above. From the center of the hold the fore mast rose up and through the deck like a great tree and all around rested the cargo; the bulk of the client's wooden boxes of earth, ballast silver sand, paper boxes of ship's supplies and sawdust, and barrels of illuminating oil (surrounded by leaked halos on the deck) for the ship's kerosene lamps.

That was all. Two-hundred and fifteen tons of water displacement with a capability for 190 tons of cargo. (He'd asked, of course.) What the hell they were doing carrying nothing more than fifty boxes of dirt... Cor blimey, Harrington had no idea.

That was it for his tour as well. He'd seen it all... or thought he had. He'd been feeling *strange* since entering the forward hold; an oppressive something that pricked his nerves, stood the hairs at the back of his neck on end. He felt... a presence. That feeling became something more when he heard a noise in the dark recess of the bow. Harrington struck another match and cautiously ventured forward.

He slowly halved the distance, his feelings turning from fear to foolishness with each step. He was ready to admit he'd been hearing things, when something took shape. He crouched, illuminating... Smirnov.

He looked a wreck, his shirt undone, his chest wrapped in a thick bandage, propped against the bulkhead, drinking from a tiny bottle. He raised his head, staring through bleary eyes. Harrington doubted the seaman could actually see him. His head lolled and the seaman *went out* at the same time as Harrington's match.

Harrington lit another and examined the label on the now-empty bottle. "Laudanum. Bless me," the Englishman whispered. Smirnov was not inebriated, he was drugged.

Harrington knew no details, but he knew he could not leave the man passed-out in the dark. He lifted the seaman onto his shoulder, thankful he was small, and carried him up to the between-decks door. He peered out, saw the newly-awakened Olgaren duck into the mess, and noted that behind the big Russian the companionway was empty. Quickly and quietly, Harrington moved – determined to get the new man abed without being detected.

So caught up in rescuing Smirnov was he, Harrington failed to notice a figure, behind the door to the midship hold, watching his every move.

Chapter Eight

* * *

With *Demeter* shipshape again, Swales called the crew, Popescu, Petrofsky, and Eltsin to supper. Olgaren was already there, asking the cook about his whaling days and making short-work of a second cuppa. The watchman (Constantin), the steersman (Amramoff), and the elusive deck boy were absent. The captain, as always, ate in his quarters.

Harrington, fresh from delivering an unconscious burden to its bunk, arrived late without explanation. On newly acquired sea legs, finally nursing an appetite, he joined the others with relish.

"Where's Smirnov?" Swales asked.

"Sleeping," Harrington put in casually. "Washing must have taken it out of him."

"This voyage is taking it out of him," Eltsin said. "Hear this. He wears a brace for his back. We saw it while he was doing the laundry. Was wearing it when he came aboard; hiding it beneath his shirt." He pointed at Petrofsky. "Was wearing it when he saved you. He's a silly-looking sort, but he's got guts. Dangling you must have hurt like hell."

"I w-won't make f-f-fun any-more," Petrofsky said.

"No more picking on Smirnov?" Popescu asked. "That leaves only Harrington."

Laughter broke out at the Englishman's expense. The jokes followed, compliments on his healthy look (his trading green skin for dusky pale), and back-slaps suggesting he'd found acceptance. Not one of their own, but one among them. They were even getting used to his endless questions.

"Why do they call it a schooner?"

"It's Scottish," Swales said ladling soup. "*Scon*; to skip on the surface o' the water."

"She'd better skip on the surface," Harrington said. "I don't know how to swim."

"C-C-Can you fl-float?" Petrofsky asked. The compartment erupted in laughter and the marlinspike waved his bandaged hand, accepting the accolades.

"Do not worry," Olgaren said. "We will never be more than two miles from land."

"Really?" Harrington asked hopefully.

"Absolutely," Olgaren said. He tapped the tabletop, indicating something well below. "Never more than two miles - from the bottom of the sea."

The crew burst out laughing. Popescu, with a tear in his eyes, noted Harrington's skin was green again.

The ship's bell sounded distantly. Constantin followed, calling them from their late supper to an even later rum ration after their day of cleaning. "Up ye go," Swales said, setting a mug of water before Harrington. "An' fer you."

Harrington brightened. "Time for the tot!"

The others froze, staring. "What is the tot?" Olgaren asked.

"Mix the grog!" Harrington replied jovially, lifting his mug. "Splice the main brace!" He nodded, trying to egg them on. "You know?"

"'Course they do," Swales said. "He means 'Tap the Admiral'?"

They were all snickering again.

"The Admiral?"

"An' ye claim ye're a Brit?" Swales feigned horror at Harrington's ignorance. "October, 1805, twenty-seven ships o' the British Royal Navy, led by Admiral Lord Nelson aboard HMS Victory, defeated thirty-three French an' Spanish ships west o' Cape Trafalgar, off the so'west coast o' Spain. The French an' Spanish lost twenty-two ships, the British none. But the cost was high, fer Nelson was killed in battle. The Admiral's body was pur-sarved in a barrel o' rum fer return to England."

"Yes. And?"

"An', upon arrival, the cask was opened an' Nelson was there but the rum was gone."

"Go on," Harrington said in disbelief.

Chapter Eight

"His pickled body was removed an' an inspection made. T'was discovered the sailors had drilled a hole in the bottom o' the cask. They'd drunk the rum an', with it, the Admiral's blood. Since then rum has been known as Nelson's Blood - an' the daily ration as 'Tapping the Admiral'.

The crew howled with laughter. Harrington set down his mug, no longer thirsty. The crew grabbed him and hauled him into the companionway. "Wait! My water!"

Swales laughed, following them out, listening to Harrington's screams as the crew carried him up – without his mug. He started up himself, then thought better of it. He didn't need any rum today. He headed back but, just inside the mess door, halted.

Swales passed his eyes about the mess and into the hot galley. All seemed quiet, but he knew better. It didn't feel quiet. He hobbled to the galley door, leaned against the jamb with folded his arms, and calmly said, "Come out." There was no response. "I'm old," he told the air, "but I'm no' daft. An' I'm no' keen to repeat masel'."

The deck boy rose from hiding behind the counter.

"Now, why is it," the cook asked, "that ye won't eat w' the crew, but ye're willin' to steal food from me hot galley?" The boy stared, green-eyed innocence. "Tha-at is food isn' it, behind yer back?" Funar brought out his hands; a biscuit in each. "An' in your gob?" Caught, Funar began to chew the fish jammed in his mouth. It looked hard going.

"D' ye know the penalty for theavin' at sea?" Still chewing, Funar examined the bread in his hands then shrugged in resignation. What else could he do? "Forget it," Swales said, fighting not to laugh. "Nevermind, lass."

The deck 'boy' stopped his chewing, swallowed (nearly choking), coughed, and looked up into the old man's knowing face. Funar's green eyes were no longer innocent. They were wide as saucers.

"Aye, lassie," Swales said, nodding. "I gawm. You... are a girl."

Chapter Nine

THE deck 'boy' stared in terror, desperately shaking his head.

"No?" Swales asked incredulously. "Ye're no' a girl? D' ye think I'm daft? Well, I'm no'. An' ye're n' more a boy than I am a mermaid." Funar's green eyes narrowed to slits. The 'boy' choked down the last of the fish, then moved to speak. "If it's a denial ye're workin' up to, save yer voice. I already told ye, I gawm ye're a wee lass."

"How. . . ? How. . . did you. . . ?"

"I've a daughter, masel'," Swales said. He stole a look into the companionway. "An' what chance had she? No mum. Left w' nowt but a poorish excuse for a father, an' her salty granddad to make things worse. Pity her stuck with the likes o' us; a ship's cook an' an old whaler. Cobbled w' one or th' other, while th' other was to sea. How many times I seen her - so much like you – trampin' round in me or me dad's rain gear an' boots. No one on earth, missy, could spot a young lady in sailor's kit like I. Ye're the spittin' image o' me own pretty when she was young. S'why I made such a fool of masel' th' other day. When I came on deck an' saw ye up in the shrouds, me mind took flight. I saw me wee Carrie in her grandpa's gear. An' I got terrible afeared. S'when I shouted, at me girl, an' that poorish soul Petrofsky took a header off the

Chapter Nine

gaff on my account. Now, we two need a heart to heart, lass. An' we'll start with, who are ye?"

"My name is Ekaterina Gabor."

Recognition dawned, but Swales hid it. "I've heard the name. Russian?"

"Romanian. My father is the Mayor of..."

"Bukovina," Swales said. "T'was yer father then, joined the dockside show as we left Varna?"

Ekaterina gaped. "How do you know...? Yes. My father and brothers."

"So?" She hesitated and Swales nudged, "Oh, come, lass. Yer secret's out an' ye've n' right to an attitude. Ye're stowed away in th' open, feignin' ye're a lad. Ye're chased aboard by armed family members. There's a story there."

"They weren't chasing me. They don't know I'm here."

"Ahh!" Swales poured a cup of tea and, with the sugar, placed it on the table. He added a plate for the biscuits in her hands, butter and molasses, and pointed Ekaterina, still in Funar's kit, to the bench. "So they're chasin' young Harrin'ton?"

"How do you know everything?"

"I gawm nowt," Swales boomed. "But I'm goin' to know! An' I'm goin' to know now. Or we're goin' to see the cap'n, we two."

It came out in a great flood of words and tears. "I'm in love with Trevor Harrington. I've never been in love before. I met him, he was a student, in the Bukovina library; a proper Englishman. He was traveling Europe studying. He spoke Romanian, and Russian, and German, and... Oh, I fell for him madly. And he for me. He said he loved me." Her voice trailed off. Swales waited. She sighed and resumed. "He said his time was short, that he might be leaving. I couldn't bear the thought."

Swales poured himself a cup and sat across from her.

"I did something stupid; horrid."

"Somethin' brought ye here? What? Why would yer family be chasin' Harrin'ton with arms? What wrong could a father no' forgive, eventually? I'm boggled. Ye need to explain, lass."

"I told my father I was with child."

"By Harrin'ton?" Swales feigned rage. "Michty me! That English swine... just left ye so? That's why that little bastard is on the run! I should have known by his first words, with lubbers puke runnin' down his weak chin. I do no' blame yer father fer tryin' to protect ye! For avengin' yer wronged virtue! Were ye my Carrie, I'd ha' rent his limbs! I'd o' killed him! Humiliatin' ye. Destroyin' yer family's honor." Swales pounded the table, as his arthritis allowed, and Ekaterina jumped. "He's done ye an unpardonable wrong!" He clutched a knife and sneered with all the bitterness the Scots had for the crown. "Fear no', bony lass. I'll stand for yer father and brothers, an' for you!"

"No! You don't understand!" She reached to calm him. "Please, Mr. Swales!"

"Oliver, lass. Just call me Oliver, yer ol' friend."

"You must hear me, Oliver. Trevor has done nothing! I made a terrible mistake. I've humiliated myself. The whole thing was a lie and I have done him a great injustice."

Swales halted his bluster and laid the knife down. "What's that?"

"I'm not with child!" Her hand flew to her mouth. Ekaterina looked nervously about; listening. Laughter filtered through the stovepipe as the crew took their rum, but the companionway was quiet.

"It's all right, lass," Swales said, pointing above. "We're alone."

"It was all a lie. Trevor did nothing. I've never been with him; never been with anyone. When I told my father I was... I made it up."

"Why in the name o' Heaven would ye do that?"

"I'm not one of the fine English ladies. Romanian blood burns hot. I did it to keep Trevor from leaving. I thought my father would insist we be married. Instead, he swore to kill him."

"As I'd a-done. As any father..." Swales shook his head. "An' the Englishman ran out - thinkin' you were with child?"

"No," she nearly shouted coming to his defense. "He knows I'm not..."

Chapter Nine

"By him."

"Of course not. He knows..."

"All he knows is he needs a new hat. The rest he's guessin'."

"Dear God! If he thinks I am... by someone else... He must think me the lowest creature. He must hate me! And my family tried to kill him! I made a terrible choice for fear of losing him. Now I've not only lost him, but put him in danger. I've made a terrible mess of everything - with a stupid lie."

"So we gawm why he's here. Why are you here, dressed like that?"

"To make sure he's safe!" She reddened under his stare. "I love him. I cannot make things right and he'll never forgive me... But if I know he is safe, I can take comfort in that. I do not deserve more."

"Don't be too hard on yerself, lass."

"He won't be punished because I came aboard falsely?"

"Let's no' get ahead o' ourselves, lass. I see no reason to rush makin' yer presence known." He considered the idea for a moment. "Ye an' Harrin'ton are no' the only consideration. Ye're a stowaway, here under false pretenses. How do y' think the cap'n will take thaat? Or the mate? A woman among the crew... who made a fool o' 'em."

"I've ruined everything!" she cried. "I cannot live with myself!"

"Here now!" Swales rose with a groan and pushed a towel into her hands. "Stop that, lass. We've no time fer it, an' no way to explain tears on a sailor. Wipe yer gob. Yer not the only sinner aboard." He took in the companionway again. "If a confession makes ye feel better, yer no' the only one here fer false reasons. Truth told, the ailin' cook I replaced wasn't sick at all. I paid him an' took his place. Spent all I had, which wasn't much; still it was all I had. Ye see, I'm pining masel'. Oh, not for a love," he laughed. "I'm too old fer that. But fer those I love an' fer that I love. I'm homesick; to see me daughter 'efore she forgets me, an' me father, if he's yet alive."

He took the towel and dried a tearful trail she'd missed on her cheek. Her eyes were rimmed in red but there was little he could do for that.

"So, lass, we're both frauds," he continued. "With secrets to keep. The crew discovers I'm here under false pretenses, they may well throw me o'erboard. An' if they find a woman among the crew, they'll sure throw you o'erboard. Meanin' fer the time bein' we both keep our dis-guises. Now... how do we let yer Trevor know ye're here, an' no' give the game away to aught else?"

"You can't. It would jeopardize his safety."

"You canno' hide the whole voyage. So you canno' keep it from him."

"We must. Please! Mr. Swales... Oliver, I swear you to secrecy."

Chapter Ten

"HERR Harrington, wake up." It was not yet dawn, Sunday morning, 11 July, and the gravelly Russian voice pulled him from sleep. Then came the grip of a callused hand. "Herr Harrington, rouse yourself. Wake up."

He made out the commander, hunched over his bunk, a smoking lamp burning his eyes in the close cabin. "What... what is it?"

"We've reached the mouth of the Bosphorus. We're at the Istanbul Strait. I warned you this time would come. Wake up."

The haze cleared and realization sank in.

The Bosphorus, with her southern sister, the Dardanelles, comprised the Turkish Straits, one of the boundaries separating Europe from Asia and connecting the Black Sea to the Mediterranean. Mythology said the Symplegades floated there by the power of the gods and would crush any ship attempting passage. But, once the legendary Jason and his Argonauts navigated this danger, the *clashing rocks* became forever fixed and Greek access to the Black Sea was opened. It was vital to the region; with a bloody history.

"Get up," the captain said. "Get dressed and collect your things."

* * *

Chapter Ten

Harrington had no complaint. The captain made it clear in Varna that his *ticket to leave* came with dictates. Now, as Nikilov led the way into the black forward hold, Harrington followed (with his re-packed kit) ready to fulfill one.

The privately chartered *Demeter*, with its fifty earth-boxes casting angular shadows by the captain's amber lamp, was forbidden to carrying anything else; cargo or passengers. Breaking the contract violated company policy and the law. A discovery of this *indiscretion* meant the captain would lose his job and the company, possibly, their ship. So, Harrington had been left off the manifest - and would not be found aboard by customs officials.

"There is no record of your passage." The captain's voice was as low as the light, as ominous as the shadows. "When we enter the strait, we will be boarded and searched by the Turks. If you are found, you will be arrested. I will say you are a stowaway. If I am not believed, I may be arrested and my ship impounded. You will NOT be found. Is that understood?"

Harrington assured him it was.

The captain lit a second lamp bracketed on the fore mast, but left it muted. "I'll have this extinguished before the inspection," he said, heading out. "Hide yourself with care."

Harrington squinted, staring the chamber over. Again that feeling! Perhaps it was the damp, the dark, but the gloom settled as if he were in a tomb. He shook it off – and set about it as instructed. He tried to stash himself between a stack of corrugated boxes and several barrels along the port bulkhead, but gave up with nothing to show for it but an oil stain on one knee. He scanned the depths for a more suitable hole and finally buried himself, uncomfortably, beneath a hard to reach tarped stack of boxes. It took time but, secreted away, it would take an industrious official to find him. There he lay, for ages it seemed, in the dark, in the damp fetid air.

The easy roll of the vessel subsided and a silence took over. Without warning, the starboard anchor was loosed. It barked metal on wood, splashed, and rattled chain to the bottom. There followed a sensation the amateur seaman did not like on this early morning, on an empty stomach; *Demeter's* movement at anchor. Over four days, he'd gotten used to the ship under way but standing, riding the swell and the wakes of passing vessels like a rolling bottle, with the rudder banging and the ship creaking like a coffin lid... Harrington breathed deeply, grateful for a calm sea.

He lost all sense of time. He may have lain there hours, perhaps merely minutes, but finally the silence in the strangely frightening hold was interrupted by the sound of the door. Harrington assumed the inspectors were descending, but reconsidered when he heard whispers. Carefully, his life in the balance, he drew back the tarp and stole a look.

Two figures of wildly differing sizes stood near the lamp – a blazing light to the scholar's dilated eyes. He blinked and, as they adjusted, made out the second mate and the deck boy. Eltsin ordered the youth to hide amid a stack of barrels beneath the stairs then covered the lot and lashed it up. "Not a sound," he told the bundle. Eltsin extinguished the lamp, as the captain ordered, and carried his own away. He pulled the door closed and the hold fell into darkness again.

Harrington drew his tarp back into place, hiding. Apparently, his was not the only unauthorized body aboard. He would not have smiled so, had he known how right he was.

* * *

Dawn broke over the Bosphorus.

The Turk's pilot boat drew near. A skiff was lowered, boarded by four officials, three reed-thin men in white and a fat one in blood red, and rowed to the starboard of Nikilov's ship. The boat was made fast, a rope ladder lowered, and the Turks assisted onto the deck. As he stepped over, the customs inspector presented a glorious sight with his knee-length red coat and curved scimitar. He had a sun dried mahogany face, a trimmed gray beard and a shaggy black mustache. An amazing looking fellow.

Chapter Ten

He spoke jovially, as if he and the captain were old friends (though Nikilov's cautious replies showed they were not). His men held their place while the customs man examined the manifest. He expressed his surprise at the scarcity of cargo then, with the captain, the second, and his men bringing up the rear, began his inspection.

With the absence of passengers, light unstored cargo, and the cleaning the ship had undergone, the group made short work of the deck and between-decks. They poked about the rear holds and, in no time, worked their way forward. Lanterns held high, the customs official studied the fore hold, the barrels of supplies, sacks of ballast, and the consignment – the stacked and tarped boxes.

"Fifty," the captain said. "Nothing else save sand, saw dust, and lamp oil."

Their leader issued an order, smiling all the while, and his men set to work. The lines were untied from one stack, a tarp thrown back from another. Within an arm's reach of the barrels wherein Ekaterina (Funar, to Harrington) was hiding, one of the customs men took a pry bar to a box. The wood groaned, the nails shrieked, and the lid came up. He lifted a moist handful, grimaced at the smell of mold, and tossed it back. "Dirt," he announced to no one's surprise.

"For why?" The leader's question was curiosity rather than official inquiry.

Nikilov glanced over the manifest and shrugged. "For scientific experiments, it says."

The inspector pointed to another some distance away. A man put his bar to work and, again, the nails shrieked... Clammy black dirt; nothing else.

The leader raised a finger, signaling 'one more', and pointed indiscriminately.

The third man climbed several boxes, stopping (ignorantly) in front of Harrington's hiding place. He pulled on the tarp, uncovered the Englishman without seeing him, then tossed it back on him again. As he put his bar to use, he stepped on the tarp – and on Harrington's hand.

Harrington clenched his teeth not to scream, fighting every instinct to yank his fingers free! The oblivious customs man, thankfully, went up on his toes to pry on the lid. The scholar pulled his fingers back - and stuck them in his mouth.

Outside of the pain, the Englishman heard the coffin nails shriek.

Inside the casket, the eyes of the recumbent vampire flashed open. The corner of his box lid was lifting and lamplight was stealing in through the crack! The voivode in him, the warrior leader, needed assistance and he thought now of the only troops at his command; the filthy rodents in the hold. Under his breath, Dracula summoned them, barking, "Rats!"

A shrill chorus erupted from the shadows in the bow. The young Turk released the pressure on the bar and turned to the hair-raising sound with eyes wide as saucers. A blur of black, brown, and gray scuttled from the darkness, squealing, claws scratching on wood, snicking on canvas, raced up and over the tarp. Beneath, Harrington heard their skitter, felt their vile wave, bit his tongue, closed his eyes, and prayed for the courage to keep silent as the rodents scurried over him.

The rats leapt from the tarp, onto the box, and at the customs worker in one scuttling horde. The young man screamed, dropping his bar, as he fell backwards off the boxes. The shrieking rats poured over him. He shouted in terror.

There were shouts too from the others in the hold. But, before panic set in, the rodents were gone, disappeared into the shadows on the opposite side. Silence overwhelmed the compartment. A stunned moment followed... then the men began to laugh. Across the hold, the lead inspector and Captain Nikilov roared too. The horrified assistant rose to his feet, fighting for breath.

"What's the matter?" the inspector demanded. "Never seen stowaways before?"

Thunderous laughter at his expense.

Chapter Ten

"Open another!" Nikilov said. "Open them all."

The man gritted his teeth. He scoured the dark floor, located and retrieved his pry bar, then turned back to the box.

"That's enough," the inspector said. "More than enough. Restore everything." He nodded to Nikilov and they started up. His assistants, one still badly shaken, and *Demeter's* second made short work of hammering the containers closed again, then all hurried out of the hold. Slightly shaken himself, Harrington was pleased to note they did so without making *any* significant discoveries.

Eltsin and the customs men stopped in the galley, where Swales served them a meal. Nikilov and the inspector disappeared into the captain's quarters to end the tour with a toast. The official sold the captain his permit for entering the strait (and pocketed the unspoken, but expected, backsheesh). No one considered it a bribe; merely part of their business.

There was rarely trouble with customs officials. Few and far between, Nikilov had found, were the countries where money did not end an inspection satisfactorily. This time was no exception. But, with good wine and better stories, the after-inspection took longer than Nikilov had planned. It was nearly four in the afternoon when the inspector and his men returned to their vessel.

Demeter's grateful, weary captain issued his brief commands. Eltsin, acting the boatswain, sounded a shrill note on his whistle, and the hands took to the capstan-bars. In no time at all, the anchor was short up and dripping at the bow. The sails filled and the schooner was again under way.

* * *

If the afternoon passed slowly on deck, it stood still in the hold.

In darkness, a stiff and starving Harrington pulled off his cover. He sat up, stifling a groan, paused to catch his breath, wiped the sweat from his lip, and shivered again at the thought of the rats. Still, it seemed they'd made it through.

"Pssst," Harrington whispered to the barrels where the deck boy was hidden. "I think we survived."

A white face, a small oval in the dark, appeared from beneath the tarp. Unrecognizable in that light, it disappeared quickly. There followed the rustle of canvas, quick steps on the stairs, a stabbing flash of shadow at the door backed by amber light sneaking in from the companionway. To raise his voice was out of the question as Harrington had no idea where the Turks had gone. Besides, it would have been useless. Funar was out the door and gone.

"Cor," Harrington whispered. "That boy hates me."

* * *

With the Turks having overstayed their welcome, Nikilov canceled the planned Sunday service but promised worship would return the following week. In its place, the commander was forced late in the day to see his vessel through the treacherous waterway. The going was, by necessity, slow. The winds were mild for a change but the currents were their usual challenge. Midway, just past the 80 degree turn at Yeniköy, came a severe (45 degree) hook to starboard followed by an immediate and opposite pivot to port between the points of Asiyan and Kandilli, the narrowest section in the strait. From the deckhouse, aft, sailors had always to be mindful of the space above their head. The main and mizzen masts, both gaffe rigged with solid booms, were swung-to and back again for these course changes. History was replete with inattentive sailors having their heads knocked off at that bend, but Nikilov's *Demeter* accomplished the corners admirably.

Afterward, in celebration of the channel's successful negotiation, and of his stowaways surviving the inspection, the captain ordered a fine supper and joined the men at table. The talk that evening was lively (with Popescu away at the helm), and the lies and laughter plentiful. Even Constantin was in a pleasant mood.

Chapter Ten

Funar, Harrington noted, was absent again, though this time with reason. He was standing his first watch. Unfortunately, he missed that meal!

Swales served haggis; a Scottish sausage of sheep's *pluck* (heart, liver and lungs), minced with onion, oatmeal, suet, and spices, simmered with stock in the animal's stomach. The description lacked appeal, but the Englishman had to admit the dish was savory. As tradition dictated, it was served with what Swales called, "neeps and tatties" (turnips and potatoes boiled and mashed separately). Tradition also called for a dram of Scotch whisky, but that wasn't happening on Nikilov's ship.

For afters, in honor of the captain's beloved Sunday, Swales prepared a delicious plum pudding. The question of whether or not the old Scot could cook was laid to rest. But Swales dampened further expectations, insisting it was a one-time in a voyage meal.

Despite several odd near disasters, the *Demeter* was operating smoothly and the crew, and passenger, were finding their places. Thoughts of accidents, gloom, and curses were laid aside for the night. Who knew... perhaps for good. The voyage, Harrington thought, might end up being more than an escape after all. It might just be a pleasant cruise.

* * *

Later, walking the larboard quarter beneath sails silvered by a brilliant half-moon, Harrington was diverted by a whispered, but unmistakably high-pitched, "Thank you." He turned to see Smirnov loitering in the shadow of the mast. The great mustache hadn't spoken a word during the captain's supper and, though he looked to have something to say, appeared to be doing so under duress.

"Glad to be of assistance," Harrington replied, offering him a chance to drop the matter.

"I owe you an explanation."

"You don't owe me anything."

"I owe you more. I'm willing to explain."

Harrington bowed slightly. As Smirnov seemed determined, what could he do but listen.

"I injured my back, ages ago." Smirnov looked the deck over to ensure they were alone. "The surgeons, one after another, wanted to cut into me, to see what they could do. Being vivisected for their enlightenment did not appeal to me. The only other answer was laudanum for the pain. It was a choice then; it isn't any longer. I used to take it to feel good, now I must have it not to feel bad. Dangling Petrofsky from the shrouds, you might imagine, did not help."

"No. Of that I'm certain."

"Will you turn me in to the captain?"

Harrington studied the little man then shook his head. "We all have our problems. . . and our secrets. Good night, Ippolit."

Harrington started away. Behind him, in the unique falsetto that only Smirnov could produce, he heard, "Good night, Trevor."

Chapter Eleven

On Monday, 12 July, *Demeter* rode the waves between Europe and Asia, tacking southwest through the Sea of Marmara, to the mouth of the Dardanelles.

This second of the Turkish Straits leading to the Aegean, like her sister to the northeast, figured strategically in the region's many wars and in its bloody legends. In 483 BC (150 years before Alexander the Great invaded Persia), Xerxes I ordered two bridges built that his Persian army could invade Greece. The gods intervened and collapsed both in a storm. The bridge builders were beheaded and the strait whipped. Fetters were thrown in, the waters were given three hundred lashes, and the waves were branded with red-hot irons as the soldiers shouted curses.

Demeter passed into the strait and dropped anchor. The captain dropped down to the passenger's cabin and rapped the Englishman awake with an air of excitement. "You need to go below, Herr Harrington. Customs are about to board - and they are accompanied by a squadron."

Harrington craned his neck at the porthole. Nikilov was right. Beside the customs vessel was a military flagboat. Sailors lined her deck with cannon peeking intermittently from their ranks; a threatening blue wall in the early light. Chilled, Harrington asked, "Have we done something?"

"No. All is well. But you cannot be found. Get below... please."

Chapter Eleven

* * *

Back in the hold, Harrington saw no need to tamper with success. He quickly found the same stack of boxes and hid (his hands tucked in this time). He was just situated when the door burst open. Eltsin scrambled down the stairs with the deck boy in tow, whispering, rather hysterically, "Hide! I don't know why the mate foists this off on me. I didn't sign you! Hide!"

The problem, aside from the proximity of the Turks, and their tardiness, was – Harrington later discovered - the boy's hiding place had vanished. The casks, in the midst of which he'd secreted himself on the previous morning, had been untied and one removed. Funar stared from the vacant space to the second in bewilderment.

"I haven't time for this," Eltsin complained. He waved the boy into the hold. "Find some place. Stay out of sight. And be quiet!"

The moments that followed sounded hilarious, the panicked lad dashing about to Eltsin's disgusted gripes. But it wasn't funny. They could all end up in prison. Out of time and patience, the second left! The abandoned boy, at the last, grabbed the corner of a tarpauline and slid beneath.

The companionway door came open and Captain Nikilov led the inspectors in.

* * *

Twenty feet away from the inspectors, beneath the canvas tarpaulin, the game was almost given away. No sooner had Ekaterina, in her guise as Funar, covered herself than she realized she was not alone. She had slid into hiding next to - another body. For his part, Harrington all but shouted when his tarp was lifted and Funar jumped in beside him. It was dark as pitch. Neither could see the other, yet both knew someone was there.

Afraid of a panic, Harrington slapped his hand over the boy's mouth and ensnared his body so he could not thrash about.

He deeply regretted, again, giving the lad reason to hate him, but could not risk an outburst. Ekaterina, man-handled, was frightened and angry, but she quietly kept her wits.

Outside their tarp, the inspection had begun. This inspector, younger than the Bosphorus man, with no beard but a fine brown mustache, in blue short coat, fez, and puffed pantaloons was less friendly, but (happily) also less thorough. His men, each with a hefty mustache of his own, were ordered to be quick. Their supervisor wanted *Demeter* off soon.

Lashings were thrown off, the scarcity of cargo discussed, cartons moved, barrels rolled, the oddity of the cargo discussed, wood pried away, tarps thrown back. Quite suddenly a portion of tarp was pulled away, exposing Harrington and the boy to the glow of lamp light but, thankfully, not to the sight of the inspectors.

Harrington and Funar, wrapped round one another, shared looks of horror. Harrington's eyes narrowed. He stared at the boy in the poor light, the cramped quarters, for the first time closely, and recognition dawned on the Englishman's face. He slowly released his hand from Funar's mouth and pulled his knit cap off. Harrington's eyes grew wide. The deck 'boy' was his hastily abandoned love, Ekaterina. His eyes fell to the cap in his hand, then to her dark sea salt smelling clothes. His lips quivered.

Ekaterina slapped her hand over his mouth.

* * *

In the spill of lamplight, partially hidden by canvas, outside the knowledge of the customs officials, Harrington and Ekaterina discovered each other. The girl took her hand from his mouth and placed a fingertip to her own. Harrington nodded. They held each other, and their breath, between the boxes and the shadowed bulkhead. In the heaven of their bodies touching, knowing what they now knew, and the hell of the same contact, she prayed (and he hoped) they not to be discovered.

Chapter Eleven

The shadows danced around the hold, cast by three customs agents, their chief, Captain Nikilov and, in the only below-deck space where he could stand upright, the big Olgaren. All within a few feet of the hidden lovers.

Thankfully, whether in answer to her prayers or his hopes, the inspector was in a hurry. A box was ordered opened and found to contain dirt as the manifest proclaimed. The cargo was counted, there and amidships, and fifty caskets agreed upon. The Turk was satisfied. He ordered his men up and, as they left the hold, accepted the captain's invitation for a drink (and, of course, backsheesh). The door was secured behind them.

It was dark and quiet in the hold again.

The couple unclinched. Slowly, quietly, Harrington climbed from under the tarp and helped Ekaterina out. He lit and turned down the foremast lamp. They stared, in silence, allowing their eyes to adjust. Then, as if a signal were given, they fell into a deep and passionate kiss.

When the kiss ended, some time later, both began excitedly whispering.

"Ekaterina! I can't believe it's you. It's been you all along. I feel like such a fool. Katya, cor!, what are you doing here?"

"Oh, Trevor," she cried, accenting the wrong syllable (the way he cherished). "I could not let you go."

"Sssh. Cor!" he repeated, as if in shock.

"I followed you... from Bukovina. I could not lose you. I did not want you to leave."

"I had no choice! Your father, your brothers... You should see my hat!"

"Your hat?"

"Never mind, it's nothing. The point is your family..."

"I know. I am so sorry. Please, forgive me!"

"Forgive you?"

"I've ruined everything. It is my fault. I told a lie to keep you - and lost you because of it. My father hates me. My brothers hate me. And I do not care. When I saw them on the dock as we were leaving Varna, I... But no. It does not matter. I could not live knowing you hated me. I had to come; to see you were safe and, if I could find the courage, to beg your forgiveness."

"The things your father and brothers yelled, the accusations..." Even in the gloom, she could see he was stricken. "You ask me to forgive you. They said you were with child; accused me of... I did not believe them. But now you ask me to forgive you? What are you saying?"

"Of course, I am not pregnant. That was the deception. But not to you. I lied to my father. I lied to be with you. You said you might leave! I could not stand the thought!"

"Leave, yes. I never planned to stay in Bukovina. But I would not have gone without you. I certainly would not have gone without a pledge between us. I love you."

She dropped her head to his chest, hit by the mistake she'd made. And, to her mind now, all for nothing. "I am a fool!"

He stopped her with a kiss and she returned it.

"The Romanian blood! I thought my father would make us be together. I never imagined he would revenge my honor. I never dreamed he would act like the Elizabethan Englander. Like the dramatist who turns his hot blood on you; on us. Oh, Trevor, what have I done to us?"

"You haven't done anything to us."

"But – what are we to do?"

Harrington laughed quietly. He grabbed the sides of his head as though he were dizzy. "There's little choice, we're going to England." He touched her cheeks, looked into her eyes, and laughed again softly, joyously, yet not quite believing. "Just look at you!"

Ekaterina pulled her cap back on to give him a good look.

The between-decks door burst open and the second mate barreled in. Ekaterina and Harrington jumped, startled. "What's going on?" He stared daggers but saw little more than shadowy outlines in the gloom. "The inspectors are gone. Funar, get back on deck! There's work to do."

Harrington raised a hand. "I was just..."

Chapter Eleven

"I have no interest in you, Mr. Harrington," Eltsin shouted. "Unless you interfere with the work of the ship. Funar! Let's go!" The eruption ended as quickly as it began and the second was gone; his exit punctuated by the slam of the hold door.

Harrington whistled softly. "Thank goodness you don't have to listen to that any longer."

"What do you mean?"

"You needn't continue the pretense." Harrington laughed. "Rada Funar! You fooled everyone. You certainly fooled me! But now you can get rid of this silly costume."

"I would love to! But, of course, I cannot. It will be a long voyage and I am stuck."

"But... now I know, surely, you can be Ekaterina again?"

"I cannot. Oliver was quite insistent."

"Oliver?"

"Oliver Swales, the cook."

"I know who he is, but... he knows who you are? I mean, he knows who you are not?"

"Certainly he knows. Everyone treats him like an old man, but I doubt he is often deceived. He will be happy you discovered the subterfuge, but he is insistent no one else must know."

"But why?"

"Because there is no telling their reaction. The world is not comprised of Libertine scholars. Women are begrudgingly allowed aboard ship as passengers, but certainly not as crew. Oliver says they might throw me overboard if discovered. He said you, a student of history, would understand. How did he say...? Yes, the irony of the Hellespont?"

Harrington considered a moment, then smiled. Of course, the original appellation for the Dardanelles; named for Helle, the daughter of Athamas. "Yes! Helle drowned in these waters during Jason's quest for the Golden Fleece. Ever since women have been bad omens; unwelcome aboard ship. Now here you are, on the Sea of Helle, dressed to avoid drowning by superstitious seamen."

She shrugged innocently, then kissed him again. "I am dressed to get aboard. And I will remain so because Oliver says I should."

"He's right. Nikilov would never have sailed, if he'd known. We have no choice. We must keep your secret; and you must be careful. Until we reach Whitby, you are Rada Funar, the deck boy."

"I'd better get on deck. The second will lose his mind if I take much longer."

Ekaterina pecked Harrington on the cheek and, as Funar, headed up. On deck, *he* helped the crew get the ship underway again. The remainder of the day was smooth sailing and, at dark, *Demeter* passed quietly into the Archipelago (the Aegean Sea).

Chapter Twelve

TUESDAY, 13 July, Harrington spent the day avoiding the deck boy. He wanted desperately to be with Ekaterina but knew that was out of the question. The last thing he needed was to react awkwardly to Funar and get them both in hot water. Ekaterina, for her part, was busy as Funar helped *Demeter* sail around Cape Matapan, south of Greece, leaving the Aegean and entering the Mediterranean Sea. The weather was gorgeous; the sea calm.

Harrington was quickly finding the voyage a torture. Unable to bear it, he stole a pre-ration moment with Ekaterina in the galley and insisted she meet him that night in the bow. Having as difficult a time with their separation as he, she readily agreed.

* * *

Harrington tied his tie, studying the reflection in his cabin's small mirror. Silently he wished for a bottle of lilac water or, might he dream, a comb; some shred of civility. He considered the clever sailors he was likely to pass between his room and the bow and decided it was just as well he had neither. The less he looked and smelled as if he were headed for a rendezvous, the more likely he was to make one. He did his best to look his best, for someone just walking the deck.

Chapter Twelve

He doused his lamp, peeked to see the hall was empty and, knowing he would need to pass the steersman, donned his most innocent expression as he headed up. He took a deep breath, stepped from the deckhouse, and found things twice as bad as he'd imagined. Not only was Pasha Amramoff there, steering, but Feliks Petrofsky as well, standing the watch. Both stared (was it his imagination?) from the helm as the Englishman stepped on deck. Harrington met their looks with a wave.

"T-T-T-Trevor, w-w-hat are... y-you..." Petrofsky shook his head, "...about?"

"Thought I'd take some air before bed. That is, if you're amenable."

Petrofsky eyed him suspiciously, nodded assent, and returned to conversing with the steersman. Harrington strolled as he rounded the deckhouse then hurried forward. To his delight, Ekaterina – still dressed as a seaman – was in the bow waiting.

"Good evening, Funar."

"Mr. Harrington. Beautiful night."

"It is now," he said with a smile.

She smiled and, as he drew near, dropped to a whisper. "I do not even know how you can look at me after all I have put you through."

Looking at her was incredibly easy. Still, she was correct, what he'd been through had not been. In that instant, Harrington was propelled back to his four day journey, on the run through the wilds of Bulgaria, to Varna and the safety of *Demeter*.

He'd hated to leave Ekaterina, that petite bauble he'd met among the library stacks. They'd had a wonderful romance that, he certainly thought at the time, ended cataclysmically. Sadly, he'd had no idea why. There'd been no tearful breakup. Barely had he arrived outside her house that night, and rapped on her door, than he was running for his life. In the distance, he heard her calling his name. He heard her father (Mayor Dragos Gabor) and brothers cursing the same name. The accusations they hurled! Cor blimey! Absolutely ridiculous. But they clearly were in no mood to debate.

Four days of hell followed; running, skulking from one rugged field to another, slowed by one dense forest after another, making his escape south through the Moldavian countryside, and south-still through the Walachian territory of Romania without being seen by day, without breaking his neck by night. He had a kit of personal effects, grabbed in haste, but no food or water save that found on the way. Admittedly, he wasn't dodging tse-tse flies in Maasailand but he wasn't on a picnic either. He was the most bookish of scholars; hunted without cause. What did it matter he hadn't broken any law, when his pursuers were the law. Harrington was on the lam.

Being an Englishman (read that *foreigner*), traveling a fiercely political eastern Europe under the best conditions was not easy. As a wanted man, he avoided the city of Bukharest, choosing the anonymity of the wild instead as if he were an American red Indian. With few options, no time to think, and a bullet hole in his once-stylish hat, he hurried south. Suspicious its smaller ports were watched, he needed to leave Romania. Despite the danger, he snuck into a wagon under cover of night and stole his way over the Danube, crossing into Bulgaria (more accurately the new principality of the Third Bulgarian State). There, he breathed a sigh of relief. Still, he needed to put Europe behind as well.

The centuries-old rule of the Ottoman's had been thrown off by the Russian and Romanian armies, with Bulgarian volunteers, in the Russo-Turkish War. But the ending Treaty had been rejected by all and the country's autonomy was in flux. (There is an old Russian proverb: *If you see a Bulgarian in the street, beat him. He will know why.*) Sneaking into Bulgaria could have gotten Harrington shot by any number of nationalities. Be that as it may, *possibly* being shot was better than *certainly* being shot, so on he ran. He spent several days hiding by light, crossing fields by night and, regretfully, remaining afoot while local farmers passed in tempting horse-drawn carts. Finally, he reached Varna. Afraid of arousing interest, and hoping to save his small purse for bargaining, he slept that night in the northern vineyards. At

Chapter Twelve

daybreak, hungry, disheveled, but rested, Harrington entered the port city.

And here he was; and Ekaterina, the love he thought he would never see again, was with him. She'd given up the only life she'd ever known, hired transport and a man to pick up his track, and followed him into the dark unknown. The two of them on the run.

* * *

Dracula came awake in his box – like a wild animal in a cage. His black soul was starved, on fire. No longer able to battle the bloodlust, he pushed up on his wooden prison. The nails at the corners gave way with a shrill bark and the lid lifted a crack. That was enough.

He closed his gleaming eyes, gave a silent command, and turned to mist. The gray cloud poured through the crack and out. It floated above the cargo, hovered over the tied tarps, then drifted down to the deck. It shifted from the horizontal to the vertical and materialized...

Count Dracula stood in human form.

This was a very different Dracula than had climbed into that box over two weeks since. Gone was the gaping wound on his forehead (inflicted in his castle vault by the hand of Jonathan Harker). It had healed and was now only a rose-colored blemish. Gone, too, was the puffed flesh swollen with the blood of a recent feed. His face now was a strong aquiline, with a high bridge on the thin nose, arched nostrils, and a lofty domed forehead. His ears were pointed at the tops. His chin was broad and strong, and his cheeks firm though thin. His mouth was fixed and cruel-looking, with markedly sharp white teeth. These protruded over the lips, whose ruddiness showed astonishing vitality for a man... of his years. For this was an old man. His hair, growing scantily round the temples but profusely elsewhere, his untamed eyebrows almost meeting over his nose, his long moustache, were all shockingly white with age. He was extraordinarily pale - and desperately in need of nourishing lifeblood.

He took in the sounds of the ship; the rushing water, the creaking timbers, the wind in the sails, the rats in the darkness; the chatter, the laughter, the whispers; the breathing, the pounding hearts, the blood pulsing through the veins of the human crew. He smelled the salt air, the odor of cooked animal flesh, the human sweat... The warm, iron-rich blood... And that other odor...

Seeing as if in daylight, Dracula moved to beneath the closed cargo doors. He could smell her above, forward of the hatch, in the bow of the ship... the woman. He would have her! He closed his eyes and raised his hands.

* * *

From somewhere abaft came the snap of wood and scrape of metal. Harrington and Ekaterina both started, turned astern and stared into the gloom around the foremast. They silently examined the deck, saw nothing, and traded nervous laughs. Barely had they returned their attention to the glassy water, when it happened again, a great snap, a scratching clank, a thud. Now both were staring aft, Harrington's hand on Ekaterina, searching for the source.

"What was that?"

"I don't know. I don't see anything." Just then, the scholar saw...

The hatch cover battens had somehow come off and lay tossed, one to each side. It made no sense. Surely they had been secured for the night and, once applied, could not have fallen off by themselves. He inched forward into the lamplight. Ekaterina followed with a hand on his back.

The hatch doors blew open, as if shoved from below by a great gust of wind, and slammed on the deck. Ekaterina jumped, Harrington shouted, and immediately after a blaze of light hit them

Chapter Twelve

from amidships. Blinded, trying to shield their eyes, neither saw a cloud of mist escape from the hold.

"What in hell goes on!" came a shout from behind the light. The voice was unmistakable. Constantin, forward of the deckhouse, came on with a lantern in his hand. He lowered the light, glaring daggers. "What goes on? Rada, why are you in the hold?"

An awkward instant passed before Ekaterina realized the mate had addressed her. "The hold? No, sir, I wasn't in the hold. Neither of us."

"It just – just came open," Harrington added. "It must have been the wind."

Constantin stared at the pair, then to the sails in the moonlight. They billowed with a steady breeze but were untouched by anything resembling a gust. The first looked past, but failed to notice, the odd mist hovering near the yard arm.

"Why are you on deck, Funar, at this time of night?"

"I, uh, was using the head, sir."

"There is a pot in the crew's quarters, yes?"

"I – I do not... I prefer solitude."

"That is childish. You need to grow up." Constantin ran his hand over his dome, annoyed, then turned on the passenger. "Mr. Harrington, we don't encourage passengers on deck at night. Does the captain know you are here?"

"He doesn't. Unless he saw me come up. It certainly is no secret; I just wanted air."

"Now you've had it, I recommend you go below. Rada, you belong in bed. You never know when the sea will call you to duty for days at a time. Sleep when you are able. Now, clear the deck."

The deck 'boy' reached for one of the hold doors.

"Nevermind," the first said. "I'll see to it. You may go."

Constantin stood, lamp in hand, as Harrington and Funar passed and started around the deckhouse. Opting for discretion, Harrington took the port rail alone. Funar took the starboard, with Constantin on *his* heels.

Behind them, the mist swirling in the foresail floated to the deck and in the dull amber glow of the mast light transformed back into the aged and hungry Count Dracula. He stared aft as the trio disappeared.

* * *

Petrofsky and Amramoff were still at the wheel when the ship's boy and the Englishman appeared from the gloom on either side of the deckhouse. The first mate came behind Funar, herding them like truants. As they started below, Constantin paused and glared at the helm. "The hatch on the forward hold is open. Petrofsky, batten it down." The door slammed and he was gone.

Petrofsky turned to his shipmate. "W-What did I d-d-do? Th-Three of them... a-and they can't batten a hatch?"

Amramoff shrugged. "Who knows."

"I kn-kn-know," the marlinspike complained. He grabbed a lamp with his good hand. "S-Same as... al-ways. Everything f-falls on Petrofsky."

"What do you suppose that was? Those two?"

"Who c-cares! I h-have to b-b-batten the hatch!"

Forward, alone, in the glow of his lamp, Petrofsky's mood lightened. He was no fanatic of the watch, neither was he so poetic as to claim his senses came alive, but he did enjoy a calm night at sea; the warm Mediterranean breeze sweeping them west, the roll, pitch, and occasional thrilling heave of the deck, the roar as the bow cleaved the water in matching arcs beneath the anchors... And, rudely infringing, Amramoff whistling at the wheel (God damn a man that whistles)!

But as he passed the forward rain barrels something came over him... Whether a sound or simply an odd vibration, Petrofsky did not know. Something about the ship suddenly felt... wrong.

Ahead, he heard a scuttling, a scratching on wood. Regardless of the hour, it was ridiculous! The ship's carpenter was at the helm. There ought be no one ahead doing any wood-working. He

Chapter Twelve

halted and held his breath, the better to hear. He lifted his lantern to peer into the dark.

The hatch was open, as the first said, a menacing black hole in the deck. The battens lay tossed aside. But why in the world at that hour? And why having opened the hold hadn't they closed it again? He could not imagine. But where was the surprise? Everything fell to him.

Something moved – and Petrofsky started.

He regained himself, lifted his lamp and searched the gloom. He saw nothing, but heard... There again; the movement, the scratching! He directed the lamp low on the deck and full upon the source. Rats! Several of them, black and filthy, their naked claws and fleshy tails white beneath his light as they emerged over the lip of the hatch from the hold below. Their eyes reflected red, they squealed and scuttled into the forward shadows.

Petrofsky shook involuntarily (he hated rats!), then shook his head – feeling the fool. For, though he despised the loathsome creatures, there was certainly nothing novel about their being aboard a sailing ship. What ship of the line didn't have rats?

He reached the hatchway, to carry out Constantin's order when, something more caught his eye. It was forward, where the port rail ought to have been (though it was hidden by darkness); something else moved. Something larger than a blinking rat! Petrofsky circumnavigated the yawning pit and lifted his lantern. There! He could just make out... a tall man standing at the rail.

Chapter Thirteen

"Y-You t-t-there!"

Who was this man? He had a thick head of white hair, but was too tall to be either the captain or the cook; the only white-haired men aboard. He was too tall to be anyone except Olgaren. But Moisey was thick as a tree with flaming red hair. Who was this thin, dark phantom? He must be one of the crew. From where else could he have come? Yet the marlinspike was certain he wasn't a crewman at all. Whoever he was, the man just stood staring at the water without any indication he'd heard.

Petrofsky was dumbfounded. "Y-You t-t-there," he called again.

Slowly the dark figure turned. Petrofsky shined his light full on him – and his throat went dry. It was an old man with a face as white as his great mustache and eyes that shined red in the kerosene light. Despite the warmth of the Mediterranean summer, a chill shot through Petrofsky as if he'd been struck by lightning. "W-Who are you?"

The old man's eyes cut through Petrofsky. He drew back the corners of his red lips, displaying outrageously sharp teeth in an awful smile. He snarled and hissed like a feral cat. Then, unbelievably, the stranger jumped overboard.

As simple as that, from his standing position, he merely jumped up and over the gunwale and disappeared. Petrofsky shouted and

Chapter Thirteen

ran to the rail. He looked over, into the sea, but saw – nothing. Nothing but swiftly passing, white-capped waters near the hull. He strained, scanning the darkness and the sea abaft, to no avail.

It made no sense! The old man had been there at the rail and had jumped overboard without a word. Petrofsky would swear to it, on a bible, before Pope Leo himself. But where had he gone? Even drowning takes time; a splash, a shout, the instinctive struggle regardless of how voluntary the act! How could he have gone so fast? The watchman was awestruck; then came the full embarrassment. What the hell was he waiting for? Someone had just... He'd done nothing about it! "M-Man o-o-over-b-board!" Petrofsky shouted, running aft. "M-Man o-o-over-b-board! E-Every-b-body on d-d-deck!"

Amramoff heard him from the wheel for, an instant later, the ship's bell rang. And, soon after, the others appeared on deck; the first mate barking, Smirnov, Olgaren, Popescu grumbling, and the second. Another moment and the English passenger was there, then the deck boy, then Swales (gasping for breath). Even Amramoff, who was supposed to be minding the helm, showed up. "M-Man o-ver-b-board!" Petrofsky shouted, leading them into the bow. "M-Man o-o-over-b-board!"

"Shut up!" Constantin shouted, grabbing Petrofsky's arm. The marlinspike stopped screaming and the mate lowered his voice. "What in hell are you yelling about?"

"T-T-There i-i-is... a man... over-b-board!"

Several went to the rail to peer out to sea, but Constantin held his ground. He scanned the gloomy deck and those standing in the lamplight. His eyes fell back on Petrofsky. "The captain?" the mate demanded. "Is that what you're saying? The captain fell overboard? I just spoke to him!"

"N-N-No, sir," Petrofsky replied in confusion. "I n-n-never... said it was. I never s-said so. I-I-It w-was not the cap-tain."

The first glared. "Look around you." The marlinspike merely returned his stare and Constantin flared. "That's an order, you stupid bastard! Look around you!"

110

Petrofsky did, without a clue what he was meant to be looking for.

"We are all here! The captain is... indisposed and will be here momentarily. Otherwise the entire compliment is here. Every soul aboard is staring at you!"

Petrofsky took them all in. "A-A-Aye, s-sir."

"We are all here," Constantin repeated. "Even those who ought not be." He turned on Amramoff and barked, "Aren't you on the wheel?"

"Aye, sir. Smooth sailing. Just tied her off to see what the screaming was."

"Return to your duty." The carpenter hurried aft. The mate returned his attention to Petrofsky, who only shook his head.

From the stern came the captain's raspy, "Mr. Constantin!" The gravel in his voice was a remnant of the quack's elixir. (The screams had taken him off guard and he'd been forced to slow his heart rate by the bottle.) He could still taste it as he snapped his braces and pulled on his coat. "What in the name of the murdering Turks is happening on my ship?"

"Petrofsky thought he saw someone go overboard, sir."

"And everyone stands here?"

"All hands are accounted for, captain. He could not have seen that which he claims."

"I d-did see it, s-s-sir," Petrofsky insisted. "I s-s-saw a m-man jump o-over! An o-o-old man."

* * *

There was no good way to resolve the conundrum. There was no evidence anything out of the ordinary had taken place. Petrofsky told the captain, the mates, and his loitering ship-mates what he'd seen. Nikilov calmly asked questions. The watchman answered – in excited bursts of what could only be utter nonsense.

An examination of the deck was made during which most everyone paused to gawp over the gunwale (Popescu, the last, nervously

111

Chapter Thirteen

crossed himself). Swales, refusing his turn at the rail, bellowed that he'd seen water before. He suggested they all head "ageeanwards to bed" where he had been "snod an' snog 'efore this quare scowderment". Nothing was found; nothing could be done.

At the commander's word, the mate dispersed the crew. Olgaren was ordered to relieve Petrofsky's watch and the marlinspike given leave to go below. He drifted behind the others and wandered aft alone, muttering. He was still talking to himself when he reached the deckhouse stairs.

"You look as if you've lost your last friend..." Amramoff called from the wheel, "to a ghost!"

Petrofsky scowled and would have replied had he not spotted the second mate nearby. He swallowed the comment, unspoken.

Eltsin frowned at Amramoff, then told the marlinspike, "Do not let it bother you, Feliks. You thought you saw something you could not have seen. I could tell stories of the tricks my eyes have played on me." He offered a friendly smile. Amramoff added a laugh.

Petrofsky went below without returning either.

The captain and mate shared a final word at the rail over rushing water. Neither believed Petrofsky. How could they? The crew was accounted for; as were the only two aboard with white hair. And, as they'd already slipped Harrington and Funar past customs, it was ridiculous to consider another undiscovered stowaway. Neither thought Petrofsky a liar, but his 'old man' had been imagined. In agreement then that the mysterious stranger had never been aboard, neither could have believed... he was still there.

Forward, clinging to *Demeter's* figurehead and hull as if he were a fly, Dracula hung trapped beneath the bowsprit and above the deadly arcs of water on either side, in the same way he was trapped between death and life. The sea splashed and burned him like acid. Fangs bared, his hatred brewing, he suffered in silence... waiting.

The Count heard every word as the captain and his mate, ignorant of his presence, blamed Petrofsky's incident on a gloom that had settled over their voyage. The first insisted the men needed to focus on their labors, while the captain said they needed to lift their mood. Their conversation closed without a concensus and they left the bow for their beds.

When the humans cleared out, Dracula crawled up, over the rail and retook the deck. He straightened his attire, brushing away the humiliation of having to hide from these rodents. Another in a regrettable line of actions taken over four-and-a-half centuries in order to survive. Count Dracula, old and white, angry and insatiably hungry, made himself mist again.

* * *

An impromptu meeting took place in the crew's quarters. It started with Popescu complaining. Smirnov, disturbed by the event on deck, joined him and they grumbled together. Petrofsky, shaken and muttering, added his voice and suddenly they had a meeting. The marlinspike related his experience again, insisting he had not invented his story. Words failed him but his fear was evident. By the time Funar entered (Ekaterina's secret was still that), Petrofsky's fear had spread.

"It is not just your strange old man; whoever or whatever he is. There's something unnatural aboard this ship," Popescu said. "Some evil. We've been under its spell since we sailed."

"Before we sailed," Smirnov corrected, his fright conspicuous in his whispered falsetto. "You were already aboard. You don't know the difficulty Constantin had signing crew in Varna."

"I can imagine. They settled for you!" Popescu laughed at his own joke.

"Play the fool," Smirnov said. "I am serious. Every experienced seaman in the city walked away saying something was wrong with this ship. Remember the fight on the quay? Those peasants threatening the dock workers. And our cargo! Has anyone ever heard of such a cargo?"

"An evil cargo," Popescu added. Wide-eyed, he was no longer laughing.

Chapter Thirteen

But someone in the companionway was; a throaty, familiar laugh followed by an equally familiar grunt of disgust. "If only me dad could hear ye lads!" Swales barged in, unlit pipe clenched between his teeth. "Fool-talk, that's what he'd call it; nowt else. Wafts, an' boh-ghosts, an' bar-guests, an' bogles only fit to set bairns an' dizzy women a'belderin'. Invented to skeer each other."

"Why?"

"Oh, aye. Why? Thaat's the question."

"We haven't invented anything. We're only saying what all on board are thinking and feeling."

"Oh, all, is it? Yer sure then? Well, I have me doubts. Feel whate'er ye like, lads. *Fear* what ye like. But take me advice – keep it to ye'sel'. For it do no' take a genius to gather that our good Mr. Constantin hates superstitions as much as the cap'n loves religion; an' if ye make either ireful wi' yer bogey stories, I fancy ye'll regret it."

Fixed on the cook's warning, the room jumped when Harrington put his head in. "Is this a private meeting?"

"Yes," Popescu said angrily. "It is."

"O' course, it ain't," Swales said. He turned on the Romanian. "Ye can't have it both ways, Bogdan. Ye can't speak for e'ery soul on the ship – an' exclude them from the conversation."

"I was speaking of the crew. We're not to be carrying passengers. He doesn't belong."

"He has a note from the cap'n sayin' he does. What have you?" Popescu scowled without reply. "Aye. So I thought." Swales waved the Englishman in and pointed to a place on a bunk beside Funar.

Harrington started for it then, aware of his weaknesses, found a seat near Petrofsky instead. "So," he said, settling. "As I gather, the topic of conversation is..."

"Ghosts an' bogles!"

"Nobody spoke of ghosts," Smirnov put in. "Not exactly."

"Gog! D' no' hedge now," Swales insisted.

"Then we will not." Popescu stared hard at the Scot, then turned on the Englishman. "There is a pall over this voyage. Something unnatural in or about this ship. Yes, unnatural! Such things exist! We wonder what it could be. And I wonder if it has to do with you?"

"Easy, lad, wi' yer accusations. I'm more than willin' to vouch fer Mr. Harrin'ton."

"That's fine. In your estimation, that clears him. I wonder who will vouch for you, old man?"

Swales leaned in to Popescu and whispered, "Lad, I gawm how men act when they're skeered. They'll do an' say anythin'. The shite runs out their gob w'out a thought, so I canno' altogether blame ye. An' no' bein' a gentleman masel', I beg yer fer-giveness in advance. But yer leapin' up and down on me last feckin' nerve. I recommend ye take this as the one an' only warnin' this old man is goin' to give ye. . . " He poked his clay pipe into Popescu's chest. "Get yer head right."

"Is there a problem?" The voice was Constantin's as he stepped into the bunk room doorway.

"Nowt to speak o'. No."

The mate's beady, black eyes left Swales and took in the others. "Have I missed a meeting?"

"Not at all, sir." Popescu said. "Just a friendly get together."

"There is nothing then that I need know?"

It felt as if any number of them had something to get off their chests. But no one spoke. A strange tension, a palpable fear, passed among them. Popescu finally ended the silence. "No, sir. Nothing at all."

Constantin nodded noncommittally. "In that case, Swales, Mr. Harrington, if you will find your quarters. Popescu, you and I have the early watch. Lights out."

Chapter Fourteen

POPESCU rubbed the goose flesh on his arms. It was mid-July, Wednesday the 14th, and they were in the mid-Mediterranen; still at that early hour, a cool breeze raced over the water, across his shoulders at the helm, and through the sails, chasing the darkness into daylight. Tired, nearing the end of his duty yet tied to the wheel, he couldn't help but shiver. He told himself it was the breeze.

He could hear the first, swearing and shouting at the hands in the bow. He'd roused them early, payment for meeting behind his back the night before, and set them to work. Annoyed with his fellow countryman's constant badgering, Popescu tried to put it from his mind, to think of something else. But the only image he found to replace it was one of Petrofsky's old man jumping off the ship.

Thus were his thoughts employed when Constantin came aft and startled the day-dreaming Popescu. "Sorry, sir," the steersman said. "I was... wandering." The mate stared, but said nothing, and the uncomfortable seaman tried to fill the void. "A bit of a nip in the air."

Constantin nodded. The rising sunlight painted the horizon; the sea and sky waxing from black, to blue, to a brilliant red-gold.

"Like the turn of the tide," Popescu whispered. "The chill which comes with the dawn."

Chapter Fourteen

Constantin scowled. "Is that poetry?" He didn't like poetry and, though he'd never met one, was certain he didn't like poets.

"Just an old saying."

"Say it again." He turned his coal black eyes on Popescu. The steersman stared back warily. "I said, say it again. That's an order."

"Like the turn of the tide. The chill which comes with the dawn."

"What does that mean?"

Popescu cleared his throat and, fearfully, answered in a whisper. "It is said those near death often die at the break of dawn, or at the turn of the tide."

The first reddened. "I'm getting tired of your whining."

"Mr. Constantin..."

"Do not interrupt me! I heard your morose mutterings last night in your farcical little meeting. I've been listening to this nonsense about a cursed ship since Varna. I'm tired of it! I'm tired of all of you whining like children. It is about time this crew began acting like men. And you are going to stop undermining them with your ridiculous superstitions – or you will feel my hand."

Popescu, wilted by the first's glare, looked away and missed seeing Nikilov step from the deckhouse. Constantin, giving the steersman hell, was likewise oblivious to the captain's arrival.

"I do not want to hear anymore about death," the first said through tightened lips. "Not another word. Is that understood?"

"Yes, sir."

"Now mind your helm." Only then did Constantin see Nikilov. He stepped from the wheel and greeted him with a nod. "Morning, sir."

"Good morning." The captain stepped casually to the starboard and Constantin followed. He reached the rail and turned, his blue eyes searching those of his mate. "Iancu, are you all right?"

"I am, captain."

They walked to the front of the deckhouse, paused and watched the crew ably but joylessly about their duties. The men were strained, anxious, and it showed. Nikilov knew them, those with whom he'd sailed before; steady fellows with first-rate attitudes. Their melancholy made no sense and he told the first as much.

"I agree, captain," Constantin said. "Something disturbs the entire crew. It is palpable. I do not know what is wrong – and they either cannot or will not say. They say only that there is SOMETHING wrong." With contempt, he added, "Then Popescu crosses himself."

Despite his religious convictions, Nikilov listened in silence.

The mate, looking aloft, noted the foot of the main top sail (damaged days before by Petrofsky to save his life) was torn again. The marlinspike's repair did not appear to be holding. He shouted to Petrofsky, bringing the damage to his attention, and ordered him aloft again.

To everyone's surprise, Petrofsky snapped back, "It is n-n-not my f-fault!" The mate's order struck him as an accusation he'd been incompetent repairing it. He waved his bandaged hand, and shouted, "This m-m-makes the work nigh imp-p-possible! And b-burns like f-f-fire!"

"Stop your whining!" Constantin demanded. "Are you angry with the work? That you damaged the sail in the first place? Or embarrassed you made a fool of yourself last night with your old ghost?"

"Was no g-g-ghost! I saw wh-what... I s-saw!"

"Shut your mouth!" the mate hollered, his patience gone. "Shut your damned mouth – and follow orders!" He grabbed a coiled line from the deck, spun on the marlinspike, and whipped it across his shoulder. Petrofsky cried out and fell to one knee.

The others halted their labors, staring.

"E-Everything h-h-happens to... me," Petrofsky cried. He shook his wrecked hand as evidence. "And n-n-now you're... a-angry about l-last night, as am... I. But it's n-n-naught to... do with me o-other than I... saw it."

Constantin, livid, raised his hand to deliver another lashing.

The captain watched, disapproving, but holding his tongue. The chain of command could only be weakened by his stepping

Chapter Fourteen

between the mate and a crewman where discipline was involved. But he was not happy with Constantin's handling of the situation. He would have a word later. For now, Nikilov fully expected the altercation to result in a fierce quarrel.

To his relief, it did not. Finding a patience even he was not aware he possessed, the mate stayed the second blow and lowered the coil. Petrofsky, too, backed down without another word. It wasn't cowardice. He simply realized his troubles, whatever they were, had nothing to do with the mate. Popescu was right, they were caused by this accursed ship. Weary, beaten, Petrofsky wordlessly gathered his gear and climbed the main mast shroud for the damaged sail.

The rest of the crew went quietly back to work. Nikilov watched them all, relieved a violent confrontation had been avoided, but deeply concerned.

* * *

Vampires do not dream.

They rest in a cold and death-like state. But when aroused, they are much like humans; they think, feel... and hunger.

Count Dracula had much to think of to occupy his wakeful hours; all he knew behind him, all he anticipated before him, and the moments at hand. One can imagine the things he had to consider.

And, while his feelings ran the gamut as anyone's might, two emotions held sway. The first was anger. Existing in a world in which he could not live had engendered in Dracula a constant state of anger and bitterness. Add the need to hide from the ship's crew, like a filthy rat in the cellar, and his thoughts grew to ferociousness. He hated them, ached for their destruction... and more.

And now a new feeling!

The recent revelation of a woman aboard the vessel had aroused in him... something he had not felt or thought of in generations.

An image of his wives, behind at Castle Dracula, flashed in his mind and the words of one in particular, spoken recently in spite, echoed in his ears...

He'd just returned to the castle with their... sustenance. He threw the bag upon the floor where a gasp and low wail escaped as it writhed with its living contents. Angry as he was, Dracula paid it no further attention. He found them – all three of his women – in a room they did not belong, doing that which he had forbidden; closing in on Harker, intent upon drinking his blood.

He'd stopped them, of course, denying their hoped-for kisses. Then Marishka, his fair-haired treasure, with her usual laugh of ribald coquetry, leveled her accusation. "You yourself never loved. You never love!" The others joined her, filling the room with their mirthless laughter. Gorgeous, ageless maidens, soulless fiends, taking pleasure in his pain. But he had loved and told them so. Long ago and far away, he had loved – deeply. Before that love, leading to that love, he had lusted.

Now, starving for life-giving blood, insanely lusting for the female creature here and now aboard the ship, he knew these were not dreams (for vampires do not dream). They were all-consuming desires. In his box, in the dark of the forehold, Dracula felt the overwhelming, undeniable ache... For, indeed, one lust fed another.

* * *

"There are so many things I want to tell you."

The night was upon them and Ekaterina, still dressed as Funar, had again managed to meet Harrington in the bow. There they whispered, wanting to hold hands, to make contact with one another, yet knowing they dared not. Society, secrecy, perhaps their lives demanded they be deck hand and paid guest passing in the night.

"And I have things to say to you. We will say them soon," Harrington assured her. "But, as you so wisely put it, not now."

Chapter Fourteen

Ekaterina nodded and smiled. Many things had to wait, but were worth waiting for. Making sure of the deck, she withdrew a necklace from beneath her seaman's jersey, a delicate gold *fleur-de-lis* that glinted in the light of the mast lamp. "Do you remember this?"

He did – and its backstory. The pendant was a stylized lily that, historically, symbolized everything to everyone (politics, dynasty, art, and heraldry). The Grand Duke of Luxembourg, the overthrown King of Spain, the House of Bourbon whose *coup d'état* replaced him, French-Canadians, all thought it part of their cultural heritage. The religious believed the petals stood for the Trinity. Harrington preferred the simple interpretation of *faith, hope* and *charity*; a charming representation of Ekaterina. He'd seen her adoring it in a shop window. (Actually, she'd admired it *and* several jeweled cruciforms but, not even understanding Christian believers, Harrington saw no reason to buy their trinkets.) He'd bought it that same day and carefully guarded it until its presentation seemed appropriate. "Of course I remember." He smiled to know she wore the gift beneath her disguise.

"I bought a dress to wear with it," she said, still whispering. "It's lovely! White as new-fallen snow, with a beautiful long gored skirt. You know, the *empire* look so popular in the cities, with a corselet. . . " He smiled. Even in the dim light, Ekaterina saw his cheeks redden. "Merely a raised waistline, silly." She giggled and laid the heel of her hand against his stomach, demonstrating the height. With impressive balance in that rocking bow, she strode away, pivoted and returned, miming modeling the dress. "It has a full blouse with three tiers of ruffles." She leaned in whispering the secret, ". . . encircling the upper bodice," and laughed again.

Harrington laughed too, quietly, as he shushed her.

"The neckline is high, the sleeves puffed at the shoulders. There are ruffles at the elbows and a cincture running here." She passed a delicate hand over her stomach.

Harrington swallowed, his throat suddenly dry. "You're lovely in it."

Ekaterina's mouth fell open. "But you have never seen me wearing it. I've... never worn it." Sadness moved in behind her bright eyes. "Except to try it on."

"Yes," he said, in equal melancholy. "On the night I... ran. I saw you, through your window, a white angel, when... somebody started shooting."

"Trevor, I'm so sorry."

"It's all right." He wanted to hold her, to comfort her, and knew he dared not. Not here. He forced a laugh, to cheer her. "You got a new dress, I lost an old hat. What could be better?"

"It's so lovely..." She paused and began to cry. "It looked so lovely against my hair."

Hacked stubbles of gold peeked from beneath Funar's knit cap. Ekaterina's gorgeous mane, once pulled forward in a fashionable pompadour, braided behind to her shoulders, passed through a bow, and draped to her slight hips, was only a memory. Still brilliant, it seemed less so chopped to a pawltry inch atop the head of a deck boy. Harrington laid a gentle hand upon her shoulder. "It's all right."

"Is it?" Ekaterina kissed his hand. "After last night, I wonder."

"You're not letting Petrofsky's fantasies, Popescu's evil spirits get to you? Sailors are superstitious by trade."

She nodded. "Still, I admit, I am afraid."

"Afraid?"

"We rush through the dark and, though it is the Mediterranean in summer, something cold and unfathomable threatens all around. The night is filled with fearful sounds. Have we a destination or are we fooling ourselves? Are we merely drifting from that we know and love to things dark and dreadful? Oh, Trevor, I can't help but feel that something terrible is going to happen."

"Darling." Harrington could resist no longer. He grabbed Ekaterina, held her and, when she looked into his eyes and kissed him, passionately returned it, as if his life depended upon it.

Had it not been for an accident they would, there and then, have been found out.

Chapter Fourteen

The mate, quietly walking the deck alone, tripped as he rounded the deckhouse and caught a rain barrel to keep from going down. The thud, the slosh of water, and the shouted oath alerted the pair. They had just the time to straighten themselves before Constantin came upon them in the dark.

He stared at the innocent looking duo, more suspicious now than on the previous night. "A bit late for another meeting, is it not?" the mate asked. "What have you two to meet about?"

"Funar and I merely stopped in passing, Mr. Constantin," Harrington said. "There's nothing more to it than that. The happenings aboard this ship that stir your suspicions, I would guess, are the same ones keeping me from sleeping."

"And Funar?"

"I was just talking, sir," the boy put in. "Conversing, as I seen Mr. Harrington here."

Constantin nodded noncommittally. "Rada, you will not be excused for lack of sleep."

"Yes, sir."

"Mr. Harrington, a word with you, if you will." It was not a request and Constantin didn't wait for an answer. Fully expecting their passenger to follow, he headed into the shadows aft.

Harrington and Ekaterina shared grimaces, smiled and mouthed good night to each other. Then she waved him away. He smiled and left to catch the mate.

She watched him go and was again alone in the gloomy bow – completely unaware of the large gray bat hanging inverted in the sail rigging above. Suspended from the lines on the foremast yard arm, the shadowy creature pinched the canvas of the fore main sail with the protruding thumbs on its folded wing-stalks, released the lines above from the grip of its clawed feet and quickly, noiselessly shimmied across the surface of the billowing sail.

It came to a stop above her head.

Chapter Fifteen

THE first mate led the way into the mess as if it were his private office. Harrington, despite being a paid passenger, followed, head hanging like a naughty child entering church.

"What exactly is going on?"

"I'm sorry, Mr. Constantin, I do not understand your question."

"This is the second time I have discovered you and the boy on deck, after hours, where you have no business. I want to know what is going on."

"There is nothing 'going on', I assure you."

"I do not accept your assurance."

"Sir?" Harrington asked indignantly.

"Come, Mr. Harrington. You are the subject of a monarchy, I of an empire. Neither of us have the right to democratic feelings or expectations of autonomy. Most especially not you. We have a chain of command here and you, Mr. Harrington, are not on it. You will follow the captain's orders aboard this vessel and, in his absence, mine, or you will regret it. Do you understand?"

"Certainly. I had no other intentions."

"I am gratified. This crew is suddenly on edge about - something. I do not understand it, but I don't need to. I need to put an end to it. I will, by insisting upon normalcy. Whatever you and Rada Funar are up to, it is not routine on this ship. It is a mystery."

Chapter Fifteen

"Our being on the deck was nothing more than a coincidence."

"Twice? After hours? No. I do not believe in this coincidence. Whatever you are about, I do not appreciate your interference with the crew and I will not have it. Walk the deck all you please, but these meetings are at an end. The mystery is over."

Ekaterina hesitated in the bow, afraid for Trevor. Not that she believed he was in any physical danger. She knew he wasn't. The first mate was prickly, but a fair man. He'd certainly been good to her. She was (rather Rada Funar was) the only crewman the mate called by his Christian name. He, along with the second, had seen to Funar's instruction as a good seaman, taught him his duties, even taught him how to steer, and looked out for his well-being. He cared about the 'boy'. That said, the first could be a hard man, brutal when it came to discipline. She hoped he was not being too hard on Trevor; that he was not throwing lightning bolts to protect his protégé.

She'd been ordered below, and knew she ought to go. But Ekaterina paused a moment more to look into the black Mediterranean, to see the ghosts of white caps on the breaking waves, to hear them slapping the ship. To listen to the wind in the sails. At least that was what she thought she was hearing.

What she actually heard was the dark gray creature, its leathery wings folded, on its stalks, its clawed thumbs pinching the canvas as it shimmied down the sail, lower and closer. She did not hear the thing let go; didn't hear it drop. She was oblivious that, as it fell, the creature transformed...

Her senses, alive with the beauty of the Mediterranean night were, an instant later, overwhelmed with horror. For something, someone, fell in a blur, landed behind and grabbed her with hands of ice. A wave of revulsion washed over Ekaterina. Cold hands, one over her mouth, the other snatching her wrists together, held her in an iron grip. A peripheral flash in the amber gloom of the face of an old man. The putrid smell of rot and decay, an awful hot breath, stifling her as her attacker's head dropped below her line of vision. A wire-brush burn as his thick mustache scratched her soft white flesh. The intense pain as razor sharp teeth violated her throat; tearing tissue, crushing capillaries, piercing a vein. Ekaterina screamed silently into her attacker's palm as her blood flowed.

Count Dracula, lusting, long starved, drank deeply.

* * *

In the first week of the voyage the crew had come to know one another and, while no great friendships emerged, the entire compliment seemed to get along. The single glaring exceptions were Popescu and Smirnov. The former, it was no secret, was no favorite of anyone. The latter, while odd, got on well enough. Both did their duty and avoided the lash of Constantin's tongue. That said, it was clear that between the grumbling Romanian and the slight Russian there was no love lost. No outright hatred, but certainly no meeting of the minds. Popescu had taken to loudly and frequently barking, "*Tu fundul prostie!*," at the little Russian. Smirnov, having secured a translation, had had enough of being called a *silly ass* before his shipmates. That would be nothing compared to the blow Smirnov's ego would suffer as Wednesday night's watch turned into Thursday morning, 15 July.

Owing to the scarcity of crew, the captain had the previous day extended the normal four hour watches to six. It complicated things, making hands seem to come and go at random, but afforded each a longer rest when their chance came. Thus Popescu relieved Smirnov at 6 am instead of 4 (four bells instead of eight) just before dawn. The Russian reported "All's well" in the monotone that generally passed between them and went below. Less than ten minutes later, Smirnov found himself back on deck – and in the dog house.

After taking the watch, Popescu, as was his routine, headed forward on the starboard to look over the bow and sails. Normally, he returned by the port completing his circuit at the helm. He didn't get that far. As he passed into the bow, he spotted something on the deck at the foot of the foremast. He drew near and

Chapter Fifteen

recognized it as the body of Funar. He kicked the lad's boot and called his name but the boy failed to stir. He could not hear and barely felt the lad's breath.

"Pasha!" Popescu shouted, calling aft in sudden fear.

He stopped himself in mid-shout, remembering the hell Petrofsky had gotten for raising an alarm unnecessarily. Better to get help quietly and let the officers raise any clamor. He hurried back to the wheel where Amramoff was talking with the second.

"What's the matter, Popescu? Seen a ghost?"

Eltsin burned the steersman with his scowl. "Shut up, Pasha. You and your damned ghosts." He turned to the agitated Romanian. "What is it?"

"Not a ghost!" Popescu whispered. "A body. The deck boy's body, forward."

"He's dead?"

"I don't think so. I think he is breathing... but only just."

Eltsin started forward. Popescu followed, trying to inform him, to defend himself, to steady his nerves.

A red ribbon of daylight broke over the bulwark, pierced the gloom, and threw the foot of the mast into deeper shadow as they reached the collapsed boy. Eltsin crouched, his hand over the lad's face. "He's cold," he said. "He hardly breathes." He looked at Popescu. "Rouse the captain, quietly."

Popescu, trembling, mumbling the 'Lord's Prayer' by rote while he recalled the superstitions of his fatherland, seemed not to have heard.

"Bogdan! Go below and quietly get the captain."

Popescu, yanked from his trance, crossed himself and hurried aft.

* * *

Smirnov heard it all; the frightened Romanian barging down the companionway past the crew's quarters to the captain's cabin, his hurried rap on the door, his excited whisper requesting Nikilov on deck and, a moment later, the captain hurrying by in the opposite direction with Popescu on his heels.

The first mate too was up and out of bed at the sound of their passing. More curious than alarmed, he grabbed his coat and followed without giving Smirnov a second look.

The small Russian was alarmed. Afraid he'd missed something on his watch, Smirnov pulled his boots back on and hurried after the three. He stepped on deck to a frown from Amramoff at the wheel. The carpenter, who'd watched the parade, pointed him forward. He rounded the deckhouse and, near the foremast, saw the captain, the second and Popescu gathered round, and Constantin kneeling over...

"Oh, hell!"

Smirnov drew near and, in the early light, confirmed the body on the deck was that of Funar. "What's happened?" he asked.

"*Tu fundul prostie!*," Popescu shouted. "The boy is near death. He's cold as the grave. He must have lain here all night, while you were supposed to be on watch. Where were you?"

Popescu may have been right. Sadly, for all Smirnov knew, the boy may have been there through his watch. Nobody knew but... he'd left the deck several times during the night. His back spasms had worsened and he'd needed, he'd taken, laudanum for the pain. He hadn't been gone long, but that meant nothing and he knew it. He'd abandoned his post. Worse, he'd returned to it under influence of drug. In the dark, in his laudanum-fog, he may have walked right past the boy. May have done several times, without seeing or stumbling over him.

"Where were you?" Popescu was baring down on him.

All Smirnov could do was drop his head. Perhaps the Romanian was right; perhaps he was a silly ass.

Sunlight cleared the sail and bathed them. The boy came to. He groaned and raised a hand to cover his eyes, as if the light burned. He moaned in pain and rolled to his side. Constantin reached to unbutton Funar's shirt and the boy's head lolled over. The mate exclaimed under his breath.

Chapter Fifteen

"What is it?" the captain asked, stepping forward.

The first lifted his hand, showing a smear of blood on his fingers. He peeled back Funar's collar throwing light on a vicious wound on his throat; a fist-sized bruise around two punctures, white with red centers, oozing blood.

"Dear God," Popescu exclaimed, behind them. He crossed himself. "The devil is aboard." He turned on Smirnov, livid, "And you let him roam the deck!"

"Shut up, you fool!" Smirnov screamed. "Shut your filthy mouth!"

"Be quiet," the captain snapped. "Both of you."

Funar began suddenly to gasp. To aid his breathing, Constantin pulled his shirt open. Under it, he found the boy's chest and midsection wrapped in a cloth brace very like Smirnov's. The mate grunted at the oddity. Surely, Funar was too young to also suffer back troubles? The captain stared, traded shrugs with the first, and said, "No wonder he can't breathe. Take it off." Constantin unbuttoned Funar's shirt to his belt, then started on the wrap. He loosened it, lifted the boy with one arm and pulled the material from around his torso – once, twice, a third time.

Behind the mate, the pressure of the morning, coupled with his fears, pushed Popescu beyond endurance. With neither reason nor excuse, the superstitious Romanian slapped Smirnov across the face. The startled Russian replied with a fist. That quickly the pair were trading blows. Eltsin and Nikilov, shouting, had no choice but to jump between them.

Ignoring their row to concentrate on the patient, Constantin pulled off the last of Funar's chest wrap. His mouth fell open. He froze in place - except for his shocked and widening eyes.

Eltsin, ordering him to stop, held the heavily-breathing Popescu pinned against the foremast. Smirnov's hair and mustache, meanwhile, were a riot. Nikilov, having given him a shake that should have sent his head flying, likewise demanded he desist. The sailors regained their senses and the fight was halted. No sooner had a quiet descended, than it was exploded by Constantin, on the deck forward, sputtering, "Good Christ!"

The commander, still holding Smirnov, barked, "Mr. Constantin! You will not take the Lord's name..." He stopped in mid-sentence. The mate, the most unflappable character the captain knew, blushed crimson in the dull light, deeply shocked. Nikilov moved to trade places. "See to the men," he ordered the first. "I'll attend to Funar."

Constantin, stunned, tried to warn his commander in passing. Too angry to listen, the captain pointed at the sailors (separated by the second) and told the mate, "See to those blackguards!"

"Mr. Eltsin," the first said, "Take those men to the helm! Wait there for orders! Go now!"

The second started aft, pushing the seamen before him.

Nikilov bent to Funar. He saw the bloody wounds on the child's throat and the cloth wrap loosened to help his breathing. He pulled the shirt open, pulled the wrap down, to see what other injury had elicited Constantin's outrageous reaction. Then he gasped too. Beneath the clothing and tightly bound chest wrap, Rada Funar, their last minute crew hire, their hard working deck boy, had been hiding a small but lovely pair of breasts.

* * *

The captain entered the crew's quarters, where only two hands lay abed, and barked, "Up! Wake up! All hands on deck!" The lumbering Olgaren sprang up, while the athletic Petrofsky growled and rolled out like a hibernating bear. The grumbling ended the instant he saw who roused them. Nikilov ordered them dressed and out, and followed them into the between-decks companionway, shouting, "Mr. Eltsin is waiting for you at the helm." They disappeared up the stairs and the captain breathed a sigh of relief.

He needed the compartment; to go somewhere with the... injured... crew... person. To tend her and to keep her secret. The crew was already agitated and ill-prepared for more shocks. It

Chapter Fifteen

made sense to get them out of the way and, with Popescu and Smirnov having traded fists, Nikilov had an excuse. Eltsin could discipline the lot, in the name of those miscreants, keep them busy and give Constantin and him time to solve this new dilemma.

With the companionway clear, he opened the door to the forehold. Constantin, having dropped through the fore hatch, was waiting on the stair landing with the injured child in his arms. Nikilov nodded and the first hurried out. He ducked into the crew's quarters and, as the captain followed, laid Funar gently on a bunk. He pulled... her shirt... closed and held it tightly between pinched fingers. For her part, the girl appeared to have lost consciousness again.

"Do you think they saw anything?" Constantin asked. "Popescu? Smirnov? Georgiy?"

"They saw the blood," the commander replied. "That was all. They were too busy with their own foolishness to... to see the... to see Funar's..." He couldn't find the words. He looked from the deck boy... the girl... to his first mate in time to hear Constantin put the day's question into words.

"What in hell are we going to do?"

Chapter Sixteen

NIKILOV needed to think.

He stared at the... heavens, what could he call her? Who in the... Who was she? He couldn't call her anything. He certainly could not let her sex be known - with the ship already in its strange uproar.

Constantin, now that they had the girl in the crews quarters, was being no help at all. He simply stared, wide-eyed, from the captain to the unconscious boy on the bunk. Boy! Dear God... girl... "Mikhail," he said, using the familiarity without thinking. "What are we..."

"Stop asking," Nikilov snapped. "We will do... what we are doing."

Though it was closed, the mate pulled the girl's shirt tighter as if he feared something might escape. He stared incredulously up at the captain, who stared incredulously down at him. Both were flabbergasted.

"Your deck boy..." The mate's mouth had gone dry, "is not a boy."

The captain's blue eyes burned. "You mean... *your* deck boy? You signed *him* aboard my ship." His voice became barely audible. "This is all we need. Can you imagine the pandemonium if the others discover there is a woman among the crew?"

Chapter Sixteen

"Yes. Especially from Popescu," Constantin said. "Couple his superstitious nature with his indiscretion. He'll incite the others. We'll be damned lucky if they don't throw her overboard."

"Not from my ship they won't."

"I am saying, sir, it might be best if we continue the masquerade until we reach a port and get rid of her."

Nikilov sighed. "We will consider that. In the meantime, what's the matter with... her?"

* * *

"Swales!" It was Constantin in the companionway. He stuck his head in the mess door, saw the cook up to his wrists in flour and bacon fat and, to his pleasure, the English scholar as well.

Harrington turned groggily from his first cup of coffee. "What's all the to-do?"

Seeing Harrington helped Constantin see other things as well, about their passenger, their so-called deck boy, and several unexplained night-time meetings between the two. It suddenly seemed a reasonable guess the secret he and the captain had just learned might not be a secret to all. Sent for the cook in his capacity as ship's doctor, the mate's theory seemed worth testing. "Swales," he snapped. "You are needed in the crew's quarters. The, eh, deck boy has been injured."

Harrington leapt from the table as if fired from a cannon. "What's happened?"

"It is not your business," the mate replied. "Swales?"

"I'm comin'," the cook said, waving his hands to explain his sloth.

"I'm coming too," Harrington insisted.

Constantin had no knowledge of what the pair were up to, but it was painfully obvious he was right; the bookworm and the girl had an alliance – perhaps more. "You are not needed."

"Mr. Constantin, forgive me. I merely meant... I'm fond of the boy and... May I come? Eh, perhaps I can be of help."

Swales, washed and toweling dry as he stepped from the galley, put in a word. "He has a medical book-learnin' I do no'. Mayhaps...?"

"Yes," the mate said, eyeing the cook in a different light as well. Was Swales also being made a fool of? Or was he a third member of this conspiracy? Thinking it best to keep them together until he knew, he turned to Harrington with a smile. "Perhaps you should come."

* * *

Constantin rapped on the door to the crew's quarters and opened it at the captain's word. Stepping in, he said, "Swales, sir, as you ordered." He let the cook pass, then holding the Englishman at the door, added, "And... at his own insistence, Mr. Harrington."

Nikilov glared a question at his first but said nothing. Instead, he laid a hand on Swales' chest to prevent his reaching the patient. "There is something you need to know, eh, before you treat the boy." He looked to the door. "Iancu, have Herr Harrington wait in the companionway."

"Your pardon, sir," Constantin said with something up his sleeve. "Perhaps Mr. Harrington would prefer to tell him."

The captain frowned, taking in the trio, mate, cook and passenger. "Mr. Constantin, what is this about?"

"Sir. It has been my observation that Mr. Harrington and..." He cleared his throat. "...Funar are more familiar with each other than we were led to believe. I have interrupted several late night meetings on deck and am convinced their relationship pre-dates our sailing. I believe our passenger is intimate enough with Funar he is aware of the fact you were about to relate to Mr. Swales."

Nikilov turned to the passenger. "Herr Harrington? Do you know something that might assist the cook in treating Funar?"

Three sets of eyes bored into him; the captain's in question, Constantin's in triumph, and Swales' in resignation. Harrington stared back in embarrassed silence.

Chapter Sixteen

Nikilov's visage grew grim. The first's showed anticipation. The poor old Scotsman appeared trapped. Harrington could not have that. He and Ekaterina were nabbed, but there was no reason to drag Swales down. He pursed his lips and took a deep breath. He nodded respect to the captain, a curt acknowledgment to the mate, and told the cook, "Oliver, you don't know this but, the deck boy is not a boy. He, uh, she... is a young woman called Ekaterina Gabor."

Swales' mind raced as he considered how to react. Finally, knowing he must, he followed Trevor's lead and feigned ignorance. "No! A lass? No! Ye don't say?"

"Captain," Harrington said. "I'm sure you have questions. At least, before you pass judgment, I hope you do. I will answer as I can. But I beg you, allow Swales to care for her now."

"Mr. Swales, you will *quietly* see to the girl's needs. The crew is not to know, understand?" The captain did not wait for the cook's answer. "Herr Harrington, you will accompany me. Mr. Constantin, you will join us."

Chapter Seventeen

APTAIN Nikilov's quarters were as austere as the commander. A bunk with one thin bran pillow, three small shelves holding books, journals, and Holy Bibles in varied states of wear, aligned tall to short like soldiers at attention, an umbrella stand filled with rolled charts, a desk chair, a worn desk (big enough to roll out his charts) devoid of clutter save for a kerosene lamp and the room's only bow to the material; a sculptured, glittering, gold mantle clock. And, like Harrington's cabin, a lone porthole.

The captain entered, sat and stared at the clock. The first followed, directed Harrington to the middle of the room, and secured the door. When finally the captain spoke, he did so as if Harrington were not there. "It appears, Mr. Constantin, we've been made fools of." The passenger moved to speak but the first raised a finger, signaling him to hold his tongue.

The captain resumed. "Am I correct, Herr Harrington? Are we your fools?"

"Absolutely not, I assure you!"

"You knew that our deck boy was... no such thing?"

Harrington nodded, feeling a little foolish himself.

"I don't like this cruise," the captain said. "While it is not exactly sealed orders, it is special orders. To have my hands tied is one thing, but to sail by the bidding of an unnamed client, as we're

Chapter Seventeen

telling secrets, I'll tell you, I don't like it. Now to add insult I find there are secrets kept from me. At considerable risk, I afforded you passage. You have repaid my benefaction with deceit."

"Captain Nikilov, I deny complicity in any ruse to hoodwink you. This is not what you think."

"You do not know what I think, Herr Harrington. Even I do not know what I think, because I do not know what is happening on my ship! Now, you will explain."

"When I bought passage on your vessel, I had no idea Katya was... That Ekaterina was in Varna. I certainly had no clue she was trying to sign herself aboard your vessel. I thought I left her behind in Romania. The whole point was to leave her safely behind in Romania."

"You have already admitted knowing she was aboard."

"Sir, I was not aware when we left Varna. Ekaterina is... impulsive. I did not learn of her presence until our seventh day at sea when we sailed through the Dardanelles. I discovered her by accident in the hold during the inspection. Until then, I too thought her just Funar, the deck boy."

The captain studied the young scholar and, inexplicably, believed what he saw. "Very well. It is not your fault, perhaps, she is here. But you cannot deny a conspiracy to deceive since that discovery. How many men before the mast know of this?"

"Sir?"

"I am asking you who else knows she is aboard?"

Harrington hesitated. His eyes fell to the floor as if searching for the answer.

"Perhaps you do not recognize the gravity of your position, Herr Harrington. Nothing will satisfy me but your complete candor. Now, who else on the Demeter knows this girl is aboard?"

* * *

For a creature nearly five hundred years old, weeks passed like seconds. True as that was, he'd been in that box, in abeyance, without feeding, for weeks. Too long!

He'd fed the previous night, for the first time in all that time, and Dracula was strong and vibrant again. Young again. Now he was back in his box, supine, glutted but far from satisfied. He'd given in to temptation, fulfilled his desire. He had tasted of the girl but in so doing had only stoked his hunger. He had spared her life, left her still aboard. The bloodlust – and the lust – remained and was intensified.

Count Dracula would have her again.

* * *

"Swales!" The captain was livid, biting his tongue. "Swales joined you in this deceit?"

"He didn't. He knew before I. There was never a question of deceit. Swales kept Ekaterina's secret to maintain calm on the ship. The crew were on edge. He was concerned they'd react negatively, dangerously, if they found her out. If you ask me, sir, he was trying to make your job easier."

"That was not his place, or yours. So far as I am concerned you've abetted a stowaway in the commission of her crime." The captain pushed his cap back. "And, for now, we will do the same."

Constantin started. "Sir?"

"My complaint is in this secret being kept from me. I cannot argue with keeping it from the crew. We are short men and experience. The crew have already borne witness to a number of strange occurrences. They do not need more surprises."

"Aye, captain."

"Fraulein Gabor will retain her identity as Rada Funar. The *boy* has a severe concussion requiring rest and solitude."

"There will be rumors, sir. How do I stifle them?"

"You don't. The subject should be changed and the rumors ignored, but not suppressed. As long as sailors are talking, they're

Chapter Seventeen

not thinking. It is a head injury requiring rest, nothing more. There will be no talk of illness or an injury – and no mention of today's discovery." He growled at Harrington. "I do not like it. But that's as is. For now the secret remains and is not to be told to the parrot."

"The parrot?" Harrington asked.

"He's telling you not to blab," Constantin barked, annoyed at his ignorance.

Nikilov's eyes dug a hole in the Englishman. "Funar will be moved to your quarters. You will bunk with the crew for the remainder of the voyage." Harrington's response was cut off by Nikilov's raised palm. "There will be no discussion. The girl's condition will be Swales concern. Beyond that, you will be entirely responsible for her. Am I understood?"

"Yes, captain."

"Then you may go and see to your responsibilities."

"I shall not fail you, captain."

"I recommend you do not," Nikilov said with menace. "So long as they are properly weighted, the ocean keeps all secrets thrown to her."

* * *

The crew were kept busy on deck while the transition was made. The girl was carried to the passenger's cabin and laid unconscious on the lower of the two bunk beds. Funar's kit followed. Harrington's kit was piled in the corner for him to deal with when he would. The Englishman became her custodian. Swales was made her doctor and, taking the assignment seriously, barreled in with a pile of books and a quickly collected bag of medical tricks.

"You are treating *him* for a severe concussion," the mate insisted. "Nothing more will be said. Anxieties are already too high." Constantin added a muted growl, and his assurance their deceit would not be forgotten, then left, washing his hands of the matter.

"I don't think he likes us," Harrington said, when the first was gone.

"'e liked me well enuff, 'efore you come along."

"We joined the ship at the same time."

"If ye've nowt but facts ye'll lose this argument." Done with Harrington, Swales turned to his patient. Her heart was racing, her breathing shallow and rapid, her pale skin cold and clammy.

Over his shoulder, Harrington asked about the bandage on her throat.

"It's nowt; two wee punctures. The mate said there were no blood to speak o' on deck. She has no other wounds, an' she's no' injured. Cleaned an' bandaged 'em as a matter o' course."

"What caused them?"

"I don't know, lad. And I do no' care. Her problem is no' her throat. She's sick, sufferin' an illness, an' I'll need follow her symptoms to gawm why."

"What illnesses strike so suddenly?"

Swales grunted derisively. "There's no end; especially at sea." He wetted a cloth in the basin and laid it over the girl's sweating forehead. "Was in the Comore Islands once, the Mozambique Channel, fer ten days. Within three or four days o' sailin' half the crew sickened an' died. It was thought a terrible pestilence had come aboard. But it struck me only those what slept on shore suffered; those what returned to the ship e'ery night escaped the plague. That's when I said t'was malaria."

"Malaria! You don't imagine she has malaria, do you?"

Swales shrugged. "That's what I am doin', imaginin'. It's all I can do. Malarial poison infects at night an' incubates for nigh on a fortnight. Yer lass was struck at night. But if it's malaria, we'll discover that, no' by askin' where she was last night, but by askin' where she slept two weeks ago."

"It's ridiculous, Oliver. She spent the last eighteen years in her father's too-comfortable home."

"Ye need put yer bias away. The girl is here, so she was on the road from Bukovina to Varna."

"Six days before we sailed, she was home. I saw her before her brothers started shooting."

Chapter Seventeen

"We've been at sea for nine. Add yer six, sleepin' in the open, Gog knows where?"

"She hasn't been within forty miles of a mosquito-infested swamp. I assure you, she does not have malaria, yellow fever, or marsh fever of the tropics." Exasperated, Harrington added, "Ekaterina has not been bitten by anything!"

Swales slipped his pipe between his teeth. "Hold yer horse, lad. I'm thinkin' out loud, to make room in me head, an' malaria isn't me only thought. There's thousands o' things it might be. Jings, there are a hundred influenzas. Add typhus, cholera, scurvy."

"Scurvy? What is that?"

"A desease Gog made just fer sailors. Some blame bad tinned meat, but I say bosh." He grabbed an old book, *A Treatise of the Scurvy*, and waved it as if he held the fabled touchstone. "Says here..."

"What is that?"

Swales screwed up his lips. "James Lind; a Scottish surgeon in the British Royal Navy. I keep it w' me cook books. They neither accepted his findin's nor implemented his treatments but, if ye ask me, they were fools. He proved scurvy was a lack o' necessary acids."

"You think Ekaterina has... scurvy?"

"Jings, lad, I do no' know. Ageean, it's a possibility. Mind ye, she hasn't all the symptoms. She hasn't the skin spots; par-ticularly the legs. Nor that we noticed, the immobility. But she's been avoidin' descent food since comin' aboard! If it's scurvy, I've no idee how far 'long she is."

Harrington grimaced at the cook's choice of words. How far along! He thought of the silly lie Ekaterina told in her effort to secure him as a husband. Cor blimey, what that had wrought. But thinking of it was pointless.

"It's early days," Swales continued. "She has the lethargy, the pale look, open wounds, an' abnormal bleedin'. None of her teeth have fallen out yet."

"Christ!" Harrington exclaimed. "Are you serious?"

"Could no' be more. Scurvy is fatal if untreated."

"Then treat her! Can you treat her?"

Swales slapped the book shut. "Citrus; lemon juice, lime juice. The right acids, that's the answer. Biscuits, dry grains, salted meats only speed the desease. I've limes and casks o' lime juice. We'll tap one for the lass tonight an', startin' tomorrow, for the whole crew. If it's scurvy, we'll soon have our deck boy on the route to recoov-ry."

"I can't believe this. If only I'd known she was here from the start."

"Ye' should o' known, lad."

"I don't deny that. But she did a fair job of staying wherever I was not. With help."

Swales wouldn't budge. "She needed help."

"Yes. And I'm grateful."

"Grateful," the old sailor spit the word like bad food. "Ye' left her alone in Romania."

"Her father and brothers were shooting at me!" The old man did not ease his stare. "I left a lot of things in Romania. You don't know the whole story, Oliver."

"I gawm more than ye', lad. Who do ye' think she's been talkin' to on this voyage. I'm aware what ye left an' why. But if her family is crazy, ye were leavin' her to 'em. I do no' say ye're the devil but ye're damned dumb, an' self-important, an' a bit o' a coward – aren't ye?"

"Yes," he said. "I suppose I am a coward."

* * *

Ekaterina tossed, sleeping fitfully through the day.

She wore a button-down, carded-wool flannel nightshirt Swales found in his kit and dedicated to her. (He'd changed her himself using a fatherly, averted eye.) It was yards too big, the girl swam in it, but offered more comfort than the work clothes she'd been wearing and made it easier to monitor her vital processes.

Chapter Seventeen

Swales tended to her with Harrington looking on like a mother hen or, give him his due, a worried lover. The Englishman, in turn, watched her while Swales tended his galley. A bowl of beef broth and bread were carried in on a tray but Ekaterina refused all entreaties insisting, in a rare moment of wakefulness, she was not hungry. With the exception of lime juice, which Swales forced upon her, she also refused drink. Everything made her sick to her stomach. Her conversations were always brusque, and followed by fitful sleep.

Then came the night...

Ekaterina snapped awake and sat up claiming she was better. That was it, as if someone lit a candle and drove away the darkness. A jubilant Harrington told her how worried he'd been. His elation was short-lived. He gently restrained her when she tried to rise, pleading she rest. She declared a need for air and argued to be allowed from the room. He refused and Ekaterina became agitated.

"I'm delighted you are feeling better," Harrington said. "That does not alter the fact you have been terribly ill all day. You've neither stirred nor taken any nourishment. You are not fit and are not allowed to go out."

"This is ridiculous!" She seemed in full vigor, though her skin color and pained-looking eyes belied the notion. "I need some air."

"I'll happily open the port hole and let in all the air you want. But you are not going anywhere. You may as well be resigned."

"You do not own me! You do not control me! I will do as I wish!"

"The master of the ship has ordered that you are to remain below deck. Your condition, and your gender, are to be kept quiet. You will do as you are told; as we all must while we are at sea."

Ekaterina stared coldly, with an anger Harrington had never witnessed before. Then, to his surprise, and perhaps even to hers, she laughed in his face; a joyless, frightening laugh. Harrington had never heard the like and it made him very uneasy.

* * *

Doug Lamoreux

Hours later, Ekaterina finally slept – deep enough that Harrington felt safe in leaving her. He gathered his kit and headed for the crew's sleeping quarters. Four steps in, as his eyes adjusted to the dark, he realized how good he'd had it in the old cabin.

The odor was foul! Until now, he'd used the facilities in the head of the ship. Here, Popescu's polished chamber pots were in vigorous use and the room smelled as if one was in each bed.

As to the beds, his was now a sailor's bunk, neither deep enough to comfortably roll over, nor long enough to completely stretch out. Most of the crew slept in their clothes to one extent or another, several wore their hats, others their boots. As uninviting as the situation was, Harrington realized he was stuck, and he was exhausted. He found an empty cot in the dark and collapsed onto it dressed. There he lay, serenaded by snores, thinking of Ekaterina; her strange illness, her unnatural temperament, and those curious wounds on her throat. Eventually, thankfully, sleep eased his mind.

* * *

Feliks Petrofsky walked the starboard deck forward of the foremast on watch – and miserable. They were short crew and now constantly on watch, or so it seemed. Add in a fog from nowhere for more grief and trouble. A dangerous situation on deck and an opportunity for a repeat of that morning's debacle. Smirnov was a wreck since the boy had been found injured. Could the same thing, Petrofsky wondered, happen to him? What had happened to the child? When – and why? What was Funar doing on deck at that hour? Who in hell would appear on deck this night, in this weird fog, to make things worse for him? Everything fell on Petrofsky!

Then, unbelievably, in a sudden flash to his right, it did!

In an instant the movement, in the form of a man, vaulted up and over the gunwale into the bow. Just appeared out of nowhere; out of the sea! A middle-aged man, dressed in black, with wide bursts of gray hair at his temples, and a dark mustache streaked

Chapter Seventeen

with gray on a white face. He moved quickly and, wherever he'd come from, wherever he was going, scared the living hell out of the marlinspike.

It took an instant for Petrofsky to realize he'd seen this man before. Yes! It was the old man who'd abandoned ship in front of him. Only younger, much younger!

The man, seeing Petrofsky with red-glinting eyes, seemed startled to find someone on deck. But he hesitated only a tick. He recovered quickly, then struck, grabbing the sailor by the throat in a vice-like grip. Petrofsky could neither catch his breath nor scream. He grasped at the hand, scratched at the cold fingers, to no avail. His wrapped hand was useless and his other failed to find a hold, so tightly did the dark man clutch him.

The stranger grabbed Petrofsky's injured hand. He ripped the bandage away and, with a vicious growl, sank his teeth into the flesh, tearing the sutures and reopening the wound. Blood spurted. He clamped Petrofsky's hand like a terrier would a rat. The Russian struggled desperately, grabbing the dark man's hair, pulling at his cloak, panicked to free himself. So blinded was he by terror, Petrofsky overlooked his one ever-present weapon, the marlinspike hanging from his wrist. Somehow he thought of it now. He whipped the lanyard around, flipped the tool into his hand, and plunged it into the villain's throat.

The tall man released Petrofsky's shredded hand. He gasped, blood pouring from beneath the imbedded tool. Yet, despite the horrible injury, the blow merely enraged him. He yanked the marlinspke from his throat and hurled it clattering to the deck. He hissed through bloody lips, eyes blazing hellfire, and snapped at the seaman's face with gore covered fangs.

Then, in less time than it takes to tell, the inconceivable happened.

Without thought, driven simply by animal rage, Dracula transformed himself into a swirling gray mist. That mist, as if forced from a bellows, slammed into Petrofsky's face. The ethereal gas, under pressure, entered the sailor's mouth and nostrils. It raced down his esophagus, into his stomach, his intestines. It raced down his trachea to his lungs, left and right bronchioles, alveoli; expanding, forcing the air out. The mist forced itself up Petrofsky's nose and through the sinus cavities in his head, the dural venous channels in the brain. It poured, through the gaping wound in his hand, into the damaged blood vessels, through the circulatory system, the chambers of his heart. In an instant, the mist tunneled insanely into the marlinspike's body. Petrofsky would have screamed from the intense pain but the gas prevented it. It pushed the air from his lungs, blocked his vocal chords, disallowed even a breath. The helpless seaman stumbled off-balance. He would have fallen had not whatever was inside of him held him up-right, bloating him beyond reason or belief. The pain was excruciating.

Then Dracula resumed his human form.

Petrofsky's body, bludgeoned by the internal pressures, exploded like a Chinese firework. With little more than a *pop* and the *rat-a-tat* of out-of-season hail, a mist of blood, bits of flesh, and minute shards of fractured bone rained down on the deck and into the sea.

On the space, occupied the instant before by the agonized Petrofsky, Dracula now stood alone - soaked from head to foot in the marlinskpike's blood. Shaken, he dropped to a knee. Reeling, dripping Petrofsky's gore, the vampire laid a hand on the deck to steady himself. He'd never done anything of the kind before and, just now, could not imagine ever doing it again. He caught his breath and transformed back into a cloud of mist. It floated, swirling above the deck for a pregnant moment, then slowly darkened, solidified, and took the shape of the Count again.

Dracula stood on the deck, renewed, the nausea and agitation passed, his person clean of Petrofsky's blood. He stepped aft of the main mast then turned and, concentrating, passed his hand over the bow. A moment elapsed, then a shift occurred as the bottom fell out of the wave beneath their bow. The vessel pitched suddenly forward (causing the ship's bell to ring). From an otherwise calm sea, a heavy wave lipped the starboard rail – shipping water and

Chapter Seventeen

washing the deck. Blood, bone, and even the offending rope tool floated toward the bulwarks, out the scuppers and into the sea. The ship righted herself, her deck free of evidence that Feliks Petrofsky had ever existed at all.

Chapter Eighteen

"COFFEE or tea, lad?" Swales asked, setting out two cups.

"Both, I think." Harrington looked wearily over his shoulder, ensuring the mess and companionway were empty and the cook's ears the only pair about, then added in a whisper, "I'll drink whichever she doesn't. If she'll drink at all."

Friday morning, 16 July, was upon them. Swales, in the midst of breakfast, paused to tend to Harrington with a tray of sugar, ship's bread, butter, molasses (in hopes the lass would brighten to a treat), and one steaming cup each of strong coffee and weak tea. "How is she?"

"I was going to ask you to look in." Harrington shook his head. "Last night I thought I'd need to tie her down. Today, she seems dreadfully ill again."

A rap at the door silenced both as the first stuck in his head. Constantin knew their secret but whether or not he was alone was anyone's guess. He looked the mess over without giving either more than a passing glance. "Has Petrofsky been in?"

"I haven't seen him..."

Without waiting for Swales to finish, Constantin was gone.

Swales and Harrington shared a shrug and returned to their business. "Try to get somethin' into arr patient," the cook said, handing him the tray. "I'll be right along."

149

Chapter Eighteen

* * *

The mate popped out the deckhouse door. The captain, speaking with Smirnov, bid him good morning. He replied hurriedly, heading forward.

"Mr. Constantin." The call arrested the first mate's progress as if he'd met a wall. "Will you come here, please." The mate turned, displaying nerves unseen at his previous speed, and approached the wheel. The commander eyed him warily. "Mr. Constantin... what are you looking for?"

The mate looked from Nikilov to Smirnov. The seaman averted his eyes, wishing he could disappear. The captain, saving him the trouble, led the first to the rail. "What are you looking for?"

"Petrofsky," Constantin croaked. He cleared his throat and started again. "I'm looking for Feliks Petrofsky, sir. He had watch last night but was not on deck when his relief came. I wanted to question him regarding his dereliction of duty. But he is neither in his bunk nor in the mess. He is... missing."

"He must be somewhere."

"Aye. That is why I'm looking." Aware of his tone, Constantin rephrased, "Forgive me, sir. I am unable to account for Petrofsky's absence. Have I your permission to continue the search?"

"No." The captain shook his head. "We'll do it right. Gather the men."

* * *

In minutes the ship's compliment surrounded the helm, taking in the captain's speech. "Feliks Petrofsky is missing from his watch. His absence must be accounted for. We are therefore going to search this ship; every corner and cupboard, every crack and crevice, from stem to stern, until we have found him." Nikilov hesitated, then solemnly added, "Or until we are certain he is no longer aboard."

That notion had not occurred to them. Constantin crushed their murmur into silence with a growl and an icy stare.

The captain continued. "Misters Amramoff and Popescu will search with me. We'll take the ship's stern, heading forward; Bogdan on deck, Pasha, you below with me. Mr. Eltsin, Olgaren, you will go with the first mate. Mr. Constantin, you will search the bow top to bottom and move aft."

The mate nodded. "Georgiy on deck, Olgaren, below with me."

"Mr. Swales," the captain said. "I trust a search can be conducted without disturbing the, eh, boy?" His hesitation was lost on the others but the cook, Harrington, and the mate had to study the pine boards in the deck to avoid eye contact.

"W' respect, cap'n, t'will certainly disrupt a sleepin' patient. An' the... lad is restin', all right. But a search o' that cabin is no' necessary, sure? Mr. Harrin'ton an' I will both avow Petrofsky is no' there. An', if the cap'n pleases, we'll, one o' us, stay w' Funar while the ship is seen to."

"Herr Harrington then," the captain answered, "you, Swales, turn your galley and mess upside down." Then, to the whole of the group, "If anyone finds Petrofsky shout the alarm."

The Scot and the scholar headed below. Behind them, the meeting broke with the master shouting final orders, "Mr. Smirnov, mind the helm. Mr. Constantin, throw off the battens and block the doors and hatches open. May as well bring light and air to the matter while we go."

So it played out, as ordered, for the next hour. The hatches were opened, light and air stole in where it rarely ventured, as the search was carried out. Nikilov and his men scoured her from the rudder forward. Constantin and his examined all she held from the figurehead aft. Each group ignored the passenger's cabin, secure its contents were accounted for, passed Swales a-midships going over the mess with a fine-toothed comb, and came up empty on opposite ends when all was done and dusted.

Feliks Petrofsky was no longer aboard *Demeter*.

Chapter Eighteen

* * *

Truth, in Captain Nikilov's opinion, usually brought with it equal amounts of joy and sorrow; knowledge, but rarely satisfaction. They now knew Petrofsky was not aboard ship. They could infer where he (or his body) was. But a world of questions had been opened as to why? The search created a bigger mystery than it solved and generated new emotions. When, following the search, the crew met again, their anxiety levels were palpable. The crew was growing fearful.

"Is there anything," Nikilov asked, "anyone can tell me about last night that can help us discover what happened? An accident? An argument?" His glances were returned with silence. "Things happen between men, that's understood. I assure you, any and all details will be taken into account." No one had anything to report. "Was there anything in the recent past, of which any of you are aware, that would suggest a reason Feliks might take his own life?"

Murmured negatives, shaking heads.

"Popescu, you were at the wheel last night. What did you see and hear?"

"Nothing, captain."

"Nothing at all?"

"No, sir, no." A sheepish look overtook the Romanian's face. Then, barely audibly, he added, "Nothing real," and crossed himself.

"What does that mean?" Constantin barked. "Nothing real! What the hell are you doing?"

A frightened smile betrayed Popescu. He tried to wave it away. "For an instant, last night, I imagined I saw something – that I could not have seen – but it had nothing to do with Feliks. It had nothing to do with anything. When you stand the wheel... you see things in the dark."

"Bogdan," the captain said. "What did you see?"

"A boot."

"A boot? What boot?"

"It was there." He pointed, past the ship's bell, to the roof of the dog house that protected the apparatus for the ship's wheel; the lines, blocks and gears working the rudder. "Just there."

"You heard someone... saw someone... atop the housing and did not report it?"

"No, captain. No, I did not hear anything. Not exactly. I just... felt it. It felt as if someone were behind me, up there, on the roof. But you cannot report a feeling. What's to report?"

"You said you saw a boot?"

"I, eh, don't know. It was suddenly foggy. Petrofsky had gone forward some time before. I heard nothing at all. But I felt something – behind me. Then, I thought I seen the end, the toe, of a boot. Over my shoulder, beyond the bell. As if someone up there were about to step off. Then it was gone."

"There was no one attached?" Amramoff asked, laughing.

Popescu reddened, feeling as silly as the question. "It moved too quick. I didn't see."

"It just vanished?" Constantin demanded, failing to hide his distain.

"There was a sound, a flutter, like a kite in the wind. The boot was gone and, for an instant, what looked like a black kite arced up to starboard. It vanished in the fog over the rail as if it had never existed." He looked the group over, ship-mates to officers, pleading. "Well, it hadn't, had it? I imagined it, I'm sure. The fog plays tricks. Could I report, 'Here, sir, is what I imagined last night?' Would anyone report such a thing?"

Popescu shrank, feeling Constantin carving him with his eyes.

"What do you know of Petrofsky?" the captain asked, breaking the silence. "His personality? Any of you? Would he have jumped overboard?"

"No," Constantin said with finality.

It was like the mate, Nikilov thought, to conclude with absolute knowledge but no evidence. Still, the crew seemed to agree. "Out of the question," the second said, making it unanimous. "It had

Chapter Eighteen

to have been an accident. I know it was calm but... it must have been."

"Very well." The captain considered the sky for a moment then, solemnly, said, "I will conduct a service for Feliks, forward on the larboard side, at six bells."

"Service?" Popescu put in.

"He is not on the ship," Nikilov said, wearily sad as Petrofsky had long been with him. "That means he is in the sea; and that means he is dead."

"I agree," the Romanian said with undisguised incredulity. "But it may not have been an accident. He may be dead by his own hand! If he committed suicide, he is not entitled to a Christian..."

"Be silent!" The captain shouted, cutting him off. His blue eyes glared daggers through Popescu. "I am not a priest! Accident or suicide matters not to me. He was one of my crew and will receive a proper burial."

* * *

Seven o'clock that evening brought the entire crew, save two, to *Demeter's* port rail forward of the deckhouse. Popescu was excused to steer (and protect his moral compass by avoiding rites on behalf of a possible suicide), while the injured Funar was in *his* sick bed. Having looked in on the patient, Harrington was the last to arrive. He took his place, out of respect rather than belief, on the end of the half-circle of sombre men.

The officers wore dress coats, made deeper blue by the glow of sunset, while the sea-green clouds to the west darkened to black. Nikilov, clutching a worn bible, saw the rain coming and hurried to start. He cleared his throat and said, "We stand here for Feliks Petrofsky. The sea has his body. Now it will have our prayers."

Constantin removed his hat, rubbed his dome, and covered his heart. With a twisted look of annoyance, he yanked off the carpenter's knotted kerchief and shoved it into his chest. Amramoff nodded sheepishly and bowed his cornet head. The rest followed, the huge Olgaren already crying, as the captain turned to the sea.

"Lord God, by the power of your word you stilled the chaos of the primeval seas, you made the raging waters of the flood subside, and calmed the storm on the sea of Galilee. As we commit the body. . . " He paused, wondering what had become of Petrofsky? If he had taken his own life, why? If not, what had happened? Where was he? "As we commit the body of our brother Feliks Petrofsky to the deep, grant him peace and tranquility until that day when he and all who believe in you will be raised to the glory of new life promised in the waters of baptism. We ask this through Christ our Lord. Amen."

There followed a spattering of "Amens"; from whom exactly, Harrington wasn't sure. There were none from him. Though he held nothing against the religious, they could keep it to themselves. The service had, he supposed, accomplished its goal. From the gleam in his blue eyes, the captain felt better. Judging by their looks, as their tension slipped away, several among the men did as well. Still to the Englishman it seemed unlikely that Petrofsky, wherever he was, had gained much from the rite.

The officers and men peeled off, to their duties or below, but Harrington remained at the rail. Feeling every bit as depressed as he had the night he ran from Bukovina, but without the flight for life to charge his spirit, he stared sadly out to sea and barely noticed when Swales joined him.

"Thinkin' o' Petrofsky?"

"Oh, hello, Oliver. No, not Petrofsky in particular. Just thinking."

"D' no' get too philosophical." Swales pulled out his pipe and pouch. He scooped tobacco, tamped the bowl with a crooked thumb and, striking a match, raised an aromatic cloud of smoke. "Eternity – thaat's a tuff nut t' crack."

"Have no fear," Harrington said. "I'm no philosopher. I don't believe in eternity."

"'ere now! What's thaat?"

Chapter Eighteen

"I don't believe in life after death. I believe in finality. It's just a shame when it ends like this. No family, no body, not even a marker to say you'd ever been. Surely, Feliks deserved a grave marker?"

"Would no' me father love you!" Swales boomed, laughing as he relit his pipe.

"What do you mean?"

"Grave markers! My Gog, how he goes off on thaat subject." He shook a balled fist in the air, aping the memory. "Tombsteans in the kirkgarth; tumblin' down with the weight o' the lies wrote on 'em." A cloud of smoke encircled his head then raced away with the breeze. "He'd sing it like a song; his indignation! A quarter of the lay-beds in Whitby, in any port village, are marked w' stones readin', *Here lies the body o'*, o'er the empty plot o' some soul lost at sea, or *Sacred to the memory o'*, o'er bodies long since forgot. An' how he laughed at the thought o' the Day o' the trumpet."

"Trumpt?"

"Judgment, lad. The Day o' Judgment! All them dead souls draggin' their tombsteans t' the pear-ly gates as proof o' who they were an' how good they was." The old man roared. "An' ye want a grave marker fer Petrofsky? Where? To mark what? We spent the whole o' the morn figurin' out he weren't nowhere. We've, all o' us, guessed he's in the Mediterranean. Well, there ye be, son." He waved his pipe over the rail and the water. "Go ahead; mark his grave." He laughed. "An' ye say ye're not a believer!"

"It's merely respect for the dead."

"The dead do no' care, lad. One day, months from now, or years from now, an old mother, or sister, or sweetheart, in some Russian village, w' a false mem-ry o' how good things used to be but prob-ly ne'er were, will set a stone readin', *Here lies Feliks Petrofsky*. An' for a time the lie will make her feel better. But the lay-bed will still be empty as old Dun's 'bacca-box on Friday night, an' the body still missin'. An' Petrofsky will still be dead as hung Haman."

Swales laid a hand on Harrington's shoulder and, together, they headed aft. They ignored Popescu's stare from the wheel and ducked below. Behind them, the green clouds completed their turn to black, the thunder rolled, and the sky, unlike the Romanian steersman, began to cry for lost seamen.

* * *

The captain didn't feel like eating and couldn't rest. Just after eight bells, wandering the larboard deck in the sprinkling rain, he found the watch and, to stem his restlessness, relieved him personally. The deck was quiet, but Nikilov walked in turmoil, Petrofsky heavily on his mind. At ten, Olgaren relieved him (while Eltsin spelled Popescu at the wheel). "Four bells and all's well," the captain said, though in his heart he did not believe it.

Still restless, Nikilov headed forward for a last look as lightning flashed in the distance. The spittle of the last four hours, he could see, was nothing compared to the storm they were fast approaching. He headed below.

The voices of the crew spilled into the between-decks companionway, Smirnov, Amramoff, Popescu (fresh below), the cook, and the mate talking on, off, and at once. Nikilov could make out no specific topic and did not try. The master of the ship didn't need to eavesdrop. He pushed into their quarters and found the men as downcast as ever they had been.

"I know this business with Petrofsky is a shock," Nikilov said.

"It isn't," Smirnov piped up. "Begging the captain's pardon, sir, but it isn't."

Popescu nodded his ascent. "We've been expecting something of this kind."

The others nodded their agreement. All but the first, who was visibly starting to bristle. "What does that mean?" Constantin growled. "You've been expecting it?"

Popescu, already on the mate's list, shoved on. "There's something aboard this ship."

The room was struck dumb and the sounds of the rain and the sea and the ship overwhelmed them for their silence.

Chapter Eighteen

Constantin, insistant, measured his words. "What does that mean?" Nobody would say or, for that matter, meet his glare. "SOMETHING!" the first suddenly yelled. "What does that mean?" He stepped to the Romanian and pushed his face into Popescu's. "You will answer."

"Something either killed Petrofsky or made him kill himself. Either way, murder or suicide, it is the harbinger of evil. More will come."

The mate shook with rage. He raised his fist over Popescu and would have landed a ferocious blow had not the captain intervened. Nikilov laid his hand on Constantin's shoulder. He spoke not a word to anyone; just the firm hand gently applied. The first lowered his arm, unclenched his fist, and nodded his acquiescence to Nikilov.

"I had hoped for clear sailing," the master told his men. "But we are coming into rain. Be prepared to be called up at a moment's notice. In the interim, please, rest while you are able." He bid his crew good-night then, at the door, asked the first to join him for tea.

Violence had been averted, Constantin's wrath quelled, but the captain's thoughts were more burdened than ever. The fears within the crew were mounting. And, though he was not a superstitious man, Nikilov's fears were growing as well. Fears that more trouble lay ahead.

* * *

The rain came – hard.

The wind picked up with a vengeance, forty knots gusting to forty-five, and the storm raised the seas to 18 feet before them. Despite the large sea, going downwind as they were, Nikilov decided to run with it. He called his crew to stations, as he'd warned them he would, and ordered the sails reduced. Then he turned the schooner upwind to slow her down.

Washed by rain, whipped by wind, his hands furled the headsails and triple-reefed the main and mizzen gaffers. All the while, the captain and mates worked alongside the men before the mast, on the deck and in the shrouds. Short-handed as they were, hard work was made light by the knowledge that together they were a good crew and, soon, most were below again and drying off.

Reefed down, Nikilov returned *Demeter* to her course. She settled into an easy motion, running on despite the gale.

* * *

In the dead hours of the night, lightning flashed, thunder boomed, the rain ticked on the mizzen deck above her head, and Ekaterina sat up in her bunk feeling like gold. The headache, the fever, the stifling sickness were gone. Her eyes ached from the lamplight but she felt rested and truly alive.

Then she felt the inexplicable hunger. Then she felt the lust.

Trevor was asleep, nodded over his folded arms on the desk.

She rose quietly not to wake him. She grabbed the linen wrap, once used to hide her shape, and quietly tore off a strip. She carried it to the mirror and stared without emotion at her pale reflection, her sunken features, the dark orbits round her eyes. She pulled the bandage from her neck revealing two bruised, enflamed punctures. Ekaterina dabbed at the wounds as her breath rose to a pant. Her heart was pounding in her petite chest. Swales' outsized nightshirt fell open to her navel exposing her breasts and hardening nipples. All she saw were the wounds. She draped the linen strip around her neck seductively covering that most desired area in anticipation of...

Behind her, reflected in the glass, she saw Harrington. Such a nice boy. A grimace twisted her lips, arched brows marred her delicate features; a look of disgust. *He is childish and insignificant. He has neither the capacity to understand, nor the strength or courage to follow. He'll have to be left behind.* But there was no need crossing that bridge yet. He was, after all, a nice boy.

Chapter Eighteen

Quietly, she blew out the lamp. The room was plunged into darkness, the ache vanished from her eyes, and Ekaterina saw - clearly indeed. She unlatched the door and returned to her bunk. She lay back on her pillow starving and, at the same time, lusting to be fed upon. She pulled the nightshirt open. She fought to still the gyration of her hips. *Must not wake little Trevor.* And she waited.

Ekaterina did not know what she was doing. Yet, she could not stop herself.

* * *

One hundred feet away, a cloud of gray mist passed through the fissures in the door to the forward hold. At first it appeared an explosion of steam had taken place and this, the escaped cloud, was finding the quickest exit. Yet it did not dissipate, but thickened into a carpet of mist that moved down the companionway. It floated past the crew's quarters and the galley, where the captain and mate were finishing a cup. The cloud stopped at the dead-end of the companionway T and hovered before the door to the passenger's quarters. Her quarters.

Even in that state, Dracula could smell the woman ready for him inside. And – something else. Someone else.

"Can you rest?" Nikilov was heard to ask. He stepped from the mess, followed by Constantin, who answered in the negative. "Then you may as well join me. We've some mulling-over to do." There were items to be discussed; the weather, maintenance, duty assignments, the mood of the short-handed crew and, no doubt, Constantin's recent flairs of temper as well. The mate accepted dutifully.

They followed the companionway to where the captain's room abutted that of the injured child and Nikilov moved to admit them. Neither saw anything out of order – as neither looked just above their heads. The gray mist, an infuriated Dracula interrupted, was abandoning the between-decks through the cracks in the overhead's aft port scuttle hatch.

* * *

Olgaren was trying to stay dry. The big Russian was hunched beneath the eave on the aft end of the deckhouse, trying to shelter from the storm; a ludicrous endeavor. Eltsin stood at the wheel, soaked and in a state of high hilarity. Black bangs matted and running with cold water, clothes hugging him like skin, coat and boots sodden, he reared his head, gargled the downpour, spit a stream like a fountain, and laughed like a lunatic. Olgaren, wiping his eyes and watching the second through the falling sheets, could not see what was funny.

So busy were they, Eltsin laughing like a clown and Olgaren shielding himself, neither noted the mist that appeared behind the helm, above the scuttle hatch. Diffused by the rain and virtually invisible at first, it soon grew dense and gray.

From his hiding place, looking aft through the onslaught, Olgaren finally saw it. He stared, straining, afraid his eyes were playing tricks. It was a cloud, yes, but something more, changing as it moved forward inside the rail. It came on, growing darker, taking on a solid form. The cloud vanished and, in its place, strode a man.

Just like that. The deck had been empty - then he was there! A tall, thin young man. (Near his own age, Olgaren thought.) He was dressed in black, had a thick mustache, an angry set to his white jaw, and red eyes that, God! seemed to burn like fire. He was a stranger, unlike anyone in the crew.

Olgaren shouted!

The tall man took no notice of the big Russian. Neither did he regard Eltsin. Nor did he hesitate in the slightest. He simply continued forward, past the agog Olgaren, past the corner of the deckhouse and down the port companionway, his cape billowing like the wings of a fluttering bat.

Chapter Eighteen

"Did you see that?" Olgaren shouted.

Eltsin shook his head like a dog sheading water and called back, "See what?"

"My God! Did you not see him?!"

"What? See who?"

Olgaren left his cover, stepped to the corner and stared into the rain down the companionway. Gone. The man was gone. Eltsin yelled something. What, Olgaren neither knew nor cared. He ignored the second and hurried forward – after the dark figure. The wind billowed the gaffe sails, whipped at the furled foresails, the rain beat down on the deck, the vessel heaved on a swell. He ignored it all. He hurried past the fore hatch, battened and secure, into the bow. There, his clothing soaked, his red hair matted, Olgaren turned in place, searching.

Gone. The man was simply gone.

Chapter Nineteen

Just before dawn, Saturday, 17 July, a hesitant rap on Nikilov's door interrupted the captain's tea and his thoughts. He was genuinely surprised when the swinging door revealed the rain-soaked Olgaren. He was the last man Nikilov would have expected to break the chain of command. Yet, here he was without being summoned and without a mate. More alarming yet was the look in the seaman's eyes. The big man appeared on the verge of panic.

"What is it?"

Olgaren's lips moved without sound. Tears welled in his eyes.

"You had better step in."

Olgaren obeyed, ducking to clear the sill. The lamplight fell on his matted red hair and his face, pale beyond the usual. "Captain, I... I just come off watch." Olgaren said, trembling. He crossed himself (something Nikilov expected from Popescu, not a countryman) and blurted, "I seen him!"

The captain lurched, startled by the outburst. "You've seen who? Petrofsky?"

"No. No, sir," Olgaren said in confusion. "Not Petrofsky." The name of the missing crewman had not even occurred to him. He shook his head. "No. Not Petrofsky. I... I do not know who he was. I saw a strange man aboard the ship."

Chapter Nineteen

"What is this? How dare you! First Petrofsky with his vision! Then Petrofsky overboard! Now you, you too have seen this mysterious old man!"

"He was not, captain. Not old. He was young, tall and thin. Pale as a ghost."

He stared at Olgaren, an experienced man of the sea, dripping on his cabin floor like a child, frightened into tears and babbling of ghosts. The captain's anger vanished, replaced by fear. "Tell me," Nikilov said. He handed the sailor a towel. "Tell me, Moisey, what you saw."

Olgaren dried his face and recounted the previous night. When he had made an end, Nikilov sat dumbfounded. What the sailor had described could not have happened. It was utter nonsense. Yet, Olgaren believed it. The man was no liar. Nor could he have invented the story being, as he was, devoid of imagination. What in the name of God was happening aboard his ship?

Petrofsky reported a stranger on deck and, soon, went to a watery grave. Now Olgaren had made a report - of a different stranger. Was some contagion raging aboard his vessel? Had it driven Petrofsky mad? Was this faithful sailor next? What if these events were the result, not of human frailty but of choice? Was someone, Olgaren, trying to interrupt the workings of his ship? To what end? To prevent the delivery of his cargo? Something more evil? Could there be a simple explanation for the fears of his crew? His own growing paranoia?

"Captain?"

Nikilov returned to the crewman staring in the lamplight. "We will search the ship again," Nikilov said quietly. What else could he do? The man was in a panic he could not allow to spread. He needed to allay those fears. "We will search the ship from stem to stern."

Relief passed over Olgaren like a wave. Somebody was doing something.

"In the meantime," Nikilov added, "You must keep this to yourself. Not a word to anyone. Get something to break your fast and await my order."

* * *

Olgaren joined Amramoff and Popescu at breakfast and, following orders, didn't say a word. Their questions were met with grunts; their jokes with indifference. Had he been anyone else, they might have taken offense. But when you are six-two, beneath a six-foot overhead, you are granted dispensation. After the meal, normally, he would have hit his bunk. There was nothing normal about Olgaren's morning. Instead, following their bread and butter, bad coffee, and worse tea, the big man followed them up; Amramoff and Popescu to work, he to wait.

Behind them, Harrington dragged himself from Ekaterina's cabin to the galley, vacant now save for the cook, and sat at the long table.

"Jings, lad," Swales said, pouring him a cup.

"If you're suggesting I look a bit haggard, I am sure you're right."

"Haggard? Ye look like ye were ate by wolves an' shite out o'er the Stonehaven cliffs. How's the lass? Sleepin'?"

"We argued all night. She wouldn't sleep; leapt about like a caged animal. Insisted she was recovered. Insisted she be let up and out. I had to hold her down to keep her in the room. She became abusive. Called me horrendous names. Said she wished her father and brothers had shot me."

Swales set down the pot, scowling. The report seemed wildly out of character for the girl he knew. "Ye convinced her t'would be best to stay abed?"

"That's just it. I didn't. She battled me outrageously, then just stopped, as if I'd grabbed her whip hand. Retreated to her bed and went out like a snuffed candle."

"She slept?"

Chapter Nineteen

"I assume." Harrington looked sheepish. "I don't know, actually. Something came over me. I failed her; fell asleep sitting there."

"Did anythin' come of it?"

"No. She's sleeping. Sometime this morning she was up, unfastened the door and pulled her bandage off. She tied a scarf about her throat and..." He hesitated, searching for the least embarrassing way to present it. "She... left herself rather unfastened as well."

"Good Gog!" Swales sat heavily. "What changes? She's...?"

"Unchanged, as far as I can see. I don't know what she was about, but I don't think she left the room. She merely fell asleep. I should not have drifted off."

Swales sagged with relief. "Let it be, Trevor. You canno' go w'out sleep. An' she's all right."

"Not at all! No more did the rain stop and the sun rise than she suffered another attack; crying, writhing about as if in a nightmare. Now she looks as pale as ever."

"Which is she, lad, unchanged or relapsed?"

"Oliver, please. I'm bedeviled as it is. I no longer think of it as relapse. She has a night condition and a daytime condition. It's daylight again, and she's sickly and back abed."

There came a rap and the first stuck in his head. "You might keep it down." Though it was not a request, neither did it appear to have been delivered with ire. "Mr. Harrington, how is Funar?"

He studied the mate, wondering if Constantin was human after all? "Not well, I'm afraid."

"Sleeping?"

"Yes. But only just."

Constantin nodded. "You are wanted on deck, both of you, if the patient can spare you."

Without waiting for a reply (his humanity was limited), the first turned and was gone.

* * *

Constantin and Eltsin book-ended Amramoff, steering, and the captain at the wheel. The crew spilled around the gear house on the mizzen deck. Harrington, having paused to check Ekaterina, arrived late and joined Swales (knocking hell out of his pipe bowl at the rail). A put-upon Olgaren was the focus of many questions coming quickly from mates and hands alike.

"You are saying you saw Petrofsky's strange man? There is someone in the ship?"

"I saw something. I do not know who or what. He was tall and thin, with a great mustache."

"What you are describing, that is Petrofsky's old man!"

"He was not old. He was young, dark and pale."

"You mean we have two stowaways?"

"You saw a ghost!" All eyes fell on Popescu, who didn't care. "He was pale? What are you saying? It was a ghost?"

"Oh yes!" Amramoff laughed. "We have two ghosts?"

"There are no ghosts – young or old," Constantin shouted angrily. "You saw what you cannot explain. That does not make it a ghost! Nor a stowaway. We mistake things; in the weather, the night, the lamplight. Shadows become phantoms, reflections become ghosts. Your eyes played a trick in the rain. This ship is not haunted!"

* * *

Ekaterina awoke, cramping, working to breathe, in an empty cabin. A blanket lay over her, her nightshirt was buttoned, and a new bandage covered her neck. She had no memory of the previous night, save flashes of an argument with Trevor. Why and what about, she did not know. All she knew was Trevor was gone.

She stood to a swirling dizziness. Feeling lost and alone, she had something to do. She stole a look beyond the door, found the companionway empty, and against orders sneaked out.

Voices settled through the scuttle from above. The crew, gathered about the helm, were loudly debating some topic she was too sick to care about. What mattered was they were busy and

Chapter Nineteen

hopefully would be for a while. Quietly, carefully steadying herself, Ekaterina lifted the cover at her feet, opening the scuttle to the aft hold. She slipped through and disappeared into the dark.

* * *

The discussion built with questions argued, fears expressed. All to the good, Nikilov thought. In the open, their superstitious terrors would not eat away at the men. When a fight threatened, when the mate shouted the men down, the captain ended it. "We will search the ship again."

The first studied the captain. Unable to contain the forces building within, he asked through gritted teeth if he might have a word. They stepped away.

"I beg your pardon, captain, but this is folly. We have searched the ship. There is no stowaway. There is no stranger, young or old. To search the first time was prudent. To yield to such foolishness again would demoralize the men."

"We cannot ignore this."

"I do not suggest we ignore it. I suggest we get ahead of it."

"You are not listening, Iancu. We must hold control of the ship – and the mens' fears."

"My point exactly, sir. Leave it to me and I will engage to do that. I will keep them out of trouble, I assure you, with the handspike."

"You would beat the fear from them?" The captain studied his first with weary eyes. He shook his head at the hot-blooded Romanian. "Take the helm, Mr. Constantin."

* * *

In the aft hold, a groggy and ill Ekaterina pulled a package from its hiding place. The package she'd hidden there on the day they sailed. Her only connection to her old life, her last hold (outside of Harrington) on the world she once knew. She opened it, peeled back the paper inside, revealing a lovely and delicate white gown;

the dress she'd carried with her from Bukovina and spoken of to Trevor that first night he'd found her out.

She held it out, remembering its beauty but straining to see in the darkness. She pulled it close, relishing its softness. She rubbed her cheek against the fabric – and began to cry.

* * *

On deck, the meeting over, the search was about to begin. Rather than split into parties, it was decided they would tour *en mass*. They lit three lanterns (watched by the disapproving mate at the wheel). Swales was sent forward to guard the bow and scream bloody murder if anyone showed his face before they ended. The rest started down the aft scuttle holes into the between-decks.

They reconvened outside of the captain's and passenger's cabins. Nikilov opened his, showed all it was empty and secured it again. Harrington begged them, in a whisper, to by-pass the other. "Funar just fell asleep. He was awake all night. I assure you there is no tall man inside."

"Open the door," Popescu said angrily. He leaned in threateningly.

"That is enough," the captain said, putting a hand between them. "Herr Harrington, your word as an Englishman? Funar sleeps? The berth is otherwise empty?"

Harrington nodded curtly, eyeing Popescu with distain. "I assure you."

"Then it is pointless to wake him." Nikilov smiled, satisfied. "There is no tall phantom in the sick room," he declared. He looked among the crew and, one-by-one, received their nods of agreement. Finally, begrudgingly, Popescu added his.

The captain led them away, moving forward, where half of the group inspected the crew's quarters on one side of the companionway, and half went through the mess, hot galley, and cook's berth on the other. Amramoff popped up the ladder, waved to the

Chapter Nineteen

scowling Constantin, and came back down again. Certain of the between-decks, they passed into the forward hold.

"One of you remain here," the captain said, leading the others abaft. "We'll start in the stern."

* * *

In the aft hold, Ekaterina, dizzy and sick, was still clinging to her lovely dress, still crying, and drowning in a flood of images from her past, in her fears for a future that suddenly felt lost, and in her own feelings of mortality. Suddenly, she was shaken from her reverie. A multitude was approaching via the forward holds and was very near.

There was no time to wrap her dress back up or to hide the package again. There was no time to do anything but run. She threw the dress over her shoulder and started up the scuttle ladder. In terror, aware of the risk from above, but sure she was about to be caught from below, she had no choice. She popped the scuttle cover and scrambled up through the hatch into the between-decks.

The companionway was empty but she had no time to bless her luck. She pushed the hatch cover back into place, just closing the scuttle hole when...

* * *

The search party entered the aft hold.

With no clue anyone had recently visited, they made a quick and thorough check by lantern light. Not that there was much to search; stacks of sand ballast and a cloying dampness from the rain, nothing more. They were satisfied. They left the way they'd come, making sure of the midship hold, and ending in the forward hold again.

It was flooded with daylight now. Swales had opened the overhead doors and, from his deck perch, watched them conduct the final leg of their search.

As Harrington had discovered in the Turkish straits, there were few good places to hide. The bulk of the fifty boxes, sand, barrels of lamp oil, and the ship's stores were all that occupied a space created to hold 199 tons of cargo. There was considerable open space and no sign of a stranger, old or young, ghost or human. The search had come up empty.

The captain thanked the second and his men. "That, I believe," Nikilov said, "ends the matter." He turned headed up. Harrington followed, hoping he and Swales could finish their tea.

Behind them, Eltsin dismissed the men. To his surprise, they seemed less than anxious to go. Popescu, as was his nature, put the matter into words. "Are you not sick yet of searching for nothing?" When Eltsin admitted he was, the Romanian pounced. "Shall we not make an end of it then? Let us open these boxes, every one of them, and complete the search."

"Don't be ridiculous. We can't tear open the cargo. Its safety is the whole point of the voyage."

"We need not tear a thing. We open them carefully; we close them again with the same care. Then we know."

"We know what? The Turks opened them."

"They did not open them all. We will open every box."

"Fifty of them? They contain nothing but dirt."

"Then we cannot hurt them."

It was ludicrous. But now the notion had settled, and Popescu's influence worked its way over them, the men seemed united. They stood in the pool of daylight from above, pleading with their eyes for Eltsin to give them hope, silently begging him to help vanquish their fears. "Quietly," Eltsin said, hesitant but relenting. "With no damage to any of the boxes, you understand!"

The men quickly agreed.

Amramoff, being the carpenter, led them in carefully prying the lids off the boxes. The first five revealed nothing but the expected

Chapter Nineteen

dirt. The lid of a sixth came up initiating a bit more excitement. Two rats, having found their way inside, were now noisily looking for an exit. Olgaren provided one, to the excited shouts from the others, with the heel of his boot. Their death-squeals jangled the nerves of more than one among them. Triumphant, Olgaren carried the dead vermin to the top of the ladder and pitched them into the sea.

With calm restored, the search of the cargo boxes was resumed.

* * *

Only a few feet away, Count Dracula lay awake. Fresh air and tiny shafts of sunlight stole in through the holes in his box. The air stirred the mold in his earth-bed, the light pricked his skin like hot needles. He could hear the humans opening the other boxes and fought the urge to explode from his casket and kill them all. What were they to him?

But he knew better. As humiliating as it was, they were his transport to England. Reaching England, Whitby first and thereafter London, was what mattered.

He felt his box being jostled, heard the Romanian language – and several variations of the guttural Russian – as the jostlers called to one another, and the thud of metal on wood. The beveled tip of an iron bar entered his box at the corner. It wagged forcefully, the wood groaned, there came a shrill exclamation as the nails and lid rose a fraction. Dracula sank his fingernails into the underside of the cover. He gritted his teeth, cursed his need to remain hidden, and held fast matching the pressure from without.

His rage grew. With whom did these fools think they were dealing? He was the Voivode; the son of the Dragon. He led his forces over the great river Danube into the land of the Turk. When they were beaten back, he led the charge again, and again. Alone, he'd come from the field of battle where his troops were slaughtered, each time to regroup and attack again. Who were these fools?

Again came the bar in another assault. He held fast to the sound of Russian curses. A second bar entered the thin gap at his right side manipulated by another Russian teasing the first. Lifting pressure was applied. Dracula held fast. He was cornered, he realized, but not helpless. He needed a diversion.

Still holding the casket lid, Dracula whispered, "E-kat-erina!"

* * *

Following the search, Swales made the mistake of staying too long in the bow. More, he'd made the mistake of looking into the forward hold. He'd gotten an eyeful of the crew starting their extended search. The dumb bastards were opening every container in the hold. He watched, disbelieving, secured the hatch doors and hurried below. Not to intervene, but to distance himself. Better to be at tea with Harrington than witness the wreck of the captain's cargo.

He was just leading the scholar into the mess when the door to the passenger's cabin was yanked open and Ekaterina ran out. Pale and sickly, but moving like an Olympian, she raced down the companionway in their direction with glazed eyes. It was obvious they were not her target, but merely an obstacle. They grabbed her as she tried to pass.

"Here, lass, whe-re ye' goin'?"

"Let me go."

"Ekaterina, what is it."

"Let me go. Let me go!"

Just that quickly there was chaos between-decks. Ekaterina screamed she needed to get by while, together, they prevented her. Nikilov stepped from his quarters, saw the tumult, and assisted them in getting the hysterical woman back into her cabin.

"We have her, sir," Swales said, as he and Harrington wrestled her onto the lower bunk.

"You've got to quiet her down." the captain insisted.

"Let go of me. You don't understand. He needs me!"

Chapter Nineteen

Harrington looked to Swales. "What is she talking about?"

"It doesn't matter," the captain said, behind them. "She must be quiet!"

"We'll see to it, sir," Swales assured him.

"Let go of me," Ekaterina shouted, struggling. "The master needs me!"

Harrington, all but on top of the young woman, clamped his hand over her mouth. Over his shoulder, he reassured the commander. "We will see to it."

The captain left, pulling the door closed. He paused for breath outside the room. "The master needs me." That's what the girl had said. Nikilov could not help but feel a tinge of pride. Even in her fever, she felt a duty to the ship and to him. The master of *Demeter* mouthed a silent prayer for the girl's quick recovery and a wish that more of his crew had her devotion to duty. If only the secret of her presence could be revealed. The crew needed...

The thought was interrupted... by another din, equally egregious, forward and below, as if he needed another difficulty. What, in the good name of God, was going on in his hold?

* * *

"Did you hear that?" Popescu asked nervously.

"What?" Amramoff demanded.

"A scream! A woman's scream!"

"You are out of your mind... and I'm busy." The agitated carpenter, sweat pouring as he bent to the stubborn casket, looked to Olgaren. "I never seen the like." Olgaren, on the opposite side, sweating twice as much, nodded in agreement. They wrenched at their respective bars, the wood barked, but the lid would not rise.

The others had ceased their labors to watch; Smirnov with amusement, Popescu under a nagging fear (the imagined screams did not help), the second in growing concern these apes would break the container. "Be careful," Eltsin warned, "whatever you do."

All were startled when the door to the between-decks flew open and Captain Nikilov filled the void. "What," he shouted, "is going on in my hold?"

His entire compliment, save the mate and cook, stood below bathed in lamplight with pry bars in their hands. Beside them, to his disbelief, several shipping containers lay open. While to his horror, only a few feet away, two men were opening another. "Stop what you are doing! Stop it now!" Nikilov descended the stairs. "How dare you touch my cargo!"

The bars were stilled, the powerful hands fell slack. "The fault is mine, captain," Eltsin said. "The men wanted to be sure and, I thought, if we took care not to damage them..."

"You thought? You are suggesting we have a stowaway inside our sealed boxes? That Petrofsky's old man... Olgaren's young man... are stored in the hold? They have been living here for eleven days without food or water? They squeeze through cracks in nailed containers to stroll the deck? And, when they are seen, they jump overboard to avoid questions?"

Nikilov's voice echoed. Then he laughed and the dam burst. One by one the men began to laugh too. Soon all were, as if they were drunk. "Come away," the captain said, a great weight suddenly off his heart. "We've searched and there is nothing here; nothing but our own mad, empty fears. Come, we have sails to set and a voyage to start anew. Close up these boxes. Put them right, that our consignee will be pleased to receive them. Know there is nothing aboard this ship that ought not be here."

Amramoff and Olgaren pulled their pry bars from the box they'd been forcing. They hammered the nails back home, securing the casket.

* * *

Ekaterina passed out. One instant she was fighting them tooth and nail. The next, she was unconscious, as if she'd been struck with a truncheon. There seemed no more reason for her losing

Chapter Nineteen

consciousness than for her having become hysterical in the first place. Swales collapsed in the desk chair and sighed in relief. Harrington, winded but grateful, tucked the girl under her blanket. He ran his fingers through her butchered hair remembering, not long ago, when it was long and beautiful; when life was beautiful. What was happening to them?

He saw something protruding from beneath her mattress, took hold and gently eased it out. It was a white gown with frills and lace, billowed sleeves and a delicate cincture. Her new dress. Funar had, no doubt, secreted it aboard in her kit. He squeezed the soft fabric, held it to him, rubbed it on his cheek (in need of a shave). He watched Ekaterina's breast rise and fall, and wondered again...

What was happening to them?

* * *

The men closed up the boxes. They covered them, tied them down, blew the lanterns out and left the hold. All... but Eltsin. The second mate could not leave, not yet. He peered into the shadowy depths... certain he'd heard something. Movement? Yes. Rats? Possibly, but he didn't believe so. It was more than the presence of vermin.

"Come away," the captain had said. Eltsin returned to the deck.

There, for the first time in days, the second heard laughter and witnessed smiles. He saw a relieved crew. Eager to maintain that mood, Nikilov allowed them a celebration of sorts before getting under way. With the captain's permission, even his approval, an early rum ration was ordered and the men brought their instruments up. There was music, singing, even dancing. The festivities ran for three-quarters of an hour before Constantin, at the master's urging, returned them to their work.

Even then, they went about it cheerfully. The singing continued with the men in the shrouds, at the sails and at the rails, while Nikilov and the mate looked on from the deck. The captain beamed.

Constantin glared. The second, passing both on the way to the helm, overheard Nikilov whisper, "You see, Iancu? You see their confidence? The search did not demoralize the men. I told you."

The first made no reply. He merely watched – and scowled.

* * *

The morning, 18 July, came earlier than Nikilov expected.

He awoke with a start, perspiration beaded on his lip, his forehead, his chest – and he didn't know why. There had been no alarm, no cries, no unwarranted jostling of his ship. All was peaceful, quiet as the tomb. Still he was wide awake. What was the matter?

They'd settled their concerns with yesterday's search. There were no murderous stowaways, ghosts, or bogies. The events of the last days had been unfortunate circumstance brewed in a cauldron of suspicion and superstition. They'd scared themselves like children. Petrofsky's fate was a mystery and, as you could not know the unknowable, would remain so.

They were in full sail and under way again, traveling without incident north of the African continent on a westerly course through the gorgeous Mediterranean Sea. Hadn't Olgaren played his accordion and sung last night? If the big man could sing, what could be wrong? All was well.

So, Nikilov wondered, why couldn't he sleep? Why couldn't he shake this feeling of doom?

He lit his lantern, bathing his desk in a flickering glow, and considered the bottle in his desk drawer. (The heart medicine he'd been prescribed.) He pushed the idea away. His problems were in his head, not his heart.

He pulled a volume (one he'd purchased ages ago but never used) from his shelf. It was not in Nikilov's nature to keep a journal. Living was enough; he saw no reason to relive events. And who else cared about the routine of an old sea dog. He could read but did not consider himself literate and he was no writer.

Chapter Nineteen

Still, strangely, he felt compelled. He opened the book to the intimidating emptiness of the first page and, putting pen to paper, scribbled in his sharp angular scrawl, *LOG OF THE "DEMETER"*. Beneath he wrote, *Varna to Whitby*. Then, in hopes of excusing himself, for who starts a ship's log halfway through the voyage, he added, *Written 18 July, things so strange happening, that I shall keep accurate note henceforth till we land*.

He paused again to decide how and where to begin. An overview seemed natural, but that brought its own concerns. He wrestled with his conscience and, finally, entered the crew compliment: *five hands*. He considered adding their names but, with one seaman missing and presumed dead, decided against it. Instead, he finished the list, writing; *two mates, cook, and captain*. It only made sense (as he had done on the ship's manifest) to leave the deck 'boy' out of it. Why admit in writing he was a fool? That Constantin had signed Funar meant nothing; the captain was responsible for that girl being aboard. He'd take the responsibility, but saw no need to proclaim it. Likewise, he decided against any mention of young Harrington. He was still in hopes of getting the Englishman off without anyone being the wiser. Both were better left off of any written record.

Nikilov heard movement in the companionway and opened his door to see Harrington step from the guest berth. The phrase popped into his head, *Pomyani chorta, on i poyavitsya*. How did the English say, "Speak of the devil... and there he is."

"How is the patient?"

"The same, captain." Harrington shook his head. "Strangely cyclical. She..." He caught himself. "He... seems to recover in the night and relapse after sunrise with little overall improvement."

The captain nodded. There were dozens of questions he wanted to ask, but the answers (what few there were) had so far offered no satisfaction. "Thank you, Herr Harrington. Please, carry on." He closed his door with a renewed determination. He'd had enough of no satisfaction. It was time for something different. The search of the ship had lightened the mood among the men. A lighter mood was what *Demeter's* master needed as well.

It was Sunday. They would hold services this morning; thank God for their blessings and their new-found mood. They would have a fine day at sea. This evening, he would dine with the crew. Together, they would sit down to one of Swales' fine meals and even finer plum puddings.

But first...

He returned to the ship's Log. Captain Nikilov would record, as best he could remember, the significant events that had befallen his ship and crew since leaving the port of Varna on the 6th of July.

* * *

The between-decks door came open and an amber sliver of light stabbed into the forehold. The second mate slipped in and secured the door. He'd been hiding in the shadows, in the mess, waiting for the coast to clear. Why Harrington and the captain were awake at that hour, and what they were discussing, was anyone's guess. Thankfully, the conversation was short. The commander returned to his cabin, the Englishman to Funar's, and the companionway was clear.

He descended the stairs carrying a roll under his arm and wearing a knife in his belt. He crossed the hold, lit the mast lamp and lifted it down. They'd been over the compartment with a fine-toothed comb. There was nothing, every man aboard was satisfied. Everyone... but him. He could not explain it, but Georgiy Eltsin knew there *was* something evil in that hold.

His mind made up, he went about his business. He turned the lamp up. He unrolled the canvas, revealing a hammock, and tied it between the mast and the starboard bulkhead. His intention may not have been sane, but it made sense to him. He would camp here. He would spend every waking moment, not occupied by ship's duties, on the look-out in that hold. If there was a secret

Chapter Nineteen

in *Demeter's* cargo, Eltsin intended to discover it; suicidal seamen, old ghosts, or restless young spirits be damned.

The second climbed into the hammock, swaying with the ship. He followed the light about the hold, the boxes, tarps, barrels, sand – the long shadows reaching for him, then away, reaching for him, then away, to the sounds of surging water and groaning wood.

"Come on, you bastard," Eltsin whispered under his breath. "Come and get me."

Chapter Twenty

FEAR and evil.

The crew of *Demeter* took a respite from the former, convinced for the moment the latter was a figment of their imaginations. The master of the vessel, proclaiming the same, secretly set his fears to paper to convince himself. The second mate swallowed his fears in pursuit of that evil. In her cabin, despite the efforts of a young scholar and an old cook, Ekaterina suffered egregiously from both. But *Demeter* was not the only canvas being painted with the unholy blackness of fear and evil.

On Monday, 19 July, as the Russian schooner continued westward across the Mediterranean, her passengers and crew were unaware that over two thousand miles away, in England, strange events were happening in a Purfleet mental hospital and, less than three hundred miles to the north, in the port village of Whitby; events influenced by the dark evil in *Demeter's* hold.

* * *

"My God!"

The exclamation echoed within the walls of the private asylum, in Purfleet near the river Thames, on the eastern outskirts of London. It rang through the halls, up and down the floors of the

Chapter Twenty

Seward Sanitarium, and out across land and sea. John Seward stood aghast. Well-kept but rumpled, weary yet alert, the young put-upon psychiatrist rocked in the doorway of Renfield's room – squinting as the morning sun stabbed through the barred window. "My God! The birds!"

They were everywhere; flitting to and fro. Thick males in gray and brown with black bibs; duller females in buff; young ones, deep brown with round heads and short tails; on the window sill, clinging to the bars. One rode the torn wallpaper like a seaman walking the plank. Several on the floor pecked dirt with their stout bills. Several flapped around a bowl of water on a writing table. One strutted a shelf above Renfield's cot while a young one warbled from his perch on the pillow. The air was alive with incessant variations of *chirrup, quee,* and *chur-chur-r-r-it-it-it.*

"No, doctor," the lunatic corrected. "Not birds. Sparrows."

Renfield was fifty-nine, according to his admission papers, but looked younger. Other than his vibrancy, too big ears, and too intense gray eyes, he was unremarkable. His collection of pets, on the other hand, was worthy of remark.

"Sparrows, yes," the flabbergasted Seward agreed. "But you've a whole colony. How many are there? One... two... And what's happened to the rest of your flies and spiders?" He nosed in Renfield's things. "They're obliterated; all but gone."

"So they are," the patient said.

"To the birds, eh, the sparrows? Don't they prefer seeds? Grains?"

"Prefer them? They're like us; opportunists. They adapt – and eat whatever is available."

"Spiders?"

"Yes. Yes, of course. Anything with life in it," the lunatic said impatiently. "But, please, I want to ask you a very great favor." Renfield's impatience vanished – as he descended into rapture. "A kitten! Oh, doctor, might I have a nice, sleek, little kitten, that I can play with, and teach, and feed..." Then came a quality of menace, "...and feed... and feed!"

The doctor hesitated, caught off guard. "I, eh, I'll, eh, see about it." To regain the upper hand, he added, "Wouldn't you rather have a cat than a kitten?"

"Oh, yes!" the lunatic cried. "I would like a cat!"

Now you're watching me. You're always watching, Dr. Seward. You tempt me with a cat. But you're the cat. You're the cat and I'm your mouse... to thump with your paw, to flick with your claws, to lay your hand upon my head and hold me – helpless – until you choose to do away with me. I'm on to you – cat. The self-important bastard lording over his lunatic. But I know, and you don't know, I'm not your lunatic. I'm the master's lunatic. The master's servant when the time is right. I know something else, Dr. Seward. I know that you are everything he has grown to detest throughout the centuries. He hates you; he's telling me even now. And, yes... I hate you too. I feel your fear.

"Renfield," Seward said, involuntarily taking a step back from his patient – and his patient's icy stare. "Renfield?"

I would like very much, I think, to kill you, doctor.

"Renfield? Renfield, can you hear me?"

This is your lucky day, Dr. Seward. The master says not yet. I cannot kill you... yet. I will continue to play the game; to be the fool. I will bide my time... as the master so patiently bides his.

"Renfield!"

"Please, Dr. Seward," the obedient one cried, surfacing as if he'd never been away, throwing himself on his knees. "Please let me have a cat. My salvation depends upon it!"

"No," the appalled doctor replied. "You cannot have a cat!"

Renfield sank into silence.

Abandoning his sulking patient to his disappointment, the psychiatrist paused outside to insist the orderly secure the man's door. "Lock it, Martin! I don't want birds flying through the sanitarium."

You're fooling yourself, doctor. You think you've accomplished something for your science. That, in goading me, you've learned something. You're fooling yourself. I'm not thinking of you; not listening to you. I'm listening to the master. He's coming. He's a long

Chapter Twenty

way off, but he's drawing nearer. As he bides his time, so will I obediently bide mine.

* * *

The following day, Tuesday, 20 July, Martin knocked excitedly on Dr. Seward's study door. The orderly was a white-suited cockney, out from London to escape the bustle, who found – with Renfield's arrival – he'd leapt from the frying pan into the fire. He'd been made the fly-eater's warder and, oh, how he longed for the old stresses of The Smoke.

The doctor bid him enter, certain (as it was only eleven in the morning) it was too early for anything awful to have happened. Seward was wrong. A crisis had taken place and the exasperated orderly began his report – as he began all his reports – with a sigh and the words, "It's Renfield, sir..."

"Yes? What is it?"

"'e's very sick, doctor."

"Sick? That's strange. I saw him this morning. He looked robust. He was humming a tune and spreading sugar on the window sill."

"Yes, doctor. Goin' about 'is old business o' fly catchin' again. An' cheerful 'e was."

"Yes, and?"

"Ye told me to report if 'e got up t' anythin' odd." Martin doffed his cap and wiped his forehead with his sleeve. "Well, sir, I got to finkin', wonderin' what 'e was up to. I didn't see none o' 'is birds first time I stopped. I went back an', blimey, if I wasn't right, 'is birds - 'is sparrows - was gone."

"Yes. They were this morning. I asked where to and he replied they had all flown away."

"So 'e says. But, I looks, see, an' there was feathers 'ere an' there about the room an' a bit o' what looked like blood on 'is pillow. Now 'e's sick, very sick indeed. 'e, uh, 'e vomited quite violently not long ago an', bless me if 'e didn't disgorge a 'ole lot o' feathers."

"Feathers?"

"It's my belief, doctor, that 'e's eaten 'is birds. The lot of 'em. 'e just took an' ate 'em raw!"

* * *

You said you wanted to talk with me, Dr. Seward. But you don't. This is not conversation. It is pontification; a lecture for your captive audience. Or should I say... your captive. What have you done with the birds, you ask. But you do not wait for a response. You don't want a response because this is not a conversation.

Again, the stare. The doctor did what he could to control a shiver, and hoped it hadn't been too obvious. Still Renfield's icy stare. No reason to drag this out, Seward thought. He'd made his point. He administered an opiate, which the patient took without trouble. Heavily but necessarily medicated, he would leave Renfield to sleep. Or, at least, to lie quiet for the night.

As he started for the door, Seward picked up the small notebook which Renfield made such a habit of scribbling in and slipped it into his pocket. It was more than curiosity. He was the man's doctor. "Good night, Renfield," he said. There was no answer.

The psychiatrist could feel Renfield's eyes, drooping slits from medication, against his back, watching him depart. Worse, and this made no sense, he swore he could feel a second pair of eyes as well, all the way out the door. Someone else watching. The doctor admonished himself for being foolish. Of course, no such thing had happened. Renfield may have been a rare case but he had the standard set of two eyes; no more. Be that as it may, he felt a wave of genuine relief when Martin turned the key, securing the fly-eater in his room for the night.

* * *

Seward jumped...

Unnecessarily, as it turned out, startled like a child by a flash of movement and color in the corner as he entered his study. He

Chapter Twenty

lit the coal-gas lamps and turned to that which had frightened him – Tabby, the sanitarium's cat.

There was nothing alarming about the animal. She was your standard British Shorthair - in calico. Renfield's orderly called her 'the clouded tiger' but others on the staff pooh-poohed the moniker declaring her tortoiseshell-and-white coat too striking to be 'clouded'. She'd been given them by a recovered patient with the declaration she would 'bring good luck'. She had done for the cook as Tabby spent her mornings mousing in the larder. Her afternoons were taken up roaming the sanitarium garden, and she spent her nights lounging in Seward's study. The doctor did not believe in luck. Neither was he a cat fancier. But he had to admit, despite the occasional startle, Tabby had become one of the family.

"You scared me. Don't do that," Seward told the cat, wagging a finger and wasting an admonition.

It was gone eleven at night and Seward had patient notes to record, starting with the interesting but exasperating Renfield. As for the tortured man... He'd explained as plainly as he was able Renfield would have to come to grips with what he'd done – from the flies through and including the disastrous end he'd afforded his sparrows. What else could he do?

"Renfield, my homicidal maniac," Seward said aloud. "You are a creature unto yourself."

At his desk, rifling the pages of the notebook he'd borrowed from the lunatic, he wrestled with his thoughts. "Peculiar... one of a kind. I shall have to invent a new classification for you. But what?" He tossed the notebook aside and took up his pen. "I shall call you a zoophagous maniac; meaning *life-eating*. For what you desire is to absorb as many lives as you can. You gave many flies to one spider and many spiders to one bird. Then you wanted a cat, presumably to eat the many birds." He eyed the skulking Tabby and the obvious question popped into his head. "What would have been your later steps? What kind of a monster are you, my friend?"

Unable, yet, to answer the question, Seward began jotting his notes.

* * *

"Yes, of course, dear. I'm terribly excited too," Mrs. Westenra said. A dignified widow, with an excitable blossoming daughter, she casually sipped her tea looking pleased but not in the least excited. "She'll soon be here. Only four days. Four days and Mina will be in Whitby."

"*Only* four days?"

How could her mother be so casual? Lucy Westenra couldn't enjoy her tea. It was all she could do to remain seated, like the young lady she was supposed to be, like the young bride she soon would be. Four days until Mina Murray, her greatest friend in the whole world arrived on the London train. Not until Saturday! Goodness, it was an eternity.

She had so much to tell her. Yes, she'd written and Mina was already aware of some of them. But not all. She'd told her; but hadn't told her, told her. All there was to feel about that wonderful, awful 24th of May when three gallant men had asked her hand in marriage. Three – in the same day. Oh, the blow she'd been forced to deliver to the good Dr. Seward, the man who helped so many disturbed people in his sanitarium. And the heartbreak she'd had to hand the handsome American Texan, Quincey Morris. But, oh!, the joy in accepting the proposal of Arthur Holmwood! She loved him so much!

There was more, things she'd not found the words to mention in her letters. Things she'd been forced to keep bottled up. She couldn't tell her mother, and wouldn't consider telling Arthur, but Mina – Mina would listen and help her... Help her to understand the urges, the terrifying thoughts, the strange dreams – nightmares; the dark and frightening nightmares that had haunted her restless sleep of late.

Chapter Twenty-one

WHILE unsuspecting minds in England were being manipulated, the Russian schooner continued westward through the Mediterranean Sea.

South of *Demeter* lay Algeria which, save for a few Tuaregs in the Sahara refusing to be conquered after seventy years of bloodshed, was now under French control. During the war, 50,000 French immigrated there, with tens of thousands from Spain, Italy, and Malta, confiscating the coastal farm lands and swarming the cities. The natives were uprooted. Poverty rose, literacy plummeted, and bloody fighting and disease erased one-third of the population. North of *Demeter's* course lay Majorca, the largest of Spain's Balearic Islands; a ghost of her former self. Six years since, in 1891, a blight destroyed her vineyards. Their main source of income decimated, the residents abandoned the island for Spain or the Americas. Whether God's plan or a curse of the devil, history was replete with stories of disease and death arriving by sea; shadowed by unimaginable suffering... and horror. And the Russian schooner continued her westward course through the Mediterranean.

Aboard, the crew were kept busy with back-breaking labors and boring routines. While that Monday, 19 July, two events began to alter that cycle.

Chapter Twenty-one

The first, while inordinate, was in danger of becoming the usual; Georgiy Eltsin was back on his self-imposed guard duty in the forward hold.

The second, and more surprising, took place in the passenger's cabin. Swales' patient was finally showing signs of recovery. In addition to lime juice, Ekaterina drank water, sipped broth and, at the cook's insistence, managed a bit of salt pork. She was weak, and slept more than she was awake, but without the violent pangs that had wracked her for days. Most encouraging, she had no memory of the hallucinations that had recently driven her raving from her berth.

* * *

Harrington's heart sang when he saw Ekaterina the following morning, Tuesday, 20 July. She was up reading at the desk. The sea was up and rain threatening, but he had the happy feeling that, had there been sunshine, she might well have been eager to bask in it. Her color had returned, rose to her cheeks, blush to her lips, and the startling green, so sadly missed, was back in her round eyes. The makeshift scarf was gone, the bruise on her throat all but faded, and the puncture wounds closed and healing nicely. Best of all, Ekaterina's gorgeous smile was back where it belonged.

Her sweet personality, so badly affected by her illness, was back. She was treating Harrington and Swales well again. Their only bone of contention remained, and neither could blame her, her intense desire to escape the confines of the cabin and breathe fresh air.

"Katya, I know you're feeling better. I'm delighted you're feeling better," Harrington said, taking her hands as she danced about the room. She urged him to join her; he urged her to stop. He laid a finger to his lips to quiet her. "Your improvement in health doesn't improve your situation. You can dance quietly, but you can't sing and you cannot go on deck."

She pulled on her knit cap. "Not even as Rada Funar?"

"Cor, no! You're not well enough. Besides, you're a stowaway. Having done so in the open only makes the situation worse as far as Nikilov is concerned. And the mate hasn't stopped growling yet. Believe me, you do not want to be caught up there."

"That can't be. I am universally loved."

Harrington smiled, delighted in her recovery. Still he felt a twinge of fear. Her infectious gaiety seemed forced and he couldn't shake the feeling Ekaterina was not herself; that she may not have been out of danger. "You are," he said, remembering to smile, "most assuredly loved by me."

* * *

Forward and below, there was no love lost at all.

The second mate, whether through real perception or gross paranoia, was certain there was something wrong in the hold. He'd taken up residence among the stores the previous day, to investigate his fears and keep vigil. He anticipated spending one night among the boxes to cure his inexplicable mania but nothing could have been further from reality. The longer he was there, listening, watching, the more he felt the need to stay. He was convinced a malevolent force occupied that space.

He was there now, fighting off the sleep he so desperately needed – and losing. He gave the gloomy hold, lit by his solitary lamp, a final look through slitted eyes, then nodded off. He was snoring immediately, oblivious to the hold, the cargo, or the scrawny gray rats that moved in from the shadows to claim the remnant of his supper.

A scant few feet away, in his casket, Dracula was less appreciative than the rats. He was seething. He'd been listening to the ridiculous human for hours; calling out impotent threats as he hovered, tinking and clinking his tea china, chomping and grinding as he stuffed his face, and now snoring. In the Count's reckoning, these fools already owed him for their insolence, their

Chapter Twenty-one

infuriating searches. And this harassment? He would pay, this little man. They would all pay.

Before dropping off to sleep, his irritating warder had opened the hatch. Fresh air filled the compartment. The clouds parted and blue beams of moonlight stole in through the holes in the lid. All of the elements that made it a beautiful night would, come dawn, spell his doom. Should the seaman sleep soundly, into the morning, the hold would be flooded with sunlight.

It took all his strength to control the centuries-old instinct to murder the man and pull the doors closed. But Dracula knew better. The seas upon which the ship bore him were unfriendly waters; deadly outside his few protections. He needed this vessel, and its crew of misfits, if he was to reach England and his new life. He would bide his time with the voyage and with the humans. Still, he'd had enough intrusions. A diversion was needed to remove this parasite; something to keep him, the entire crew, busy. They needed some place to be other than the hold. He needed the hatch doors closed.

Dracula laid his hands upon the underside of his box lid – and concentrated.

* * *

The second was deep in a dream, on land, under the soft moonlight, hand-in-hand with his sweet Orina. The dream played out as it had so many times before, the details no one's business but his own. The end came too quickly and, as always, in tears. Orina died, long ago. The moonlight, the sweetness, the kisses were the phantoms; the dream cut from wholecloth. Death, the impending grave, that was the only reality. The tears came...

... in torrents, running down his cheeks, his clothes, everywhere. Drowning him...

"Mr. Eltsin!"

A voice, dull, insistent... beyond the wash of tears. A voice new to the dream.

"Mr. Eltsin!"

He struggled to the surface, to wake, to sit. He was in the hold soaked from head to foot. His hammock swung madly, the ship buffeted by heavy waves. Water poured in through the open hatchway. A silouette, so expansive at the head, so thick at the shoulders, it could only belong to Olgaren, hung over the lip of the hatch above, pelted by rain, backlit by flashes of lightning, shouting down at him. "Mr. Eltsin! The captain's... called ship's officers... to stations! You are needed." Out of nowhere, the sea was churning and *Demeter* was in what sailors euphemistically referred to as *rough weather*.

Later, when the storm abated and they were able to breathe, each of the crewmen would have wild stories of how a gorgeous night erupted in blasts of lightning, wind, and rain. Of how each courageously battled to save the ship. Later. For now it was upon them.

Eltsin scrambled up the hatch ladder and, gaining the deck with a hand from Olgaren, was awed by what he saw. The ship had not merely surged into a surprise blow. She'd entered a hell of water instead of fire. A quick look over the pitching deck showed Constantin, Amramoff and Popescu, damned as well, suffering above trying to reef the foresails. The first and the carpenter were lashing the canvas, Popescu was lashing out – cursing heaven and hell in the same stolen breath. Eltsin and Olgaren would join them but first, fighting the wind, buffeted by waves lipping the bulwark, they wrestled the hold's hatch doors closed and fitted the battens into place.

* * *

The head had torn loose on the square-rigged foresail and it had to be put right, rainstorm or no, to successfully shorten the sail and before the canvas was ripped to ribbons by the wind. It need not be mentioned the repair would have to be accomplished

Chapter Twenty-one

without the ship's rope and sail expert, the late Petrofsky, their marlinspike.

"It's *All hands to stations* now," a dripping Smirnov (with a drenched mustache) cried, as he called Swales, and even Harrington, up from the mess. "The captain asks you both to relieve him at the helm. He needs every man for the sails."

The men before the mast rode the heaving yards as if riding some fearsome beast. Eltsin had gone aloft to join them. Olgaren, with his great strength, remained on the pitching deck to work the lines at the pinrails. Nikilov stood alone at the wheel, trimming the rudder against the blow with difficulty. He was needed forward with the men and, with only an arthritic cook and a weak bookworm from which to draw, Nikilov decided to make steering a two man job. The salty Russian wondered now after his replacements. Happily, through the downpour, he made out his relief coming.

Smirnov led Swales and Harrington up, onto the deck. The Russian and the Scot struggled abreast for the helm; the former for new orders, the latter to relieve the captain. Harrington, his heart racing, lagged behind. What the two in the lead thought or felt, he didn't know. But Harrington was terrified, entering a level of hell he'd never imagined. If there were gods or devils, both seemed in league against him.

The ship was running downwind, driving into a trough between two massive waves. Swales took the wheel and, as Nikilov stepped away, the rudder kicked. The bow began to yaw and, turning windward, to rise up suddenly. The stern slid down the face of the wave, outrunning the bow, and the schooner broached (turning broadside into the trough). The vessel was virtually knocked down, listing well over 45 degrees, and threatening to lay on her beam ends. Water rushed over the port gunwale and *Demeter* came near to capsizing.

Drenched, Harrington fell to his knees between the deckhouse and the port bulwark. With the ship on her side, he felt the spray and saw only the foaming, white horses atop the waves where the sky ought to have been. And how to describe the motion? To be in full contact with the pine deck and still feel as if he were falling through the air!

To a chorus of terrified shouts, the main sail boom swept across the deck. Had not the massive Olgaren (and now Smirnov and the grumbling Popescu as well), been there to stop the sweep, the boom might well have plunged into the sea, main gaffe sail and all, and the schooner gone into a death roll. But the might of the straining seamen, and not a little luck, halted the event and saved the ship.

"Hard over," the captain was heard to yell. "Hard over! Head her off!" Nikilov and Swales, fighting together, forced the wheel over and abruptly turned the ship to the lee.

Harrington reached for the chainplate, where the main mast shroud met the rail, in a desperate effort to prevent falling into the sea. But, as he grabbed hold, the sea dropped away – out of sight. The ship, answering the helm, pitched up in the opposite direction, as she fell off downwind and back into the trough. The water disappeared as the schooner righted herself and the whole of his vision was filled with rain coming hard at him and boiling gray-black sky. Lightning flashed!

The ship rolled the opposite direction on her keel, the main boom swung again – threatening all on the deck coming back to the starboard – and the hands pulled for their lives.

Harrington's knees left the deck and the deckhouse bulkhead stopped him as he fell up the other way. To his surprise, there was no pain, merely a fleeting shock at the contact and a desperate need to catch his breath. He inhaled, got a mouth full of salt water for his trouble, then (coughing and choking) was off again, sliding down the wall of the deckhouse back toward the floor. I'm trapped! was all he could think; a rider on a horse of the apocalypse!

The ship pitched back again, picking up speed now she was running. Rain, rat lines, the raucous roll of the vessel back to the port, hurling him toward the bulwark, the pinrail through the blur, the wide, black, angry ocean – everywhere – ready to swallow him, and a monstrous gray wave hammering him on the

Chapter Twenty-one

head, driving him nearer his watery grave. The ship may have been saved but Harrington was done. He gasped and closed his eyes for the last time.

It was a complete shock, a moment later, when the young Englishman realized he wasn't dead. He wasn't drowning either, though it felt like it. He suddenly understood he couldn't breathe because someone had hold of him, around the chest, in a bear hug. The shock continued as his rescuer dragged his limp, drenched body aft of the deckhouse, around the corner, to the hollow beside the door to the between-decks. There they dropped, exhausted, his rescuer sagged between the rum tanks and the sloshing rain barrel with Harrington in his lap.

"Th- thank... you," the scholar shouted over the tumult. He gasped, grateful to take in air, and shouted again, "Thank... you."

The ship continued to pitch beneath them, down at the head then up, down at the heel then up, rolling from side to side, threatening life and limb with each evolution. The rain poured, the thunder boomed, and the monstrous waves jumped the rails. Harrington took it in - alive. When he finally caught his breath, he turned his head to look his rescuer in the face and met the knowing blue eyes and soaked solid features of the ship's commander.

Harrington began to shake, crying. Nikilov slapped his arm, squeezed his shoulder firmly. "Fear not, Herr Harrington," he shouted over the din. "A character-building storm for everyone!"

* * *

With the compliment, captain and mates, crew and passenger, running the schooner before the wind, none were left between-decks to witness the strange gray mist pour through the cracks in the forehold door. It glided the companionway and, as it moved, took the shape of a human being. But only the shape.

Count Dracula, an old man again, with wiry hair and a white mustache, now that their parasitic watchmen were occupied, saw no need to suppress his rising bloodlust. He strode aft, in perfect balance, oblivious to the pitching and rolling of the floor, and all but floated to the door of the passenger's cabin. Behind it, he could sense, smell, feel, Ekaterina.

He could sense something more. She was resisting. Not, the vampire imagined, for long. Silently he called, knowing that within the cabin, within her head, his voice was booming.

The door came open and there she stood... wearing an expression of abject terror. She stared, unblinking, breathless at first, then breathing, then panting. *Invite me in*, she heard him say, though his bright red lips remained unmoving. She fought to block the insistent voice, now booming, *You must invite me in*, like cymbals crashing within her head.

Then he spoke, actually, in a commanding bass, "You must invite me over the threshold."

Her defenses crumbled at the same instant something wild took command of her spirit. She met his stare with gleaming eyes and threw the door wide. "Please," she said, trembling. "Come in."

Dracula crossed the sill and pushed the door shut behind him. He took the girl in his arm, grabbed her firm round bottom and, without waiting for an angel to pass, lifted her and bit her throat. He drank to her moans relishing her life force. Contrary to his nature, tamping his animal urge, ignoring her pitiable cries, he consumed only so much then forced himself back. Dracula sliced a razor-sharp fingernail into the flesh of his wrist, into a vein, to release a watery ooze of red-cells and separated platelets (his tainted blood resisted its own coagulation), and lifted it to her. Ekaterina pulled back but the vampire would not be denied. He grabbed the nape of her neck and pressed his wrist to her mouth. "Drink."

When still she hesitated, he forced her head forward, pressing her lips against his bleeding wrist until she had no choice but to suckle. A moment and holding her was no longer necessary. A moment more and she began to feed hungrily.

* * *

Chapter Twenty-one

Following its initial surge, the sea calmed markedly. The crew remained busy but the threat of imminent foundering passed as the blast ebbed to governable rough weather. The operation of the vessel was gotten in hand and *Demeter* rode through the night.

Swales, beaten and bruised, had been relieved several hours since and sent below to sleep. He must have done, for now something startled him awake. As consciousness returned the old Scot recognized the cause of his alarm; a slamming door. He lifted his head, ignoring a stiff neck, and saw Olgaren's hunched form coming in. A kerosene lamp burned in the companionway and, in the ambient light, he saw a deluge of water running off the seaman's gear. The exhausted Russian spoke not a word but, in his soaked kit, fell onto a bunk and began to snore.

Swales sat up rubbing the sand from his eyes and wondering what in hell Olgaren was doing in his room. Then reason returned and he realized he was in the crew's quarters. But why? He'd been relieved, he didn't know when, sometime Wednesday morning (21 July), and came out of the rain. He was exhausted and cold. Yes, it was summer in the Mediterranean, but he was nearly seventy, soaked, and in the wind for hours. He had no memory of lying down. But he had – in the crew's quarters.

Swales heard the BANG and the room went dark. And again, and the dim light was back. Olgaren had failed to secure the door and, with each roll of the ship, it slapped either the sill or the bulkhead. It continued to do so, back and forth, BANG and BANG, as the ship rode the waves.

Swales grabbed the bunk frame and weathered a swell while the door smacked the wall again. He was unsure of the time but clearly up for the day. Should he feel like lying down again, it would be in his own bunk. He pulled his boots on, gathered his coat as he stood, and headed out. Still in possession of his humanity, he closed the door for Olgaren.

Harrington, relieved, soaked, and coming down found Swales in the companionway. "Aren't you on the wrong side of the hall?" he asked. His smile belied his exhaustion. "Or shouldn't I ask?"

"Ask what ye will. I've no answer fer ye, as I've no' one for masel. I joined the crew an', after last night, I'm grateful to wake no matter the bed. Is it the light or could ye use a bed yersel."

"I could use a cup. . . if you were making some."

"Don't light the stove in a storm, but it feels we've e'ened out. A couple o' hot kettles will go a long way toward rightin' the whole crew. Ye keep me company, I'll keep ye awake." Swales crossed into the mess.

"I shan't be long, Oliver. I'm going to look in on Ekaterina."

Swales muttered an acknowledgement. A moment later, as he ladled two kettles of water from the larder cask, he heard a commotion. It was difficult to identify for, though the storm had lessened, it still made itself known. As he struck a match to the kindling, Swales heard it again; louder, longer, rife with terror. Harrington was shouting! Cursing himself for ignoring the first, he doused the match in the sand and hurried out. He reached the aft end of the companionway as fast as his arthritis allowed and saw the door to the passenger's cabin ajar. . . "Trevor," he said, as he pushed the door open.

Swales looked in with disbelieving eyes and gasped, "Good Lord!"

Chapter Twenty-two

HARRINGTON was on her bunk, clutching Ekaterina, rocking her and crying. She was unconscious, bleeding from her reopened throat wounds. Blood smears marred her lips and chin. "The door was open," he bawled. "She was like this, her head on the floor, dropped there like so much rubbish."

They settled the girl in bed and Swales tended her. He examined the inside of her eyelid, peeled down her lower lip. What should have been healthy pink tissue in both were a dull blue. He pinched her fingernail turning it white, released it, and waited what seemed an eternity before the pink returned. "It's as if she were drained," he whispered. "Drained o' blood."

Harrington grabbed his arm. "What does that mean?!"

"Calm yersel', lad. It means what I said. Somethin's drained the girl's blood... fer a second time. An' there's damn little I can do."

"You must do something! Give her blood. Give her my blood!" He ripped his cuff open, yanked his sleeve up. "You don't imagine I'd object, surely?"

"T'is no' aboot yer objectin' or no."

"Then give her my blood. I've read of it; a transfusion. It can be done!"

"It can, aye, but no' here. Jings, lad, think. We mended Petrofsky's hand with a filed fish hook. D' ye think I'dda done that if I

Chapter Twenty-two

had the wherewithal to cross blood? I have neither the equipment nor the knowledge and I'd likely kill her quick as any shipboard malady. I'm no' a doctor! I'm a cook, tryin' to get home like thee! There's precious little I can do." Swales squeezed Harrington's shoulder with all the strength in his gnarled hand. "But I will do all I can."

The wounds on her throat, more worrying now because of their inexplicable re-opening, were cleaned and bandaged. Extra pillows were collected for props to assist her breathing. Swales eyed the porthole, certain the child would benefit from fresh air, but the wind and waves precluded the idea.

Harrington hovered. "How is she?"

"She's sickly. Trevor, ye need a lie down."

"Damn blast it, Oliver! How is she?"

"She's near death! An' I'm sayin' nowt ye don't know already. I can no' treat her an' attend to ye as well. Now, listen to me. Listen! Ye've been a-deck all night, near drowned. Ye need rest as..."

"I can't rest!" Harrington insisted.

"Ye can't go on, no' an' do her any good. I'll do what I can. But I'm too old to go on fore'er. When I fail, ye'll need be there for her. An' ye won't be if ye do no' get some sleep now." Harrington tried to speak, but Swales interrupted. "It's clear, we canno' leave the wee lass alone. One o' us must be w' her. I'm rested now. Ye must ge' rested to spell me. Now, argue with that an' ye're nowt but a fool."

He couldn't and didn't. With Swales' assurance there was nothing to contribute, he kissed Ekaterina's clammy forehead and left to get some sleep.

Swales returned his attention to the girl who surfaced to semi-consciousness in agony. He mixed a powder for her pain and helped her drink. He paced for a time, watching, wondering what if anything he could do. It was then, while most helpless, he made a fascinating discovery.

The girl moaned, rocking, as if she were lying on broken glass. Swales paused between her and the outer bulkhead and noted that, of a sudden, she seemed to relax. The medication had taken hold. Relieved, he stepped away, and was startled as Ekaterina cried out. He turned back but, before he reached her, saw her relax. Swales stared, perplexed. Again he moved and again the girl cried out and cringed. "Jings," Swales whispered. It was damned strange. Something was turning the girl's pain on and off like a lantern.

Beyond her condition nothing about her appeared out of the ordinary. He examined himself, seeing only that which he expected, and too the cabin. All was as before, with the exception of a beam of sunlight dissecting the room from the porthole. Swales approached noting that a crease had opened in the storm and a startling gold beam of light stabbed through the gray clouds like the blade of a knife. The morning was proclaiming itself and the port focused the brilliant light on Ekaterina's face. When he stood between, and the girl lay in shadow, she was at peace. When he stepped away and the beam hit her – she cried out!

"Michty me," Swales muttered. He stepped away again, letting the sun touch her. She moaned in pain and rolled to escape the light. He grabbed Funar's cap and held it over the port, blocking the beam. The girl fell quiet again. "Daylight?" Swales whispered.

As his experiment required torturing the girl, he could not continue. (He was embarrassed he'd treated her as he had.) Still, Swales had seen it! But what in the name of Robert the Bruce had he seen?

* * *

As quickly as it had parted, the cloud-cover returned. The sunlight vanished and gloom reclaimed the sea, the ship, and the cabin. Swales dispensed with Funar's cap and, free from the debilitating effects of the sun's rays, Ekaterina found fitful sleep.

Demeter rode the storm. The young woman struggled for every breath while Swales watched. Hours passed. The cook and scholar, the latter only slightly less exhausted than the former, changed places. Swales went to bed (his own this time) determined to sleep.

203

Chapter Twenty-two

Harrington sat up determined to stay awake. The young woman wrestled with nightmares while Harrington willed her to recover. Hours passed. *Demeter* rode the never-ending storm.

Harrington answered a rap and admitted Swales, carrying food, with books under his arm. "She's still sleeping," the scholar whispered. "I shouldn't think we ought to wake her."

"Nor I. It's no' for her."

"Oh, I'm not hungry."

"Wither or no' ye lack belly-timber is no' the question. I need no' remind ye o' the importance o' keepin' up yer strength."

"No. I'll eat." Harrington set the plate down and pointed to the books. "What are those?"

"I borrowed these. Been doin' some readin'. Thought ye might take a look." Harrington reached but Swales, now the moment had come, hesitated handing them over. The Englishman eyed the old man suspiciously. Swales relented, speaking rapidly as he surrendered the volumes. "I've been curious aboon things happenin' aboard ship. Wither any are connected or all coincidence. An', natur-ly, I'm suspicious aboon the cause o' our lasses affliction. The affair w' the sunlight only made it more so."

Harrington nodded. Swales had told him of the effect the light had on the girl. Her cap, as a porthole cover, had been replaced with the lid from a flour barrel. It all seemed rather silly.

"I'm no' in step w' the skeered yabblins o' the crew. Nor do I think any knowledge ought be rejected out o' hand."

Harrington nodded, slightly amused. Two days of seriousness from Oliver Swales was almost more than one could bear. He turned to the books. The first was a well-used bible. He screwed up his lips and stared a question at the cook.

"He would no' let me borrow one w'out th'other."

"The captain?" Harrington asked, thinking of the ship's zealots. He missed the shake of Swales' head as he took up the second volume. The title, in worn gold, read *Aberglaube und das Volk Gottes* which, if he could trust his German, meant 'Superstition and the People of God'. The author's name, Rev. E.P.H.

Wagner, added nothing to his knowledge. Neither it seemed, as he flipped the pages, would reading the work. Every '*das jedes* Monster, *Undeadgeschöpf* (undead creature), *Nosferatu*, Werewolf, *Gewindebohrerkobold*(hob-goblin), *Bluttrinker* (blood drinker) and *Günstling des Teufels enthält*" (minion of the Devil) that had ever dragged its knuckles across the mountains of Europe on a cold *Walpurgisnacht* appeared. And, as written by a minister, only devotion to God could save their victims from death, eternal suffering or, worse, undeath and an eternity haunting the earth.

Harrington rolled his eyes. "Where in the world did you... No. Allow me to guess. You borrowed these from Popescu?" Swales nodded. "You think we have a monster aboard?"

"I dinna know what t' think. I have heard a lot o' fearful grumblin' an' I am curious. Aside that, if ye need somethin' to keep ye awake through yer vigil w' the lass, this ought to do."

Harrington couldn't argue with that.

* * *

By Thursday, 22 July, *Demeter* had been in rough weather for three days during which her short-handed crew struggled past the southern tip of Italy, north round Africa, and fought their way into the western Mediterranean south of Spain. Exhausted hands were busy with the sails round the clock; furling and reefing them short when the rains came, resetting them when the rains abated and the blows ebbed. After each storm, the captain earned his bones fixing his course as if they were just starting, with limited visibility, a useless sextant, and trusting to instinct.

Strangely, for the crew, the dangers were a blessing. The more they feared the storm, the more they fought to stay atop it. The harder they worked, the less they thought of nightmares and shipboard phantoms. As they won the battle with nature, they forgot their fears of the supernatural. And, as they left their ghosts behind, even the mate grew cheerful. It was almost perverse. With each storm, working on the verge of destruction, the ship

Chapter Twenty-two

pitching and rolling until hell wouldn't have it, the mood of the men improved. The mate, not a genial man on his best days, laughed and praised their labors.

His compliments were timely, as they approached the straits of Gibraltar. Countless armies had failed to destroy or conquer the famous rock at the southwest tip of Spain. 'Solid as the Rock of Gibraltar' had become a maxim. Constantin felt the same about his crew.

Harrington, with his academic's mind, wandered from the heroic symbolism to the mythical and mystical aspects of the location. Had they shared his knowledge of what Plato called the realm of the Unknown, Constantin and his crew might well have trembled. The strait and the Rock, one of the fabled Pillars of Hercules, was believed by the Romans to have been created when their hero smashed through the mountain of Atlas, connecting the Atlantic and the Mediterranean. The Greek historian Siculus argued the opposite, that Heracles (as he knew him) narrowed an existing strait to prevent sea monsters entering the Mediterranean. Tradition said the pillars bore an inscribed warning for sailors, *Nec plus ultra* (nothing further beyond).

The schooner passed through the straits in visibility so poor neither the rock, to the north, nor Jebel Musa (Hercules' southern pillar), could be seen. The rain still fell, but what had for days seemed an assault from the weather had quieted. Considering all she'd been through, a relatively shipshape *Demeter* entered the Atlantic Ocean.

Nikilov ordered the carpenter to begin frequent soundings and, correcting his course to N.N.E., instructed the steersman to keep them as near to Spain as he was safely able. "Rather than venture any further out to sea," he told the helm. "We will give ourselves a respite and turn her into a coaster for the time being." The captain stared into what, despite the rain, looked like a new curtain of fog settling over them, and only partly in jest, added, "That is... if Spain is still there."

"Aye," Popescu said, adjusting the rudder. "And assuming we stay afloat."

Nikilov frowned but said nothing. Beaten as they were – how could he?

* * *

Harrington no longer needed to peek outside. He could gauge the time by merely watching Ekaterina. In the day, she struggled for breath, fought for life. Following each sunset, her symptoms fell away and some wild and repellent new personality came to the fore. The change was frightening to observe and as regular as clock-work.

Swales entered and was just closing the door when Ekaterina's eyes snapped open. They seemed almost red though Harrington thought it a trick of the light. She looked from her lover, to the cook, about the room, and back to Harrington. She bared her teeth, markedly longer and sharper than before, and hissed. Harrington and Swales reeled back in spite of themselves. Then, ignoring her mystifying temper and his own fear, the Englishman took her hand. The hatred vanished from her face. Ekaterina fell back – and to sleep.

"Cor!" Harrington spluttered. "Did you see that?"

Swales shuffled closer. He pulled her lips aside displaying her normal white teeth, her eyelids to show her beautiful green eyes. He and Harrington read each other's emotions; the fear and concern, curiosity and relief.

Ekaterina's eyes snapped open again. Her hands shot up before her, arms bent as if she were pressing up on some invisible flat surface. "Help me!" she shrieked. "It's dark! It's cold! Oh, God, help me! I'm in a casket! I'm buried. . . in a wooden box!"

Ekaterina screamed to freeze the blood of the young scholar, to stall the heart of the old seaman; to frighten two brave and stalwart men nearly to death.

Chapter Twenty-two

* * *

During the night, Ekaterina, who needed sleep, slept fitfully while Harrington, there to protect her, was having a time staying awake. Even Popescu's book of superstitions was unable to keep him alert. He pulled the lid off the porthole (the night offered no threat) and stared out. The latest storm seemed to have ended but a thick fog hid the moon and stars.

He splashed water on his face and grimaced at the heavy-lidded reflection in the mirror. He splashed again, showed little improvement, and toweled off. Inexplicably, a shutter ran through him. The hairs erected themselves on the back of his neck and Harrington was overwhelmed with the feeling someone was watching him.

It was an insane notion, but he checked the glass again. There was no one watching; nothing there but the dimly lit cabin, Ekaterina in her bunk, and the uncovered port (backed by swirling fog) staring back like the opaque eye of a blind cyclops. Still… the cloying feeling persisted. He turned to examine the room. It was empty and he felt foolish; scaring himself for no reason. Then his eyes found the port again – and the bone white face, framed sideways, staring in.

Harrington started in disbelief, then knocked over the ewer, splashing water, as he darted back to the mirror. There was nothing! Ekaterina, the cabin, the port reflected in reverse, but nothing else. The mirror cast no reflection of the face, nothing in the port at all. Turning, it was clear either his eyes or the glass were betraying him. The face remained, on a bizarre horizontal angle; stark white, with red-looking eyes above a heavy mustache. It sneered with red lips and raging white teeth.

He took a step toward the porthole – and the monstrous face disappeared.

Stunned, moving on instinct, Harrington threw open the door and raced out. He hit the stairs running and burst from the deckhouse to the deck, scaring the hell out of the helmsman.

"What is it?" Amramoff asked, one hand on the wheel, the other clutching his chest.

Harrington was too busy thinking to answer. The realization had struck that, in order to look through the port at that angle, the spy had to dangle at arm's length from the mizzen deck. Ridiculous! The only alternative would be to cling to the side of the ship. It was absurd! He could not have seen what he thought he saw.

"Harrington! Harrington, what is wrong?"

"Did you see anything?" the Englishman asked, passing the wheel.

"What? Did I see what?"

Harrington, leaning over the mizzen deck rail, peered into the gloom at the port to Ekaterina's cabin. That's all there was to see, a small circle of amber in the hull. Nothing else. The man, the thing with the white face, was gone. "You've been here all the time?" Harrington demanded.

"For an hour, I just came on."

"But you've been here since?"

"Of course. What is the matter?"

"Who has the watch?"

"Smirnov, for what that's worth." Amramoff laughed. "He's wandering the fog in the bow."

"When did he go forward?"

Amramoff wrinkled his nose, pulled his yellow beard in annoyance. "I saw him when I first came on. He's been forward since. What is the matter with you? What are these questions?"

"Has there been anyone in the stern with you in the last few minutes? Have you seen or heard anyone; anything?"

"There has been no one. What or who, in the name of the Emperor, were you expecting?"

"Nothing," Harrington said, coming back to the wheel. He felt slightly dazed. "No one." He headed below, muttering to himself, "My mirror played a trick on me."

But the Englishman knew it was not the mirror. It was his eyes or, perhaps, his mind.

Chapter Twenty-three

FRIDAY morning, 23 July, Swales brought the girl's breakfast and, two steps in, halted in alarm. "Are ye sick?" Harrington was a pallid sight. "Ye' look like ye've seen Popescu's boh-ghost."

"I have," the scholar said, securing the door. "I've either seen the ghost or I've lost my mind."

Swales deposited the plate on the desk. "I think, lad, ye ought make me wise."

Harrington did, as best he could, relating the events of the previous night; the bone-white face in the porthole, the absence of a reflection in the looking-glass, his race to the deck, and the vanishing act. "There is a monster on the ship."

Swales lifted Popescu's book. "Ye get thaat from this?"

Harrington arched his brow. "I've been reading that, yes. You gave it to me."

"Aye, t' keep ye awake."

"Well, I'm finally awake – to what is happening."

"There are no ghosts."

"I'm not talking about ghosts. I'm talking about something that happened. Did you read it?"

"I thumbed it 'efore I dropped it off."

Harrington took the book. "You weren't convinced?"

Chapter Twenty-three

"O' what? I dinna study it? I'm no scholar. An' though I've travelled from here to there, I'm no' a man o' the waarld like yesel'. That German is mostly Greek to me. Besides, the subject matter is no' science? It's hy-pear-bole. Superstition. An interestin' read, if ye're no' too par-ticular an' ye like that sort o' thing. Better still, a serviceable paperweight. There's nowt to convince me o' anythin'."

"Where's your open mind?"

"D' ye no' hear me?" Swales laughed derisively. "I've sailed this whole damn waarld, lad. Seen queer things in queerer places; snake charmers to cannibals, shite t' turn yer hair white an' stand it on end. An' I've learned a thing or two – in me own dense sort o' way. My mind is open. But if I'm to be convinced – aboon anythin' – t' will require substance; no' folklore."

"That's all you think it is?"

"O' course. D' no' tell me ye' believe this nonsense because o' Popescu's book?"

Harrington frowned. "It isn't just his book. I've read of these things... before my trip to Europe."

"What things?"

"Ekaterina's loss of blood. Phantom's walking the deck and disappearing at will. Men vanishing in the night." He searched the floor, thinking. "There was one... The subject matter was similar to Popescu's book; superstitions, ghosts, ghouls..." Harrington snapped his fingers. "The Magia Posthuma by von Schertz. A... Catholic lawyer who studied the case of an earth-bound spectre that attacked the living. It detailed incidents of a plague called... vampirism in Serbia, Moravia, Transylvania. Blood drinking... and the mastication of the dead!"

"Masti-cation?"

"It means to chew..."

"I gawm damn well what it means, lad! It's a fairy-tale!"

"The stories were supposedly true. The locals believed them. They were literally exhuming their own dead, disfiguring the corpses, reburying them with charms to ward off the evil eye and prevent..."

"Prevent what? D' ye hear yersel'?"

"I'm telling you what the book said; to prevent their rising from the grave. To prevent their attacks on the living. To stop the spread..."

"O' a non-existant disease."

"I admit, the authorities saw it that way; passed laws to curb the vampire hunters' activities. Made it illegal to open graves and destroy corpses."

"Just so. It's insanity. There's no evidence; can be none as it's all superstition."

"There is a vampire aboard the Demeter."

The young scholar said it so plainly, so calmly, the sentence stunned the listener. The cook stared agog - unable to respond. To end the deafening silence and keep an upper hand in the argument, Harrington soldiered on. "Even before we left Varna there was talk of this voyage being cursed."

"Talk, yes! There's nothin' new in that. Sailors grumble."

"This is different. Something *is* wrong; I saw it last night. I didn't read it in a book, I saw it! Oliver, there is a vampire aboard this ship. Weigh the facts."

"What facts?"

"In Varna, the first had difficulty signing crew."

"These are facts?"

"Listen, will you? It is a fact he had unusual difficulty signing crew. Experienced seamen walked away claiming there was something wrong with this ship."

Swales took a frustrated breath, then nodded. "O-right."

"A week and a half ago, Petrofsky reported a stranger on deck who, when he called, jumped overboard. He swore to it. Several days later, Ekaterina was found ill with wounds on her throat. That same night Petrofsky went missing. Do men simply disappear?"

"He killed his-sel'!"

"There is no proof one way or the other. So, to continue... The night of the 16th, Olgaren reported another strange man on deck

Chapter Twenty-three

who also vanished without a trace; a different man, younger. Now, was he younger? Or merely revitalized?"

Swales growled in disgust.

"Since that night," Harrington said, carrying on. "We've had four forsaken days of weather that every man in the crew has called 'otherworldly'."

"Storms a' sea happen all the time."

"In the cloudless Mediterranean? You know as well as anyone this is not storm season for these waters. Yet we've had four days of unrelenting rain and wind. It's unnatural. It's evil."

"Ye're bein' ridiculous! Ye're tellin' me some... monster... aboard ship, is controllin' the weather? Go on! Pull t' other one!"

"Wednesday morning, Katya was sick again. On the verge of recovery, her wounds reopened and she suffered a relapse. Why? And how do you explain last night? The face suspended outside the port that does not reflect in the glass? And, like the others, vanished into thin air?"

"It's nonsense!" Swales exploded. "Shear an' utter nonsense! If ye' believe any o' this, ye're out o' yer mind! An' ye' can't think fer one minute I'll have anythin' to do w' this?" The cook turned angrily away, caught the edge of the desk and took a breath. Silence consumed them.

In her sleep, Ekaterina moaned. Swales and Harrington both stepped toward her bed. She relaxed as the spasm passed and they looked at each other - embarrassed.

"I'm sorry, Trevor," Swales said. "I did no' mean that. Me father, for all I love 'im, is a bully, unable to admit he's e'er wrong. If he can't out-argue ye, he'll tongue lash ye a double share, insult and brow beat ye, embarrass or frighten ye into silence; then take yer silence for agreement. Despite my best efforts, there's too much o' the old whaler in me. I... I do no' want what ye're sayin' to be true."

"But you know it is. You believe." He waited and, finally, Swales nodded. "You knew before I did. That's the reason you borrowed that book from Popescu."

"Aye, because I'm an old fool. Ye were meant t' talk me out o' it. But ye're a fool yer-sel."

"We must find this monster and destroy it."

Swales sagged into the chair, nodded and sighed. "We'll have to do it alone. T'would be pointless to try t' convince the cap'n. We'll no' be believed. An', o' the crew, the only one would hear us would be Popescu, who'll rant an' rave but no' help."

Harrington squeezed the old man's shoulder. "Then we do it alone. We give Ekaterina what protection we can, then we find this thing."

* * *

A cold dinner was eaten by wet sailors. After, their rum ration was again passed-over due to the still-dangerous weather conditions. The crew went unhappily about their duties while Swales, his mess cleaned, returned to the sick cabin with a flour sack in his hands; the collected spoils from a private quest. He found Harrington changing Ekaterina's bandage. The sleeping girl looked tiny and frail.

"There was no blood on her hands."

"What's that?" Swales asked.

"The morning we found her, there was blood on her lips, in her mouth, on her chin... none on her hands. If it was hers, how did it get on her lips?" Harrington turned looking pale. "If it wasn't..." Hate filled his eyes. "She's been forced into some awful baptism... some black communion. There is a poison flowing through her, changing her."

"Enough, lad," Swales said, depositing his sack on the desk. "We have work."

Swales was right, there would be a time. Harrington bit it off and moved to the desk. "I want you to know," he said stiffly. "I made these because you asked." He drew a cloth-wrapped package from the bottom drawer and, laying it out, added, "They go against everything I believe in."

Chapter Twenty-three

"Aye, so ye said already." Swales frowned. "Let's see 'em."

Harrington drew back the top wrap. Beneath lay three handmade wood crosses.

"Oh aye, a fine job," Swales said. "Ye'll make a ship's carpenter yet."

"Then I'll die a happy man."

Both let that go without comment. It wasn't the first time either had spoken without thinking.

"If ye were no' a heathen bastard... If ye'd bought the lass a cross like e'ery other man in the waarld, 'stead o' that fine french necklace, ye'd no' have had to take the trouble w' these." Swales tapped one of the crosses, then pointed across the cabin. "Tie one o'er the lass. An' do no' look at me so. T'was the whole feckin' point."

Harrington secured a cross to the bunk frame above Ekaterina's head. He'd bickered with Swales upon receiving the assignment, and wrestled with himself while putting them together, for he still refused to believe in an all-powerful Being controlling the world. But he had to admit, inexplicably, he felt safer with the icons in the room and satisfied with this one keeping Katya company. "What have you in the bag?" he asked, turning back to Swales. "Steal anything useful from the galley?"

"If it's my galley, it's no' stealin'." Swales drew out several bulbs of garlic. "My last two," he said, grudgingly.

Harrington's smile threatened to become a laugh. He'd surrendered his atheistic sentiments for the cause, Swales could unhand some garlic. "Don't forget the port."

The old man separated the cloves and, using them like chalk, smeared the meat and juices into the wood around the porthole frame. He did the same on the top sill and down the door jambs. He finished scratching a garlic cross on the inside surface of the door.

He returned to his bag and withdrew a box. He opened it, sniffed, grimaced and made his distinctive grunt. "Mustard seed. Does it work if it's goin' bad?"

"I don't know if it works when it's fresh. We're following Popescu's book. There," Harrington said, pointing to the deck in front of the door. "On the floor, the width of the sill, so... it... cannot pass."

Swales shook out the contents of the box, a line of mustard seed across the opening that – superstition said – the creature could not cross. Behind him, Harrington pulled a wad of string from Swales' bag. "What's this?"

"D' ye no' remember? Tie a knot in the string e'ery three or so inches, as ye're able, so the fiend will be forced to pick it up an' count the knots one by one 'efore he can pass..."

Harrington rolled his eyes.

"We're shy most o' the things the German book calls fer," Swales explained. "... a wild rose, poppy seeds, a thorny switch o' hawthorn, holy water. Disgraceful really. With so many damned seaman aboon, ye'd think we'd be better prepared to ward off evil."

Harrington tossed the string back in the bag without tying any knots in it. "That's the lot," he said. "And a sorry lot it is."

"No' if any o' it works."

"Your confidence overwhelms."

"Oh, lad, it's no' as bad as all that. Ye're goin' to see to a few other important items."

"I am? Such as?"

"Later, lad. One t'ing at a time." Grinning like a demon, Swales reached into his pocket. "Fer instance." He withdrew a string of blue and white rosary beads and a crucifix that glinted in the lamplight.

"Where did you get..." Harrington stopped himself as a look of alarm blossomed. "Popescu! He'll lose his mind when he finds it gone."

Swales snorted a laugh. "Luv to see that! Assumin' he has one. Pure silver or I'm a mermaid."

"It's beautiful. He will go crazy."

"Fek 'im, he's already crazy. 'esides... by the time he comes off watch, it'll no longer exist. It's goin' t' vanish just like poor Petrofsky. We're goin' to melt it down."

Chapter Twenty-three

"For what?"

"Trevor, ye know more than any one man I e'er met. So how is it ye're so damned dumb? Ye read the book. We're goin' to make silver bullets."

Harrington screwed up his face. "Those are... for werewolves, aren't they?"

"Oh, aye. But if they work fer the one, why no' t' other? Particular if they come from a silver cross! Can ye argue thaat?"

"No, but - now I am confused," Harrington said with a scowl. "We haven't a gun."

Swales shook his head. "We have no gun, yet," he whispered. "But unless I miss me guess, an' unless he's diff-rent than e'ery other master to e'er put to sea, Captain Nikilov does."

"You said earlier it would do no good to tell the captain; that he would not assist us."

"Aye. So I believe."

"You mean you intend to steal a gun from the captain?"

"Jings, lad, no! I'm too old for that shite." Swales laid the rosary gently on the desk, then turned to Harrington in all sincerity. "Ye're goin' to steal it."

* * *

The gray cloud seeped through the fore hold door into the between-decks companionway. It hovered, then started aft. It passed the crew's quarters (undetected by those speaking inside) and floated on to the hall's dead-end and the door of the passenger's cabin; the girl's room. The mist began to seep into the cracks in and around the door. An instant later, the mist exploded back into the companionway.

It swirled and transformed into the dark vampire. Dracula gasped, shaken. Tears ran down his cheeks. He staggered and caught the walls to hold himself. As he recovered, he grew livid. He smashed his fists against the bulkhead. Beneath his black and iron mustache, he sank his teeth into his lower lip until his own fluids ran. "Damn you, sheep," he whispered. "You cannot protect this girl. She is already mine!" He coughed, the fetid odor of garlic clinging in his flared nostrils. He fought to catch his breath.

The door to the crew's quarters came open and Amramoff's voice rang out, "I've got to relieve Smirnov." He stepped out, turned abaft, and shouted, "Mother of God!" He fell back into the dorm. "My God!" he screamed, from the floor, pointing through the door. "My God!"

Exclamations erupted; Popescu above the others, demanding, "What is it?"

"A rat!"

"You are screaming like a woman over a rat?"

Olgaren, ducking for the sill, stepped over Amramoff and moved into the companionway. He looked aft, saw it too, and gasped, "Oh, it is huge!" A remarkable comment coming from the massive Russian. Amramoff, back on his feet, jammed the doorway with Popescu trying to pass at the same time. They wrestled out for a look.

"Lord!"

The gray-streaked black rat, twenty-five pounds at least, stared from the floor at the juncture to the captain's and passenger's cabins. It bared vicious fangs that, Olgaren didn't wonder, could have ripped the head off his *Ovcharka* (the family's sheep dog). Its beady eyes glinted red. It squealed – a noise to ice the spine. Its vile claws scratched the deck as the creature darted to the starboard. Its leathery rasp tail, the last of the animal visible, snapped the bulkhead like a bullwhip, then it too disappeared around the corner.

* * *

On duty at the wheel, the second mate had let his mind wander. Lost in thought, he was startled when the cover on the starboard scuttle, behind him, shot into the air as if an explosion had taken place below. There was no concussion merely a *poof*, as if a magic

Chapter Twenty-three

trick had been performed, and the lid went flying. Only luck and the wind dropped it back on the deck instead of in the Atlantic.

So taken aback was he, Eltsin failed to notice the mist that followed as the cover left its place. What he did notice, a beat later, were the seamen piling out from below like circus clowns; Amramoff, the character, Olgaren, the auguste (just squeezing through), and Popescu, the aggrieved whiteface, bringing up the rear as usual.

"Did you see it?" the ship's carpenter demanded.

"Again with 'Did I see it?'," Eltsin shouted. "What is everybody seeing that I see nothing?" He arched his brow. "What are you talking about? What are you men doing?"

"The rat," Olgaren put in. "The big rat; did it come this way?"

"Nothing 'came this way'!"

Amramoff shook his head, looking the deck over. It wasn't that he didn't believe the second, he just didn't believe what he'd seen. Olgaren joined him. Popescu stood and crossed himself. Eltsin watched them, certain all three had lost their minds.

Smirnov, on watch, appeared around the deckhouse moving aft. He saw the sailors probing the shadowed deck and asked what was happening. Eltsin shrugged. "I have no idea."

"It was there," Amramoff muttered. "Then it was gone."

Eltsin and Smirnov watched the hunters scour the deck then looked nervous questions at each other. What in the world was 'It'? Where in the world could 'It' have gone?

Chapter Twenty-four

"MAYBE we did not really see it," Olgaren said.

"You know we did. It's just not here."

They scanned the deck as if none had ever been there before. The rain had ended but everything within sight remained soaked, heavy, smelling of wet wood. The wind billowed the sails.

"If it did not come on deck, maybe it went below." Olgaren turned to the others. "Do you want to look in the hold?"

"I'm going to bed," Popescu said, not even considering the idea.

"You should all go to bed." The second straightened, tall at the wheel, as he remembered he was in charge. "Whatever you saw is gone. Get some rest while the storms are abated."

"You do not think we are going to hit more rain, do you, Georgiy?"

"I don't know, Moisey. I don't know anything. Go to bed."

Popescu and Olgaren headed below in silence. Amramoff remained. He'd been on his way up to relieve Smirnov of the watch when they saw... What they saw. He did so now, asking for a report.

"I have nothing. But you do. Tell me what that was about?"

"I thought I saw something," Amramoff said. "I don't know."

Smirnov frowned and turned his questioning look on Eltsin. "Don't ask me," the second said. "Like I said, I don't know anything."

221

Chapter Twenty-four

"I left my kit in the bow," Smirnov said, bitter at being left out. He turned on his heels, raised his lantern and headed into the darkness forward.

He reached the bow, set his lamp on the cathead over the starboard anchor, and leaned against the rail. His back ached terribly. His annoyance pricked him as well. Beyond the hearing of the others, the little Russian grumbled, "Everybody sees things; nobody knows anything." Had he looked over the rail, and down the hull of the schooner, he'd have been in the know.

Dracula was clinging to the side of the vessel. He'd been to the stern, to the covered port of Ekaterina's cabin and had tried to gain access. Again he had been repelled. The porthole, like the inside door, was protected by garlic. Voices at the wheel had prevented his regaining the deck and the Count had been forced to crawl the length of the ship forward. Nearing the anchor, in the quiet of the bow, the still enraged vampire started up to the rail.

Smirnov's annoyance passed quickly. True no one had let him in on the night's events but, he asked himself, did he really care? His back was killing him and his nerves were a-jangle. But his watch had been uneventful and he was relieved to be relieved. It only remained to visit the head and he could call it a day.

He pulled out a small bottle and drank. He sighed, anticipating relief, then reached to undo his belt - when something flashed in his periphery. He snapped his head to the starboard, sending an arc of pain through his back and legs, in time to see a figure, in black with a bone white face, come up and over the bulwark as if out of the sea.

He took in air but there was no time to scream. The dark figure stared, with eyes of fire, looking almost as startled as Smirnov. It lasted less than an instant before he veered at the Russian. He clamped his hand on Smirnov's face, yanked his head hard to the side and, without ceremony, sank his sharp teeth into the flesh of his throat.

The bottle fell from Smirnov's hand and bounced into the shadows on the deck. He flailed his fists, trying to fight, but the blows landed without effect and soon ceased. Dracula pulled back, dripping blood, as Smirnov began to lose consciousness. Limp as a child's rag doll, the sailor felt himself being lifted and was helpless to prevent it. The deck disappeared beneath his feet and he was airborne. Dracula dropped him over the rail at the ship's bow.

Smirnov bounced off the block and tackle, smacked the ship board and anchor, and landed caught on the swaying anchor chain. He was lodged there, feet above the racing sea, fighting to hold on to consciousness – and the chain.

Dracula growled from the rail above; cursed the sailor and whatever malevolent god or grinning devil had intervened. He yanked a handspike from the capstan and returned to the rail with murder in his eyes. He leaned, towering over the gunwhale and the terrified Russian. He brought the weapon down with all his might, smashing the handspike across the sailor's knuckles with a hair-raising crack.

Smirnov's high-pitched scream, like a terrified bird in distress, would have curdled blood had it not been lost beneath the sound of the waves pounding the prow of the ship. He lost his grip on the anchor chain and dropped into the sea. The starboard bow rammed him as the schooner raced past. The seaman bobbed like a cork then vanished into the darkness abaft.

Dracula, staring aft with red glistening eyes capable of seeing in the night, smiled as the speck of a human disappeared beneath the frothy waves.

* * *

Saturday, 24 July, Harrington was up early, wrestling with the notion of stealing a gun from the captain's cabin. Dying for air, he took his worries on deck. The first mate was steering with Amramoff nearby, technically on watch, but practically repairing a scuttle cover broken (the Emperor knew how!) in the night. Harrington acknowledged them, then headed forward to conduct his business.

Chapter Twenty-four

On his return aft, the Englishman stepped on a small bottle lying on the deck. He held it to the mast light and examined the label, reading: *Laudanum.* "Smirnov," he whispered. He whispered the name again in curiosity; and a third time with growing sadness. He looked the deck over, relieved not to find the Russian inebriated. That he'd resumed sedating himself on duty suggested that both the sailor's pain and his addiction were getting the better of him. It was reckless. And discarding the empty on deck was madness. Harrington shook his head and slipped the bottle into his pocket. Wasn't he risking his own neck by helping to hide Smirnov's condition, after all? At the first appropriate moment, he intended to give the seaman hell for his stupidity. Resolved, he started below.

But Smirnov was not in his bunk, nor the mess, nor the hold (where Harrington had memorably found him once). His impromptu search unsuccessful, the Englishman returned to the deck and initiated a new conversation with Constantin and Amramoff; short but not at all sweet. The carpenter denied seeing Smirnov since relieving him the night prior. The first had not seen him since the previous day. The little Russian, and his gargantuan mustache, had vanished from the ship.

Amramoff took the wheel, following the mate's ordered course of N.N.E. (for they were in the midst of rounding the northwest coast of Spain). Constantin left them both to rouse the commander.

* * *

Nikilov stood alone at the wheel, deep in thought, staring into nothingness. Another storm was brewing in the distance. Something equally as dark was brewing here. For the first time he was feeling it too, doom hanging over his ship.

Already a hand short, entering the Bay of Biscay with weather again threatening and now - another man lost. Smirnov, disappeared after his watch, and not seen since. Constantin, Eltsin and Harrington were giving the ship a going over, but he knew in his heart they would find nothing.

Suddenly the first was there, seemingly from nowhere, with consternation in his coal black eyes. "There's trouble brewing," he said, rubbing his bald pate with angry energy. "The men are below; meeting, grumbling."

"Seamen always grumble."

"No." The mate shook his head. "Sir. This feels... different."

Nikilov took him in. It was not like Constantin to...

The BANG of the deckhouse door interrupted his thoughts. Olgaren appeared in the doorway. He ducked to avoid hitting his head, stepped out and looked to the helm. He frowned, seeing Constantin with the captain, but did not falter. The moment was too important and not to be postponed. He inhaled, stealing himself, ducked again under the main mast boom, and stepped to them. Olgaren nodded to the mate, then addressed the commander. "Captain. The men... we talked. They asked me... Well, to speak to you... for them."

"You?" Constantin asked, incredulous, stifling a laugh.

The captain frowned at his mate, though his point was taken. Olgaren did not strike one as a spokesman. As for their grievances, he'd meant it when he told Constantin sailors always grumbled. That said, the few, Amramoff, Popescu, Swales and Olgaren were all that remained of his crew. Though he would never surrender his vessel to their whims, the situation certainly dictated they be heard. He returned his attention to the nervous seaman. "What is it, Olgaren?"

Without indulging in an outright snub, the big Russian gave the first what shoulder he dared and met the captain's eyes. "Sir, with respect, the men feel there is something wrong on this ship. And especially... there is something wrong in the hold. We, the crew and me, do not think we are going to reach port. Not as things stand. We, the crew and me, we want your permission..."

"My permission for what?"

Chapter Twenty-four

"To take the boxes from the hold... and heave them into the sea."

As if on cue, lightning burst across the blackening sky. Thunder cracked and rolled.

Nikilov ignored the dramatic weather. He cocked his head at the seaman, certain he'd misheard. "Did you say... throw our cargo into the sea?"

Olgaren, captivated and terrified by the approaching storm, as if it were an omen he'd long-feared, failed to answer.

"Olgaren," the first barked. "The master asked you a question."

"Did I hear you?" the stunned Nikilov repeated. "You want to throw our cargo into the sea?"

Olgaren washed his ham hands in the air, searching for an answer in the boards of the deck. Finally, he managed a nod.

Constantin jumped in, sneering. "Fortunate for you those Slovaks are not here!" He turned to the captain. "The peasants that delivered the boxes the morning we sailed from Varna. They threatened to kill anyone mistreating their cargo."

"The men are frightened, captain," Olgaren said.

Constantin refused to be ignored. "This is my countryman, yes?" he angrily demanded. "Popescu, yes? He's the ringleader of the round robin that sent you up here? Like a superstitious old women! He's made you absurd! Go back and tell Popescu, and the rest, they are ridiculous. The cargo is the only reason any of you have work. Without it, you might all jump into the sea!"

"Iancu." The captain patted the air to tamp the mate's fury. "Mr. Olgaren, I was not always a captain. I understand, and I am not disposed to anger. Tell the crew that. The men are concerned. We are all concerned; for our crew, our ship, and the property for which we have all put hand to paper, in pledge, to see safely to its destination. We shall not shirk our duty."

The mountainous sailor nodded sullenly. His eyes grew misty and, for a moment, it appeared the man would burst into tears. He did not. Neither did he leave the helm. Olgaren stood his ground.

"Was there something more?"

"Yes, sir. We... the crew... we wondered, sir, if... we might stand a double watch?"

"What in hell for?" the mate barked.

"That will do, Mr. Constantin. Moisey, why are exhausted men asking for extra duty?"

"The men... well, sir," Olgaren licked his lips, to no avail. "They... they are afraid to be alone."

"God dammit!" Despite knowing the captain's repulsion to foul language, Constantin could stand no more. He was mate to a bunch of children!

"You may." Nikilov told Olgaren, ignoring Constantin's outburst.

The first mate's mouth fell open. Nikilov raised a hand and looked his first unflinchingly in the eyes. "Inform the crew they may double the watch. Help them work out a schedule. Help them, Mr. Constantin. After you finish, return here."

Black eyes blazing, Constantin strode away. Olgaren, ducking the boom again, hurried to catch him. The lightning flashed as they disappeared below.

The captain leaned heavily on the wheel. The men were not alone, his fears too were growing. There would soon be trouble between his volatile mate and his increasingly agitated crew. Their frustrations, their fears, would soon drive them to violence.

* * *

"The blood is the life."

Lucy Westenra repeated it, in a whisper, and felt evil and awful for having done. It wasn't, after all, her thought; hadn't been meant for her. She'd stolen it, eavesdropped and taken it off of the wind...

It had been intended for the laughing lunatic. (That's how she had come to think of him.) She did not know who he was, where he existed, or even if he existed. He may well have been a creation of her own troubled mind, a character from her recent dreams. She'd spoken of him to no one and never would. But she thought

Chapter Twenty-four

of him, whoever he was, as the laughing lunatic, and she could not help but listen when someone, something, spoke to him on the wind. She'd heard these strange solicitations for some time now; a deep and resonant voice calling to him from the sea. She knew neither the speaker nor from whence he spoke. But she felt his God-like power.

"The blood is the life."

She listened and she envied the lunatic. Secretly, she hoped what she heard was only a preamble. In her dark thoughts, perhaps the spot wherein her dreams originated, Lucy thrilled to think she too might soon have a role to play - in whatever was to come.

"Lucy! Lucy!"

She stared out to sea from the cemetery on Whitby's eastern cliff. The tombstone against which she leaned was cold beneath her hands; the moon hidden by clouds. The dark frothy sea looked empty but, Lucy knew, that was not the case. Something was out there.

The harbor was quiet below; it too waiting.

"Lucy! Can't you hear me?"

A voice she recognized but, just then, could not place. A sweet voice full of curiosity, confusion, and not a little fear. It was at her side, calming, trying not to frighten or alarm. "Lucy. Dear Lucy..."

Mina, of course. It was Mina Murray, her closest friend. But how did she (Lucy) get to London? How, in the dark of night, had she found Mina? Silly, no! Mina had come to her, in the north, in Whitby... by the train. She and mother had met her at the station that very day; brought her to their rooms at the Crescent.

"Lucy. Come, dear. Let's not wake you. Just let me take your hand. We'll get you home again before you catch your death."

Mina had come to visit! Or was she part of the dream? If so, why was she here? What part had she to play?

It was not a dream; it couldn't be. Why, if none of it was real, were the cool winds off the North Sea fluttering her nightgown? Hardening her nipples? Turning her skin to goose-flesh? Why was her long dark hair an airborne riot? Why were her naked feet wet with dew and padded with mud? Why was her heart racing; her pulse pounding? Why were her lungs starved for air? How was it she could feel Mina's warm hand guiding her away?

If it was a dream, why was she walking amongst the graves of Whitby in the dead of night?

Chapter Twenty-five

THE following morning, Sunday, 25 July, found Lucy again in her cemetery (it was beginning to feel like hers) staring out to sea. The harbor was alive. But the workers seemed unaware they were merely marking time until... what, Lucy wondered? Lately, she'd been feeling so far away and thinking the strangest thoughts.

"Lucy!"

It took a moment to realize the call was coming, not from the sea, but from the curved staircase behind. Lucy turned to see Mina, flushed and breathless, waving a letter, running her way.

"I've been looking all over for you again!" Mina smiled, relieved. "I wanted to show you. This came in the morning post. It's from Mr. Hawkins, Jonathan's employer. He's coming home! Isn't that wonderful, Lucy? A letter from Transylvania, from Castle Dracula. Jonathan's starting for home!"

Mina threw herself at her friend. She hugged Lucy and danced around her in delight. Lucy joined her, laughing and dancing until both needed breath. Renewed, Mina began again, waving the letter, chattering her good fortune. Despite Lucy's wish to share her joy, Mina's words began to fade while Lucy's own attentions were drawn away to the north and east. Mina droned happily.

Lucy stared hopefully out to sea.

Chapter Twenty-five

* * *

What a marvelous show!

Dracula lay in his box, delighted by how deliciously events were coming to fruition. He laughed quietly, cruelly, relishing the moment. He'd felt her presence for some time but, busy with the crew of *Demeter* and with Renfield, had not pursued the contact. Now, assuredly, he would.

Her name was Lucy. She was easily as sensitive to his thoughts as the lunatic had proven to be. She lived in Whitby, which was paramount to his needs, and she was a close friend of Jonathan Harker's fiancée. Through Lucy, he'd heard all... Mina ecstatic over one of the three letters written by Harker at his insistence (which the Count himself posted). Her joy at Harker's supposed return. There would be none; his wives would long-ago have seen to it that Harker was dead.

Now, here was their beloved Lucy. She would be his first... taste of England. It was all he could do not to roar with laughter at the irony. There was only one word – delicious!

He surrendered the idyllic scene in the cemetery, for the voices around him required attention.

Dracula could hear the frightened whispers of the crew, their terrified mouthings. He relished the fear growing round him like crops. But there was a vexatious undercurrent that concerned him; weeds in his garden. Serious mutterings among some of the whisperers. Their fears were generating a desire to lash out at their unknown enemy. Their panicked activities, searches of the ship, prying eyes gaping into the hold, had been annoyance enough. Now came threats to cast his boxes into the sea. Dracula knew human nature (like no human on earth). Most of the remaining crew would cower in the corner of their floating cage like frightened rabbits, but a few among them were starting to kick in a misguided attempt at self-defense. That could not be allowed; not when he was so near his destination. He had to prevent them – by keeping them in jeopardy.

So it was the vampire, vibrant with Smirnov's blood, again turned the powers of darkness upon the elements. Soon thereafter, *Demeter* was in the midst of another devastating storm with a wind that buffeted her from ever-changing directions. The sea rose up and pounded the schooner. The waves broke over her bulwarks, washed her decks and set the crew battling for their lives.

Secreted below, pitching and rolling with the ship, but no longer pestered by the humans aboard, Dracula could concentrate on other things.

* * *

Renfield rose quietly and crept to the barred window... to gaze at the moon shining on the sanitarium garden and, in the distance, the deserted Carfax Abbey estate. Its untended grounds were hidden by a separating stone wall, but the top of the desolate main hall was visible and, beyond, the peak of its attached and partially ruined chapel.

"Yes. Yes," Renfield whispered, replying to a message only he could hear.

"*Prepare ye the way of the master.*"

So little to ask really, adoration, obedience. For this devotion... a promise of the world and all the blood-filled creatures in it. All would be given him, if he would obey. But fail the master and he would be punished with excruciating death, damnation, and all of the eternal tortures the demons of hell could conceive.

Renfield gripped the iron bars... and swooned.

* * *

The devastating weather continued unabated on Monday, 26 July. The waves tossed the ship and overwashed her decks. Despite the hatch covers being closed, sea water sluiced down the hatchways. Everything between-decks was as wet as everything

Chapter Twenty-five

up top. The spirits of the brave crew-members flagged, unaware as they were that...

Count Dracula guided the earthly elements of water and air. Then, turning his focus on his human disciples, from his dark, damp box of earth, he heard what Lucy heard:

* * *

"I saw her from the window last night. Already across the drawbridge, she had climbed the stairs to the Abbey cliff. Her slippers, the hem of her nightdress, were soaked. I could think of nothing to do, so I simply followed her. I feared waking her. You do hear it's wrong to wake a sleepwalker. She paused in the graveyard staring out to sea as if she were waiting for something on the horizon. But there was no horizon; it was as black as pitch. Finally, she dropped her shoulders as if in surrender and turned for home."

"I'm so grateful you were there. Do you think, Mina, it would help to lock her door?"

"I do, Mrs. Westenra, but was afraid to suggest it for fear you might think –"

"That you were being cruel? I think nothing of the kind. I know how much you love Lucy. But I am so afraid, Mina, some terrible dark force is trying to exert itself over my daughter; her life, perhaps her soul. Please do, lock her door at night until these nightmares subside."

"Every night, Mrs. Westenra, I promise you. I'll do all I can to protect our dear Lucy."

Lucy pulled her ear from the drawing room doors and hurried away. She should not have been eavesdropping, she knew. But some dark part of her needed to know. Clutching her night gown, her bare feet on the polished floor, she hurried up the stairs – before she was caught.

She wanted to scream, to cry, but knew she could do neither. It was so embarrassing. By definition, she had no control over her sleepwalking. If only Mina and her mother understood how frightening it was. If only they could hear the voice from the sea. The whispered words of admiration, the warnings against disobedience. If, somehow, she could explain the dreams that made her walk the halls of the Crescent, to venture the streets of Whitby. The frightful nightmares with the dark man (Arthur Holmwood certainly?) in shadow. His promises of an eternal love, if she obeys.

She closed the door to her room and leaned trying to catch her breath. It was all so confusing. But she knew one thing, she was not sleepwalking now. They intended to lock her in at night. She'd heard every word.

Lucy was unaware that Dracula had heard every word as well.

* * *

"'ain't ye ashamed now?"

"Ohhh, Mar-tin!" Renfield tripped, nearly falling, as the outraged orderly dragged him from the garden, through the side entrance, toward his room in the ground floor rear (where his antics were least likely to bother others). Renfield stumbled, while Martin grumbled all the way.

"It's no good, mate," the orderly insisted. "'avin' at flies an' spiders in yer room is one fing. Scaring 'ell out o' the other residents is quite an'of-er. Yer've no call makin' a nuisance, in-truptin' the of-ers treatments." The orderly, more than usually angered, had searched the whole property. "Yer not the only one tryin' t' get 'is sense back. When ye come over that big wall, ye scared the livin' daylights out of everyone what saw ye. The nurse will never be the same. Yer've no business at the old Abbey. That's private property, see. Ye'll be killed in that ruin and never found." Martin sat Renfield on his cot. "Ye' 'ear? Yer've no right. What ye doin' at Carfax anyway?"

Renfield scowled, a look he generally reserved for Dr. Seward, but said nothing.

Chapter Twenty-five

"'ave it yer way. But that's it, ol' fly eater. Now, yer goi-in' to fink a-bout what yer've done."

A slam and a snick of the key in the lock. Renfield, alone, threw himself against the door. He tried the knob, knowing it was locked, then sagged to the floor in a heap.

"Forgive me," Renfield whined. "Forgive me... master."

In his box, in *Demeter's* cellar, Dracula laughed, enjoying the game, then replied without anything like laughter. His message, across the distance, echoed in Renfield's tortured mind. "*I do not forgive. I do not forget. Do not fail me. Obedience brings reward. Failure brings death and damnation. Prepare ye the way of the master.*"

* * *

The devastating weather continued all of Tuesday, 27 July. *Demeter*, hopelessly windlocked for a full day now, was running the Red Queen's race. Even stubborn Nikilov was forced to admit it and surrender. The sails were dropped; and both anchors. The ship bobbed between the swells, riding out the blow, her bare poles and furled spars pointing like skeletal fingers at the lightning-streaked sky.

The air between-decks was growing stale but, with the waves still breaking over the ship, going topside for fresh was out of the question. Watches, despite safety lines tied about the deck, had been curtailed because of the dangers. The steersman, lashed to the deckhouse by an afterline, manned the helm and deck alone in vastly shortened (one hour) shifts. The schooner was miraculously holding together. But cracks were appearing in the psyches of her crew.

Popescu, always grumbling, did so now under his breath. (His mother's rosary, it seemed, had been misplaced.) He used the little energy not sapped by the storm to cast suspicious stares around. He prayed often, but only for himself. Amramoff and Olgaren, the two longest with captain and ship, were thick as thieves but growing distant from the rest of the crew. Olgaren spoke only to Amramoff and slept every moment he wasn't on deck. The carpenter feigned good humor but failed to convince. His familiar laugh was gone.

As for the mates... Eltsin moved about as if he were a cat – silent, alert. For what, nobody knew. Constantin was more brooding and unapproachable than ever. Captain Nikilov, hardly gregarious in the most social settings, grew even more introspective.

Swales, the eldest, was also the busiest. With their dwindling numbers, the watch and meal schedules had gone to smash. With the weather pounding hell out of them, no fires could be lighted – and no hot food be had. Swales saw to it that cold meals were available. When he was not preparing food, he was tending the girl (still thought a boy by half those left).

The ailing Harrington suffered in the extreme and, were it not for his concerns for Ekaterina's welfare, would have given up completely. Like the others, he was cold, wet, miserable, and had had virtually no sleep in days. Unlike the others, Harrington was no seaman. When he was up and about, the scholar fretted at their interrupted efforts to find the vampire in their midst.

Swales could only agree. They'd had no time to hunt, to melt the crucifix, to make the bullets, to steal the gun. The weather was marking both as woefully inadequate menaces to the monster.

At the same time, the rumor solidified among the men that the ship's curse was responsible for the weather that plagued them. The captain would not accept it and the first would not hear it. Swales and Harrington believed the whispers were closer to the truth than any aboard imagined. But that conviction brought with it an alarming paradox; the devastating sea made it all-but impossible to slay the monster, yet destroying the creature was precisely what had to be done to end the horrible weather.

* * *

Chapter Twenty-five

Though it couldn't be told for the clouds, night fell again on the sea, somewhere between the Bay of Biscay and the English Channel, and on *Demeter* lost therein.

On her tossing deck, unseen by human eyes, a swirling vapor escaped from beneath the battens on the forward hatch. The fluctuating cloud took shape and an aged, gray Dracula strode the bow alone. Washed in rain, wrapped in fog, he stretched out his hands... concentrating across the miles...

Lucy's eyes came open, though she still slept, as Mina left the room. Stealthily, as if in a dream, she rose from bed and padded to the door. She laid her ear against it and listened. There, again, outside, Mina and her mother conspiring.

"Lucy? Is she..."

"She walks more than ever, Mrs. Westenra. Every night I'm awakened by her moving about. Pulling on the door; trying to get out. To where, for what, I don't know." Mina sighed, sounding weary.

Lucy felt a pang for the anxiety she was causing. Her nocturnal activities were awakening Mina. Her friend was growing nervous; finding it difficult to sleep herself. But what could she do?

"Thank God, Lucy's health has kept up." So good. Mina was always thinking of others. "Her cheeks are a lovely rose-pink. She's lost the anemic look she had. It's just that... Lucy seems in such great anticipation of – I don't know – something."

"You mean something – good?"

"Yes," Mina said reassuringly. "Oh, yes, Mrs. Westenra. I just pray it will last."

They moved away and the hall fell silent. Lucy tried the door and, as expected, found it locked. She knew they were only looking out for her welfare. She knew they meant only the best for her. But...

Why are they doing this to me! Why are they trying to keep me from you!

Lucy sank onto the floor beside the door – crying softly.

* * *

Martin had had it! London was a thirty minute train ride west. Why in hell was he still there?

Renfield was gone again. Martin had searched the sanitarium and grounds, top to bottom, and come up empty. The orderly was back inside, wondering how he would explain the man's absence, when he heard screams on the ground floor. He made out two voices as he hurried that direction; Dr. Seward's, and the high whine and hideous laugh of the ole fly-eater himself.

"Renfield! Put it down! I will not tell you again!"

Martin, out of breath and patience, passed into the doctor's study without knocking. There stood Seward issuing orders. On the other side of his desk crouched the laughing Renfield, ignoring the psychiatrist for all he was worth. The lunatic clutched the sanitarium's calico cat by the nape of the neck, licking his lips while Tabby struggled.

"'ere now! 'ere now! Come along, ole fly eater!" Martin grabbed the cat away.

"Ohh, Martin!"

"Listen 'ere." The orderly set the terrified animal down. It raced from the room. "Ye're go-in' t' leave off that cat, see! Tabby belongs t' the lot, see. An' ye are go-in' t' leave off chasin' her. Ye scare 'ell out o' that poor fing."

"Ohh, Mar-tin!"

"Not an-ofer word! I've had me fill of ye'. Come along."

"But he gave her to me!" Renfield blubbered.

"What're ye talkin' about?"

"The calico cat!" Renfield whined. "The master gave her to me!"

"Renfield, please," Seward said, wearily. "I did no such thing."

Renfield stopped in his tracks. Struck dumb, he turned and stared at the doctor – as if he were a bug. Then he broke into laughter.

"Come along, ol' fly-eater."

Laughing hysterically, Renfield allowed the orderly to escort him out and away.

Dracula was laughing as well.

Chapter Twenty-five

Forward of the foremast, the ship pitching and bucking at her anchors in the raging sea, the vampire stood in flux. He surrendered his human form, becoming a mist, as each wave lipped the bulwark and dashed the deck. The water passed through him. Between the blasts of water and foam, he resumed his solid form.

Just so, like the phantom the crew feared, the aged Dracula stood his own watch in the bow.

* * *

Wednesday, 28 July, brought more of the same, persistent rain, spasmodic bursts of lightning, and a hapless schooner tugging at her anchor chains with every indication she would do so all day long. No progress whatever was made, and no one aboard had the least idea of where they were. But, late in the afternoon, hints appeared their luck might be changing. The weather, while miserable (particularly for the green lubber among them), began to slacken. Near sundown, or the time the sun ought to have set, the storm arrested itself enough that the deck finally saw human traffic.

The wheel was lashed. The captain stood the helm in lamplight, lost in thought as was becoming his habit, when a shout from the deckhouse caught his attention.

"Four days of this!" The second mate stepped out, his oilskins shining as if he'd been for a swim. "Four days," Eltsin repeated, "in hell!"

Maybe he was tired, maybe he'd been dulled by the weather and the days, either way Nikilov ignored the junior officer's impertinent oath. Besides, he was right. Even heaven would not debate they'd been knocked about. The captain laid a hand atop the wheel, nodded, and sighed, "Aye."

"I'm so stiff and weak I can scarcely move."

"I feel for you, Georgiy; for you and with you. Try doubling your age."

His complaining was idiotic, Eltsin knew. They'd been through it, the evil days, together. He'd endured nothing that the others had not. It was a poor beginning to what he'd actually come to discuss. "Captain," he said, searching for the words and the courage to start again. "The talk going round. Do you not think it possible something aboard the ship is causing the weather?"

"We've had this out, Mr. Eltsin."

"Yes, sir, but..."

"What does it mean, causing? Are you asking if someone here is controlling the weather?"

"You said, captain, you've never seen such violent weather, for so long, in these seas. Nor I, nor anyone, I imagine. Late August storms, on the Banks, yes. But here? Now? It's not natural, this endless tempest. Maybe whatever is aboard the ship... this nameless horror..."

"There's nothing aboard my ship, Mr. Eltsin!" Nikilov, rarely a shouter, saw the fear in the second mate's eyes and regretted his tone. He lowered his voice. "There is nothing aboard this ship that ought not be. Nothing but fear. Fear is our trouble; the most destructive cargo a ship can carry." The captain's eyes hardened with determination. "Georgiy, I need your help. The men are not wrong, but they have the wrong target. This fear is the cargo that must be jettisoned, thrown into the abyss, that the heads and hearts aboard this ship can right themselves."

The second trembled involuntarily. Fighting to still it, he nodded and said, "I will help you, captain, however I am able."

Nikilov smiled (the first time in four days). "Why are you not sleeping... when you have the chance?"

"Everyone is abed. But no one sleeps," Eltsin said. "They are, perhaps, too exhausted."

"Aye." The wheel bucked. Nikilov unlashed her, took firm hold of the spokes, and talked to the rudder with his hands. The stern came round, climbing off an angry hill of water, and quieted the growl of the anchor chains. He returned to his conversation as

Chapter Twenty-five

if they'd never been interrupted. "Between us, Georgiy, I hardly know how to set a watch anymore. No one is fit to go on duty."

The second nodded. "I'll watch, sir, and steer when need be. You've been too long. And the others... Let them rest a few more hours. Perhaps they'll sleep."

Nikilov looked over his sodden deck, criss-crossed with lines, rain barrels puking their overflow with each swell, dripping reefed sails on the mizzen and main, furled spars on the fore (looking like Christ's cross on Golgotha against the rolling clouds). The wind gusted sporadically but appeared to be waning. The seas remained terrific, but the captain could feel them calming. Tomorrow, he thought with relief, tomorrow we shall get underway again.

"Yes," Nikilov heard himself telling Eltsin. "Perhaps just a little rest."

* * *

Night fell. *Demeter* remained at anchor in a rough – but easing – sea, and Eltsin remained at the lashed wheel alone. He wasn't complaining. He'd volunteered as watch and unsteering steersman. The crew were too exhausted to double up as they had been or even walk the regular watches. They'd earned a break, and their sanity demanded it. The captain and mate were certainly pulling their load and more. Eltsin was not complaining. He was able and it was his duty. That said, he didn't like it one bit.

He had a *feeling*. Eltsin was the kind of man who got feelings. When he did, he usually acted upon them and rarely regretted having done. Something now was giving him a feeling. There was a vibration in the air he did not like. (The fog which had increased despite the winds was not helping.) He'd sensed it before, on this voyage; the queer feeling around the forward hold. It was insane, Eltsin knew, he'd already proven it. All those hours standing guard, with nothing in the hold but fifty boxes of dirt and one idiot. He laughed at his own foolishness.

He was still laughing when he walked away from the helm.

***

Eltsin found himself below, at the foot of the deckhouse stairs, as if in a dream. His shadow stretched, long and thin, down the companionway owing to the dim light from the deck lantern above. He was halfway forward, without realizing he'd taken a step, when something within roused the second to consciousness. What was he doing? He'd left his watch! He'd left the helm! They may have been at anchor, but they were still at sea, and there was nobody on top to keep the ship trim. He could not be that irresponsible. And yet...

Eltsin entered the crew's quarters, felt his way to the carpenter's bunk, and slipped his hand over Amramoff's mouth. "You're needed," he whispered. "Get up."

Amramoff drug himself from the depths, shook his cone head and hair like a party favor, and groggily pulled his boots on. He grabbed his kerchief, dangling from his shelf, and shambled out, closing the door behind.

"Take the watch, Pasha," the second said. "We're still berthed. Just keep her trim. If God ever rejoins the voyage, well... we'll see." He turned his attention forward, down the dark companionway.

"You all right?"

Eltsin did not answer but pointed, absently, to the stairs and the deck. Amramoff obeyed, climbing up and out into the fog. The second turned back into the ship feeling the *feeling*, whatever it was, stronger than ever. He moved slowly forward in the dark between-decks.

Something beyond the hold door - was calling him.

***

Eltsin struck a match. Its glow, though he didn't know how or why, found him already standing in the forward hold. He put the flame to the lantern then lifted it from its bracket. He scanned the dark; boxes (tarped and not), barrels, cartons, and stark shadows

Chapter Twenty-five

all around. The door to the companionway was closed, and he had no memory of having passed through it. The *feeling* had carried him there.

"What are you?" Eltsin whispered. "I know you are here! You are responsible for... what's happened to the crew. You are the cause of this weather. You have beaten us to death." He cleared his throat, his voice rising in anger. "I'm not afraid of you! I am going to find you! I will destroy you!"

Behind him, unseen, in silence, a spider descended from the overhead on a silken thread.

She was a Mediterranean black widow, roughly the size of the new 10 ruble gold coin, and she glinted black with thirteen red spots on her round abdomen. Her eight legs flexed like skeletal fingers as the creature spun her way to the deck. Her tiny body teemed with deadly venom. To her side, on her own thread, descended a second spider as if they were running a race. Beside the second, came a third. And another. And another yet.

The hairs stood up on the back of Eltsin's neck. His arms turned to goose-flesh. And, for the life of him, he did not know why.

Then, before him, he saw a black spider drop from the overhead. It descended on a silken tether, spinning as it fell. Beside it came another. And, beside that, another still. He drew in a lung-full of stale, wet air and, with a shaking hand, lifted his lantern. The amber glow ushered in his horror. Dozens of them! Black widow spiders falling from the overhead like rain, trailing silver bars of silk to the deck.

"My God!"

So engrossed was Eltsin in his terror, he nearly missed hearing the laughter altogether. Finally, it settled in his ears and on his psyche; a rich timbered laugh that shook the second to his core. He turned, bringing the lamp's yellow light, to see the web wall and spiders behind him and, beyond that, the figure of a man standing in the shadowy depths of the hold. Eltsin halted, his lantern shaking as he fixed the beam upon the stranger, and gasped!

The light was reflected by red-looking eyes set in the white face of an old man; the tall, old man described by Petrofsky – dead and gone Petrofsky. He was looking at the ship's ghost!

Too horrified to form intent, Eltsin moved on instinct fueled by blind fear. He had to escape the hold! He ran – smack into the vertical webs behind him. He screamed, disgusted by their sticky grasp, tripped, and fell violently on his face. His lamp hit the deck with a clang; still intact, still lit. Rising, clawing at the web silk, the second stumbled again and fell into his hammock – still swaying in the same spot he'd hung it so many days before.

The spiders attacked, dozens of them skittering over the hammock, his clothes, his flesh in the gloom. They began to bite. Eltsin screamed, repeatedly, shocked by the agony. Their attack was relentless, excruciating, and covered his body; arms, legs, chest and face. They bit him and injected their venom.

Eltsin groaned from the pain. Welts rose quickly around the bite wounds; dozens of them, swelling, seeping blood. His muscles began to cramp. His breathing to falter. His bleeding lower lip tripled in size. His left eye disappeared behind a swollen lid.

A new pain stung his widely dilated right eye. Tears welled, further blinding him, as a bright light stabbed. Gasping for breath, struggling to see, he could just make out the stranger's silhouette – the devil in the hold – standing above him with what must have been his own dropped lantern.

"The spiders," the devil said, laughing. "They spin their webs for the unwary fly... for the blood is the life." He held the lamp near his white face, his red eyes, his sharp teeth – and he blew out the flame.

In the pitch black of the dank hold, Georgiy Eltsin screamed.

Chapter Twenty-six

EVEN Popescu found reason for cheer Thursday morning, 29 July. The ship lay steady at anchor and the storm, as far as he could hear and feel, was finally over. He wasn't cheerful, of course, but he had reason for cheer – until he stepped on deck. His discovery of Amramoff at the wheel, instead of the expected second mate, put him right on edge again, "What are you doing here?" he grumbled.

The carpenter stared back – stricken – offering no reply. Terror filled his eyes.

"What's the matter with you? Where is the second?"

Amramoff's lips quivered. Popescu grabbed the steersman by the shoulders. "Pasha, where is Georgiy Eltsin?" The Russian began to cry, shaking his head uncontrollably. "All right. It's all right." Popescu squeezed his shipmate's arm. "I'm going forward for a look..."

"N-No!" Amramoff sputtered, tears running into his beard. "No, don't go! He went forward and he never came back!"

"The second mate?"

"He went forward. He never came back!"

"He is not below. He's not in his bed."

Amramoff merely trembled and cried.

"Stay here; stand the helm. Can you just hold the wheel? I'm going forward to look. I will be right back." Popescu was not a

Chapter Twenty-six

courageous man. But the carpenter was not helping and, frankly, was frightening him so the Romanian wanted to get away. "Stay here. Hold the wheel."

Popescu headed forward. He made the foredeck quickly, then slowed. Beyond the deckhouse, he paused for a handful of water from a starboard rainbarrel (his mouth had gone dry). He splashed his face, took in a chest-full of air, and... advanced ten steps when he stopped cold.

The forward hatch doors lay open.

"Mr. Eltsin? Hello. Georgiy, are you there?" He inched forward until the whole of the hatchway opening came into view and froze at his own gasp.

An enormous spider web, in an intricate pattern of silver-gray, covered the inside of the hatchway. He crossed himself and strained to peer into the hold beyond the cloud of web work. "Mr. Eltsin, are you there?"

Popescu reeled back, dizzy with vertigo. He gulped air to clear his head. He turned to the stern, his heart racing, and shouted, "All hands on deck! Everybody on deck!" The ship's bell began to ring. Amramoff had, apparently, emerged from his stupor. "All hands on deck! Everybody on deck!"

* * *

Within minutes, what remained of the crew were on deck; the captain, mate, Swales (looking ancient), Olgaren, Harrington, Amramoff (still at the helm, but alert again) and the shaking Romanian who'd called them up. Popescu led all to the open forward hold. Their exclamations as they drew near, from awe, to alarm, to abject terror, made it obvious all were as startled and impressed by the silken web work as he. All except the first mate.

"It's a spider web!" Constantin said with distain. "So what!"

"Mr. Eltsin is missing."

"What has one to do with the other?" The mate tore away the edge of the web above the ladder. He kicked a hole through it, ghostly whisps clinging to his boot, and started down. For a moment, his lantern glowed warmly from the silent dark. Then Constantin screamed, not in terror, but in anger; unbridled rage. A blue fire oath flew from the hold, followed by the repeated sounds of his heels against the deck. Then came a shout over the stomping. "*Karakurts!*"

It was the Balkan name for a deadly spider and looks of horror traveled around the deck. The collective shock was interrupted by another shout.

"Get down here and help me!"

Olgaren dropped down, stomping the black widows to paste. The others filtered down, joining their dance, stomping the remaining spiders, chasing those that tried to escape, struggling through and tearing down the web work curtains stretched through the hold.

"Watch yourselves! Be alert, in numbers they kill!"

It was good advice, delivered almost too late, as one particularly large black widow dropped on Olgaren's shoulder. He hollered, stumbling off-balance, as he slapped at it. He fell over... something... Eltsin's hammock. Olgaren shook the spider off. He turned to catch his breath - and froze in horror. The Russian let fly a scream none aboard could ever have forgotten; the terrors of his soul rising at once.

In the hammock (rocking beneath him to the swell of the anchored vessel), wrapped with the hammock in a cocoon of spider's silk, gray as a marble statue at the gateway to hell, was the ship's second. What little of Eltsin was visible showed him horribly bitten, swollen; one eye staring lifelessly out in terror. Ignoring Olgaren, the black widows scrambled over their web-enclosed work of art.

* * *

The details can be guessed, the exclamations as each man was made aware of what lay there; the wails, the whispers, the dumbstruck stares that followed! Popescu's self-righteous claim Eltsin bearded the lion in its own den, Harrington's snigger at the

Chapter Twenty-six

pompous Romanian mixing his biblical metaphors, Constantin's irate oaths as he ordered Popescu, then everyone, to shut their heads. Eltsin's hammock was cut down. The decimated, silk-wrapped corpse was lifted to the deck, hauled to the bulwark, and wrapped in anchor chain.

"Throw it over," Nikilov said in a whisper.

"Sir?" Olgaren asked. "What about a burial?"

"The captain did not require a body for Petrofsky's service," Constantin growled. "He doesn't need one now." The men, silently staring at the deck, only made him angrier. "You were all so eager to lighten the ship's load before... Throw the damned thing over. Get it off the ship!"

With a handful of spiders still weaving on Eltsin's hammock cocoon, and without ceremony, the late second mate was chucked into the sea. The glum lot stared after it until the captain asked for their attention. "Mr. Swales, Mr. Popescu, eh Mr. Harrington, if you are willing, young man," Nikilov said. "Please return to the hold. Make sure of these... spiders. Every one of them must be done away with. Diligence, with all care." The three started below, and even Popescu kept his dissent to himself.

"Mr. Constantin, it is past time we got underway. Set sails, while I figure where in heaven's name we are."

The captain went for his sextant, while the mate, Olgaren and Amramoff went aloft.

* * *

Finally underway again, on a smooth N.N.W. heading, captain and mate took the helm and watch and dismissed the crew to eat. Nikilov might not, and Constantin assuredly would not, have done had they known the crew would turn the quiet meal (no one was hungry) into a clamorous meeting. Not surprisingly, the superstitious Popescu led and, in short order, had the others near panic.

"Wurdulak! What is that?" Amramoff stroked his pointed beard. "What is the Wurdulak?"

Popescu, who'd introduced the word, now hesitated. Harrington answered for him. "The vampyre. The dead man who drinks blood."

"What? Why a blood drinker?" the carpenter asked the scholar. He turned his question, and his questioning eyes, on Popescu. "Who has had their blood drinked?"

Harrington opened his mouth and Swales kicked him under the table. "Hey!" he yelped, twisting in the cook's direction. Swales shook his head. The rest of the group, intent on Popescu and his outrageous claim, ignored their antics.

"Whose blood," Amramoff reiterated. "Why this... Wurdulak?"

"Can you explain three men dead?" Popescu asked.

"Accidents happen at sea. That's not news. They say the Gloucester fishing fleet alone loses a hundred-fifty men a season on the Banks."

"But they know how and when; ships and dories lost, men overboard in storm, accidents. We float. We have had no accidents, save Petrofsky's hand, and the head knock from which young Funar seems unable to recover." Popescu ignored Swales cold stare. "These are our only accidents. Funar lives. Petrofsky did not die from his hand. No. He disappears, without a peep, on a calm night. Smirnov too; no ripple, merely gone. Who or what killed them?"

"A monster killed them? Who then? Who is this blood drinking corpse that haunts us, Bogdan? Who is this Wurdulak?"

"Feliks Petrofksy."

The wind whistled down the stove pipe. The sea raced past the side of the vessel. No one breathed in the mess. Until... Olgaren spoke the first words, outside those to Amramoff, he'd spoken in days. "Petrofsky," he said, simmering, "was a friend of mine."

"Yes, of course," Popescu replied, unphased. "That is the point. The Wurdulak befriends all of his victims. He attacks only friends and family. He made friends with everyone in the crew. Yet, he

Chapter Twenty-six

harbored darkness and sadness. Because of this ship, the rumors of a curse..."

"Spread by you!"

"Was I alone?"

Olgaren looked to the others then, embarrassed, shook his head. Energized by this minor victory, Popescu continued. "Petrofsky killed himself because of his fear. In doing so, he fullfilled his own prophecy. He is cursed and returns from the dead to feed off of his friends. He will kill us all."

"Nonsense!" The room was abuzz with cries of "Ridiculous superstition!" One raised his hands for silence. "The second did not die by some blood drinker. Eltsin was killed by spiders."

"Aye." Popescu spit his disgust. "The devil's spawn. Petrofsky is a Wurdulak because he killed himself. His suicide made evil manifest. Because of him, the devil commands this vessel – and the legion of hell to attack it."

Amramoff joined Olgaren with a derisive noise of his own.

"Have you ever seen so many black widows? So many deadly vermin? You saw it."

"We all saw," Amramoff said. "So what? What are you talking about?"

"This ship. The curse on *Demeter*."

"Blah, blah," Olgaren said, slapping the table with a frightening BANG. "You make us out idiots. What are you? The curse. Blah, you talk. I ought to cut your lying throat!"

"Go ahead," Popescu said. "Or just wait and the curse will do it for you."

"What are you talking about!" Olgaren jumped up, rapping his crown on an overhead beam. He growled and gripped the top of his skull. No one dared laugh. Through gritted teeth, he demanded again, "What are you talking about?"

"We are a doomed ship. Those that the Wurdulak does not kill, the devil will."

Cries went round again. "Easy, lads," Swales said. "T'is a strange waarld. As fer masel', I believe 'im."

A clamor again. Harrington, afraid for Ekaterina, worried their plans would fall apart, returned the favor and kicked Swales. "Here!" the cook yelled. He raised a hand to the Englishman, signaling all was well, then turned to the others. "Here now, all of ye! What I meant was..." He turned to Popescu. "I believe *you* believe this super-stition. But thaat's what it is, lad. E'ery country, e'ery village has them. My own adopted town, Whitby, our destination, has a haunted Abbey where a White Lady is said t' walk the broken halls. Fer centuries they've seen her in the top window."

"Then she is real!"

"She's a reflection o' the sun off a bit o' metal flashin'. I'll show ye when we get there."

"I fear we will not get there," Popescu whispered. He crossed himself. "You may not believe in your White Lady, but I do. And I believe in *Demeter's* monster."

* * *

The meeting broke up. The men floated out, to the deck or their berths. Popescu delayed his departure to keep an eye on Swales and Harrington. Something about them had spurred his curiosity. He peered out to see the cook following Harrington to the passenger's cabin. Swales darted a look back as they turned the corner but Popescu had already retreated. The Scot saw only empty hall. Swales returned his attention aft, speaking to Harrington; both unaware they were overheard.

"Why in hell did ye kick me?"

"For the same reason you kicked me. Oliver, no one believed Popescu. They won't believe us either; and we cannot have interference. We must protect the ship and crew, but Ekaterina comes first."

Popescu pricked his ears at the unfamiliar name. Who was Ekaterina? Before he was able to give the question voice, he got his answer. Harrington opened the cabin door and greeted someone

Chapter Twenty-six

inside. The eternally ill deck boy replied. Yet, something about Funar's voice was... different.

Popescu slipped toward the juncture to better see and hear. The cook and the English passenger were just entering. Popescu stole a glance between them, managing a look, as they closed the door. He could not believe his eyes. A sickly looking Funar was on his bunk in a flowing night shirt. But dressed so, without a smudged face and his trademark knit cap, it was plain as day...

Funar was... a young woman!

* * *

"How are you?" Harrington asked, his hand against Ekaterina's forehead. She was pale, her skin clammy and cool.

"Tired. I was about to lie down."

"That's an excellent idee," Swales said, over his shoulder. "Get yer-sel' settled, while I bend Trevor's ear." He led Trevor across the cabin, and whispered, "There's no time like the present, lad."

"I'm sorry?" Harrington asked, lost.

"The gun. Unless this undead thing is daft he'll know we're comin' for 'im. We need that gun. The sea's calm, the crew, cap'n and mate are on deck. If yer're e'er goin' to get it, t'will be now."

"But we haven't made the bullets."

"I ha' no' been keen t' light a fire, have I? One thing at a time. An' right now, the cap'n's cabin is toom!"

"I need to think about this."

"There's no time left fer thaat! I'll look to the wee lass. You get the gun."

The details of the Englishman slipping into the captain's berth to search could be stretched in the telling. But it isn't necessary. He accomplished it quickly and quietly, on his toes, without being seen. Nikilov and the mate were plainly heard, through the scuttles, at the helm, in a rousing discussion with the crew. Popescu was shouting his head off.

Popescu spilled the beans. The crew laid down their work and, as one, approached the con demanding – with the Romanian as their mouth piece – answers to two pointed questions. Was there a woman aboard the ship? Had she come aboard as a member of the crew?

"Who the hell do you think you are?" Constantin bawled. "Go back to your work. Or is this a mutiny?"

"No, sir," Popescu sneered. "Is no mutiny. Neither, sir, shall we go back to work."

"How dare you!" Constantin raised his hand to strike.

And would have had Nikilov not intervened. "Belay that, Mr. Constantin." He watched his first lower his hand, then turned to the crew. He saw anger, embarrassment, and fear in their faces – and felt it his responsibility, his failing.

"The answers to your questions are, yes, and yes. There is a woman aboard. She came aboard in masquerade, as Rada Funar, without our knowledge. She was discovered following her injury. If any of you feel *lied to,* I apologize. But, understand, I was fooled, and made a fool, before the rest of you."

"I knew it!" Popescu turned to his shipmates. "I told you!" He crossed himself. "I told you in Varna this ship was cursed. Now it unfolds!"

"There is no curse on this ship. There is a stowaway aboard, nothing more."

The men, led by Popescu, were grumbling.

"Our problems started with that... that girl... being allowed aboard."

"Let me be clear about this," Nikilov said. "The girl is not to be touched. I am responsible for her and you will leave her alone. She will be dealt with when we reach Whitby."

"She started it, but it does not end with her," Popescu said. "There is a curse upon this ship. Right or wrong, those boxes must be brought up from the hold..."

Chapter Twenty-six

"We will not let superstition get the better of our thinking," the captain said.

"You have an obligation to your crew," Popescu insisted. "We demand those boxes be thrown overboard!" He turned to Olgaren and Amramoff and raised his hands. "Do we not?"

Olgaren and Amramoff nodded jointly.

"You heard the captain," Constantin shouted.

"Aye, but!" Olgaren was a wreck. "It cannot be left there! Would it not..."

Constantin grabbed a handspike from the deckhouse. "Damn you!" he screamed, and struck Olgaren aside his head. The big man toppled like a tree. The others backed off, the deck grew silent. The mate drew a tin of water from a rainbarrel and doused the unconscious seaman. Olgaren came to. Another moment and the stunned Russian stood with his head in his hand.

"Evil eye or no evil eye," the first said. "The trust of this ship's owners is in the hands of Captain Nikilov, not in the sea. If the Devil does have cargo aboard this ship, then it is consigned and will be delivered."

"That will do, Mr. Constantin," the captain said. "Moisey, you are not badly hurt?"

"No, captain," the big man answered in a monotone.

"Mr. Constantin has your attention," Nikilov said, addressing the group. "Might I assume I again have your order?" He received nods all around and, a tick later, three conclusive – if disheartened – barks of, "Aye, captain".

"Nobody will go near the passenger's cabin or the young woman below. She is injured and in need of rest. No one will lay a hand on the boxes in the cargo hold. Is that understood? Neither are to be molested or interfered with. Now, attend to your duties."

The captain signaled his first mate to follow and headed below.

* * *

Harrington had already rifled Nikilov's book shelves, his kit locker, and had his hands in the top drawer of his desk, when he heard the unmistakable approach of footsteps. The scholar panicked. He had no legitimate excuse for his presence, and no way out save the way he'd come in. The door to the companionway was, even then, being pushed open from the outside. The Englishman took the only action available. He dropped to the floor and slid under the captain's bunk.

Nikilov ushered the mate in and secured the door.

Harrington would not have shown himself for the world but lay there sweating from the heat, trembling from fear of being found, and listening from curiosity – and an inability to do anything else. His search had been cut short; his opportunity to secure a gun was gone. In but a few sentences, he learned how much deeper it went, the degree to which the events lay on the captain's mind and how seriously he was taking the tensions of the frightened crew.

Nikilov lit a lamp, illuminating their footware for their unseen guest, and cleared his throat. Before he could speak, he was interrupted by the mate.

"I apologize, captain," Constantin said (without sounding terribly apologetic). "For losing my temper just now."

"Yes," Nikilov nodded. "I appreciate your saying so. I would appreciate also your withholding corporal punishment until I order it."

"Aye, sir."

"That said, I did not call you down, Iancu, to issue a reprimand." He stooped to the bottom drawer of his desk. Harrington drew back not to be seen. From it, Nikilov withdrew a substantial wooden box. "I regret having to do this but am afraid we have no other choice." He laid the box atop his desk and lifted the lid. Inside, unseen by Harrington in his hiding place, facing each other, lay two shining blue revolvers.

"Captain?" Constantin asked.

Nikilov lifted a pistol from the box. "It is my feeling you and I should arm ourselves." He examined the cylinder to see all seven

Chapter Twenty-six

chambers were loaded, closed it and extended the weapon to his mate. "And remain armed until we discover the cause of our... tensions."

"We've searched the ship again and again. There's nobody aboard but the crew."

"Yes." The captain nodded at the gun. "Take it, if you agree with me."

Under the circumstances, how could he not? Constantin pocketed the revolver.

Under the bunk, Harrington cursed himself for not having checked that drawer first. Then again, they'd surely have been caught – before they'd had time to use it.

Above him, neither Nikilov nor Constantin spoke again. They left the cabin and returned to the deck and their nerve-wracked crew. Harrington came out of hiding, to stare at the outline of two pistols carved in a, now empty, box.

Chapter Twenty-seven

A KNOCK at the guest cabin put both Harrington and Swales on alert. Ekaterina had had no visitors and little intrusion since her consignment. They had no reason to expect a change. Harrington opened the door and Constantin entered with something preying on his mind.

"Swales, you're needed on the wheel." He hesitated, then turned to the Englishman. "The captain asks, Mr. Harrington, if you too would be willing to go up? We need someone to stand the watch and the rest of the crew are done in."

"I have no problem helping out, certainly," Harrington said. "But I am concerned about Ekaterina being left alone. Can the crew be trusted to leave her?"

"The crew?"

"I assume, with the cat out of the bag, they are still angry? Their superstitions..."

"I would not put it down to superstition. I am not superstitious – and I hate her presence. Would not you be angry if you'd been lied to? Thank whatever higher powers you ascribe to I do not command or you would all have been whipped. Be that as it may, the captain has ordered she not be touched. Therefore she will not be touched. It is that simple." He spread his coat, arms akimbo, and Harrington saw the pistol in his belt. "Should anyone try,"

Chapter Twenty-seven

the first added, "I will kill them. Now, if you will, as soon as you are able, on deck."

* * *

The heavy gray mist that was Count Dracula rose from his box. It hovered for a moment, in flux, then drifted forward and upward to the forehold's door to the between-decks. The cloud met the door, and its many cracks and, an instant later, was on the other side – in the companionway.

The mist shifted and became the tall black-clad vampire. He paused a moment. All was quiet, save for creaking wood, the muffled sounds of the wind-beaten canvas, and the thump and splash of shunting water at the bow. The officers and crew not on deck were in their beds, dead to the world, as ravaged by the voyage as their ship. The tall man strode the companionway to its end. Dracula laid his hand on the door to her quarters and mentally summoned her.

On the other side of the door, Ekaterina broke the cross off the frame of her bunk. She threw the pieces across the floor and hurried to the door. She threw it wide open. Vampire and lover stood facing one another.

She grabbed the cross above the door frame and pulled it down. Dracula averted his eyes as she snapped the icon into pieces and threw them with the others on the floor. She raised her arms inviting her lover to her.

Dracula smiled and stepped forward, then growled and retreated again. His eyes stung, his sinuses burned. The garlic remained still pressed into the wood around the door. Enraged, he turned on his heels and strode back to the hold. He made no attempt to slow as he approached, nor did he move to open it, but hit the door at full speed – as his body vaporized. Dracula was gone; the mist as well. The door was intact and undisturbed.

In the hold, in a rage, Dracula threw up his hands. "Ekaterina," he hissed, his voice dripping acid and anger. "Come to me. Here, now, come to me!"

* * *

"Have ye ever been to Whitby, Trevor?" Swales asked, leaning on the ship's wheel.

"No," answered the scholar. "The north country has always been a bit cold for me; especially on the coast. I'm a man of The Smoke."

Swales shook his head. "Ye can have all o' London an' then some fer what I care."

"Why did you ask? About Whitby, I mean."

"Was just thinkin' o' her, Whitby, that's all." He stared out to sea, his eyes lost in the distance, without seeing it. "There's a great reef rises outside o' the harbor, runs out into the German Sea..."

"The what?"

"The North Sea t' you; I was raised by an old whaler," Swales chuckled. "So, this reef runs from behind the south lighthouse. At its end, floats a bell buoy. It rides the waves an' swings with the weather an' puts such a mournful sound upon the wind. I heard it, in me mind, the Whitby harbor buoy, when I rang the hour just now. There's a legend says when a ship is lost – that bell buoy is heard out t' sea."

"You believe that?"

"Meh. Fool-talk. That's what me dad would say. Lies for the comers and trippers, an' the like."

Harrington laughed. "For who?"

"The tourists!" Swales said. "Them feet-folks from York and Leeds that be always eatin' cured herrin's an' drinkin' tea."

* * *

The stairway door creaked slowly open and the slim amber light of the between-decks lamp threw a shadow into the darkness

Chapter Twenty-seven

of the forward hold; Ekaterina's long, thin shadow. She stood motionless, her body swamped in Swales' out-sized nightshirt, peering into the depths with unseeing eyes. Still she stared. She pushed the door to its limits and the slim light reaching around her illuminated the tall figure of her master below.

"Come to me," Dracula said.

Ekaterina moved down the steps, unsteadily, but eagerly. She hurried across the hold. The wet wood chilled her feet, the odor of mold and cloistered air stung her nose, the pitch and roll of the schooner nearly flipped her to her knees. None of it mattered. She reached Dracula and fell into his arms.

He pulled her to him and her short squeal became an extended moan. His right hand cupped her soft rear, his left pulled her shirt open and explored her small, firm breasts. He brushed her hair over her shoulder with his thin nose and great mustache and nuzzled her neck. His grip was icy cold but immeasurably powerful. His breath, a font of acrid rot, was hot and enveloping. None of Ekaterina's thoughts were her own. She had only a single driving need – to give herself body and soul to the master. The vampire was pure lust as he stroked her; pure hunger as he sank his teeth into her throat.

Chapter Twenty-eight

THE morning of Friday, 30 July, arrived with Swales still at the wheel, physically exhausted and eye-sore, trying to see through the blasted fog. The sails were reefed again and the ship was going nowhere fast. In such a state, he wasn't even startled when Harrington, yet at the watch, stepped from the gray nothingness of the swirling mist like a performer in a magic act. The scholar joined him and they stood, silently, one in their weariness and melancholy.

They'd been warned to keep a sharp eye out for land. They could barely see a hand in front of their faces. Then something came out of the fog; not a sight, but a sound, a moaning cry like the pathetic mewl of a wounded kitten. It floated aft from somewhere nearby.

They looked at each other in frightened awe. Trembling, Harrington lifted his oil lamp. Near useless in the heavy fog, it created an amber nimbus about them but failed to illuminate anything farther than a few feet away. Moving to investigate, as was his duty, Harrington heard it again. It was a weak cry of pain and terror but this time it sounded human.

To the Englishman's reckoning, it could only have come from the deckhouse, below deck. He approached with trepidation and, as he reached the door, turned for support from Swales. Less than twenty feet forward of the helm, and he could see nothing of the

Chapter Twenty-eight

old cook through the swirling fog. On his own, Harrington opened the door and put in his lamp.

Ekaterina lay collapsed midway down on the stairs in agony. Even in the poor flicker of his lamp, he could see her too-large night shirt torn open, her breasts exposed and spattered crimson, a stream of blood running from her throat. "Cor! Oliver!" Harrington shouted over his shoulder. "Oliver! Come quickly!"

"What is it?" came the frightened question from the fog.

"Come quickly, please!"

* * *

It would seem incongruous that later that day a celebration was held aboard *Demeter*. Yet that was the case.

The girl was gotten quietly back to her quarters. Replacements were secured for both men, and Harrington and Swales disappeared below to tend to Ekaterina's injuries. Actually, beyond the understanding of the others, they fought to keep her alive, with one bright spot in the affair; they no longer had to pretend they were nursing the deck boy.

Meanwhile, with no inkling about their undead cargo, the captain and first mate met in the commander's quarters. And, while no one knew the weighty matters discussed, rumors flew among the remaining men before the mast. They emerged soon-after, to everybody's surprise, in the most jovial of moods. A meeting of the ship's compliment was called and, with the captain's permission, Constantin made an announcement.

"We have gone over our maps," he said, with a rare (though still cruelly angled) smile playing on his lips. "Despite this ridiculous fog, the captain and I believe, we're certain, we are nearing England. This will be our last night at sea!" Cheers went up from all around and Constantin let them play out before he proceeded. "We have every expectation, despite the fog, of reaching port tomorrow." The cheer went up again and, this time, he merely shouted through it. "We've neglected our rum ration for days. Captain wants to make it up to you!"

The delighted men scurried for their mugs. The half-hogshead tapper was opened and the rum ran again. With Nikilov's permission, Popescu brought up his violin and, in a rare show of comradeship, carried up Olgaren's accordion as well. For the first time since their first week at sea, there was music, there was dancing. For the first time in as long, there was an absence of fear.

* * *

Away from the celebration, Swales and Harrington had stabilized the girl and struggled to find some way to protect her from the vampire.

Swales lifted Ekaterina's eye-lids noting their once-brilliant green had been reduced to a pale yellow that – when the light struck them – gave off a red reflection. He peeled back her upper lip and, though the change was slight, saw that her eyeteeth were longer and sharper. She was restless, in pain.

"How is she?" Harrington asked hopefully.

"She is changing. This thing, this vampire, is o'ertakin' her, changin' her. He is turnin' her into a creature like himsel'. Her teeth grow sharper, her eyes harder. She longs fer the dark."

She stirred briefly to find Harrington at her side. "Trevor..." She reached for him. Her strength failed and her hand slipped to her breast. "I've had a dream," she managed in a whisper. "The most awful dream..."

"Yes, dear, it was only a dream. A bad dream," he assured her. He tucked her hand under the blanket and she was asleep again. "I do not understand this..." Harrington looked up to see a change come over Swales as well. There was something on his mind; something he was hesitant to reveal.

"Trevor, we must talk."

Chapter Twenty-eight

"She doesn't remember anything," Harrington said. "At least nothing she recognizes as having been real. Maybe we're making too much..."

Swales shook his head. "I know, lad, ye'd like it to be a dream. But ye know better. You found her. An' I do no' need to list the evidences. The relapses. The effects o' the sun. Ye remember, I dare say better than I, her attempts to escape the room. That episode – laying abed when her whole pair-sonality changed... the ferocious look, the feral nature what o'ertook her. Ye' were here. Ye saw what I saw. That was no' yer lass layin' there."

"Yes." Harrington nodded, defeated. "It was as if someone, something had possessed her."

"More than 'possessed'..." Swales wandered, considering. "It was as if whate'er it was traded places w' her. Physically changed places; took o'er her body. Ekaterina was no' here, *It* was. An', fer an instant, she went - where'er It is now."

"That's insane! How? Why? Where?"

"Fer-get it's insane. The whole fekkin' thing's insane. Her takin' down that cross an' lettin' 'im in was insane. Ye heard her." Harrington tried to turn away but Swales grabbed him, making him face it. "Ye heard her, Trevor. Ye heard her yersel'. It's cold. It's dark. I'm in a casket..."

"I'm buried in a box."

"Aye. That's what she said. Packed up like a cold corpse in a box. She was seeing, no, she was in, his hiding place. He possesses her and, when it suits him, takes her place."

"Cor," Harrington said breathlessly. "For what reason?"

"The why is easy... to spy on his enemies. While she is where'er It hides. He is here, seein', hearin' through her. Gog, lad, do no' stare at me so. Do no' go askin' me what I mean. I do no' gawm a thing." He grunted. "I saw a thaumaturge once..."

Harrington's questioning glare stopped him.

"Jings, lad, fer a fella what claims scholarship as his stock-in-trade, ye know shite. A conjurer... a magician. I envied him then.

I envy him more now. I'd give all I have to pass my hand o'er her eyes an' magic-ly make her tell all she knows o' this devil."

"I agree. But we're not magicians," Harrington said. "So, what are we going to do?"

"NO! Not here!"

They started, for neither had spoken. The demand had come from the bed. They turned to see Ekaterina, sitting up, with fear in her eyes. "Do not," she implored, "discuss it here!"

"Darling," Harrington hurried to her. "We're sorry. We didn't mean to upset you." He tried to take her in his arms but she resisted.

"No, Trevor, it isn't that. You don't understand." The fear in her eyes was real, but far away. She was looking both into the past and into the future – and was horrified by what she saw. "It wasn't a dream. NO! It wasn't a dream at all." Harrington tried to quiet her, but she wouldn't have it. "It was real. I felt... what I felt... the cold, the damp, the darkness... through him. Oh, forgive me, my love, but I fear that he can feel, and see, and hear through me. Oliver is right. You mustn't say or do anything in my presence you do not wish... him... to know." She faded back onto her pillow exhausted.

Swales took the scholar by the arm and led him away, whispering. "If she can see an' hear what this creature sees an' hears, if she can lit-rally be where he is, can he no' do the same in reverse? She canno' be part o' our conversations. She canno' know our plans."

"Katya would never betray us!"

"She would no' choose to betray us. But ye know at times she does no' control hersel'. We must remove the opportunity and speak outside her hearin'. She canno' tell what she does no' know. You must accept this, Ekaterina has. She knows her safety, all our safety, requires she be kept in the dark." He saw the flash of panic on Harrington's face. "Be strong. She needs ye. I need ye."

"I don't need you!"

They spun back to Ekaterina's bed – to an unbelievable sight.

Chapter Twenty-eight

The girl was crouched, holding the frame above with one hand and pointing at them with the other. Her eyes gleamed. Her teeth were fangs. "You are nothing!" she shrieked.

The voice was not that of Ekaterina. It was a deep male voice, filled with hate. Harrington reached for the girl. "Katya!"

"Stay back, bastard," it hissed. "Who are you to challenge me? I was a prince, a soldier, a statesman. Mine is a learning of ages, a heart that knows no fear... no remorse. What are you?"

"Ye're fine, lass. Let us lay back..."

"Fools! You would pit your knowledge against mine?"

"Ekaterina," Harrington began... but she heard nothing.

"I despise you. Weakling!" Her eyes focused somewhere beyond the room. "I have tasted her blood... and she mine! When I call, she will answer. Where I go, she will follow. You, all of you, are nothing more than our sustenance. You will all die horribly – at the time of my choosing!"

* * *

Swales poured Harrington a cup of tea, returned the kettle to the stove, and joined him at the table. Both were shaking and shaken by what had happened in Ekaterina's cabin. The girl had collapsed after the vulgar puppet show her so-called master had put her through. She was back in bed now, sedated with laudanum (from the late Smirnov's kit), and thankfully asleep.

"She was right. 'efore her last trans-fermation, what she told us was correct. She's changin', to some new order o' creature like this thing she calls her master. He kills... takin' his victims somewhere beyond death. We must consider Ekaterina's affliction in light o' what she told us. Ye were right to call it a baptism o' blood..."

"I can't even think about it."

"Here, lad. I was wrong to ignore it when ye raised the point; an' ye have no' the luxury o' ignorin' it now. But we can use our knowledge against him. We can find this monster through her."

"How can you even suggest it. It's too horrible, unthinkable!"

"Calm yersel'." Swales took a sip, and his own advice. "Very well, let it be as ye say. Our task will be more difficult. But it remains our task all the same. So let us ferget the lass now an' consider our adversary. He's only been seen at night and, apparently, does not venture from his box until the deathwatch hours. I dinna gawm if he fears discovery an' so tries to avoid us or if, like the lass, he's effected by the sunlight itsel'. It does no' matter. Between dawn and sunset he confines himsel' below. Thaat's when we must find him. That 'efore anythin'. Find him in daylight an' strike."

"This ship has been searched repeatedly."

"At the risk o' agreein' w' Popescu... This creature is hidin' in one o' those wooden boxes."

"Then we must find him... for Ekaterina's sake."

"Aye, but it goes deeper than thaat, lad. There's more than the girl at stake. Fifty o' 'em, each a hidin' place! An' we're takin' this thing an' his boxes to our homeland. Once there, scattered in attics, basements, buried in the ground, hidden throughout the town - or the country. He'll ne'er be found ageean. An', if Popescu's book is right, time is on his side. He'll have centuries t' wait."

"Cor!"

"Aye. Now, add t'other thin's that book says. That he can change form; alter his physical bein' to that o' the mist, the wolf, the rat, the bat to attack unsuspectin' folk in the night. W' the evidence of our eyes alone, must no' this man, this monster, be ut-terly stamped out?"

"It's horrible," Harrington said, nodding. "These boxes, this evil, cannot reach England. We must find him and destroy him. But, Oliver, we cannot go about this foolishly. We must carefully plan how we'll proceed."

"Oh, aye. We must make the necessary preparations an' we must go armed."

"But what chance have we now of getting a gun?"

"A gun is no' the only weapon in the waarld."

"You used the last of your garlic."

Chapter Twenty-eight

"There's yer handiwork," Swales said. He produced one of their homemade crosses and pushed it into the scholar's hand.

Harrington scowled. "I made those at your insistence. As for using them, I'm afraid you have the wrong vampire hunter." He tried to hand it back.

Swales refused. He curled the scholar's fingers around the icon and patted his hand. "Take care, lad, lest yer stubborness be the death o' ye."

"Oliver, I can't pretend belief in god."

"I dinna ask it o' ye. The cross is no' only a symbol of God; it's a symbol o' good. Surely, ye believe in good an' evil?"

"I don't understand your question."

"Ye're avoidin' my question. Ye either believe in good an' evil bein' two vastly diff-rent thin's or ye do no'. In which case ye accept as fact there is no marked diff-rence between yer lass an' the creature tryin' to claim her. Now which is it?"

"Don't be ridiculous! Of course there's a difference!"

"An' one o' the two is good?"

"Certainly!"

"An' t'other?"

"All right, your point is made," Harrington said, slipping the cross into his pocket.

"Armed against evil, we identify the right box, we secure it so this thin' canno' emerge and, when the opportunity comes, we open it an' do what must be done."

"If we make a mistake, is there a danger of his getting off the ship? If he can take the form of other creatures, couldn't he become something... a bat?... and escape?"

"He canno' cross runnin' water, so he canno' leave the ship.

"I remember reading that. But that means the men were right. They were right all along! We should have just thrown the boxes into the sea."

"They were right, but to what end?"

"If running water will destroy him, we can find him, carry him up, and throw him over."

270

"The cap'n and mate would no' allow it then and they will no' allow it now. Precious little good it'll do to survive this trip only to be hung for mutiny. No, lad. We find him alone an', w' protection at hand an' him at our mercy, we destroy him where he lies."

"The book says his head must be cut off and his heart pierced."

"Then that's what we do."

Harrington nodded with determination. "For Katya, I am ready to suffer the consequences of murder."

"It's no' a question o' murder and the only consequences will be if we fail. Does no' the book say also thaat, treated so, the monster's body will fall to dust? There would be no evidence o' murder."

"I'm merely saying I am prepared to meet the rope for Ekaterina's safety."

"That's grand, lad. But I'm no'." Swales squeezed Harrington's arm. "Still an' all, it is agreed we'll do this. We shall leave no stone unturned findin' him. An' shall stand or fall destroyin' him." He stepped into the galley, clinked about, and returned with a stout brown bottle. "Shall we seal our oath?"

Harrington grunted. "I've had enough Golden Mediasch to last a lifetime."

"Golden... pah," the cook said, pouring. "This is slivovitz. Sweet blue plum brandy; the Serb cure-all."

Harrington swallowed the brandywine, pursed his lips to exhale as the shot sent a heat-burst through his chest, and inhaled deeply to recover. "That's... good."

"Ye said yersel', the prize should be worth t' risk."

"If you had this all the time," he said with tears forming, "why did we drink the other?"

"I didn't know ye then," the old man said, catching a breath of his own. "Slivovitz ought only be imbibed w' the worthy."

* * *

The music ended. The fog cleared in late afternoon, revealing a blue sky. For the first time in weeks a small but exceedingly happy

Chapter Twenty-eight

crew went back to work. The captain ordered all sails set and, in deference to their jovial moods, kept what he knew to himself.

Nikilov had taken a sextant reading, the first in six days of blind sailing, and had consulted his charts. The results were devastating. He and his first had been egregiously in error; fooled, no doubt, by the abominable weather. But that poor excuse offered no solace. *Demeter* was nowhere near Whitby – and would not be for days. They were still hundreds of miles south in the English Channel.

The frustrated Nikilov considered coming hard over, taking the ship north to England's southern coast and her nearest port. But, he knew, he could not. Sailing into Dover on a beautiful sunny day with a ship in good repair would be impossible to explain to the owners. The cost of hauling the cargo overland to Whitby would be more than they would be willing to bear... without a permanent change as far as he was concerned. Yes, he'd lost crewmen. But theirs was a dangerous business and, as far the company was concerned, fatalities part of the cost of conducting it. He could point to nothing – except fear – to justify abandoning their contractual destination. He could not divert the ship.

It had been a difficult journey. But they were nearing Whitby. At the moment, the men's hearts were light and the weather was finally in their favor. They were a good crew and they deserved this enjoyable respite. Tomorrow he would break the news... They had yet several more days at sea.

Chapter Twenty-nine

SATURDAY, 31 July, began like so many others on this – *Demeter's* most dismal journal. The damnable fog had returned. There was a sunrise but, behind the shifting mists, it appeared as little more than a diffused glow intensifying the suffocating gray. The gay mood of the previous day had vanished, replaced with a pervasive feeling of doom.

Their fast broken and on deck, the men were let in on the captain's secret. The storms and fog had contributed to what Nikilov confessed was his navigational error; for which he apologized. They had made less progress than he had earlier imagined and, no, they would not reach Whitby this day. The mumbles and groans of the crew (Popescu, not surprisingly, more than the others) were received with silent understanding. When they subsided, the captain did his best to bolster their spirits again. They were in the English Channel, would soon pass Dover's brilliant white cliffs, and would make their last major course correction. They were almost there!

That ground covered, Nikilov moved on to their ship's duties. It was Saturday and, though he believed it would do the men good to busy themselves cleaning, he simply hadn't the heart to order it. They were dead on their feet and aching in spirit; they needed rest. Other than Funar (funny, how Nikilov still thought of the

Chapter Twenty-nine

girl as Funar) there was no sign of illness aboard the ship. They would survive another day or two without soap.

The master dismissed the men, to their duties or their bunks as assigned, and went for a walk to mull his thoughts. He began in the bow, where he undid the forward battens and lifted the hatchway covers. Then, wandering his ship alone, pondering the voyage, he propped doors open as he passed. It was Saturday after all, he could at least air *Demeter* out.

The day passed quietly... as far as Nikilov and his remaining hands knew.

* * *

Below deck, outside of the knowledge of captain and crew, a new and very different battle for the schooner was begun. With the others at their duty stations or in their bunks, Harrington and Swales, carrying lantern and kit, quietly entered the midship hold. It contained only a handful of the Transylvanian boxes; making it, they'd agreed, a good place to start their process of elimination. As quickly and as quietly as they were able they set to work.

Harrington took a pry bar to the first box while Swales stood holding a cross in his admittedly trembling hands. The scholar loosened the lid, then took up a hammer and one of the wooden stakes they'd fashioned. He and the old man shared an anxious breath and a nod of readiness. Harrington jerked the lid open. Dirt. Nothing but.

Both sagged, Swales lowering the cross, Harrington the hammer and stake. Both, realizing they'd been holding their breath, exhaled lungs-full.

"Only forty-nine to go," Harrington said.

Swales made his famous grunt of disgust. "I'm too old fer this shite."

The box was resealed as quietly as they were able. Harrington scratched a small mark in its forward end and they moved to a second casket. Then another, and another; repeating the routine.

Each unveiling started with nervous dread... and culminated in embarrassed relief when the box was found to contain only soil. Tension... relief... frustration. Again and again. A feeling of hopelessness grew.

Soon, they'd gone through all of the cargo in the midship hold finding nothing more evil than mold. Each container was resealed, marked, and pushed back into place. Now they were certain, the vampire was in the bow. Collecting their tools and lantern, Harrington pointed to the forward door and asked, "Shall we?"

"One minute," Swales replied. He slid the cross into the lamp bracket on the main mast footing and left it there. "Let us keep it out o' bounds."

Harrington smiled nervously, nodded agreement, and led Swales into the forehold.

* * *

Just before sundown, or when sundown would have been had the fog not prevented his seeing it, Nikilov circumnavigated the ship again, retracing his steps and resecuring the doors, the hatchways and his own porthole. He wound up his patrol in the mess.

There, the tired old Scot was hard at work. He and Harrington had barely gotten started in the forehold, when he'd been forced to return to his duties. With the sick girl, the searches, the calls to deck for the weather, the meals he'd served already that day, and his and the scholar's covert activities (of which the captain was unaware), the cook was behind the times. His galley and mess were... a mess. His hopes of getting on top of the matter... were about to be dashed.

"Mr. Swales," the captain said wearily. "I'm sorry to ask it of you, but there is nobody else. Would you... could you stand the night watch again?"

Swales, like everyone else, was exhausted. Unlike the others, he was decades past his best years. His rheumatic joints, his

Chapter Twenty-nine

oft sprained back, the old calcified breaks to his bones; all were conspiring to put him out of commission. For the captain, he'd ignore them. He smiled at the weary ship's commander. "O' course, sir. Glad t' assist any way I can."

Bleary-eyed, the captain retired. He considered making a notation in his ship's log but, in the end, decided there was nothing new to add. He checked the time on his prized clock, immediately forgot what it read, and fell onto his bunk. Nikilov was sleeping the moment his head touched down.

Swales grabbed his oilskin in the event the unaccountable rains returned, his clay pipe and a tin of '-baccy, and (from its hiding place in the larder) Popescu's rosary. He set them aside to pour a steaming cup of tea. He stuffed a ship's biscuit into his breast pocket, the thoughts of the day running through his head, and hurried topside sipping his fresh brew. Behind him, Swales' slicker, pipe, and the borrowed crucifix lay side-by-side, forgotten, on the counter of his galley work space.

* * *

Popescu stood at the wheel - terrified.

He wasn't alone. The cook was on watch, forward, in a suffocating fog that, like the previous four days of rain, had risen from nowhere. But he may as well have been alone. He could see the wheel in his hands and little else. He knew the mizzen mast was immediately before him, and the deckhouse and main mast before that, but none were visible. Nothing and nobody existed, save the dank fog.

He thought of a prayer his mother taught him as a child, closed his eyes searching for the words after all the years and, as they came to him, whispered them quickly out loud. Then again. Over and over, with his eyes clamped shut and his grip tightening on the spokes. He began to relax, feeling better. Popescu opened his eyes – as a tall stranger stepped from the fog.

It was Olgaren's ghost. It had to be. Draped in black, with a pale white face, Olgaren's ghost! "*Ajuta-ma, Dumnezeu,*" Popescu gasped, beseeching God. He lifted his trembling hand, twisted into the sign of the *mano fica,* to deflect the fiend's evil eye.

The stranger smiled, laughed, then leapt. Popescu screamed but the vampire, already upon him, cut it off. He pulled the Romanian from the wheel as if he were a child and, wrenching his head to the side, bit him viciously in the throat. When he pulled away, several minutes later, Popescu hung limp. Dracula gasped, blood running down his chin. He snarled, for he'd sated his hunger but not his rage. He dragged Popescu from beneath the mizzen boom to the side of the rudder gearhouse. He lifted the seaman's body above his head and heaved it mightily over the rail. The corpse splashed, thirty-feet astern, in the cold English Channel and vanished in the dark as the ship raced on.

* * *

Swales, moving slowly down the slippery deck, was headed aft through fog thicker than his own pea soup when he heard Popescu scream; first in terror, then in pain. Goose flesh erupted on his skin and the old man froze in place. "Dear Gog," he whispered under his breath. His instinct was to run – but to where? He was in the middle of the English Channel. And, damn blast it to hell, he was too old to be running. He started again, straining to make out the port side corner of the deckhouse. He found it by feel as much as sight and continued aft, left hand on the deckhouse bulkhead, right hand fingering the bulwark pinrail – trying to stay in contact with something solid, something real – his fear growing exponentially with each step.

"Popescu." He'd meant to shout, but his voice failed, and it arrived as a gravelly whisper. He cleared his throat and gave it some air. "Popescu! Give a shout, lad, so's I gawm ye're there."

Silence and the sea. Nothing more.

Chapter Twenty-nine

Swales reached to his pocket, looking for his pipe (as much to chew on as to smoke), and found only a ship's biscuit. He furled his brow and swore under his breath, mentally kicking himself for his forgetfulness, as he cleared the aft corner of the deckhouse. He paused by the rum casks, just below the main boom and, staring aft, whispered, "Bogdan, what's the scowderment, lad?" He ran his hand along the boom, to guide him, and took three wobbling steps aft when the fog parted like a theater curtain. At center stage, he could just make out the lolling ship's wheel rocking on its axis; to the port, to the starboard, with the motion of the waves. He strained his eyes and realized the rudder was unguided, for the wheel was untended. The steersman was nowhere to be seen.

"Popescu?"

Nobody and nothing to see for the fog. Swales swallowed hard and hobbled to the wheel. He took a breath and control of the helm. He wiped the moisture from the face of the compass with his sleeve, then snorted at his own ridiculousness. By the needle, their bowsprit was pointed east. But he hadn't the slightest notion where the ship was or what course had been ordered.

"Popescu!"

He may as well have been standing on the moon and, a moment later, wished he was.

The fog billowed and the starboard corner of the deckhouse became visible. Taking shape beside it, in the mouth of the companionway, stood a dark cloaked figure. It was not Popescu, nor was it anyone the Scot had ever seen before. It flashed through his mind that, were it not for the fellow's beard, he looked exactly as Olgaren had described his ghost. Then it spoke. "Popescu?" the ghost said, aping him. "Pop-es-cu!" It laughed; guttural, rumbling.

The fog cleared further, as if driven off by magic, and the old cook realized that the figure mocking him was no ghost. It was clearly the monster for which he and Harrington had been searching. As evidence he saw now that, what he had mistaken for the creature's beard, was in fact his lower lip, chin, and throat awash in dripping blood.

"Crivvens," Swales gasped in a whisper.

The creature's eyes gleamed. He recognized the Scottish slang for *Christ defend us!*, smiled, displaying bloody fangs, and answered, "He can't."

Swales throat had gone dry. He could not speak, but could only stare.

"You would cross swords with me? I commanded legions centuries before you were born. You are, all of you, my jackals, to do my bidding or to die by my hand, as I see fit."

As angry as he was afraid, Swales met the monster's leer with the Scottish version of the stiff upper lip. He eased his hand from the wheel, reaching...

Dracula saw the move and, still mocking, the blood congealing on his lips, asked, "More gar-lic?"

Swales grunted and answered, "More effective than garlic." He reached for his coat pocket, intent on defending himself from this hell-spawned demon. Only then, as time stood still and an age seemed to pass, did the old man realize his oilskin, his faithful pipe, and the rosary crucifix for which he reached lay useless in the mess below.

The fear dawned in Swales' eyes and, like a cat on a mouse, Dracula pounced. The Scot struggled, fighting a match would have swelled the breast of Robert the Bruce with pride. But Swales was a seaman (an exhausted, arthritic old seaman at that), not a warrior. The vampire bared his fangs, snapped, and savagely tore Oliver's throat out.

* * *

Harrington heard a scream of terror and recognized it instantly as that of his friend. He raced on deck, scanned the darkness, cursed the fog and, soon, found Swales alone on the mizzen deck behind the wheel. He lay in a growing crimson pool, his hand on his throat trying desperately, uselessly, to stem the flow of his own blood. The fiend, whoever or whatever had attacked him, was gone.

Chapter Twenty-nine

There came a shout behind.

Like spirits, the first mate materialized starboard of the deckhouse coming aft through the fog, while Olgaren carried an oil lamp up from below. They moved cautiously and, together, discovered the wheel untended. When Swales groaned and Harrington moved, behind the rudder gear box, both jumped. Olgaren raised his light. Constantin raised his voice. "Who are you?" the mate demanded, waving a handspike as if it were a club.

"It's Harrington," the scholar called out from his knees.

"Who's the other? Amramoff?"

"Pasha is below," Olgaren said, butting in. He laid a meaty hand on the first's tunic. "He's sleeping; dead to the world. It was Popescu steering."

Constantin rounded the gear box and stepped onto the mizzen. "Who have you there then?" He was nearly atop them when the fog allowed the mate a look. He could only gasp. The big Russian behind stared in mute horror. The Englishman was cradling their cook in his arms. Swales, from the chin down, was soaked in his own blood. The details of the old man's injury might only be guessed at but they were extensive.

"It's Oliver Swales," Harrington said, laying his cheek on the old man's head. "He's been attacked. I did not see by what."

"Popescu?"

"I don't know. I haven't seen him."

"What can we do?" the first asked.

"Nothing." Harrington considered for a moment, but knew better. "No, nothing."

"Come," the mate said, taking Olgaren's lamp. "We'll find Popescu." He faded into the fog. Olgaren followed without a word and he too disappeared. An instant more and the glow of their lamp vanished as well.

"Hang in there old man," Harrington cried. He pulled a kerchief from his coat pocket and tamped his throat. The effort was useless but he tried all the same. "You're going to be all right."

"No," Swales gasped, clutching at the young man's sleeve. "I must... gang ageeanwards home. My daughter... does no' like... be kept waitin' when it's tea... it takes me time t' crammle aboon the grees, for there be a many o' 'em." Swales was staring past Harrington, beyond the fog and the sails. He was staring out to sea - from the east cliff of the Whitby cemetery. In his mind's eye, he threaded the tombstones, headed for the long curve of concrete steps (how many times, as a boy, he'd counted all 199 of them) leading from the kirk-yard, to the drawbridge below, over the river and on to home. To a daughter and a father he hadn't seen in years, and now never would again. His breath came in gasps, blood bubbling from his lips, his words in weak bursts barely audible above the billowing canvas and the churning sea, "So many steps... so many steps... 'efore I'm home."

Swales died in Harrington's arms.

Chapter Thirty

THE captain started from sleep and sprang up sitting in his bunk; all of his senses on fire. He was not alone. There was someone else in the cabin. He caught his breath. "Who's there?" No response, no movement. He darted his head, straining in the dark and, as his eyes adjusted, could just make out a human form sitting nearby. It was Constantin - just sitting and staring at him.

"Iancu! Lord, you. . . " He stopped himself. "What are you doing?"

Still no answer. It was unsettling. The captain rose, grunting. He stepped past his frozen mate, struck a match at his desk, and held it to the glittering face of his ormolu clock.

It was Nikilov's one bow to materialism and his only valuable possession; the mantle clock inherited from his parents. The French sculpture featured Napoleon and his Archduchess bride seated upon thrones with an angel, and the clock face, between them. As art, it meant nothing. Nikilov didn't know chiseled rococo from his knee and had never heard of François Linke. Its supposed allegorical allusion to the pagan gods Mars and Venus meant even less. What mattered to the breathless seven-year old he was (when first he heard its story), were the thrills received, the horrors conjured by the details of its manufacture. The clock was covered in nitrate of mercury, layered with powdered, high-karat gold, and fire-gilded; the mercury burned off and the shining gold perma-

Chapter Thirty

nently adhered. The process created eternally beautiful art – and killed the artist. The fumes from the burned quicksilver poisoned the gilders. They lost their hair, their teeth, their sanity, and their lives by the age of forty. And so the time-pieces became *death clocks*. What could be more appropriate, the captain wondered, with the first mate of his doomed ship sitting there like a corpse, than to check the time using a death clock?

No! Nikilov was suddenly angry. Not his ship! Not his mate! He lit his lamp and examined Constantin in the amber light. Swollen, red eyes; the man had been crying. "What has happened?"

"They are gone," Constantin whispered. "Swales from the watch. Popescu the wheel." The first began to cry again. "Popescu is missing, his post abandoned. The cook is there, near the helm, dead. His throat..." Constantin faltered.

Nikilov considered the news in silence. "Who is at the wheel now?"

"Olgaren and Amramoff both. One wouldn't go without the other." He ran his fingers over his dry lips. "They're there together in the fog. They're the only ones left."

"The only ones? The Englishman? The girl?"

"They're all right... I assume." Constantin waved them away. "I was not speaking of them. I meant the crew. Of nine, only four remain, Olgaren, Amramoff, you and I. We are the only ones left."

The words reverberated in the captain's mind. "The only ones left..."

* * *

Oliver Swales' weighted, canvas-wrapped body, barely visible in the fog, sank into silence. Buried at sea without a grave marker, just the way Oliver would have wanted it.

It was Sunday morning, 1 August. Harrington stood numb as he watched all that remained of his friend vanish from sight into the depths of... who knew where? They were supposedly in the English Channel. If true, they were somewhere between the

Atlantic Ocean and the North Sea, somewhere between England and continental Europe. In the neverending fog, who knew exactly where?

Harrington turned to see Nikilov behind him, a bible in his hands, unopened, unused. The Englishman had not waited for a ceremony, merely sewed up the canvas, lifted the cook's body over the gunwhale on his own, and released him into the deep. Neither Ekaterina nor the other three seamen aboard had attended. That was fine with Harrington. The captain made no interference. He merely watched until Swales was gone. Now his eyes were closed and, the scholar assumed, he was praying.

Harrington walked away.

* * *

Nikilov had hoped, it seemed now without reason, that reaching the English Channel would cure all their ills. From the Mediterranean, to the Atlantic, to the Bay of Biscay they had been beaten and bruised by the wind and rain, more than any captain could have expected his ship and crew to endure. Through it all not another sail or ship had been sighted; not one. He'd hoped that reaching the channel would change that, that they would have to see another vessel, could signal for help, and get his ship into port. Any port, anywhere. But the fog had prevented their seeing, or signaling, anyone.

To make matters worse he could no longer, to any great degree, control the course of his ship. The sails were fully set and, God help them, would have to remain so. They dared not lower them, for they had neither the strength nor manpower to raise them again; not with their square-rigged foremast. He had no choice but to run the ship before the wind and steer her northwesterly as best he could. The only factor in their favor was his knowledge the coast of England had to be to their port – somewhere.

Blind, deaf and dumb, through two more relentless days of fog, with no way to determine their progress, the captain sailed on.

Chapter Thirty

No sun, no moon, no stars. His sextant and maps useless, with only his experience and guesswork to guide them. But Nikilov had no good feeling about it. His senses told him Demeter was racing to some terrible doom.

"Captain?" Nikilov lifted his head, aware for the first time someone else was present. It was Olgaren, with his cap in his hand. "Captain, you all right?"

"Yes. All right."

"I come for church. Amramoff is steering, but I come for church."

It was Sunday, wasn't it? How could he have forgotten? A Holy Bible in his hand and, yet, he'd forgotten the Sabbath. "Thank you," the captain said, with something akin to a smile. "There'll be no worship today, Moisey. If Pasha can spare you, try and get some sleep." The man nodded his massive red head and hesitantly started aft. "Mr. Olgaren," Nikilov called after him. "You are a good man."

Olgaren reddened and was gone. Again, Nikilov had the bow to himself. Only three of his crew remained, Olgaren, the ship's carpenter, and his first mate. The condition of each, physically and mentally, was questionable at best.

Olgaren and Amramoff soldiered on. Not that they had conquered their fear – they were all, Nikilov included, terrified – but that they reached some place in their minds beyond the fear. They accepted the situation as it was, without the necessity of understanding, and now went about their work stolidly. They would take the future as it came; God's best or the devil's worst. Despite his nagging despair, the captain couldn't help but feel pride for his stalwart men.

Nikilov was less than proud of his first. Truth be told, resentment was beginning to brew. They were near England but far from safe. He needed every man and now he doubted his mate. Constantin was no longer eating. He'd taken to silence and long bouts of sleepless wandering about the deck. He stared blankly into the darkness by night, the fog-enveloped sea by day, without appearing to see anything at all. Once the hardest (most stubborn?)

of all of Nikilov's men, he seemed now completely demoralized, as if his strong nature had, in the end, worked against him. His inability to control the situation, to rise above it, was eating away at him. Nikilov feared for the mate's sanity and was at a loss as to what to do about it.

Not that he didn't have compassion for his first mate; he did. But what had he really expected? Olgaren and Amramoff were, after all, Russian. Constantin, it went without saying, was Romanian.

* * *

In the middle of the afternoon, following a brief respite, the rain came again. The few remaining hands were called on deck to sail, to save, the vessel. Everyone responded... except Harrington.

It was not cowardice that made him ignore the call to stations. If anything, it was a new level of courage. To fight the storm and keep the ship afloat was important, he knew that. But, obviously, not the answer to the cause of their difficulties. Without meaning to be clever, they were merely treading water. With everyone else busy on deck, Harrington would answer the call in another way. To truly save the ship and those left aboard her, he knew, they needed to rid her of the parasite below. The vampire had to be destroyed.

The deck work was made more difficult with the crew depleted. Likewise, his duty was more difficult without his friend and colleague. Be that as it may, he was in Swales' room, little bigger than the old man's bunk, just off the hot galley larder, making sure of the materials they had put together; a cross (he'd had to fashion a new one), stakes, carving knives, matches, and a hammer *borrowed* from Amramoff. It was all guesswork, of course, based on superstitious writings, half-remembered scholarship, and shots of slivovitz. He grabbed the kit and started out, but paused in the galley. There, on the counter, collected and forgotten, lay Oliver's oilskin, his pipe and tobacco, and Popescu's rosary.

Sadness swept over the Englishman. "Your death shall not be in vain, Oliver," Harrington whispered, as he slipped the rosary into

Chapter Thirty

his waistcoat pocket. "I won't allow it. This creature will suffer for what he did to you and Ekaterina! I swear it, my friend! I swear it!"

"Have pity on him, Trevor."

Ekaterina's voice, whispered and feeble, nevertheless startled him. He spun round to see her, in Swales' nightshirt and bare feet, beside the mess table. She could barely stand for the pitch and roll of the ship, was pale as a ghost, with desperate sadness in her eyes.

"Katya, you should be resting." He hurried to her side and led her back to her cabin.

"Have pity on him, I beg you."

"Pity?"

"This man. This monster that haunts us. Whatever he is, he was once a creature of God and must be pitied."

He hadn't told her of Oliver. She had no way of knowing the depth of his hatred. "After all that he's done to us," he said, helping her into her bunk. "I pray for the chance to send him to hell!"

"Don't say that, Trevor. Dear Lord, please! One day soon, I could be a creature like him."

"Katya, don't even think it!"

"It's true. It could well be true. Soon you may need to destroy me! Would you send me to hell? Dear God, Trevor, am I doomed to the pits of hell? Will God deny me his heaven! Destroy him if you must. But, please, don't hate him."

* * *

The rain was again a storm, thunder rolled and lightning flashed. It was nearly ten at night before Ekaterina finally fell back to sleep and, for the first time in a long while, seemed free of the nightmares. The calm looked good on her.

During his vigil, he'd torn linen into strips and hid them away. Now, he pulled these bandages from a desk drawer and put them to use. Quietly, and ever so gently, one limb at a time, he tied Ekaterina's wrists and ankles to the four posts of the bunk. Whatever was to come, he had no intention of Katya being pulled into the mix, either by her own stubbornness or by the evil thing in the hold. He needed no more trouble or interruptions. He'd already lost the daylight and there was no more time to waste. What he'd planned would be difficult enough. Secure in the knowledge she was safe, he slipped from the cabin.

Harrington retrieved his kit from the galley, for Oliver's memory, for Ekaterina's life, for England's salvation. It sounded like high melodrama but was also true. The dangers increased with every moment, every mile, that passed. He threw the bag on his shoulder and headed for the hold.

Chapter Thirty-one

HARRINGTON pushed into the forehold. He descended with a firm grasp on the stair rail as the thunder boomed and the ship heaved and rolled with the heavy sea. Harrington ignored the storm, lit the kerosene lamp, pulled a pry bar from the kit, and started at the boxes.

He was overwhelmed with an eerie feeling of already having been and done as he opened the first box and found only dirt. Then again. And again. Nothing but dirt. The odd feelings were soon replaced by the old frustrations. He panned the lamp about the hold, thinking this endeavor was going to take forever and feeling sorry for himself. He barely finished the thought before he shook his head in shame. The earlier inspections found nothing but dirt and the monster had been there all the time, waiting to begin his reign of terror. From this lair he'd perpetrated his abominable horrors against Ekaterina and methodically killed the crew. The monster was here. If it took forever to find him... it took forever. He would find the hellish creature!

He bent to another box and began prying on the lid, oblivious of the mist escaping from a casket across the hold. He continued to work, unaware of the change in that mist as it materialized into the vampire behind him.

"I am glad you found your way here."

Chapter Thirty-one

The voice was deep, melodic as a church organ, beautifully spoken English, with a decidedly eastern European accent, likely Romanian. His scholar's mind deciphered this on its own, while the startled Harrington jumped and caught the top of a barrel for balance. He clutched the pry bar and stared into the gloom at the phantom. Olgaren's young phantom!

Renewed, Harrington guessed (if Popescu's book were right), by his recent attacks on Ekaterina, Swales, and the missing Popescu; his vigor restored by their blood. These thoughts passed through his mind in a flash. In the same instant, he took in the cloaked figure, as the frightened crew had described. His eyes were piercing, face and hands stood out white as chalk. Then it dawned on Harrington, it had spoken to him. The Englishman cleared his throat. "Excuse me?"

"I am glad you are here. You will find much of interest before the night is out."

"Interest?"

"You appear to be searching for something." He waved his hand at the opened box on the deck behind Harrington, then at the bar in his hand. "I understand, being a curious creature myself."

"Creature?"

"The usage is incorrect? Forgive me. I have made a long study of your language. But it is quite possible I am a poor student."

"Who are you?"

The creature smiled, showing sharp teeth. "Forgive me again. I am Dracula. Count Dracula."

The vampire returned the startled Englishman's stare and, taking him in, was reminded of the young man he'd left behind in his Transylvanian castle over four weeks since; a play thing for his brides. Jonathan Harker... now dead or something worse. He abandoned these thoughts and returned his attention to this one.

"You are a scholar also, yes?" Dracula asked. His smile vanished. "But your curiosity puts you in danger. From books, you acquire knowledge but not understanding. You learn of things best left alone but have not the wisdom to leave them. Thus, you foolishly trespass."

Harrington opened his mouth to speak. Dracula stopped him with a gesture.

"Your presence belies any denial, please. But allow me to sate your curiosity. Like you, I too am a reader. Through books I have come to know and love your great England. I long to go through the crowded streets, to be in the midst of the whirl and rush of humanity, to share its life, its death, and the drama, the pleasure, the pain that makes what lies between. I am but a little way on the road I would travel. Soon, very soon, Whitby. Then. . . London. The great city that invites those willing to join in her. . . life. Unlike you, I will not be trespassing. I will be welcomed; celebrated as nobility."

"Nobility?" Harrington looked at the caskets about them. This was the Transylvanian nobleman spoken of, the owner of the boxes. How much worse the affair suddenly seemed to think this loathsome creature could pass itself off as human. He intended not only to feed off England but to walk among her people as one of them. "You are responsible for what has happened to the crew of this ship?"

Count Dracula did not even consider the question but waved it away as a trifle. Though terrified, Harrington recognized his duty. Feigning a casualness he did not feel, he stepped toward his sack on the floor. "You are responsible for what is happening to Ekaterina?"

"Delicious!" the dark one said with a laugh. His eyes glinted red.

In that instant, Harrington's fear left him, replaced by fire. "I am going to kill you!"

Dracula laughed again, a booming laugh to match the thunder.

Harrington dove for the kit, from his knee grabbed the handmade cross and slid it across the deck in the monster's direction. It came to rest at his feet and, in the lamplight, threw an elongated shadow onto his legs. Dracula howled and jumped back shielding his eyes. He lashed out at a stack of cargo over his left shoulder, tearing the bindings and throwing down the boxes. A brown cloud

Chapter Thirty-one

erupted and the offending icon disappeared beneath a wave of sawdust. Dracula lashed out again, at the containers to the right, shoving a barrel over into the mix. As it toppled, the lid flew off spilling illuminating oil. The kerosene splashed, yellow and cold, across the deck, the fallen cargo, the tarped boxes, the cross lost somewhere below, and Harrington on his knees.

The scholar sputtered, moving to rise, soaked in kerosene.

The ship rolled. The pool of oil rushed back across the deck and splashed over the vampire's feet and up his legs. Dracula ignored the deluge, turning on Harrington, shrieking, "I am master. None... will master me!"

Harrington, covered in oil and beyond caring, jumped forward and yanked the lantern from its bracket on the mast. "I will destroy you!"

"And this ship? And her crew? And... your lady fair, your Katya," the vampire said, mocking him. "Will you burn her as well?"

Harrington stared helplessly at the flame in his hand, the splashed oil, and the vampire. Swales was dead, the crew all but lost, Ekaterina on the verge of becoming one of these things! His home waited unknowingly to be next. He was out of weapons with which to fight this creature. If he didn't destroy him now, what else mattered? He raised the lantern and shouted, "I'll kill us all before I'll allow you to reach England!"

Dracula snarled and stepped toward him.

Harrington smashed the lamp on the deck. The kerosene erupted. The hold was aflame; the vampire on fire. Screaming, Harrington was burning too.

"No," Dracula shouted, stretching his arms, stretching his fingers to the overhead. "NO!" There followed a series of loud CRACKS, heard over the blaze and the storm as the battens above snapped and blew off. A tremendous gust followed as the hatchway doors flew up and open.

Lightning flashed above the billowing canvas on the square-rigged foremast towering over the open hatch. The cold rain poured in and, while Harrington and the vampire screamed their lungs out, extinguished the fire. Harrington teetered in the gray mist, badly burned, and fell to his knees groaning. Dracula, burned as well, instead of buckling to the pain, glared and gritted his sharp teeth.

Then Harrington, on his side in agony, witnessed the unbelievable again.

The monster was there, then he wasn't. The wounded Englishman, his consciousness slipping, didn't know what happened. Suddenly all that remained were the red eyes and vicious fangs embodied in the form of a huge black wolf. On all fours before him, it growled fiercely, dripping saliva. The wounded scholar thought he was hallucinating. Then it happened again, this transformation. The wolf was gone and the vampire was back. But, with his return, Harrington saw that his ruined flesh was repaired, as if he'd never been burned.

With an angry hiss, Dracula leapt at Harrington.

* * *

On deck, Amramoff stumbled, swimming as he walked, fighting to the fore of the ship against the wind and the waves. He'd spotted the open hatch doors. The Emperor alone knew how they'd come undone, but the battens were matchsticks. They had to be closed before the ship foundered and he was going to close them. Olgaren, holding on for life at the corner of the deckhouse, saw him and followed. Nobody, he thought, ought to face this sea alone. The storm was too devastatingly loud for either to hear much of anything, but they found each other with a nod of respect at the brink of the opening.

Lightning flashed and Amramoff paused as they lifted the doors closed. "Did you see that?" he shouted, pointing below. Olgaren shrugged and waved at his ears. "DID YOU SEE THAT? Something moved... in the hold. SOMETHING... IN THE HOLD!"

Chapter Thirty-one

Olgaren, pushing the rain from his eyes with a soaked hand, stared. The hold was black as pitch. There was nothing. More, there couldn't be anything and he shouted as much back.

They threw the doors shut. Amramoff grabbed a coiled line from the main mast pin rail and together they tied the covers down. The hatch secured, they fought their way back toward the stern.

* * *

Despite the blaze, *Demeter's* hold suffered surprisingly light damage. The rain had so quickly extinguished the fire that, outside of the spilled oil, little else had been consumed. The same could not be said for Harrington. His clothes were blackened rags, he was horribly burned and in agony.

With the hatchway secured above, and the lamp broken, the hold was again in darkness. The downpour had stopped but the cargo was soaked and the air thick with steam. Dracula stepped from the swirling cloud, seeing as if in daylight, with murder in his eyes. He grabbed Harrington by the remnant of his coat front and lifted him, yowling, off the deck.

Nearing madness, perhaps to block the soul-searing pain, Harrington's mind was flooded with questions. How could this creature accomplish such a transformation? What was he? Why did his clothing change with him? Then again, why not? Were not his clothes, all clothes, organic; made of clay like him? But how a wolf? And why a wolf? What had Oliver said, a rat, a bat... Poor Oliver!

He was snapped from his delirious wanderings by the monster drawing him near. Their noses all but touched as he stared daggers into the Englishman's agonized eyes. Harrington saw the hate. He felt the heat, smelled the rot, of his acrid breath.

"Impudence," Dracula whispered acidly. "To match your wits against mine. I promise you a most terrible death." Unable to escape, or even struggle, Harrington was helpless as the Count held him dangling above the deck. The vampire closed his eyes and quietly called, "Ekaterina."

"What do you want with her, you fiend?" Harrington cried. "Leave her alone!"

Dracula merely smiled.

"She won't come. I've seen to it," he screamed through the pain. "She loves me. There's nothing you can do. She is released from your influence."

Dracula answered, "You are a fool," and the between-decks door came open.

Harrington gasped. There, on the ladder platform, free from her bindings, stood Ekaterina. Her right wrist was bruised, her left bleeding. She had not only come at the monster's call, but had injured herself in doing so. More, she had cast off Swales' shirt and now wore the white flowing dress she'd secreted aboard. Lit by the companionway lantern, she looked an angel. But could an angel be summoned by a demon? Despite the pain, and the vampire's grip, Harrington gasped, "Katya!"

"Ekaterina," Dracula said, beckoning the girl. "Come."

She seemed almost to float down the stairs and, as she drew near, Harrington was overcome by the sight. It was a bastardization of one he'd witnessed before. That fateful night her father and brothers began shooting, Ekaterina had looked down on him from her window wearing the same lovely dress. Now everything was different; tainted. The bodice hung untied, the cincture dangled loosely about her hips, the high neck was torn exposing the milk-white skin at her throat and shoulders. Beauty... dragged through hell. She continued to move, as if floating, across the hold; her full attention, her adoration, on Dracula as if the Englishman did not exist.

Forcing Harrington to his knees, Dracula stared into Ekaterina's eyes, bored into her mind, commanding her without uttering a word. She obeyed, drawing the cincture from her waist, and letting her skirt dance on drafts of air in the cool hold. She stared unblinking at her master, twisting the ends of the belt around her fists, then turned to the crippled scholar.

Chapter Thirty-one

"Katya!" Harrington screamed. His scorched wounds weeping blood and fluid, Harrington lifted his hands to protect himself. Dracula slapped them down and he hadn't the strength to raise them again.

With no indication she'd heard him, Ekaterina looped the sash about Harrington's neck and held the ends waiting. Dracula, holding the helpless Englishman, raised his red lips in a cruel smile and nodded his assent. Ekaterina obeyed, drawing tightly on the ends of the cincture. Harrington gasped, gagged. She pulled with all her might; harder, tighter. She gritted her teeth, and pulled. Sweat burst from her pale forehead, and she pulled. The garrote dug into Harrington's throat and was swallowed by the swelling flesh. All the while Ekaterina stared, unblinking, into the eyes of the vampire.

Harrington's already burned throat turned white, then red. His breathless face went ash-gray, then cyanotic blue. His gagging halted; his breathing ceased. His dilated pupils disappeared as his eyes rolled into his head. Pin-point red petechial hemorrhages burst in clusters in his eyes. Accompanied by rumbling thunder, his lifeless eyes rolled down. His chin fell slack. His bloated, blue tongue dangled.

"Excellent."

Ekaterina, smiled gratefully, relishing Dracula's praise. Her eyes still locked on her master, she loosed the cincture and let the strangled Harrington fall to the deck.

Chapter Thirty-two

IN the hold, lamplight stealing in from the companionway, overtop of Harrington's burned and strangled corpse, Count Dracula lifted Ekaterina to him. Breathing heavily, she swooned and turned her head offering her master her naked throat and the bruised site of his earlier violations. He groaned and sank his teeth into her neck. The flesh tore as the wound reopened and Ekaterina cried out. There was a spurt of blood, her groan matching his, and the vampire drank.

He drained her blood nearly to the end. The girl collapsed into Dracula's arms and still he drank. She moaned again and the vampire, feeling her life ebb, forced her away from him. He eased her to the floor at his feet.

He turned from Ekaterina, grabbed Harrington as if his corpse weighed nothing, and lifted him onto his shoulder. He carried him up the straight ladder, pushed the hatchway open (breaking Amramoff's lashings), and stepped from the hold. The rain had stopped, the fog was thicker than ever. No one, save a vampire, could have seen their hand before their face. Dracula lowered Harrington into his arms and, moving through the dark and fog as if it were mid-day, carried him toward the port rail. (Intent on his mission, the vampire failed to notice Popescu's crucifix and rosary slip from Harrington's torn waistcoat pocket and fall to the deck.)

Chapter Thirty-two

At the bulwark, like the old cook throwing out galley scraps, Dracula chucked Harrington's body into the cold English Channel. He smiled triumphantly, watched the corpse disappear into the waters astern and for the longest time stared after it.

When Dracula finally turned away, Ekaterina was behind him. It was no surprise. While her step was now as stealthy as that of a cat, he'd heard her as if she were the stomping Olgaren. Rivulets of blood ran down her neck and chest. She smiled. Her eyes glistened red by the light of the oil lamp and her now-elongated teeth indented her soft red lower lip. They stood together in the fog, on the foredeck, the wind whipping his black cloak and her white gown; the masters of the night.

* * *

Again in the hold, Dracula threw a tarp off the stacked cargo, pulled a lid off one of the boxes quite near his own, and dropped it to the side. Then with a grating scratch of wood he lifted the box, dumped a portion of its dirt onto the floor, and laid it back flat. Behind him, watching, covered in blood, Ekaterina hummed and ran her fingers through the tangles of her matted hair. Dracula stared, thinking of his wives and, strangely, taking the measure of his regret. The lusts that led him from his casket to this woman were gone.

She caught his stare, stepped toward him with eyes aglow, and raised her arms for an embrace. He turned away and gestured toward the box. "You were never buried," he told her. "The soil from my homeland shall be yours. Find your rest."

She returned his stare in marked confusion. Angry, lonely, and fearful, *Demeter's* newest vampire did as she was told. She climbed into the box and lay upon the moldy soil. Count Dracula lowered the lid and closed her in.

* * *

Midnight, and Sunday became Monday morning, 2 August. The fog did not frighten Amramoff but it was frustrating. How could he maintain a decent watch when he could not see a thing? He was making his way slowly forward around the deckhouse when he thought he saw something near the hatchway to the cargo hold. What it was he didn't know.

He raised his lantern, moving stealthily in that direction, and panned the mouth of the hold and the foredeck. There was nothing as far as he could see. He held the lantern, diffused and glowing in the fog, over the open hatch and peered into its depths. Nothing but darkness and the ghostly outlines of tarps, lines, boxes, and barrels. Yet, he was certain (he was not the sort whose eyes played tricks) he saw something. It was his duty to ascertain what. He started into the hold.

"What the hell?" The carpenter stared, in shock, startled by the disaster the hold had become; barrels shoved open, oil and sawdust spilled, dirt poured out, scorches on the ceilings and overhead, and the tarps thrown off of half the cargo.

He saw something, a gray mist, swirling above one of the stacks of boxes and one box in particular. He approached throwing light on the ghost-like cloud with the lantern. The mist looked to be dissipating but, upon closer examination, he saw that was not the case. The swirl was disappearing like water down a drain through the fissures in the box, forcing itself inside.

Amramoff stood gawping and unable to move. Then his sensibilities returned. He spun on his heels, lifted the lantern, and scanned the hold looking for... There! He grabbed a heavy iron bar from the floor and turned back to the cargo set to batter the box open. Then he froze -

At the sound of a deep, spine-chilling voice, "Rats. Rats. Rats!" that echoed through the hold. There followed a series of high-pitched shrieks, and the voice again, "Rat. Rats! Rats!!" And they came out of the shadows!

Georgiy Eltsin had told him all about it; how he should have been there that morning, in the hold, to see it. How the Turks,

Chapter Thirty-two

while inspecting the cargo in the Bosphorus, had the living hell scared from them by rats that appeared out of the dark. Now here they were again. There was nothing new about rats on a sailing ship. But what was the voice, calling for them!

Now again, he watched as they came squeaking, scratching, closing in.

A rat squealed, leapt on Amramoff's arm, and sank its teeth into his flesh. The carpenter shrieked in horror. He jerked his arm back and, without thinking, swung the bar at the vicious rodent. The rat dug its claws into his wrist and jumped to his shoulder, avoiding the iron switch. Amramoff smacked himself, snapping the bones in his forearm. He screamed in agony, dropped the tool with a clatter and, as he tried to turn, tripped and went down. There was a collective shriek, a riot of high pitched cries. A riotous rush forward. They attacked in a wave, scratching, tearing, biting. The seaman fought his way to his feet. His broken armed dangled uselessly, but he fought the rats off, threw them off, with his good arm. He fought to reach the ladder.

Monstrous shadows danced about the hold to the tune of squeaks and screams. The rodents bit Amramoff as he gained the ladder, clawed at him as he climbed, tore at him as he dragged himself out of the well and crawled onto the deck. On hands and knees, he moved away with rats clinging to his clothes, his limbs, his flesh. Behind, the rats poured up and out of the hold like a waterfall flowing in reverse. Red-eyed and squealing, they skittered across the deck after the carpenter.

Amramoff was up again, unable to scream for he was unable to catch his breath. Still the monsters came on. Dozens of them, shrieking, clawing, tearing. His clothes, those that remained, already damp from the fog, were now soaked with blood. The feral rodents, having tasted his flesh, were ravenous for more.

The carpenter retreated, tripped and fell again, screaming before the rushing monsters. He fought to rise and retreated to the port rail. When there was nowhere else to run, he fought his way up onto the gunwale. What terror, compared to the bloodthirsty rats, held the sea for him? Covered in the clinging, writhing beasts, he found the breath for one final shriek of terror and fell into the pitching froth. Though no one heard him, Pasha Amramoff thanked God for a death in the cold sea.

Chapter Thirty-three

THE captain woke to a scream.

He had not been long abed; a scant few minutes. Not long enough to dream. He was... mentally disheveled; his vision, his hearing, his brain all were cloudy. That said, he knew he was right. It was a cry, a shocking mixture of pain and terror, near by. Just outside, it seemed. But the passageway was silent now.

He rose, considered a dose from the quack's tonic bottle as his heart was racing, then decided not to take the time. He headed up, quickening his pace with each step and, by the time he reached the deck, was nearly in a panic. He burst through the deckhouse door and ran into a figure moving in the fog. They grabbed one another, ready to fight.

"Iancu!"

"Captain! I heard someone cry out. I ran up as quickly as I could."

"Have you seen..."

"The night watch?" Constantin asked. "Not a sign."

"Come," Nikilov said. "We will find him together."

Like phantoms themselves within the fog shroud, they searched the deck. To no avail. The watchman was nowhere to be found. Amramoff was...

Chapter Thirty-three

"Gone," the captain said, a tremor in his voice. "One more gone. Lord, help us!"

"Just after I made the deck," the first mate said. "Just after I heard the man scream..." At the rail, he pointed out over the port bow. "The fog... It lifted for a moment. I swear, captain, I could see clearly for an instant. We're past the Straits of Dover." His voice dropped to a whisper. "We're past the straits. We must be."

Nikilov stared at Constantin, dumbfounded the man had so quickly forgotten the missing carpenter. Yet, he could also understand. They were lost at sea. Could it be that land was indeed nearby? He followed the mate's indication, to the surging but invisible sea, seeing only the same gray nothingness that had been their constant companion for days. If the fog had lifted, it had fallen again immediately and surrounded them completely; a swirling pall.

"I'm certain I saw the North Foreland," Constantin persisted. The captain heard it now, in the mate's voice; not excitement but agitation, rising terror. He was still looking to the port, but aft now, where there was nothing but fog. "I saw it," the mate said. "If so, if I'm right, we are now off... in the North Sea."

"Do not let us jump to conclusions."

"Conclusions? Do you not see it, Mikhail? Do you not feel it? The Devil is driving this ship!"

"Stop it, Iancu. What is the matter with you?"

The first turned staring, his swollen eyes glistening with tears, and Nikilov could see what the matter was; his first mate was frightened to death.

In matters of discipline, he'd always tried to be fair, but Nikilov had never coddled his men. The notion of having to nursemaid the fiery Constantin would not have occurred to him. But here the man stood, distraught, bewildered. What could he say? "We've been in bad weather before."

The first nodded absently and started slowly away.

"You know we have, man," the captain shouted, suddenly desperate to convince him. "How many times coming into the Bosphorus have we been unable to signal anyone? Or hail a soul for the weather as we drew nigh the rock of Gibraltar? It is bad weather, Iancu. My God, that's all it's been all along, just bad weather!"

"Bad weather?" Constantin repeated. He shook his head in disbelief. "From Cape Matapan to here and now... not a moment's rest. The Devil's breath in the sails every instant. Rain and seas, rain and pitching seas until hell wouldn't have it. And every time it ends... comes a frightening calm as dead as hanging Judas and this miserable, suffocating fog that holds us, travels with us! If we are traveling anywhere at all!"

Nikilov could hardly argue. Even as he spoke, the fog curled in closer making Constantin all but invisible; a shadowy phantom in the gray swirl with the voice of his first mate.

"Nine days since we entered the Bay of Biscay! Eight to pass through the English Channel, through rain and blasting wind. It's unheard of, by any reckoning! In all that time, not a headland, nor a port, nor a ship, nor a single living soul to see anywhere along the way. And six men dead! Vanished, from the ship and the earth, as if they'd never existed! At least six for that's just the crew. When is the last time either of us saw your Englishman? Or the girl?"

"Iancu..."

"Are they dead too, captain? Do you even know?"

"Iancu..."

There was no answer. Nikilov could no longer see Constantin for the fog. Whether the mate was still there, whether he'd walked away, or whether he'd simply vanished like the others, the captain did not know. "Iancu?" He stared wordlessly into the fog.

A man of faith, his only comfort for days had been his knowledge, his belief, that he and his crew were in the hands of God. Now his mind was playing tricks, telling him he was alone. But he knew better. Constantin had merely left the deck. Frightened and despairing, he had walked into the fog, gone off to be alone, nothing more. He, Mikhail Sergeyevich Nikilov, was not alone. Iancu was still aboard. His passengers were still aboard. And the Lord, his Lord, still held sway. To that end, he would be

Chapter Thirty-three

steadfast in his belief, in his duty. "God," the captain told himself, "is guiding us."

But the fog continued to swirl on the dark, cold deck... and Nikilov, despite his faith, felt desperately alone. Something black as the night, palpably evil, something outside of his body and soul was shouting at his mind, worming its way into his heart, insisting, *God has deserted you!*

* * *

The figurehead of the goddess *Demeter* undulated through the night. Beneath her, white foam burst from the blackness highlighting the crests of arcing seawater that twinned her bow as the schooner cleaved the surface of the cold North Sea. The gray fog parted by the bowsprit, the triangular flying jib, the jib, and the fore staysail, swirled in again around the tall, darkly-robed form behind the anchor capstan. Count Dracula stood like a statue, his hands raised in concentration.

While his body stood in the bow, riding the bucking deck as if he were attached, Dracula wasn't there at all. Beneath his physical being, all that constituted the vampire was in Whitby, in the Crescent, in Lucy's bed, Lucy's body.

He'd left her alone, undisturbed, for much of the week and the initial jolt was considerable. It took a moment for Dracula to recognize that he had again achieved the transition. In that thrilling instant he started as he took in the surroundings. There was a marble-topped washstand over a small section of brick floor (to catch the jets of splashed water), two small chairs, a large elbow-chair covered with dimity, a chest of drawers with brass handles, a dressing-table with a looking-glass and, on the far side of the room, a large window; its heavy curtains drawn back, its lace curtains aglow with a blue beam of moonlight stealing in. The initial sensation passed, and he recognized his surroundings for what they were, Lucy Westenra's bedchamber. Dracula lay in a clumsy British four-poster, in the softness and warmth of her bed-clothes, of her body, feigning sleep and studying the dark room. A canopy stretched above like the lid of a sarcophagus, lined with chintz, a fringed valance depended all around like spiders' webs, with curtains drawn back to the posts. A coverlet and blankets shrouded him in the warm fragile body he inhabited. He stretched, gripped the round buttocks, ran her hands up over the sharp points of her hips, felt the flat softness of her stomach, and over the swell of her breasts. He squeezed her lovely soft breasts and relished the sensation. He slipped her hand inside the top of her bed-clothes and was cupping the breast again when...

He looked up to see Mina, staring at him, staring at Lucy in curiosity, as she squirmed upon the bed fondling herself in her sleep. She too was in her night frock, flaxen hair draping over the shoulders, with soft points and softer curves interrupting the flow of the fabric from beneath. Dracula was overcome with bloodlust. More, with lust. He reached out to her... and remembered he was in Lucy's body. He was, at that moment, neither man nor vampire.

He could see it in Mina's eyes, the confusion, the growing fear; aware something was different about her friend, but unsure what. Then a wariness came over her as if suddenly she knew Lucy was watching her.

In a flash, Dracula was back in the bow of the schooner, surrounded by damp fog, sprayed by sea water, in his own body, cold as the grave.

He looked to the sky, concentrating. The roommate, Mina, needed a diversion. "Lucy," Dracula called aloud, summoning the woman that had a moment before been his physical host. "Lucy. Prepare for me. I will soon be there. Prepare ye the way of the master."

* * *

Across that great distance, his call roused Lucy from her bed but not from her sleep. She had, an instant before, stared in confused terror through red-looking eyes, his eyes, at the whipping sails

Chapter Thirty-three

above and before her on the fore of a fog-bound ship. She was frozen, wind-blown, horrified! Then it was over and she was back in her bed.

Now he was calling. "*Prepare ye the way of the master.*" She had no choice but to answer.

She was up immediately, in her sleepwalking trance, past the startled Mina and hurrying for the door. She turned the knob, found it locked, and began frenetically searching the room.

Mina could only guess at her goal, to find the door key, and followed on her heels. She was worried about her companion, but terrified of waking or frightening her. So worried, Mina was no longer even contemplating her friend's strange activities just a few moments since.

* * *

Constantin, walking the watch in the starboard companionway, paused at the corner of the deckhouse. He felt... something and strained his eyes, scanning the foredeck. He could see little in the fog-diffused lamplight, and nothing at all that appeared out of order. Still, he had that feeling. For an instant, he thought of Eltsin and his endless *feelings*. He started again, one slow, silent step at a time, stalking whatever was responsible for the palpable presence.

The fog seemed to part and, suddenly he was there; tall, thin and ghastly pale – the phantom of the ship. The tall man from the crew members stories. But which was this? Not poor Petrofsky's vision, for this man was far from old. His hair and thick mustache, striped with gray, but otherwise black as the night. Younger even than the man Olgaren reported. A third stranger! He stood in the bows, looking out to sea first, then strangely turning his attention to the deck beneath his feet. He was whispering and Constantin could only just hear him.

"Ekaterina," the phantom whispered. "E-kat-erina... hear me."

Constantin couldn't believe his eyes. In his agitated state, the phantom's words meant nothing to the mate. What the man was saying was of no consequence. What mattered was his presence. His? He? He... was not a man! Could not be, with the things he'd done. What then was – It?

Finished with It's chant, It stood like a statue looking out to sea.

The first quietly pulled his knife from its scabbard. Even in the fog the lamplight glinted off the blade as Constantin's hand shook. He inched forward, drawing a breath as quiet as he might, creeping up behind... It. Constantin gritted his teeth and, with a violent thrust, stabbed the creature in the back.

At least he tried.

The first mate's mouth fell open with horror and shock. For the knife met no resistance whatsoever and passed through the tall stranger as if he... It... were not there. It was as if the tall man were himself merely empty air. And, in that instant, It became empty air. Before Constantin finished the thrust of the blade, the dark man was gone. There was nothing, no one, there.

Constantin strained his eyes and only then saw a cloud of mist, lighter than the fog, hovering. Then it was gone. GONE! And, to Constantin's horror, a big gray bat beat the air in its place. Where it had come from, how it could have traveled this far out to sea, he could not answer. Nor did he have time to wonder, for the flying terror emitted a shrill screech and dove at him. Constantin covered his bald head and hit the deck. There was a flapping of its leathery wings, another shrill cry, then the bat too was gone.

Constantin breathed a sigh and listened intently. He heard the wind in the canvas, the sea pounding the prow as the vessel cleaved its way forward, and the creak of the ship as it rolled with the waves, but the hellish sounds of the gray monster were gone. Constantin pushed himself up to look around. He rose unsteadily. The tall man and the flying creature were gone.

* * *

Chapter Thirty-three

Flabbergasted, the mate ran, tripping through the fog, back to the tied-off wheel. His mind raced but there was no way to release the tension for he was all alone. Who would believe him? He stared forward, as if he could see through the fog, untied the wheel and leaned heavily upon it. There he remained, trading unseeing glances between the fog before him and the deck planking at his feet.

He was still there hours later when Olgaren relieved him. The big Russian was a shell of his former self. He'd spent the day searching for Pasha Amramoff; searching in vain. A restless sleep followed and now, with nothing else to do, he reported for watch. Defeated and alone, Olgaren failed to notice the mate's stricken condition. He asked by rote if anything worth mentioning had occurred. The first mate said nothing. "Mr. Constantin?"

Constantin merely stared into the fog.

"I'll take the wheel, sir," the big man said.

The first surrendered it without a word.

"Is this our heading, sir?"

Without replying, the mate started for the deckhouse.

"Mr. Constantin?" Olgaren called after him. "Are you all right?"

The officer disappeared, leaving Olgaren alone, ignorant of the strange occurrences on deck, and unsure even of the ship's course. He checked the compass, making sure of his bearings, and corrected for N.N.E., the last course as far as he knew. There was nothing else to do. He stood, stricken, holding the wheel, blind, deaf and dumb.

* * *

Time went by too slowly for the nervous Olgaren. The fog was making him claustrophobic. He missed his shipmates. He missed his friend Amramoff. He was terrified in his loneliness... until he felt the presence of another and his real terror began. Nothing about the deck had changed. All was as it was before. Yet he felt another in his midst.

A gap opened in the fog, and a beam of brilliant moonlight sliced through setting the rear of the deckhouse aglow. In that ray of yellow light, at the mouth of the port companionway, a young woman emerged. He thought he must be dreaming. The clouds of mist rolled as she moved and Olgaren saw she threw no shadow on the deck. She was fair, as fair can be, desperately thin and pale, with short and abruptly cut golden hair and eyes that seemed almost red in contrast to the light.

She wore a flowing white dress stained with what looked like blood. Her face was familiar, though he could not recollect when or where he had seen it. Then it dawned! The face was that of Funar, the injured deck boy. An instant later, it all flooded back; the boy had been no boy at all, but a girl, a stowaway who was injured and not seen again on deck. That explained the blood.

"You should not be on deck."

There was something about her that made Olgaren uneasy. He'd come to know her as a boy, had forgotten her altogether, and now saw her as a woman. Though she was thin, with little in the way of a shape, still he saw now she was every bit a woman. He felt like a monster for his sudden evil thoughts. Worse, on top of longing for the girl, he also felt a deadly fear.

She smiled at him with brilliant white teeth that shone like pearls against her ruby lips. Olgaren felt a stirring, a wicked desire for her to kiss him with those red lips; a strange mixture of terror and an agony of delightful anticipation.

She stared at him for several long seconds, then whispered, "I don't know what to do."

"What?" Olgaren said. "I do not understand you."

She laughed, a silvery, musical laugh, and said again, "I don't know what to do." Only then did the big Russian realize that the girl was not speaking to him. A blind fear swept over him as Olgaren became aware of another presence on the deck. No sooner did he recognize he and the girl were not alone than another figure appeared out of the fog starboard of the deckhouse.

Chapter Thirty-three

It was the tall man. His tall man! He was real! He had not been a hallucination! Or had he, Olgaren wondered? Was he hallucinating now?

"What do I do?" the girl asked.

"Feed," Dracula told her.

"But... how?"

Dracula gestured toward Olgaren. "As you will."

Olgaren did not speak Romanian, the language they seemed to be speaking to one another. But he didn't need to. All of his, what others referred to as 'dulled', senses were sending out alarms. He was terrified. But, despite his fear, Olgaren could not take his eyes off the dark couple. "I'm not afraid of you. I'm not afraid of ghosts!" In spite of his declaration, Olgaren's knuckles were white as he strangled the spokes on the ship's wheel. "Neither do I fear stowaways pretending to be ghosts." He nodded as if he'd made a discovery. "You've made monkeys of the others, but you won't make a fool of me."

Ekaterina looked to her master. Dracula gave no indication he'd heard Olgaren. He simply gestured again urging her forward. "He is yours."

She laughed again and stared intently. Then the laughter faded and her look of innocence disappeared. She leaned into a subtle crouch and moved to the bulwark on her right, her step as silent as a cat. She continued in an elliptical circle that brought her back toward the wheel on Olgaren's left. The tall man, the Russian saw, was doing the same on his side, mimicking her movements. As they closed in, Olgaren heard a rumbling in the base of the tall man's throat and a feral hiss from the girl.

Dracula halted his step while the girl continued on, gloating. Olgaren's eyes locked on hers. Then he found, despite his best effort, he couldn't turn away. His entire frame was both thrilled and repulsed in the same instant. As the fog swirled back in, the curtain of yellow moonlight faded, and the darkness overtook them, the last thing Olgaren saw was the glint of moisture as she flicked her tongue and licked her red lips and sharp white teeth.

314

Chapter Thirty-four

ENDLESS, billowing fog was the only thing visible from the captain's porthole. It was Tuesday, 3 August, just after midnight by his clock. He'd lost track of the watches, if they could be called that any longer, and wondered who was at the helm. The first now, Nikilov thought.

He gulped a draught of heart tonic, grateful for the awful taste (at least something was normal). He laid the bottle back in its drawer, beside his last, empty, prescription bottle and suddenly had an inspiration. He tore several blank pages from the back of his Ship's Log, wrapped them around a pencil, and slid the roll into the empty tonic bottle. He tucked all into his pocket. He was going up with no notion of when he'd return. No reason now he shouldn't continue his observations.

Nikilov left his cabin and toured the between-decks. The passenger's cabin was empty. Where Harrington and the girl had gone, he did not know. He couldn't remember now when last he'd seen either. There was no one in the mess, and no food, coffee or tea. They could dig something out later, salted meat, raisins... Nikilov did not remember the last time he'd eaten. It did not matter, he wasn't hungry. But how he would love a hot cup of tea.

He crossed the companionway into the crew's quarters and found he'd been mistaken about the steersman. Constantin was

Chapter Thirty-four

there, unconscious in his flannels, one hand and one foot draped on the deck. Olgaren, he decided, was probably at the wheel.

Nikilov massaged his forehead. "What is happening to me?" He'd never lost control of a ship. Now he seemed not to know whether he was coming or going. He paused, struck. Of course, it had to be Olgaren at the wheel. There was no one left!

He exhaled, fought back the tears, and pricked his ears to listen. The mate was breathing. Of course, he was. He was sleeping. Thank God for a deep and well-earned sleep. Constantin bucked, moaned and the captain saw how fitfully he slept. Nikilov burdened his God further, silently asked Him to grant his mate peace. Hoping (rather than believing) He might, the captain decided to let Constantin sleep. He would take the first mate's turn at the wheel.

* * *

He stepped from the deckhouse into a gray pea soup of fog. Strange too, for the wind was strong and steady; he could feel the vessel running smoothly before it. He peered through the clouds, in the direction of the helm, but saw nothing. He touched the boom and headed aft. But as he drew near, his eyes grew wide and his mouth fell open. His heart stopped and the blood froze in his veins. The wheel lolled gently with the roll of the ship, untended and untied.

"Olgaren?" he croaked, barely audible. He cleared his dry throat and tried again. "Moisey Olgaren!" He took the wheel and shouted forward into the night air. "Olgaren!"

He would wait. Olgaren would return.

Hours passed...

During which Nikilov worried for the big Russian and fought his fears alone. Finally, when he could no longer simply stand there, he lashed the wheel and took the starboard companionway past the deckhouse. Minutes later, he returned on the port side, having seen no one and nothing but fog.

Back on the aft deck, he leaned on a rum barrel to consider a full search. But what would be the point? How many times had his schooner been searched? To what end? Nothing had ever been found. Olgaren, the captain feared, would not be found either. He returned to the helm and took the wheel in hand. He was in command and would not, could not, leave the helm untended again. He remained there the rest of the night, the events of the cruise mixing with the swirling fog to stimulate his fears and play tricks on his mind. As dawn approached, Nikilov could contain those fears no longer.

"Constantin!" he bellowed. "Mr. Constantin!"

Scant seconds elapsed, certainly not a full minute, the deckhouse door BANGED on the bulkhead. The fog parted and the ship's mate appeared wild-eyed and haggard. He wore only the flannels he'd slept in, not having bothered to dress, and ran his hands maniacally over his dome.

The captain was concerned his mate's reason had given way.

Constantin spied the captain, recognition dawned in his crazy eyes, and he stepped toward him. He gripped the master's coat sleeve, drew to within an inch of Nikilov's ear, and whispered, "It is here."

The captain, without a clue to his meaning, told him, "Moisey Olgaren is missing."

Constantin ignored him, as if he hadn't spoken at all, and repeated, "It is here." He pulled away, looked the captain in the eye, and nodded at their shared secret. He leaned in again. "I know it now. On the watch last night I saw It. It was like a man, on two legs like a man, tall and thin. But it was ghastly pale. It stood in the bows, looking out forward, as if It could actually see the sea through the fog. And I thought I had It. For all of us!" He pulled away, remembering. "I drew my knife..."

Nikilov drew breath, suddenly aware his mate was holding a keenly sharpened blade. He was afraid, not for himself, but for the sanity of his mate and friend. He tightened his grip on the wheel, warily watching as Constantin slowly carved the air.

317

Chapter Thirty-four

"Oh, so quietly, I drew my knife. I crept up behind It." He viciously stabbed the air and shouted, "And I gave it my knife!"

The ferocity vanished as quickly as it had appeared. The madness, if that's what it was, left his eyes. He looked to the captain in disbelief and utter dispair. When he spoke again, he barely muttered, "But the knife went through It. Just... right through It, as if his body were as empty as the air."

He didn't mention the cloud of mist. Did not tell the captain about the huge bat. Could not admit he'd run from the deck like a frightened child! There was no need, not now. If he had been cowardly, he'd already decided, he would make up for it now.

"But It is here," Constantin said going on. "... and I will find It. It is in the hold, perhaps in one of those boxes. I'll unscrew them one by one and see. You work the helm."

Constantin seemed not to care, or even realize, he had just issued an order to the master. With a look of warning, and a finger to his lip to ensure their shared secret, he turned and disappeared back into the fog. The deckhouse door was heard to close.

For a moment, the captain was of a mind to follow but the wind was building again and starting to come in gusts. The fog remained but the sea was growing choppy. No, regardless of what the first was about, the captain knew he dared not leave the helm.

A short time later, the mate re-emerged carrying Amramoff's tool chest and a lantern. He ignored Nikilov and disappeared around the deckhouse headed, if he followed his stated intention, for the forward hold. Constantin was mad. The captain was certain now. He was stark raving mad and it was no use trying to stop him. He could destroy the cargo, Nikilov realized, but why should he? He wouldn't hurt those big boxes hunting an imaginary fiend. To pull them about was as harmless a thing in his present state of mind as he could do. Let him go about it if the exercise kept him busy.

The captain drew the bottle from his pocket. He unrolled the paper and pen and, beginning with his finding the helm untended and Olgaren gone, recorded these most recent events. There

Nikilov stayed, minding the helm, writing his notes, feeling the wind pick up, and trusting in God that the fog would clear soon.

If he could only see. He could steer to a harbor, any harbor.

But he needed another plan. If the fog did not clear. Or, if the wind rose too much and he couldn't steer... Nikilov considered the matter. He could cut down the sails! Yes, close as he had to be, he could lie by and signal for help. Someone would eventually see him. If the wind got up, he had the option. One way or another, this hellish crossing was nearly over!

Soon he heard Constantin, forward and below, knocking away at something in the hold. Let him pound. The work was good for him and (dared he hope?) might help the mate to come out calmer.

Dawned arrived, softened to a glow by the stubborn fog.

* * *

The mate, panting with fear, pumping with adrenaline, dropped Amramoff's tool box into the hold with an explosive BANG and slid down the hatchway ladder. He collected a hammer from the scattered tools, moved immediately to the nearest stack of cargo and began smashing the top box. It was less a search than it was an attack. Wood cracked, splintered and the lid was pitched aside. Dirt flew. He kicked through the clods as if an evil stowaway might be hidden within any one of them, spreading mold and soil across the deck.

Nothing! Nothing but dirt.

Disgust registered on Constantin's mad face. He turned to a second box and again lashed out with the hammer. The lid burst open under his assault. Dirt flew, as did a startled rat that hit the floor running. Constantin ignored the squealing rodent as he rifled the box. Nothing.

The first mate cursed an oath.

He grabbed the handle on another, pulled it out and, even in his mania, reeled in horror. Stuffed behind, was the dead body of Moisey Olgaren. His mortal remains lay twisted, with waxen

Chapter Thirty-four

blue-tinged skin and a torn-out throat of sallow fat, red muscle, and white vocal chords. The eyes were a lusterless gray. The whole was drained of blood.

Determined to go on, the mate willed his terror into anger. He smashed the box with his hammer, busting through the lid. The broken slats parted revealing a pair of staring eyes within. Constantin shouted. It was the Romanian girl, wide-eyed and lifeless, looking up through the hole.

The shock drove him back, physically from the box, mentally from the moment. In that instant, like one of the amazing Lumière actualités he'd seen in Paris, the past was projected before his eyes. It had been nearly three weeks since they'd caught her, disguised as a boy, making fools of everybody aboard the ship. She had paid for her lie, the evil in this hold had seen to that. If only he'd known... If only he'd listened to the score of experienced sailors who refused to sign aboard this cursed ship. Now, here lay the poor child, dead and buried away with the dirt and the rats.

But, as the first mate stared, he realized that the seemingly lifeless form beneath his gaze was full of color, vivacious, almost bloated. Between her slightly parted, brilliantly red lips, the pointed ends of sharp canine teeth showed. Her staring eyes, even as he stood over her, had somehow altered. They were suddenly aimed in his direction and filled with hate. The girl was not dead! She had been possessed by the evil in the hold. She was one of those awful creatures Popescu had always been on about. The girl was one of the undead.

In a panic, in a rage, Constantin screamed as he tore the lid off. There she lay, in a flowing white gown, a wounded throat awash in dried blood, herself a murdering monster that must be destroyed. He grabbed a handspike from Amramoff's kit and approached the box with gritted teeth. He raised the deck tool above his head and, with a trembling hand, drove it down and into her stomach.

The girl came up in the box shrieking like a banshee and grabbing for him with clawed hands. The first mate struggled to free himself from her icy grasp. He yanked the handspike from her body then turned on the attack. He swung the hammer with one hand, blasting her solidly in her white forehead with a dull *thwack*, and stabbed her again with the handspike. Screaming and clutching at her wounds, Ekaterina dropped back into the casket.

Constantin crossed the hammer and the blood-soaked handspike, one over the other, and brandished this makeshift cross over the monster in the box. Screaming and hissing, Ekaterina did all she could to shield her eyes.

He threw the broken lid over her, closing it as he was able. Beneath, visible through the crack, her hate-filled eyes gleamed, while her fangs were bared in a shriek. He laid the gory tools, still in the shape of a cross, atop the lid. Inside the box, the eyes closed. The fangs disappeared, as the shriek became a low moan, behind agonized lips. The motion within the box ceased.

Constantin closed his eyes and tried to catch his breath. His heart was racing. His hands were trembling. Stealing himself, he returned to Amramoff's kit, took up a pry bar, took another breath, and surveyed the depths of the hold. Whatever the girl had become... Whatever this thing was... it was trapped for the moment; caged if it couldn't be killed. But, the mate knew, she was not the cause of this evil. Somewhere in one of these caskets he still had the devil to find.

Behind him came a riotous eruption, tumultuous sound and motion. Shadows danced, rats squealed, wood slapped hard against wood. Constantin spun, raising the bar defensively, to face the din. There stood the phantom, his feet still in one of the partially-filled boxes, the tossed-off lid laying half-way across the hold. He was young, vibrant, bloated with blood. He stared at Constantin with livid, hate-filled eyes that gleamed red in the dull light. And he spoke... "How dare you?"

The first mate's eyes grew wide as saucers. His mouth fell open in a silent scream as his mind snapped. He dropped the pry bar with a muted clang. He backed away from the tall one, fell on the stairs, and scrambled to the between-decks above.

Chapter Thirty-five

A SCREAM echoed throughout the ship, from the fore hatch, through the between-decks companionway and up the scuttles. The startled captain looked up from the wheel. His blood ran cold, the hair on his arms and the nape of his neck stood on end. "Dear God," he whispered.

The deckhouse door BANGED open! Constantin exploded from below as if shot from a gun. "Save me!" He landed on his feet, teetered, and would have fallen had he not grabbed the top of a rum barrel. He steadied himself, in body, but it was beyond debate the first was now a raging madman. His eyes darted and rolled, his face contorted with all of his wild fears. He looked about, caught sight of the captain through the shifting fog and shouted again. "Save me!"

He stumbled to his left, turning a circle in the swirling fog. He scanned the heavy mist, as if expecting some THING, some unnamed horror, to reach from the gloom and grab him. In this manner, spinning, darting his head, unintelligible cries escaping his trembling lips, Constantin moved toward the starboard rail.

Nikilov stood his place at the wheel, straining to see his shipmate, his friend, completely undone. Should he seize hold of the man? Or would that harm more than help? Could he say something, anything, to sooth him and stem the madness? What

Chapter Thirty-five

would he say? How would he say it? Tired and not a little terrified, Nikilov stood mum.

Constantin sprang up onto the rail and teetered on the bulwark. He grabbed the main mast rigging and turned to face his commander wearing the shifting fog like a shroud. A change came over the mate. The fear drained from his face like rum from a barrel (the blood from Lord Nelson). The boiling anger, so much a part of his make-up, likewise evaporated. His shoulders sank, his arms fell to his sides. He looked slowly out to the sea, though there was precious little visible through the heavy air, then turned back to the helm. He was finished; nothing left but exhaustion and despair. "You had better come too, captain," Constantin said, in a sad but steady voice, "before it is too late."

"Iancu," Nikilov said... But his first mate was beyond hearing.

"He is there." Constantin pointed past the deckhouse, to the innards of the ship. "He's there! I know the secret now." Then, even through the fog, he smiled. It was a smile, not of happiness, but of relief as if he'd reached the end of a long and miserable journey.

"Iancu." Nikilov could think of nothing else to say.

The mate stared into the swirling mist to their starboard with the rushing water providing background music to this his final scene. "The sea will save me from Him," he said with certainty. "It is all that is left!"

Without another word, Constantin jumped.

Nikilov stared, wide-eyed and disbelieving, at the ship's empty bulwark. For a long time afterward, he could do nothing else. He merely stared.

Slowly, with much force of will, the captain's mind wrapped itself around what had taken place. Constantin claimed he knew the secret. Now Nikilov knew as well. The mystery to the horrors that had taken place aboard his ship was solved and the truth in the open. Iancu Constantin, his mate, the man to whom he had given responsibility near-matching his own for his ship, his crew, and his cargo, the man to whom he had given his trust and his friendship, to whom he had given a loaded revolver when every other soul aboard was unarmed, was mad. He had killed everybody aboard *Demeter*. Now he had taken his own life. "God, help me!" The captain prayed.

How was he to account for these horrors? For an instant he imagined himself being tried and convicted for murdering his crew. He imagined himself dragged before a crowd eagerly awaiting his execution. He saw himself swinging from the gibbet. He imagined all these things happening when he brought *Demeter* in to port.

Then the ridiculousness of these thoughts sank in and Nikilov laughed, screaming to the heavens, "When I get to port!"

* * *

Presumably the sun rose on Wednesday, 4 August.

Nikilov knew it was there because he was a sailor. But he could neither see it nor appreciate its arrival. He could not feel its warmth or rejoice in its purity. The sun could not pierce the veil of fog surrounding the ship all through the day. Its rays, diffused by the thick swirling mists, managed little more than to glow with a smothered daylight, a gray nimbus that vacillated wildly in brightness and was often as dark as night.

The captain was beginning to feel his 'nocturnal existence' tell on him, and scribbled as much on the note pages he carried in his pocket. The nights were destroying his nerves, he wrote. He started at his own shadow and was full of horrible imaginings. God knew there were grounds for his terrible fear. The schooner no longer felt like his ship and, more and more, he found himself thinking of *Demeter* as nothing more than *this accursed place*!

For most of the day, Nikilov remained at the con. There was nobody left to take the wheel; he was the last man standing. And, of course, he was the ship's captain. But he made up his mind, eventually, that the only way to remain at the helm long enough to save his ship was to leave it briefly now. Things needed tending to... So he tied the wheel off.

Chapter Thirty-five

* * *

Nikilov entered his cabin with thoughts of returning to the helm with his pockets swollen with booty from below; a bible, the Russian colors, a coil of stout rope, food and drink, his log book, perhaps even a pound of Swales' tobacco and a bottle, if the old boy had one hidden. (He never knew a cook who didn't.) His great plans changed when he reached his berth. The bible and colors seemed superfluous. They were ever his strength and courage but, as he always carried both in his heart and head, what sense did it make to overload his hands? Food and drink, though he could not explain the feeling, seemed out of place and somehow wrong. The rope seemed foolish as there was rope a-plenty on the deckhouse wall. More ridiculous yet was the idea of tobacco and a mug. He did not smoke and, as he was the only one here to be responsible for the ship, would not drink.

In the end he settled for his spyglass and his sextant. They'd been taken below, along with the ship's hour-glass, when the seas got up rough. He left the time piece. (What difference could the time make now?) He took the glass and measuring device under his arm and started back.

He paused in the mess and, searching Swales' galley, located and confiscated a tin of oil. The deck lamps had been neglected (with no deck boy to refill them) and were all but dry. He'd a notion to grab some biscuits, cheese or a handful of raisins. But Swales had been so fastidious in cleaning up there was nothing edible in sight. With the ship sailing blindly, unguided, through the fog, Nikilov would not take the time to look. He returned to the deck with the items he had.

Several times more during the day Nikilov lashed the wheel and left the helm to stand at the port bulwark and search for land or ship, equally impossible. Following each sortie, he returned to take the wheel again into his hands and regain some sense of control.

But the fog had left him blind. What, dear God, kind of fog was it? It seemed the whole western North Sea (for didn't he have to be in the west of the North Sea?) was covered in this swirling blanket. Or was it his own private fog moving with the ship?

Nikilov left the wheel one other time that bleak and foggy Wednesday. He secured the ship, on a course he'd only guessed at and went to the head. He could have accomplished the same over the near pin-rail but, though everything else was gone, he still had his dignity.

Going to and coming from the bow, Nikilov walked past the rosary that dropped on the deck from the tear in Harrington's waistcoat pocket, without taking notice. He returned to the stern ignorant of its presence.

On his return, he diverted to the deckhouse rain barrels, washing his hands and face in one and stealing a cool drink from the other. He'd eaten nothing since the afternoon of the previous day. A momentary twinge of annoyance passed through his frame for the memory of his late cook. The man had been tidy to the point of starving him to death. Of course it was nonsense and Nikilov knew it. Cleanliness had always been, by his own pronouncement, next to godliness. He had no one to blame for his rumbling innards. (How would the loud Scot have put it? *He "lacked belly-timber".*) He accepted the rumble and ignored it. Nikilov found himself refreshed by the water and chose to be content with that. He resumed the wheel with a lighter heart, determined to push away the spiritual darkness.

Morning became afternoon became evening. Throughout, Nikilov's mind ventured over many topics, envisioned many faces, debated furiously with itself, and worked to still itself against the effects of many fears. To say these thoughts all passed in silence would be to mislead. For the old seaman, to his own embarrassment, caught himself more than once laughing, singing, even arguing to the air. All the while, the wind blew (without clearing the fog!), the sails billowed, waves buffeted the ship, and the deck creaked endlessly as it pitched and rolled beneath his feet, his desperately aching feet.

Chapter Thirty-five

* * *

Outside of Nikilov's activities, the day came and went below deck as well. The gray glow left the fog with the setting of the sun. With no one below to light the lamps, darkness overtook the bunk rooms, the mess and galley, and the cellars of *Demeter*.

In the pitch black of the forward hold, Dracula emerged from his box. Following the bloodbath of the previous night, his vitality had returned and his youth was again in full vigor. He stepped to the coffin he'd created for Ekaterina the night before and, even in the blackness, had to quickly avert his eyes. He hissed in annoyance. The ship's tools, left atop her box by that miserable sailor, were still there, over-laying each other in the shape of a cross. He reached blindly down and flipped the lid open, sending the offensive cross (inoffensive tools again) flying across the hold and out of his way.

Ekaterina lay within, wide awake, in agony.

She was ghastly pail and fighting for breath. Her eyes, like Dracula's, had the reddish reflection of some wild animal but, unlike his, were lusterless and lacked the startling brilliance that made the Count's so frightening. She was starved for blood, her body wracked and emaciated, a viscous mixture of blood and clear fluid seeped from the wounds in her stomach. He lifted her, upsetting the casket and disgorging moldy dirt about the deck at his feet.

* * *

The captain heard something below. He feared his ears must be playing tricks. He was the only person alive on the ship! The crew was dead or gone, and days had passed since he'd seen either of his passengers. Yet, to his growing alarm, he heard someone; something.

What had Constantin said just before he jumped to his death? "He is there!" They were the ravings of a madman, surely. They couldn't have meant anything. Who was left?

"Who," he whispered aloud. "Who is there?"

As if he'd spoken a cue, the door to the midship deckhouse burst open. Nikilov gasped.

There, in the dimness of the lamplight, stood the fiend, tall, thin and draped in black as his terrified crew had described him all along. A young man. The ship's phantom with, and there Nikilov gasped again, the Romanian girl in his arms. All indications of her former incognito, the deck boy, were gone. She was clothed in a white dress, the origin of which the captain couldn't begin to guess. Otherwise, her appearance did not match her elegant attire. She was conscious, but only just, and lay wounded and splattered in blood, supine as he cradled her, and at his mercy.

"Who are you?"

The dark creature, the shadow man, ignored the question and stepped out. Behind him, the deckhouse door slammed closed with the roll of the ship.

Nikilov stared on, unable to hide his awe. "What have you done to the girl?"

The monster that haunted his ship paused and glared at Nikilov. Then, dear God, he smiled, showing frighteningly sharp teeth below his mustache. With no more answer, still cradling the girl, he rounded the starboard corner of the deckhouse and vanished into the fog headed forward.

"What are you doing with her?" Nikilov cried in impotent fury. "In the name of God, what are you doing with her?"

* * *

Dracula strode into the bow with Ekaterina gasping in his arms.

There had been much for him to consider the preceding day as he lay in his box. He thought of his brides, rising from the vaults, floating through the halls of his castle in Transylvania. He thought of Lucy, the dark-haired beauty whose mind he'd touched ahead of them in Whitby, wandering the night, aching for his arrival. He thought of the maniacal servant in Purfleet, addicted now to

Chapter Thirty-five

blood, waiting impatiently to serve him. And he considered this young thing in his arms.

"Stop there!"

His thoughts interrupted, Dracula turned to see the ship's captain emerge from the fog.

His blue eyes pierced the veil of gray to stare at Dracula with all of his pent-up anger. He could not merely stand by at his wheel while this demon had his way with the child. To that end, he'd drawn his gun and come forward brandishing the revolver. "Give the girl to me."

The vampire would have laughed had not the rest of the crew been so obstructive, so tiring. He'd had enough. He eased the girl to the deck and turned on Nikilov.

The terrified captain did not wait to see what the monster next intended. He raised the gun and pulled the trigger repeatedly; seven explosions in rapid succession. His shaking hand sent the first shot wide, through a spritsail, but the remaining six struck their target solidly in the chest and stomach. The phantom bucked slightly as each shot tore through him and a dark nimbus of watery blood appeared and grew around each puncture in his black clothing. Beyond that, the assault produced no discernable effect. The tall man merely glared at Nikilov, his eyes glinting through the fog and black smoke.

Dracula swatted the gun from the old man's hand sending it flying over the rail. He tore the captain's shirt clutching at him then threw Nikilov somersaulting away. Dracula moved in again, eager to send the old sea dog to whatever afterlife awaited him.

Nikilov was helpless. Face down on the deck, hungry, exhausted, disheartened beyond the breaking point, he'd been in no condition for a fight from the start. He recovered his senses only to realize he was about to meet his doom.

It was then he saw the miracle.

Surely it was; a rosary *miraculously* glinting in the soft glow of the deck light. He had no way of knowing that it wasn't a miracle at all, that the icon had fallen from the pocket of the murdered

Harrington, that it had lain there all day. He had himself stepped past it several times. But he saw it now and, like the miracle he presumed it to be, Nikilov clutched the rosary in his fist and drew it close.

Dracula reached for him. Nikilov rolled to avoid the clutching hand. He stared up in blind horror at the white face, the sharp teeth. Emboldened by fear, Nikilov lifted the rosary as if it were a shield. The silver crucifix, the depending beads, shone in a brilliant flash of reflected light. Dracula shouted in pain and backed away.

Nikilov did not know why he'd been spared, nor did he care. The monster had released him! Instinct told him to flee, yet, he could not without the girl. With the tall man turned away, he looked to her wondering how he could save her. But she was staring back at him with something akin to animal hunger in her eyes. She appeared badly wounded and wobbly on her feet but had a set of fangs every bit as frightening as those of the phantom. Only the crucifix, Nikilov was certain, kept her from him. Dracula joined her, baring his teeth. The pair hissed and Nikilov backed away in terror. Like everything else about this voyage, he was too late to do anything at all. He turned and ran.

Dracula pictured the captain, shaking like a wind-blown leaf, hiding somewhere in the fog. He would deal with him later. With Nikilov and his detestable Christian symbol gone, Dracula lifted Ekaterina back into his arms.

"Am I dying?" she asked, struggling for breath.

Dracula smiled in spite of himself. "You are already dead. You are beyond death."

"But I feel like I'm dying."

"The cross," he said, "left atop your box all day, prevented your wounds healing."

"Will I heal now?"

"In time. Were I to allow it."

She gasped against the pain, holding him tightly. "I do not understand."

Chapter Thirty-five

"You are a delectable little toy." The vampire smiled cruelly. "But I have many plans for when this ship reaches England. None of which include you."

"I love you. I am yours."

Dracula chuckled, then roared with laughter. He set her bare feet upon the deck and, supporting her weight, stood her against the pinrail. "Companionship... a pleasure, but always a fleeting one."

Anger flashed in her eyes driving the pain, temporarily, from them. She grabbed the rail to brace herself. "You don't want me?"

"I cannot use you. Still, to show you that I too can love, I offer you something I have never offered another in all these many centuries..."

Breathless anticipation took over, the wounded vampiress was wide-eyed. "You offer?"

"My pity." He stroked her hair, watching the anger flash in her eyes, and allowed his hand to trail to the nape of her neck. "And a second, even more rare gift... my mercy." He snatched her throat with lightning speed. (So quickly she hadn't even time to gasp). "I shall not miss you," Dracula told her. "But I will most certainly remember you." Showing neither hesitation nor emotion, he lifted her off the deck and snapped her neck. Her lithe body went limp as a rag doll. Her face was still alive, her eyes blinking, her protruding tongue lolling to one side, a stuttering gasp escaping her lips in an unsuccessful attempt to talk – or perhaps to scream.

He grabbed a handful of her flowing dress with his free hand, bunched it at her knees and lifted her over the gunwale. Then he dangled her above the churning North Sea like a goose in a shop window. "We are undead," he told her. "We cannot die. But we can be destroyed. This is the gift I now give you."

He dropped her with a splash. The living water of the cold North Sea churned around her as if she'd been dumped into a vat of acid. Without muscle control, she could not work her lungs, could not scream (though her mind was shrieking), could not struggle. All Ekaterina could do was vanish beneath the foam-topped waves.

* * *

With nowhere else to run, Nikilov was back at the ship's wheel trying to maintain his sanity. He was shaken to his core and shaking. Terrified, trembling, he gripped the crucifix and cried in shame at having done so little to help the girl. He was still crying when the tall man appeared from the fog again on the port side of the deckhouse. He was alone. His arms were empty.

"The girl!" Nikilov hollered. "What have you done with her?"

Dracula stared a threat at the captain. "Like your crew," he said, "her usefulness was behind her." He punctuated the remark by washing his hands in the air.

The captain raised the crucifix. The vampire averted his eyes. He lingered a moment more, threatening at a distance, before he turned and vanished below.

What nightmare could be more terrible than this awful, unnatural thing aboard his ship. He dared not go below, dared not leave the helm, dared not even sleep. He determined then and there to stay awake at the wheel all night. He was resolved, but he was also more frightened than he'd ever been before. Nikilov began to shake, crying in despair, for the girl, for his crew and for his lost ship.

Chapter Thirty-six

"FORGIVE me, Iancu!" Nikilov laid his head on the wheel. "Forgive me."

He'd misjudged his mate, his friend, he'd accused him of murder and (though he'd pitied his insanity) had breathed a sigh of relief at his self-immolation. He'd been so desperately wrong. God forgive him, Constantin was right. There was a horror below, a monster in the flesh.

Nikilov had seen the creature, a sight he could never forget. He'd spoken with him, an experience he could never get over! He'd cowardly allowed him to take the girl forward to her destruction. Now he stood alone, at the helm of his doomed ship, awaiting death. If only he'd listened!

The first had been right to jump overboard. What man of the sea could object? But a death in the waters that had been his life, would not be granted Nikilov and he knew it. A comforting sea was for others. His was a cruel sea with its own rules. He was captain of *Demeter*. Cursed or not, possessed by demons or not, she was his ship and he could not leave her. More than that, he would not surrender her. He would take a stand. It was his duty. He owed it to his friend and mate, Iancu Constantin.

Nikilov refilled his fading lamp with the kerosene he'd collected on his sortie and considered his position. He was weakening and felt it. Had he a plan, would he have the strength, the courage,

Chapter Thirty-six

or the time to act? Could his mind last? Could he even look the monster in the face again?

He licked the point of his pencil and, in his notes, in a weary hand, wrote.... *God and the Blessed Virgin and the Saints, help a poor ignorant soul trying to do his duty.*

Should the ship fail to make Whitby, should she be wrecked, perhaps the bottle would be found, and those finding it might believe. Even if they did not, at least men would know he had been true to his trust. He rolled the pages and slid them into the bottle. He corked it like a repentant sot and pushed the bottle into his pocket. Then he sighed deeply. The time had come for his final offensive action as commander of *Demeter*.

Well Nikilov knew, he could not escape the fiend that had brought ruin to his ship. He was, he knew, as dead as his crew. But he was not finished. He could not save himself, but he might yet save his ship. And, if God was willing, he might even save his soul and his honor as a captain.

He scanned the deck, as far as the shifting fog allowed, and the sails in the heights. Convinced he was alone, he left the wheel. He scarpered forward to the deckhouse, grabbed the thinnest, strongest braid he could find among the hanging lines, and returned to the helm. He took the miracle rosary from his neck. He looped the beads over the top spoke on the wheel and, with the line, tied his left hand over them. Carefully, if awkwardly, with the crucifix clutched in his palm, he tied his right hand over the left. He tested his work, making sure of the slack to flip the crucifix over his hand, toward the bow, and back again. Satisfied, he fastened the knots with his teeth.

* * *

Night became morning, became day... All day Thursday, 5 August, Captain Nikilov stood his station tied to *Demeter's* wheel.

The cost of saving his ship, Nikilov realized, would be high but not tragic. The only human left aboard, he'd had to surrender his humanity. He would not leave the helm, therefore he could not eat, attend to his ablutions, or see to the calls of nature. It hardly mattered. There was nobody left to impress, for whom to be an example, or before whom to be embarrassed. Direct sunlight was no worry owing to the fog and, as they'd traveled far enough north, the heat was no difficulty either. In fact, as day dragged into evening, the captain developed a chill (and a fear of the impending cool of night).

His major physical concern was thirst, which grew as the hours wore on. More than once, he was tempted to untie and drink of the nearby rain barrel or even, forgive him, of the half-hogshead of rum. He resisted. The water was a matter of character. The rum, under the circumstances, would be as wrong as surrendering the helm. And that, he would not do, until he reached land. His thirst unsatisfied, Nikilov could only pray for the fog to lift and a British port-of-call to show itself.

With the setting of the sun (presumably), came the gloom and, from forward and below, the sound of hammering. The source was beyond question. There was no one else aboard *Demeter* except that thing. There it was again, sharp hammering, metal on wood. What was he doing?

* * *

In the dark of night, as Nikilov knew he would, came the monster.

Thirsty, hungry, exhausted and fighting to remain awake and upright, Nikilov was just nodding when the demon rounded the deckhouse. The captain snapped instantly awake. The tall man stopped and stared toward the helm with a cruel smile on his lips.

He removed a handspike from among the hanging gear, waved it in Nikilov's direction in a playfully threatening manner, then rammed the tool through the lower side of the tapped rum keg. He pulled it free and the rum spilled out. He watched the captain while the container gurgled empty. He repeated the action with the

Chapter Thirty-six

full, untapped keg. Again, even more forcefully, the perfectly good rum poured out, followed the roll of the deck to the scuppers and spilled into the sea. When the second was empty, he threw the handspike at the helm. Nikilov ducked and the makeshift dagger rang the ship's bell and hurtled away.

The dark man snapped the lines holding the rain barrel to the deckhouse. He lifted it over his head, dumping the water on the already rum-soaked deck, then heaved it over the bulwark into the sea. Still smiling, the monster spoke. *"Apa, apa, fiecare in cazul in care ... Nici vreo picatura de a bea."*

Nikilov stared sullenly. He understood the Romanian easily enough. And it was not necessary he be a scholar like Harrington to recognize the quotation from *The Rime of the Ancient Mariner*. Every ship's commander and seaman that could read knew it by heart. "Water, water, everywhere," the villain had said. "Nor any drop to drink." It was not necessary, either, he be a genius to realize the monster was doing more than taunting him. That he intended his speedy demise was beyond doubt, but it was increasingly clear the demon sought the captain's mental breakdown first. He *was* evil incarnate.

The monster disappeared around the deckhouse and, a moment later, was throwing the forward rain barrels into the ocean. Nikilov could hear the splashes and could only watch as, ten yards out on the port side, one of the barrels bobbed past in the fog. He flinched, tied as he was, when a third barrel hit the foredeck with a tremendous smash, splash and splintering of wood.

The phantom reappeared in the opposite companionway. He was coming aft, quickly, with the last rain barrel above his head, puking its water as he came. The terrified Nikilov raised the crucifix. The dark one averted his eyes and blindly hurled the barrel at the captain. It hit the binnacle before the wheel. Nikilov ducked as his bindings allowed. An explosion of wood and water followed as the barrel chipped the housing, shattered the crystal compass face, and burst. Nikilov dodged a flying wheel-spar, but was hit instead by a broken barrel slat that tore his coat sleeve and his arm. The ship yawed hard to port, answering the erratic rudder, and only the wheel prevented the captain falling on his face.

The creature smelled the blood before he saw it; a moist stain growing on Nikilov's sleeve. He hissed, hungry and seething. He paced madly in an arc before the helm with murder in his eyes, yet was unable to approach. The crucifix shown like fire in the captain's hands, the rosary beads glinted in the lamplight. Nikilov raised his head and, with what little strength he possessed, spoke to the creature in his native Russian.

The demon glared hell-fire! He threw his head back, howled like a wounded animal, and vanished through the deckhouse door headed below. The vampire understood the guttural mouthings of the bastard Russian plainly enough. *"All this blood,"* Nikilov had said, waving his pathetic crucifix. *"And not a drop to drink."*

* * *

Terrified, in pain, the captain sagged against the wheel. His heart pounded in his chest (with his quacksalver's tonic below). He fought to slow his breathing, to govern his fears. He thought of the monster, unsure even after all that had happened, if he could make himself believe. He felt a chill in his soul and, as he stood through the night, it came home... He was the only human on board. More, having seen it with his own eyes, he finally understood that he was also the only thing aboard with a soul.

The captain lost track and, though he saw the glow of sunrise somewhere beyond the fog, was unaware when the morning of Friday, 6 August, arrived. More than three full days had passed since Iancu Constantin immolated himself. Since Nikilov had left the helm, washed himself or shaved. Three days since the captain had eaten a bite of food. Two days had gone since he'd first tied himself to the wheel and swore his oath to remain there until *Demeter* reached a friendly port. Owing to that promise, he'd had no choice but to wet himself again in the night. It made no difference, there was nobody aboard but the demon. Urination

Chapter Thirty-six

was no longer a concern. Two days had elapsed since his last drink of water.

Nikilov grew tortured with thirst. His throat burned, his mind was on fire. The mist of sea water, ever upon him, ever drying, caked his bleeding lips with salt. The sun was both ally and traitorous enemy. Its pure light kept the dark creature below, while those same rays, and their reflection off the water, would have cooked him had they not been refracted by the fog. It was bitterly ironic... the miserable fog preventing his finding land was also keeping him alive.

Demeter, like Nikilov, barely lived. A sea-worthy schooner the day they left Varna, she'd been sorely mistreated by the devastating unseasonable storms. Buffeted at anchor or forced to run before the wind, the short-handed crew had been kept from making badly needed repairs by the unseen monster. Repairs that would not be made now until she reached a port. The fore sail, the fore top-sail, and one of the jib sails had tears in them. These would rip further should the storms return or the winds gust. The rigging was loose on the main sail. The gaffe vang (replaced following Petrofsky's long-ago injury) needed to be tightened. The rudder was responding awkwardly and Nikilov was concerned. The whole ship, redolent of fear and death, needed cleaning and airing. Add the knowledge all vessels leak, even if they haven't been near cap-sized as his had.

The threat of misfortune and disaster was a constant companion on any voyage. How much more should something occur to further disable his vessel? He was alone, at the mercy of the fog, the wind, the sea, and the devil in his hold. His only tool was the ship's wheel and, among his many worries, was the thought his vessel might not hold together. He wrestled with one scenario after another; all that was wrong, all that could go wrong. In the meantime, not a bite of food, no water, none of the quack's prescribed tonic. Not even a chair.

And so the day passed.

Night fell and fear rose in the fragile heart of the ship's captain. For he knew that soon the monster would come, looking grayer, more pale than on his last hellish visit, to stare and to growl, to glare hatred with his eyes gleaming like ignited rubies, to hiss and bare his sharp white teeth, to attack and (dear God please) be repelled by the blessed crucifix.

* * *

Dracula could hear them, through Lucy, as clearly as if they were beside him, the dogs howling in the night throughout the village of Whitby. They sensed his approach. They howled. And Dracula, in *Demeter's* cellar, remembered the wolves in the courtyard of his own castle.

"The children of the night," the voivode whispered. "What music they make!"

He remembered also the expression of bewilderment on the face of the young estate agent, the late Jonathan Harker, when he'd made that comment in his presence. What was it he'd told him? Yes, that being a city dweller, Harker could not possibly enter into the feelings of the hunter.

Whitby first, soon after Purfleet, and then the great city of London... all stretched before him. His for the taking to do with as he pleased. Dracula arose from his box, aging and white, but victorious. The ruling kingdom of the world was about to meet its conqueror. The hunter had come to England.

* * *

"Put it away."

There he stood again; the demon. Where he came from, how, or when he appeared, the captain did not know. He was simply there, standing on the deck, fading in and out of the thick fog. His head was turned, his glance averted, his hand raised to his

Chapter Thirty-six

brow shielding his eyes from the crucifix in Nikilov's hands. "Put it away," he said again. "I will not approach."

The captain eyed him, wearily, warily.

"I am Dracula," the vampire said, still facing away. "Count Dracula. You are?"

"Nik-i-lov." The captain licked his split, white lips. "Captain Nikilov."

"I will not approach you... captain. Why would I? It makes no sense to harm you. I need to reach England. You need food and drink. Put the crucifix away. Let us strike a bargain."

Like a soothing balm, the thought of food, the image of clear, clean drinking water, the idea of sinking his throbbing head onto his bunk pillow overwhelmed the captain. He heard the deep, inviting voice again, "*Let us strike a bargain.*"

The tempting visions, the words of promised peace, reverberating through his brain, vanished suddenly, pushed back into the darkness from which they'd sprung by another phrase, ingrained in him since boyhood; a scripture from the New Testament book of James. "*Submit yourselves therefore to God. Resist the devil, and he will flee from you.*" The devil was staring icily at him, trying to sway him toward... what? It did not matter. Nikilov had his answer and, with no desire to debate pure evil, he passed it on to Count Dracula in the only way he could. With all the energy he could muster, he began to loudly pray the Lord's Prayer.

Dracula hissed his anger, raised his arms, and was gone.

One moment he was there, tall, dark, evil. Then came a blur, a bending of his physical being that caused Nikilov to gasp. An instant later, a huge black wolf – with the same red-burning eyes – stood growling on all fours in his place. The creature moved, panting as it padded the deck in a whirl, then vanished in the fog. Unable to see it, still Nikilov could hear it circling the helm.

The panting, the padding feet, a low growl... A flash in Nikilov's periphery and the wolf popped out of the fog to his right. It growled and was gone. There again, out of the gray swirls on the left. A snarl and it was gone. Nikilov's terror was intense. The panting, the padding feet, a yelp... Out of the fog again, forward of the wheel, eyes gleaming red, great globs of saliva dripping from its vicious white fangs. The monster howled to chill the captain's blood. It leapt at him.

Nikilov jerked back, unable to retreat for his bindings. He flipped his wrist and the crucifix flopped forward. The monster landed beside the dented compass, howled at the proximity of the holy icon, whined in pain and darted away. Breathless, Nikilov halted his scream, searching the deck. He knows, Nikilov thought. The demon knows I'm sick. He smells my fear. He's trying to frighten me...

The wolf appeared again from the fog. It leapt, snapping and snarling, landed to his left, spun and disappeared.

Nikilov began to cry. "Stop this," he yelled. "Stop this!" Like the wolf, the captain's breath came in pants. His dried lips cracked, bleeding, tears ran down his sun-baked face. Somewhere within the fog, he could hear the growls, the howls, the panting, as the creature chased circles round him. It seemed very far away, for pain seized him. It started in his left arm, a shooting pain, followed by crushing pressure in his chest. Nikilov gasped but could not catch his breath. He squeezed the crucifix, his knuckles turning white. Again, before him, the wolf appeared, growling, dripping saliva.

The captain's erratic racing heart suddenly seized. Unable to hold his head up, he nodded and, had it not been for his bindings, would certainly have dropped to the deck. But the lines held, the ship's wheel stood, and Mikhail Sergeyevich Nikilov – the last man aboard the Russian schooner *Demeter* - died standing at the helm.

Chapter Thirty-seven

Now the tale returns to where it started, Friday, 6 August, in the village of Whitby.

Hopeful of her fiancé's homecoming following Mr. Hawkins letter, disheartened at not having heard from Jonathan since, worried, even frightened by Lucy's sleepwalking, Mina sat on her cemetery bench overlooking the sea.

Sir Oracle, Mina's old whaler, hobbled up the steps and made straight for her. His approach, his expression, the way he lifted his hat, made it plain he wanted to talk. Mina had been touched by the sad change in the poor man of late. This day he looked more melancholy yet. He twisted his hat and wearily said, "I want t' say somethin', miss."

He was so ill-at-ease Mina could not help but take his hand and gently whisper, "Speak freely, Mr. Swales. Please do."

"I'm afraid, my deary, I must have shocked ye by all th' wicked thin's I've been sayin' aboon the dead." He began to cry and begged her forgiveness. He related the sad tale of his life, in Scotland, at sea, and here in his adopted home. He poured out his heart, his fears of a rapidly approaching eternity, his fears for the return, the life, of his son, Oliver.

So it played out in the cemetery.

Soon after, Mr. Swales started home, passing the alarmed coast guard racing across the harbor bridge and up the great stairs. He

Chapter Thirty-seven

put his spyglass to use and drew Mina's attention to a sailing ship, a Russian schooner, bobbing lost and confused on the distant sea. "We'll hear more of her before this time tomorrow."

* * *

It seemed the coast guard was mistaken.

The following day, Saturday the 7th, was according to many one of the most beautiful in memory, sultry (not uncommon for August) but otherwise unusually fine. Balmy enough that residents and tourists alike took advantage. Holiday makers, in their best, on sight-seeing day trips to Rig Mill, Runswick, Mulgrave Woods, and Robin Hood's Bay, while all the day, in and out of the harbor, the Emma and the Scarborough were under full steam tripping tourists up and down the coast.

In late afternoon, when a breeze arose from the southwest, some of the gossips on the east cliff called attention to a show of *mares tails* high in the sky to the northwest. These early storm clouds did not startle, but rather added to the overall beauty. The approach of sunset was grand. Masses of splendidly colored clouds, flame, purple, pink, green, violet, and all the tints of gold, separated by masses of black in all sorts of shapes, delighted the assemblage in the old churchyard.

Out of sight and out of mind, was the befuddled Russian ship that had appeared on the far horizon, and so alarmed the coast guard, the previous evening. The vessel must have found her bearings (when, headed where, was anyone's guess) and passed by Whitby, for the schooner was nowhere to be seen.

* * *

But she wasn't gone at all. *Demeter* was there, drifted from sight back into the North Sea, less than ten miles east of the village. There she bobbed on the swells, windlocked, as the sun sank below the horizon.

Evening settled in the rigging and a blue dark fell on the deck. Captain Nikilov's corpse stood, tied at the wheel, while the ship's new master watched it loll to and fro with the roll of the waves. Each time the body flexed to port, Count Dracula was forced to turn away from the glint of the crucifix clutched in its hands. Dead... and still the seaman vexed him. Dracula would not be able to steer the ship from her helm. He would need another way.

He turned, his black cloak billowing like wings, and strode forward on the port side, *Demeter's* phantom, the only creature aboard save the rats, walking the deck alone.

The Count stopped just aft of the foremast shrouds. With one hand on the mast rigging and the other on the port rail, he stared out over the sea. Whitby lay beyond sight to the west. The current was wrong, the wind was wrong, the sails were wrong, and he had no governable rudder. None of it mattered. He was the voivode, the war leader, and he was taking this vessel to England.

Dracula lowered his head as the clouds in the east began to roll in and darken. He concentrated on the winds as they passed over the port side and dropped to skate on the surface of the sea a quarter of a mile west of *Demeter,* and on the elements in the water therein. In his mind's eye, he saw, slowly but coming on, the genesis of a massive rotation. The winds rose up and bore down. At Dracula's command, the sea began to churn.

* * *

In the time it took the old whaler to climb the steps to the cemetery on the east cliff, the breeze had strengthened to gusts. Swales had been watching storms roll in from that vantage point for fifty years. He did so again now, at the elbow of the young coast guard. "She's comin'," the old man said. The coast guard eyed the blackening sky and nodded.

Both thought it, but neither added, 'Looks like one hell of a blow'.

The steamers had ceased their trips along the coast and come in for the night. Captains planning departures, up and down the

Chapter Thirty-seven

quay, reconsidered, choosing to keep their mules and cobbles in. All were waiting with no intention of taking to sea until the storm passed. As evening turned to night, the only lights on the water belonged to fishing boats racing for shelter. Like diamonds against blue velvet, they rose and dipped in the swell, rolling to their scuppers, as each swept into the harbor ahead of the blow.

Shortly before ten o'clock the air grew oppressively still. Sheep could be heard bleating inland and the barking of dogs throughout the town sounded frighteningly like a concert of wolves. The band, courageously playing on the pier, had lost its lively French air and now seemed less an entertainment than an intrusion. While many of the cavorting storm-watchers missed it altogether, to the more sensitive among the crowd something supernatural (silence preceding it like a rushing spectre) seemed on the verge of overwhelming them.

* * *

Dracula stared over the ship's port rail, concentrating.

Black clouds rolled in, gale force winds billowed *Demeter's* sails and bent her masts, yet the water's natural swell fell away and the waves stood up in short, quick, angry cross-dashes. It seemed the sea was an orchestra, each foamless wave a musician rising to tune his instrument then retaking his seat. Soon the ocean lay down as smooth as glass. The concert looked about to begin.

Lightning flashed as Dracula stretched out his hand. The sea groaned as if some living monster were awakening in its lair. Then, to match the sound, came a spectacle right out of hell.

A quarter of a mile away, the vast bed of water suddenly convulsed. The wind's short, sharp gusts turned to a steady and fierce blow. The water began to chop, standing up. Prodigious streaks of foam rose and spread, at a great distance, into one massive counter-clockwise swirl. The gyration grew to a huge vortex; circling northward and westward. Moving with the wind, heaving and hissing, whirling and plunging, on a course directed by the devil, building with a mind-boggling velocity. Each moment added to its speed, its headlong frenzy. The whole sea was surging around in ungovernable fury, north and west, north and west, a train of violence on a circular track.

From this motion came the thunderous backlash of a gigantic wave. It struck *Demeter* on her port bow, rolled under the ship, and lifted her up to touch the electrically charged sky. The swell continued its massive outward roll, beyond *Demeter* into the sea, while the schooner bobbed on the top then slid down her inner face as if plunging off a mountain. She hit the bottom of the wave in bubbling foam. A man on deck would have been sick and dizzy, but Dracula stood without moving.

As wide in diameter now as it was distant from the ship, the massive whirl had come fully into existence. Now, at its center, as if a drain had been opened in the sea floor, the water fell out and the vortex became a whirlpool, increasing in speed and drawing the surrounding waters into its rotation. The edge of the whirl was a belt of gleaming spray. The mouth of the incredible funnel glistened jet-black, speeding dizzily around, roaring to the winds, a cylindrical wall of water descending to hell.

Demeter groaned and rolled on its keel. The bowsprit and carved torch of her ornate figurehead yawed to port, to the northwest, picking up speed, as it too was drawn to the maelstrom.

* * *

Just at sunset the coast guard and his technicians, on the east cliff, got the new searchlight working. They'd lit it for the first time when Mr. Swales had come up to view the weather and continued their experiments as darkness fell and the old whaler abandoned them.

Sir Oracle descended the stairs, heading home to his granddaughter, when the shore light was turned. With no desire to blind those on the docks, they swept the beam across the misty ocean startling nothing more than a few storm-tossed seabirds whose

Chapter Thirty-seven

wings flashed white then disappeared. Little did they realize as they played how quickly the searchlight would prove useful.

Outside the harbor, the storm had the sea running high. Each wave broke skyward, throwing white foam that was whirled into space by the tempest. The men chased these wet explosions until their light crossed the path of a lone fishing boat still a-sea and in jeopardy. She'd lost her way and, with the angry waves washing over her gunwales, was nearly swamped.

The coast guard took the light over from his technicians and trained the new beam on the troubled vessel. This man-made miracle did the trick. Guided by the light, and steady hand of the coast guard, the boat found her way, rushed into the harbor, and made the pier; the fishermen aboard sodden but otherwise none the worse for wear.

* * *

Swales saw the rescue as he reached the drawbridge. Confident the fishermen were safe, and aware there was little he could do if they were not, he hurried home (his son's home actually), where both kept after, and were kept by, their little Carrie. A daft way to think of things, really. His grand-daughter was nearly fifty years old. Still she would always be their little Carrie.

Mina's Sir Oracle quietly cracked the door to her room and stared in at his sleeping grand-daughter. She hadn't felt well after supper, had excused herself to lie down, and was there now. His rheumy eyes were not what they once were. Swales could not discern her face in the gloom, but he recognized her form and could hear her peaceful breathing. He closed the door quietly.

He returned to their small sitting room and his worn rocking chair. He lit the lamp creating a soft glow, then lit his clay pipe (a gift from Oliver; *the only thin' worth a damn to e'er come from Ireland*). A robust cloud of smoke filled the room. He stared at the empty rocker on the other side of the table, Oliver's chair, and relit his memory.

Soon, Swales was trembling.

Something was wrong. For days he'd felt it, feared it. It was unshakable, the sadness that drove him to the cemetery, to make himself foolish before young Miss Mina. Here it was again... the *feeling* that Oliver was gone. Not merely away on a long sea voyage but truly gone; dead. He felt it, believed it absolutely in his heart. Oliver was dead and gone and he would never see his son again.

More than that, far worse, something inexplicable, something evil was headed their way. Lightning flashed turning the room, for an instant, to daylight. Thunder rumbled. Spittles of rain, a deceptively weak opening salvo of the storm yet to come, marred the room's two small windows.

Sir Oracle's tears fell too.

* * *

Mina sat up again. Not in bed, for she'd abandoned her bed, but on the settee in Lucy's room from which she'd watched her restless roommate all through the evening and into the night. The storm, it seemed, would be fearful and Lucy too was making Mina afraid.

Twice already, she'd risen from her bed – quite asleep both times – dressed herself and tried to get out of the room. Good fortune had awakened Mina in the nick of time and, on both occasions, she'd undressed Lucy without waking her and gotten her back to bed. Not that there was a struggle, there never was. Each time Mina stopped her, led her back to safety, she yielded without a struggle.

But the evening had taken its toll. Mina could no longer sleep, worried as she was for Lucy. The storm, rattling the windows, drumming the roof, booming among the chimney pots only made it worse. Now again came the thunder like the sharp puff of a distant gun. Mina shuddered.

* * *

Chapter Thirty-seven

Call it fate, call it coincidence, but it was storming in Purfleet every bit as hard as it was in Whitby, coming down in sheets with the lightning only starting but promising much. It had come out of the blue. Equally unexpected was the storm inside the lunatic asylum.

"He's mine!" Renfield screamed.

Dr. Seward, making notes at his desk, was frightened out of a year's growth; caught off guard when the patient burst through his study door shouting. True to the recent form his mania had taken, Renfield went for Tabby, their calico cat, with bloodlust in his mad eyes. The doctor tried to intervene and tumult followed.

The cat escaped as the lunatic grabbed and missed, the doctor was knocked over his desk, and Renfield too went down. The orderlies, an exasperated Martin brandishing a straight-waistcoat, and his right-hand man William (heavy on muscles, light on brains), charged in, as the calico charged out, and overwhelmed the patient.

"Blow me down dead, doctor," Martin said, riding the man on the floor. "'ow 'e got out of 'is room, I don't know."

"It doesn't matter now. Just get him under control!"

Renfield fought them with his considerable strength. Despite resistance, his protests, and his nonsensical ravings, the lunatic was eventually bound into the canvas and leather straight jacket, his arms crossed over his torso, and the elongated sleeves belted behind his back.

"No! No! I've got to prepare! You don't understand! He's coming! The master is coming! I've got to prepare!"

Trussed like a felon, Renfield was dragged (he refused to walk and screamed all the way) back to his room. He was deposited on the floor, howling like the madman he was. "Set me free! You've got to set me free! He's coming! I've got to prepare!"

"Come away," the panting Seward said, ushering his orderlies out and locking the door. "Leave him alone."

Renfield lay, lit by sporadic bursts of lightning, muttering and alone.

"Set me free. He's coming! The master is coming!"

* * *

Midnight arrived, Sunday, 8 August, the witching hour, and round and round *Demeter* careered, barely displacing water as it made the circuit, flying rather than floating. With the black wall of ocean on her starboard blocking out the storm to the east, and her port side riding the inner edge of the whirlpool, the schooner's tormented sails emptied and fell flat for lack of wind. It seemed *Demeter* would any second plunge into the abyss. She lay almost upon her beam-ends as she raced round in dizzying swings and Dracula stared to the bottom of the profound gulf where the walls of the vast funnel met and clashed in a roaring mist lit by lightning flashes.

More than *Demeter* was caught in the whirl. All around the ship raced barrels, broken yards, water-logged tree trunks, a splintered mast and, there suddenly ahead, the bow section of a wrecked vessel, churned up from the bottom. Each item in turn missed or struck the ship as the fates would have it, ran the massive circular course, took the plunge, and disappeared into the abyss.

The maelstrom drew the schooner, faster, on around. The ship creaked, the masts groaned, *Demeter* cleared the wall of water and the wind gusts billowed the sails in the opposite direction. The vampire, still conducting in the bow with lightning flashes all around, clenched his fists. *Demeter* groaned, climbed the lip of the funnel's edge to starboard and, as if shot from a catapult, left the whirl.

Behind, the mist in the depths of the funnel were swallowed up, replaced by churning sea, as the bottom of the gulf filled. The whirl slowed; the maelstrom closed and disappeared. But the deed was done! By the force of the vortex, *Demeter* had been driven in a westerly direction. The storm raged on and the jettisoned schooner was on course for Whitby.

Chapter Thirty-eight

SUPERNATURAL silence muted the voices of those out and about in the rain and stifled the band on the quay. Then, at midnight, came a hollow booming from over the sea. Flashes of lightning lit the distant ocean, revealed breaks in the heavy mist. The sky trembled with thunder. The crowd on the shore, still cheering the rescue of the fishing boat, was drowned out by the gale.

On the cliff, the coast guard stretched his aching back. So intent had he been on following the boat with his beam, he hadn't realized how near he was to giving out. He leaned against the light, almost falling when it rotated to sea under his weight. He looked seaward following the beam then paused, certain he'd seen... something.

He maneuvered the light with purpose and saw it again; something on the swell. The object veered in its course, battering the waves and, drawing near, took shape. It was a sailing ship! She was square-rigged on the fore, ridiculous in this blast, and full gaffe rigged, main and mizzen, with no reefing whatsoever. Surely, she was piloted by a lunatic! Then a realization struck. This was not just any ship. It was the foreign schooner he'd seen the evening before. She'd vanished from sight all the long day and he'd assumed she'd gone on her way. Now here she was again. All her sails were set (dangerously!) and idly flapping in the wind. She was heading west, straight for Whitby harbor.

Chapter Thirty-eight

The coast guard began frantically to signal her. He warned the ship, over and over again, of the storm. He'd begged her with the light to reduce her sail. All of his effort was to no avail.

The wind had backed to the east and up and down the harbor, on the piers, on the eastern cliff, the cemetery walk, and the grounds of the old Abbey, a shudder passed among those who saw the schooner. Shouts of alarm rose, gossip spread, about the ignorant and foolish officer at her helm.

* * *

Demeter's captain, Mikhail Nikilov, dead and lashed to the ship's wheel, lolled back and forth with every roll and yaw of the ship. His waxen eyes stared sightlessly from the full, in some spots torn, sails to the sodden deck, from the starboard sea to the port sky. He had grown cold and white, stiffened with rigor mortis, then flaccid as the rigor passed. The corpse stood at the helm – ignored.

The ship's new commander, Count Dracula, white with age, pale from lack of blood, stood in the bow of the forlorn schooner. The deck pitched beneath his feet, the winds blasted the sails. The boiling sky of emerald and black exploded with a CRACK of lightning.

Demeter ran on.

* * *

In her bedroom in the Crescent, Lucy's lovely but still sleeping eyes came open. Like an automaton, she threw back the covers and quietly, so as not to disturb Mina, climbed from her bed. Asleep but aware, she stole to the rain-spotted window and stared at the town and harbor.

The tempest broke over land and the whole aspect of nature at once convulsed. The waves rose in growing fury, overtopping each other, until the sea outside of the breakwater was a roaring monster. Whitecrested waves beat madly on the sands and rushed up the cliffs. Others broke over the piers, battering the lighthouses that guarded the mouth of the harbor. The wind roared and blew with such force even strong men had difficulty keeping their feet.

Lucy watched through the rain as the authorities chased away the brave onlookers and cleared the pier, no doubt saving at least some of their lives. To add to their difficulties, and the danger, wet masses of fog were drifting inland like the ghosts of the North Sea dead. She shuddered at the thought.

Then came the voice from the sea; the voice of the master. Lucy left the window and quietly, with one eye on the sleeping Mina, found her night coat.

* * *

In Purfleet, within sight of the dilapidated Carfax Abbey, within the cold stone walls of the sanitarium, the orderlies (whispering amongst themselves) shared a sense of relief. Renfield, still in a straight-waistcoat, had finally fallen asleep. It was the first time in forty-eight hours he'd ceased ranting. The calm was refreshing. Martin took one last look then, satisfied, closed the peep hole in the door, thinking, 'It's about bleedin' time'.

On the other side of the door, Renfield heard the hatch close... and opened his eyes. He could always fool ol' Martin! Now, quietly, quickly, in the same way he amazed his childhood friends with demonstrations of his 'double jointed-ness', he pressed his confined shoulders against the hard wall and pushed. His arms slipped from their sockets with two barely audible pops. That accomplished, he sank his teeth into the waistcoat and tore at the canvas as a tiger would its prey.

* * *

With the lighthouses of Whitby harbor visible in the distance, *Demeter* had veered slightly off course; heading N.N.W. now when

Chapter Thirty-eight

a westerly path was called for. Damn the ship's captain at the helm! And damn the crucifix in his cold dead hands!

Dracula raised his hands again, summoning the most terrifying of all sea events; a massive squall. The schooner bucked and heeled over. A tremendous whistle roared through the sails and shrouds as a train of cold air raced off the North Sea following an upward gesture of his right hand. Then, to a sudden downward movement of his left, came a microblast that hit the sea east of the ship like a hammer.

A twenty-foot wall of wind-driven water climbed angrily into the air and slapped the ship on her aft starboard side. Like a toy shoved across a park pond, *Demeter* was blasted hard to port, rolling on her beam ends and nearly cap-sizing. She rolled back to an even keel headed west; on course again for Whitby harbor.

* * *

The coast guard and his mates followed her with their searchlight, shouting in excitement and terror. It was nearly the hour of high tide and, unbelievably, the schooner was rushing straight at them with all sails set.

Spellbound as the vessel bore down, one of the old seamen watching from the cliff behind the light was overheard to whisper, "She must fetch up somewhere, if it's only in hell."

* * *

Draping her night coat, Lucy did not bother to tie it closed as she tried the door. She found it locked. Like always now – locked. She would not be a prisoner, not here, not now. She was being called. The meaning of the last weeks, the answers to her dreams, was at hand. She had to get out.

Mina was still sleeping. Just as well.

Lucy slipped to the window. She parted the curtain. She tugged for all she was worth and, with a great effort, threw up the sash.

The window shrieked. The lightning flashed. The thunder rolled. Rain poured in, soaking her robe, the front of her sleeping gown. It did not matter. Nothing mattered now but escaping the confines of that room and reaching the cemetery over the sea. She forced the window open further, her saturated night clothes sticking to her breasts, her stomach. She ducked her head, determined to get out and away.

"Lucy!"

She froze, as she was, half-way out the bedroom window of their apartments. Mina had her by the shoulders, pulling her back inside. Rain water cascaded down her long black hair, her soaked gown, forming a puddle on the floor.

"Oh, Lucy! Oh, Lucy!"

Lucy offered no resistance, put up no struggle, said nothing. She was yet asleep.

* * *

"He is come!"

All good things must come to an end, Martin thought. Renfield's silence among them. Sadly, the peace and quiet hadn't lasted long.

"Looney's screaming again."

The lead orderly stared daggers at his assistant. "Ye think I'm deaf? Ye think I don't 'ear 'im?"

Martin pulled the peep open and peered through. Renfield was there, at the window, staring out at the storm, yelling his head off. "He is come! He is come!" It took the orderly a moment to realize the patient was no longer bound up. His straight-waistcoat lay, in shreds, across his bed. More, the iron bars in his window were twisted away as if they'd been made of cheese. Renfield was climbing out.

Martin swore an oath, wrestled his key in the lock, and yanked the door open. He and his partner rushed into the room. Ahead by a step, Martin grabbed Renfield as he sidled out between the twisted bars. Renfield growled and lashed out. Martin screamed

Chapter Thirty-eight

as blood arced across his white jacket. He let go and the lunatic slid away, through the bars, and dropped into the dark outside.

"'e stabbed me!" Martin shouted in pain.

"What with?" William asked in horror.

"'ow the bloody 'ell should I know what wiff?" Martin bellowed, waving his crimson-splashed mitt. "'e bleedin' stabbed me! Ain't that enuff?"

William tried the window but realized there was no way he or Martin would make the squeeze. And it wasn't likely he could bend the bars further. Besides, they were too late. Renfield was gone, lost in the rain, in the pitch black of the garden.

"I'll get an-ofer straight-waistcoat," Martin said. He wrapped a handkerchief tightly about his hand, staring out at the grounds. "You get yer Wellingtons, mate. Got t' go after ole loony, yeah? Ye don't want t' get yer feet wet."

In the dark, beyond the reach of his tormenting warders, Renfield ran a straight line through the rain soaked grass into the trees at the edge of the sanitarium property. Without a ladder or the least hesitation, he scaled the wet wall separating the asylum grounds from those of the deserted Carfax Abbey. He flipped over the top like a circus performer and dropped on the other side into the grounds.

* * *

In what to men would have been blinding fog, Dracula moved between the main and mizzen masts, his cape billowing in the rain and wind, his eyes averted from the crucifix in the dead man's hand.

In their turn, mizzen then main, he tore the restraining lines from the pinrails and let them fly to the winds. The great booms, unleashed, swung madly, sweeping across the deck to starboard. Dracula threw his hand into the air and knotted his fist. The booms halted their swing in answer to his silent command. Redirected, each billowed fat and the schooner veered to port, picking up speed.

He returned to the foredeck, raised his arms like the maestro and, conducting the elements of the storm, wind, rain and raging sea, drove the vessel on. The mist began to thin and the lighthouse beacons at the mouth of Whitby harbor appeared dead ahead.

* * *

Moments before, the troubled schooner had disappeared within the shifting gray banks.

Now the soaked crowd on the east cliff, and those near the harbor, saw and felt the wind shift to the northeast taking the fog with it. From that fading mist, like the legendary Flying Dutchman, the schooner emerged... running before the blast. Buffeted from wave to wave, the vessel miraculously found a line between the piers, coming on.

"There's a flat reef there between her and the port!" The coast guard shouted to relieve his own terror. "A good many ships have suffered there. With the wind blowing from this quarter, she'll never fetch the entrance of the harbor. It's impossible!"

He hit the ship with the light beam – and waited for destruction.

The wind beyond the breakwater shifted. The booms on the vessel's main and mizzen masts swung, untended, grabbing the shifted wind gusts. The ship came round and skirted the edge of the murderous reef. The booms swung again, the sails flattened and refilled in the opposite direction.

Another wave of dank sea-fog settled like a blanket and the crowd was forced to strain its collective ears for they could not see a thing. The tempest roared. The thunder crashed. The sails of the hidden ship snapped – booming like cannons! The coast guard fixed the searchlight on the harbor mouth and east pier where the shock of the impending crash was expected. Soaked and stunned, everyone on land waited breathlessly.

The schooner reappeared!

Chapter Thirty-eight

To shouts, gasps, and screams from the crowds, the derelict ship threaded the needle between the lighthouses and their extended piers. Many thought they'd witnessed a miracle from God. They could not have known the exact opposite was true.

The schooner raced through the beam of light as it passed into the harbor. For an instant, it showed the man at the ship's wheel. He flopped from side to side like a marionette, his head snapping, swinging with the motion of the vessel. He looked to be drunk and ready to fall over. Somehow he kept his balance, remained upright; teetering but never losing hold of the helm.

In the southeast corner of the harbor, what the locals called Tate Hill Pier, was a beach of sand and gravel left by the tides over the years. The nearby residents were either asleep, ignorant of the excitement, or out of their homes and watching from the east cliff above, for the pier was empty. Thankfully so, for this was the target of the rushing schooner as the wind drove her across the harbor. The crowd shouted, exclaimed, watched in awe as, with a great swoosh, a crunch and an alarming explosion, the ship hit the sand and was driven aground...

Harrington's books flew from their shelf like a cricket googly, bowling Smirnov's empty laudanum bottle from the desk top. Funar's oilskins tumbled from the upper bunk. A cask in Swales galley smashed the wall tossing limes like marbles. Petrofsky's marlinspikes sailed like darts. Amramoff's tools erupted. Popescu's chamber pots disgorged their contents. The personal effects of Eltsin, Olgaren, and Constantin heaved and crashed. Nikilov's death clock ricocheted off the cabin door and landed as broken and dead as the artisan who'd crafted it.

The ship's timbers shook. Her shrouds strained. The lashings gave way as the torn top sail crashed down. Everything loose on the deck took flight, everything secured came loose. Captain Nikilov's body slammed against the wheel, slumped, but stayed on its feet.

The ship climbed the sand, throwing up water and gravel, tossing jetsam. The schooner slid over the rocks and ground to a halt.

Lightning flashed, thunder rolled in a crescendo! *Demeter* had arrived in Whitby, England.

* * *

Despite the storm and the crashing waves, the excited crowd shocked at seeing the ship run aground, moved back towards the harbor. Two, the coast guard, who left his spotlight, and a newspaper correspondent, from the west cliff, were good runners and rushed ahead of the rest.

The technicians still working the light scoured the harbor entrance as if searching for the demonic forces that had driven the ship. Finding nothing, they turned the light on the derelict to see the coast guard and the newsman had gained the beach. They made their way quickly, carefully, towards the grounded ship, through broken spars, wreckage and jetsam scattered across the rocks and sand.

The coast guard was nearly to the canted wreck when SOMETHING, a blur, leapt over the bow rail and landed on the beach before him. He pulled up, startled, and took a moment in the blazing light and long shadows of the search beam to see it was – a huge black dog! He signaled a warning and the news man, coming behind, swore an oath and stopped short too.

The dog (or could it have been a wolf!) snarled. It bared vicious fangs, saliva dripping from red lips, then snapped a threat with heavy jaws. Neither man moved. The animal, its eyes red as fire, gave vent with a tremendous and spine-chilling howl, then raced away. The creature cleared the rocky beach and vanished into the dark.

Epilogue

THE monstrous dog, vanished in the night, had scared the living hell out of the coast guard and the news man. Now, as they drew near the wrecked ship, the gloomy figurehead did the same. Gouges in her face, in the face of the fanged creature nestled between her breasts, and in her breasts, marred the sculpture and gave the carved image an aspect of menace. At one time the figure meant discovery and new life, now it only frightened, proclaiming a derelict's arrival to England's shores. They forced themselves past the eerie wooden maiden.

A torn line from the collapsed foreshrouds hung down over the gunwale, a deadman, dragged through the water and lying on the sand. The coast guard grabbed it and climbed; the first living soul aboard the schooner in two days. The journalist was hot on his heels. They made their way aft, through the debris, and around the deckhouse. On the other side, past the mizzen mast, they pulled up together staring in shocked awe at the helm. Never had man seen such a sight.

A seaman, the captain if his coat and cap told the truth, stood unmoving at the helm. His hands were tied, one over the other, with a crucifix and rosary in-between, to the ship's wheel. The binding cords had cut his wrists to the bone and the poor fellow was dead.

Epilogue

The crowd had reached the pier hoping for a closer look; some, by the chaos, even a chance to get aboard. On one end of the pier, the coast guard's technicians and police personnel were stopping all who advanced and refusing them access to the ship. On the other, the harbor's chief boatman was letting friends and relatives climb aboard. The coast guard chased them back, hoping to keep to a minimum the number who saw the dead man.

"Pay him no mind," a toff told the crowd. "Jealous he is, as he's got no salvage rights. I'm a law student; I know what I'm on about. The right of salvage belongs to the first civilian entering a derelict. The coast guard, being official, has no claim in the Admiralty Court. And the rights of the owner are already sacrificed," the would-be lawyer said (as if he knew). "His property being held in contravention of the statues of mortmain, since the tiller, as emblemship, if not proof, of delegated possession, is held in a dead hand."

The confused crowd nodded their complete understanding.

"Dr. Caffyn," a police sergeant called to a local surgeon in the crowd. "Would you be good enough to make a cursory examination?"

The doctor did and, in little time, declared, "The man must have been dead for quite two days."

"There's no crew!" The harbor boatman shouted, interrupting. He'd stepped from the deckhouse with three men behind him, a brother and two nephews, drawing the attention of the crowd.

The sergeant tried to quiet them. "What's that?"

"We've searched the ship. There's no crew. Nobody. There's not another soul aboard."

The murmur started again. This time the officer let it play.

"He must have tied up his own hands," the coast guard whispered to the doctor. "And fastened the knots with his teeth."

The doctor searched the body and removed Nikilov's corked bottle. He held it to the sergeant's light, seeing note paper and pencil inside. "Hallo. Unless I miss my guess," the doctor said. "That ought be an interesting bit of scroll."

The ropes were cut (they'd sliced too deeply to be untied) and Nikilov's corpse removed from the wheel. His honorable watch, from this world and the next, had lasted nearly five days. A makeshift litter was fashioned from the debris and, on the magistrate's nod, the captain was reverently carried away. An inquest and burial with honors, in Mina Murray's clifftop cemetery, were all that remained of Nikilov's voyage.

The fierce storm was abating, the crowd scattering, and the sky beginning to redden over the Yorkshire wolds.

* * *

Martin and William, soaked by the storm and dry again now the sun had risen that bright Monday morning, had searched the grounds to the Thames and back, all night long, with no sign of the escaped lunatic. Headed back, in weary defeat, the pair were startled by a distant howl of idiotic glee; the laughter followed by... singing. The orderlies shared nervous looks of surprise. "Blow me down dead," Martin said. Someone was singing a rousing rendition of 'The Roast Beef of Old England'.

> "When mighty Roast Beef was the Englishman's food,
> It ennobled our brains and enriched our blood.
> Our soldiers were brave and our courtiers were good
> Oh! the Roast Beef of old England, And old English Roast Beef!"

The stanzas were disordered and the song off-key, but Martin wasn't surprised. Renfield was the singer and his enthusiasm made up for any lapses. The ballad danced happily on the air.

> "But now we are dwindled to, what shall I name?
> A sneaking poor race, half-begotten and tame,
> Who sully the honours that once shone in fame."

Epilogue

They followed the music through the trees to the high wall separating the sanitarium property from that of the deserted Carfax. But, as the orderlies closed in, they found the song coming, not from the wall or beyond, but from the branches of an old English Oak tree on their side. Renfield was nestled, out of reach, in the saddle between the top of the trunk and the base of the branches. He was facing Carfax and singing with all his heart.

"Oh! the Roast Beef of Old England, And old English Roast Beef!"

Having heard him long before seeing him, and certain he was off his top, the orderlies moved in slowly. William had the straight-waistcoat ready; Martin carried only determination.

"When good Queen Elizabeth sat on the throne,
Ere coffee, or tea, or such slip-slops were known,
The world was in terror if e'er she did frown."

"Renfield!" Martin called up. "Wha' in the name o'..." He paused, mouth agape. Horror halted the orderly's question.

"Oh! The Roast Beef of old England..."

The lunatic turned in his seat. "Hello, Martin!" He was clutching a cat (with its throat torn out), his mouth and chin awash with blood. His fountain pen protruded from the animal's neck.

"Lor' 'ave mercy..." the orderly whispered. Not wise, that, giving a dangerous lunatic a fountain pen! Martin withered as he looked from the stabbed cat to his own bandaged hand.

For what it was worth, the lifeless body did NOT belong to Tabby. The calico cat, long a target of the lunatic's bloodlusts, had survived the storm (and Renfield) intact. This one wore a mangy striped coat of gray and black, probably a stray that passed the gloomy Carfax at just the wrong moment. Still, by his grin, his gore-splashed face, and his song, Renfield thought he held a delicacy.

All night they'd feared this moment would be a violent confrontation, but nothing could have been further from the truth. Renfield was delighted with everything; the sunny morning, the request he vacate the tree, the notion of returning to the sanitarium. All was right with the world and he happily came down from his perch. The straight-waistcoat, unnecessary for this amiable patient, was instead employed to wrap the poor cat. (Renfield's offer to carry the bundle was politely turned down.)

William was sent for a towel for Renfield's face, while the patient talked Martin's ear off. The one-sided conversation consisted of the lunatic's own brand of circinate babble, centered on the Abbey and his insistence the deserted mansion would soon live again. Martin understood none of it, but would admit Renfield's glee, his gory chin, and his claim that, "He's come! He'll be here soon, you'll see," left him... uneasy.

* * *

Lucy was up early, at her bedroom window, staring to the east and the distant harbor. There'd been a dreadful storm, and a thrill throughout the village with the arrival of the stray ship. It was all so exciting, who could sleep? And yet, she remembered little of what had occurred. She remembered being dried off, dressed and put to bed... It was all so strange.

She was not, Lucy knew, the woman she had been only yesterday. Something had changed. What, she could not say, but she could feel it. Would Arthur still love her, she wondered, still marry the Lucy she had become?

"Oh, Lucy," Mina exclaimed, entering the room. She joined Lucy at the window, chattering gaily from one subject to another. She'd just looked in on Mrs. Westenra who was sleeping like a baby. The color, she said, was back in Lucy's sweet cheeks. (No wonder three men had fought for her hand.) Lucy must be getting better.

Epilogue

Perhaps last night was the end of the dreams; the nightmares. Mina was happy, for the first time in days. She hoped she would soon hear from Jonathan. Perhaps today? And what a night, a storm, and how terrible was that sailing ship so dramatically running aground!

They stared together at the harbor and the tilted wreck of wood and canvas on the rocky beach. "They say she's Russian. It's horrid. That there was only one seaman aboard; and he was dead."

Lucy listened without hearing, her attention drawn from the broken vessel to the distant east cliff and the gloomy ruined Abbey beyond. Something... someone there... was calling her name. She could feel it. Tonight, she thought, secretly... Tonight.

* * *

The authorities conducted their investigation of the derelict ship, gathering information but finding factual conclusions strangely elusive. Most stunning of all was their discovery that her destination had been – exactly where she wound up, their own port of Whitby. How, in the name of a good and loving God, she had gotten there without a living crew... The mind boggled.

What happened to the crew was a subject of wild conjecture. Had the captain committed mass murder; *done the crew to death*? The rumors ran from suicide to the supernatural. The discovery of bottled notes in the pocket of the corpse, and later his Ship's Log, turned Captain Nikilov into a hero and turned suspicions instead upon the missing first mate. Ultimately, the facts mattered little as those involved had been *foreigners* after all.

In contrast to her unbelievable arrival was the disappointingly ordinary cargo she carried. Nothing whatsoever to stir the imagination or answer the mystery of the ship's crossing. Other than normal provisions, and a god-awful supply of sand ballast, the ship held only fifty boxes of ordinary dirt. These were turned over to Mr. S.F. Billington, a Whitby solicitor acting for an unnamed party. A rather confused representative of the Russian consul arrived, paid the requisite harbor dues, and claimed the battered schooner (to the chagrin of a know-it-all law student). And, though a surprising number searched for some time, no trace was ever found of the black dog that abandoned the vessel, and scared the coast guard, upon its arrival. Wrecked and desolate, *Demeter* had, at the cost of captain and crew, accomplished her task and delivered her cargo. Outside of everyone's knowledge, Nikilov had also accomplished his; the ship had been saved and his honor as a captain salvaged.

The figurehead on the prow of the schooner, broken and run aground on the sands of Whitby, stared vacantly inland. Trevor Harrington, gone with his love, ruined and lost upon the sea, among the first to meet Count Dracula on his journey to a new land, was well-studied and knew much that was hidden. He knew, for instance, Demeter was a Greek goddess, a mother earth figure who controlled the crops, fertility, and the beginnings of life. But Harrington was ignorant of the rest of her story. Or perhaps on that bright morning in Varna, as he planned his own new life, he'd simply chosen not to remember… that Demeter was the mother of Persephone. That her beautiful daughter, ravaged then kidnapped by Hades, was forever after permitted to visit this earth only four months of each year, when the land bloomed with spring flowers. When the growing season ended Persephone was yanked back to hell by her diabolical husband for eight cold months. Harrington had failed to recall that the torch in Demeter's outstretched hand illuminated, not only the seas before a cargo ship, but the goddess' way as she searched the darkness and the depths for Persephone, stolen in the night and made the bride of the monstrous king of the underworld. What better name could grace the bow of the ship that brought the night stalker, the king of all vampires, to the shores of England?

None more fitting than Dracula's Demeter.

About the Author

Doug Lamoreux is a father of three, a grandfather, a writer, and actor. A former professional fire fighter, he is the author of four novels and a contributor to anthologies and non-fiction works including the Rondo Award nominated Horror 101, and its companion, Hidden Horror. He has been nominated for a Rondo, a Lord Ruthven Award, and is the first-ever recipient of The Horror Society's Igor Award for fiction. Lamoreux starred in the 2006 Peter O'Keefe film, Infidel, and appeared in the Mark Anthony Vadik horror films The Thirsting (aka Lilith) and Hag.

Other Books by the Author

- The Devil's Bed
- The Melting Dead
- Corpses Say the Darndest Things (A Nod Blake Mystery)

Co-authored:

- Apparition Lake (with Daniel D. Lamoreux)

Contributed:

- Horror 101: The A-List of Horror Films and Monster Movies (Edited by Aaron Christensen)
- The Best of the Horror Society 2013 (Edited by Carson Buckingham)
- Hidden Horror: A Celebration of 101 Underrated and Overlooked Fright Flicks (Edited by Aaron Christensen)

More horror from Creativia

- The Blackstone Vampires series by Carole Gill – gothic romance and horror.
- Moribund Tales by Erik Hofstatter – a short story collection of raw and visceral horror in tradition of Edgar Allan Poe.

Contents

A Penultimate Moment as Prologue	1
Chapter One	7
Chapter Two	13
Chapter Three	25
Chapter Four	35
Chapter Five	43
Chapter Six	51
Chapter Seven	61
Chapter Eight	69
Chapter Nine	77
Chapter Ten	83
Chapter Eleven	93

Chapter Twelve	101
Chapter Thirteen	109
Chapter Fourteen	117
Chapter Fifteen	125
Chapter Sixteen	133
Chapter Seventeen	137
Chapter Eighteen	149
Chapter Nineteen	163
Chapter Twenty	181
Chapter Twenty-one	189
Chapter Twenty-two	201
Chapter Twenty-three	211
Chapter Twenty-four	221
Chapter Twenty-five	231
Chapter Twenty-six	247
Chapter Twenty-seven	259
Chapter Twenty-eight	263
Chapter Twenty-nine	273
Chapter Thirty	283

Chapter Thirty-one	291
Chapter Thirty-two	299
Chapter Thirty-three	305
Chapter Thirty-four	315
Chapter Thirty-five	323
Chapter Thirty-six	335
Chapter Thirty-seven	345
Chapter Thirty-eight	355
Epilogue	365
About the Author	373
Other Books by the Author	375
More horror from Creativia	377

Printed in Great Britain
by Amazon